EARTH 101

TIME TO RUN

EMAE CHURCH

Korudaz
Ink

Earth 101 – Time to Run

ISBN 978-1-9163003-1-6 (eBook)
ISBN 978-1-9163003-0-9 (Paperback)
ISBN 978-1-9163003-2-3 (Paperback IngramSpark)
ISBN 978-1-9163003-7-8 (Hardback)
ISBN 978-1-9163003-3-0 (Audiobook)

Published by Korudaz Ink, an imprint presenting this work by Emae Church

For more information, address: enquiries@korudaz.co.uk

First printed edition 20th July 2021

Book cover design by Andrei Bat

https://emae.church

For
the
J.A.M.I.J

EARTH 101

TIME TO RUN

By
Emae Church

CHAPTER ONE

My lungs are on fire. My heart hammers. Muscles burn with fatigue, and my ankles threaten to twist and throw me sideways onto the muddy grass.

But I must keep going. Up and up, dodging the mounds and dips which almost got me last time.

My running suit feels cold against my chafed, swollen legs. The blood pumping through me reverberates in my ears, almost drowning out the residual pitying whispers which accompany the sidelong glances. They greet me everywhere I go now.

Except here.

My solitary wilderness.

One stupid mistake, and I'm Jayne, reduced to cold and judge-mental gossip at the school lockers. Not front-page news but not forgotten either. Never. Forgotten.

I stamp harder into the soft ground with each thought and push onward. The sky is a menacing grey on the hill's horizon.

I look up and take a fresh icy gust to the face.

I'm not what they think I am. No way will I let them relegate me to town freak before I'm even eighteen. I'm so much more than that, and everyone will see. I'm sure of it.

I gasp against a razor-sharp breath. My chest finally refuses to open to full capacity. My lungs don't feed my muscles the oxygen they need for my next step.

Thunk.

The refreshing grass embraces my tired body with a sweet scent of approaching summer, and I roll onto my back, heaving for air. The blurry stopwatch ticked over my previous record nine seconds ago, and I'm not even at the top yet.

A scream wants to rip out of my chest, but I hold it in, too tired to think, let alone shout at the wind. I'm alone on this barren hill. Windswept and almost dark, no one comes here but me and the occasional blackbird. But I resent showing my weakness even to the birds.

I lay for a few seconds and then stand on wobbly legs. A blanket of lights stretches out flickering ahead of me, all the way to the harbour on the other side of town. My pulse slows a few paces, and I inhale deep again, in through the nose, out through the mouth. First thing I learned in cross-country running. That and don't lose.

I swipe a wet smudge of dirt off my knees and take tentative steps down the hill. So, I didn't beat the record I set for myself eight months ago. I'll still trash anyone who tries to race me. Let's see the condescension on their faces then.

I'm on the steepest part of the slope. It can be perilous even in daylight to descend it without knowing exactly where to place each step. A tiny tug on the pit of my stomach dares me to jump. I almost smile at the thought, but instead, I scramble down the steep, slippery bank.

The wind flattens my bangs across my forehead and whips the ends into my eyes. I rub the water out of them. Freeze.

My first instinct is to duck down as the tail end of a voice carries across on the wind. Somewhere near the bottom, out of sight. I don't know what it's saying, but it's female, and it's getting closer.

Tucking my long hair back behind my ears, I strain to listen above the wail of the wind. Can I catch a word or two of the approaching conversation? Hunkering down in a small dip, my black running suit camouflages against the darkening foliage. My mind lurches with paranoid thoughts.

The walls of my anxiety close in until I'm crouching so low, I'm almost embedded in the grass. My hair flicks up in the wind, and I grab it back down, though the coloured streaks will probably signal my location anyway.

"You can't force me to do anything!" The last word tapers off, shaky and weak.

I recognise the voice. It's Laura from school. I crane my neck and squint over the top of the nearby scattered boulders. But where is she? And who is she talking to?

Are they here because of me? Laura knows my running route – she's been vocal of my attempts to scramble up this hill – but this can't be a follow-on to what happened in school today? What will they think if they see me hiding?

The urge to stand up tugs at me. To carry on down the slope and mind my own business. But what if Laura sees me? How could I pop out of nowhere and continue along my way, pretending I don't notice her? I don't need even more hushed conversations and lowered eyes in the corridors of Hill Derry tomorrow.

I'm also not in the mood for another run-in with her.

I wipe away a lone, wind-induced tear on my cheek. The howl of the wind is picking up and carrying away Laura's words.

All I hear is the despair in her voice. "Why are you doing this?"

The fear. "Please, wait. Let's go back–"

Who is she with? I've seen her hanging with a lanky fella with white hair after school, but… should I go after her?

Do I want to find myself in another argument and fight?

The feet and voices grow faint and are replaced by the whistle of the wind. Billowing clouds chase across the dark sky. Peering down from my hiding place, an urgency compels me to follow Laura, as a gust of wind echoes with her voice.

Wait a minute, was that a shout? A scream? I'm on my toes as I move forward quickly but warily.

I search the street around me, but I'm alone. There's nobody to ask for assistance. Even if there were, would I bother asking? Probably not.

There, another shout. I should leave them to it, but a worrying curiosity sweeps me along, following Laura's voice. I can't make out what she is saying, but it's an angry, albeit shrill tone. I know Laura, and that is a scared voice. She's hiding fear behind a veil of angry words.

I stop at the corner to an alleyway. They'll see me should I turn the corner, and all the anger will become aimed at me. A bus charges past and almost erases the shouting, but between the sounds of heavy wheels and metal, I catch a snippet of Laura's words.

"Why don't you just jump in your stupid sh... and ...-off to another galaxy!"

Whoever she is with has not uttered a raised word. All I hear is a male mumble of sorts. He's obviously trying to calm her. But then an unwitting cough escapes me. I grasp my mouth, but then it happens.

My knees buckle, and my head spins as my vision darkens. What's going on? It's as though my head has been dipped in water but then comes a flash. I can't see where, but I'm sure it came from the alleyway.

Has Laura spotted me and has taken a picture of me, cowering here in the darkness, with her cell phone? I'll be a laughing-stock in school tomorrow. Before the night's out even.

She'll upload this to her digital landfill of social media with me the victim. Oh, why did I follow her? Have your stupid argument, but leave me out of it.

What's that? Footsteps.

My head stings and buzzes with the dark, thickness of the air around me. I'm paralysed, but I'm aware of someone crouching over me. My mouth won't form words. I can't raise my gaze towards whoever is looking at me. Leaden lifelessness pins my arms to my sides.

Then the darkness is broken by a voice. Hushed and distorted by the giddiness ebbing through my head.

"Stupid human."

A boy's voice.

It could be seconds or minutes, but the wave passes, and my head clears as the chilly air slaps me back to attention. My lungs burn as I gasp through chattering teeth. I must have been holding my breath.

Did I pass out?

I scan around me. Alone again. I push myself to shivering legs and peer down the dark, lonely alleyway. Empty. Laura and the boy are gone.

Where did they go?

What has just happened?

My tired legs hobble along the street and past the hill.

Dense trees, arcing from the top to the bottom of the hill, and to the left of me sway. Their leaves play eerie music of their own.

Shadows from the thicket stretch out long across the open grassland, threatening to reach me soon.

CHAPTER TWO

What was that last night? Did I blackout? I lost all control of my body and senses.

And that voice: *"Stupid human."*

I massage my temples and forehead, then run my fingers through my hair. I checked the web last night, but there were no pictures of me online, shivering by that alleyway.

More curious, Laura has taken down her social media pages. Why would she do that? She sees herself as the voice of the school, of the town. The gossip-queen of Dereton.

But she's deleted it all now. Is that what she was arguing about? Who was that boy?

I jump as a bag drops to the floor beside me.

Isla arrives right on the first bell and sits down next to me, breathing heavily.

"Roadworks held the bus up," she gasps. "They're building a huge crane on the high street. Think they'll let me have a go at it?" She smiles, looking mischievous, but this falters when she catches my expression.

I feign normality. "For you, probably yes."

Despite her weird thing for tractors, diggers, and cranes, Isla is super popular. People warm to her in an instant, while I seem to put people on their back foot. They are wary of me, but I don't know why. I'm a friendly, approachable person – well, I think so anyway. Yes, there's always been a *thing* with Laura and her mates, but that's it.

Then again, there was *that* episode in class the other week… I roll my neck, dismissing the thoughts.

The hum of the room reverberates with hushed tones and giggles. The little paranoid voice in my head draws my attention to the small group huddled at the front. Then I notice, Laura's not here. Nobody's mentioned yesterday's argument. In this place?

Laura's rarely late. She walks to school, so the construction work on the high street won't hinder her. I guess her argument, at the base of the hill last night, has seen her calling in sick today. Or getting her mom to do it for her. At least I'll get some peace today from her bitching about anything she can think of.

I wish I could jump back in time and undo yesterday.

The bubbling tension between Laura and me erupted and ripped through the Richter scale. Two years of constant digs, brushes in the hallway, and toxic stares resulted in a nose-to-nose slanging match.

Thankfully, this was in art and design class, so the audience was small, but it all became ugly. We exchanged venomous taunts and shoves but somehow held it together, so it didn't become a hair-pulling, face-scratching fight. But then I went too far.

Laura called me a dog repeatedly. As she walked away, I noticed she had left her cell phone on the desk. Picking it up, I was about to chuck it in her direction, but then she said it, "A little dog, just like her sister."

"Why don't you go and *fetch* this, Laura?" I shouted and held the cell up. Adrenalin gripped my throat with tingling dizziness.

As she turned, I threw the cell with all my strength. Not in her direction but the classroom window. The sickening splinter of the pane was applauded by dozens of plastic components raining to the floor. Laura's gasp met my own.

The crack in the glass didn't spread, and the window held, but a teacher's voice broke the scene. "What's going on here?"

The room emptied as though a starter-pistol had fired. Laura shot a final glance at me and hastily retreated. Leaving me there to face the music.

<hr />

A shiver reminds me of last night; Laura's words echo around my head.

But that other voice? *"Stupid human."*

I must have imagined that when I blacked out. I suppose I was teetering on the edge of a dream; nightmare more like it.

Isla's voice snaps away my thoughts.

"Here, Miss," Isla responds to roll call with our house teacher.

"Anyone knows where Alan is?" the teacher asks, searching the faces after calling Alan's name twice.

With that, he enters the room with apologies for being late.

"Here, Miss," I respond to my name called, keeping my head down. I don't want to catch her disappointed gaze. I'm sure she'll have a *quiet word* at the end of roll call and advise me to see the Principal before classes. I couldn't go yesterday as Principal Georgeson was away on some board meeting.

Mom and Dad will be hit with a bill for the window repairs. Probably the cell phone, too. There goes my allowance… forever.

My gaze shifts to Laura's empty chair, as the teacher skips straight from me to Leslie, missing Laura altogether. Why hasn't she asked about Laura? The guilt in the pit of my stomach burns from yesterday. Is Laura absent because of me? No, even more reason she would turn up today: to see me hung out to dry. She'd get immense pleasure seeing me in trouble. And I'm in deep.

But what happened last night? Did I imagine that?

Has nobody noticed the omission? I quickly scan the faces in the room, and despite a few curious looks in response, everything is normal.

This reminds me of that one other time... Apprehension crawls up my spine.

I mouth, *no Laura*, to Isla's questioning glance, but her brow creases and she raises her right shoulder slightly. *Who?* She mouths back. I shrug away the question. Who indeed?

Roll call ends, and I wait to be called up front, but nothing is said. I stand so our teacher can clearly see me. I even exchange a warm smile with her, but she says nothing. Maybe they expect me to be the *adult* here and instigate matters on my own. There is still half an hour before the first session.

"Sorry, Miss. I need to pop upstairs, to the school office," I tell our teacher, waiting for confirmation of an appointment with the Principal but she just nods. They're taking this well. The last time a window broke, an article appeared in the local press.

As I make my way to the second floor, I discretely scan the faces of other students, searching for that knowing expression of *look who's in trouble*. But the reactions are the standard friendly or stay-away responses.

Like a criminal, returning to the scene of the crime, I peer through the glass panel of the art class door. I'm thankful the room is empty, and it greets me with the musky odour of a thousand dried paintings.

If I were a cartoon character, my lower jaw would drop to the floor. The window is intact. Tracing my fingertips across the glass, there's no sign of breakage, but there are smudgings of dirt, greasy fingers, and splatters of paint. It hasn't been replaced.

This is the original window, and there's no damage? I clearly remember breaking it.

Two students enter the room, and I make a hasty exit. I pause at the stairs to the third floor. If I were a betting person, I'd wager the Principal is not expecting me, so I make my way to the first session class and sit at my usual desk.

What's going on here? Magic windows? Nobody asking about the fight with Laura. Her name not called out by the teacher and no questions as to her whereabouts?

I flinch as a stab of pain in my forehead pulses adrenalin through my body.

This happened before.

With Chloe.

—

Chloe and I were joined at the hip. She enjoyed the same music and bands at *The Pit*. Every Saturday, she would shed her withdrawn, reserved school persona, and jump around the dancefloor with her posse. Sure, in classes, Chloe kept herself private from the masses, but we were close. We could read each other's nods, breaths, tone of sarcasm, rolls of the eyes. But it's like nobody even remembers her existence. It's been more than a month since Chloe was in school.

Last Saturday, I made an ass of myself when I asked Jeff, one of her mates where Chloe was. The conversation became pissy, as this supposed friend pretended never to have known anyone called Chloe. Surrounded by the Goth posse, we screamed at each other over the shrieks and crashing of the live band music. Why was he lying? Chloe was such a great mate, but I'm the only one here who cares she exists. Who hasn't forgotten that she existed.

In class, our teacher doesn't call her name at rollcall. And on my cellphone, her number erased. But now, there's not even a text or call history.

One day Chloe was there and the next? It's as though she's deleted from existence.

I could shout out, "Anybody seen Laura or Chloe?" But I fear the backlash. The looks.

I had an outburst in school over Chloe. It echoed the argument I had in the club with Jeff.

I was frog-marched to the Principal's office after I caused a *scene*, demanding – more like screaming – why the people in my class were conspiring to make me look like an idiot over her absence. Pretending she doesn't exist.

As if the people here don't already see me as odd. That didn't help my case much.

As I search the faces in the class, I wonder who will be next? Whose name not called out tomorrow? Or the day after?

It could be me.

Forgotten.

CHAPTER THREE

It's been a troubling week since *that* night with Laura. The storm which threatened to attack brushed us by, but the dark clouds linger in my head. My heart pounds during roll call each morning in school, as omitting Chloe and Laura's names still goes without a hint of curiosity from anybody. Chloe should deliver her usual grunt to acknowledge she's here when calling her name. Laura always responds with a "Present, Miss."

But not today. Or any day.

Someone's playing a game with me. I know Laura and especially Chloe. Laura was there that night, and she's been in this school, making my life hell.

Hasn't she?

I rummage through my locker again for anything linking Chloe or Laura to this school. A piece of paper with their name on it, a class timetable, or the recent outing to the visiting maritime sailboats schedule, but I come up empty. I've let this pass for too long. I must act.

"Hey, Jayne. What've you lost?" Isla shoulders her locker next to mine.

"Oh, nothing. Looking for a note from Chloe."

Isla grabs a textbook from the back of her locker. "Chloe Stirling? I didn't think you two were speaking?"

"No. Chloe Bates," I respond with a heart-skip, as Isla's expression drops into a frown.

She dips her chin. "Not this again, Jayne. Chloe, who?" Isla raises open hands, palms up to emphasise her question. There's no malice from Isla.

Exactly, *Chloe, who?* I spin the wheel on the combination lock and tap my head. "Ignore me. Got to get the papers for Hunneford's class. As per usual, he volunteered me. Catch you in a minute." I head for the third-floor admin office.

I can tell what Isla's thinking. But I had my *accident* over a year ago. My head trauma has gone. Hasn't it? Just because I forget silly things like shopping lists, doesn't mean I've invented classmates.

And I'm running late. The session start bell insists I hurry along the empty courtyard to Hunneford's Psychology class.

There's the usual Monday morning hum about the room as I enter. I place the stack of papers on Hunneford's desk and deliver a feeble, "Sorry, I'm late." He returns a grin and gives me a flamboyant, "Thank you, Jayne." He always stresses the trailing "e" more than most.

Yes, I am *Jay-nee* to my family and friends, but he takes it an irritating step further. I sit at my desk and flick the neckline of my top back and forward to help cool myself.

"Body language," Mr Hunneford announces to bring us to attention. Then he begins his rehearsed lecture in how animals communicate without words and how eighty-five per cent of our communication comprises tiny gestures of our bodies. I've already stopped listening and pay even less attention to the DVD presentation, which follows afterwards.

I can't solve Chloe or Laura. Why do I remember people who don't exist here? But I heard Laura's voice that night. I've known her and Chloe for years.

Laura and I were friends throughout school, but then matters took a tangent in various directions. Boy troubles. She liked Iain, and he liked me. To cut a long story short, I got the guy. But with it came the name-calling and anger. Laura hated me, and her bitterness branded me as *easy*; Iain was a senior, two years older than me.

The rumours spread, and too many small-minded people assumed my older boyfriend and hanging with the Goths, equalled me sleeping with Iain. I never did, unless holding hands and kissing qualifies.

Tired eyes prevent me from focusing on the presentation. I was up all night again on the web: search engines, social media, you name it, I've looked. Chloe and Laura are not on any of my friend lists, but I know I've seen the pictures. The showing-off and whatever. Laura's blogs don't exist anymore.

But now gaps, vacant spaces occupy the photos which Chloe or Laura was part of. Laura's name is missing from the engraved nameplates on sporting trophies, in the glass cases of the school reception area.

I tap my forehead like that'll help, but my fingertips trace across a small plate hidden below the skin. A metal memento from the accident I had a year ago. The tissue feels cooler there and numb. I hate it.

When the presentation ends, Hunneford holds up one sheet of paper I brought to the group. We're called a group, not a class, as a mark of respect to our seniority. Yeah, right.

"I'd like you to partner up!" Hunneford smiles.

We groan.

"Read through the sheet and carry out the exercise." Hunneford motions for us to move.

There's the usual chaos moment where everybody decides who to sit with. Still, I can't help but notice Alan is partnering with Jess. He always sat with Laura. And Chloe, she would sit with Leslie or me. I twist to see Leslie sat next to Steve. The skin over the plate in my forehead stings. This happens a lot more of late, and it's annoying. I rest on my elbows and tap my fingertips against my head to help soothe the irritation.

Within the disarray, Aithen enters the room.

I straighten and watch Aithen pass elegantly between the bodies around him. Whenever he enters the room, a delicate sensation tightens my upper chest. It causes me to breathe just a little harder. It's normally now that Chloe and I would exchange that knowing look. She knows, knew I have a thing for Aithen. But it was our secret. No way would I share a crush with this lot.

When Aithen joined this class at the start of the last semester, a multitude of hearts skipped a beat; mine included. I wouldn't consider him a *pretty boy*, but more someone who can handle themselves.

For all his airs and graces, Aithen's always late. He doesn't show up late for effect – a grand entrance – quite the opposite. Head down, trying to make himself small. Bit pointless as he must duck as he enters a doorway. At first impression, you'd call him a naughty boy, but he's studious. He has a casual but confident stride, which betrays the *don't notice me* stance he tries to deliver. The hood from his cotton sweater pulled up over his head, shadows his features.

He passes through the throng and his fingers trail across the edge of my desk. I look up, but his eyes watch the floor.

As usual, he parks himself at the back of the room.

Aithen tends to back off from the group and not get involved in small talk, any conversations. But he's often the first to jump in to answer questions in math.

It bugs me.

I've had free reign in Durham's class until Aithen showed up at the start of the semester.

My gaze becomes glued to where he touched the desk. What's that all about? I should have paid attention to Hunneford's earlier body language lecture. I won't be obvious about it, but who sat with Aithen? I turn under the pretence of seeing who Sally partners with.

I catch my breath. Aithen's staring straight at me. Even as a student passes between us, Aithen moves his head to remain focused on me. My cheeks flush, and I nibble my bottom lip.

This is not the only time he's caught my gaze. The first time was when I entered the school library, and I held the door open for Aithen as he was leaving. I could see he was struggling to say something; his mouth trembled, and he appeared to swallow nervously, but his eyes: they smiled for the rest of him.

"Thank you," he said, and his mouth joined his eyes in the smile when I replied, "You're welcome."

It was hard to describe, but the impact on me has been compelling since. Often, I'll catch him unawares, watching me. But he'll snap his gaze away before I can acknowledge it. Isn't there a rule somewhere that says it's okay if a cute boy is giving you the stares, but a not so cute guy is…?

The group settles as the pairings finalise, though Isla fusses from desk to desk, deciding who to sit with. She already knows I won't join in on this exercise; I don't like Hunneford's silly games and without Chloe, who do I want to play stupid, psychology games with?

Like a buzz against the side of my face, I can sense Aithen's stare. He's continuing to watch me as I cast him a glance.

I raise my eyebrows at Aithen and can't stop the quiver of my smile breaking through. He looks at his desktop, then back to me. *Go on, give me a smile*, I will him, but he drops his gaze again.

I spin back to my desk and pretend to read the paper. Aithen usually ignores every person and me in this school – besides the teachers – and now, and now what? It's probably nothing. I'd like it to be something though.

More than once he's held a door open for me. I've seen him

standing alone in *The Pit* and once he gave up his place at the bar for me to jump the queue.

And yet, I've not spoken to him outside of school.

Perhaps I should have given him a playful wave and entice that smile from him.

But then the negative thoughts play around my head. Has he heard about my accident and chosen the judgemental side? He was there that day I had my Chloe meltdown in school. That's the thing about this place – opinions spin on a coin: on the one hand, the small-minded idiots who think they can guess your every move and motive. On the other, the handful of genuine and caring people whom I love to know.

No, Aithen may be quiet, but I don't see him as flocking to silly rumours and opinions. He's too sophisticated for that. Now that I think about it, he began this whole watching me thing since that meltdown. Before that, I was blanked like the rest of the school.

Partner up, Hunneford said. I angle my head, pretending to be mulling over one of the questions from the sheet. From the corner of my eye, I can see Aithen's still alone. The girls in this group usually flock like vultures with a new guy, but he's kept them all at bay.

I turn towards him, and his eyes catch mine. I give him a questioning shrug, and he nods towards the empty seat beside him.

Really? Why's he suddenly showing interest? Is this a trick?

But I can't fight this urge to talk to Mr Never-speaks-to-anybody. I grab the sheet with a trembling hand. I don't know if I imagine it or if the room becomes quieter.

When I stand, Hunneford raises an eyebrow. I stopped joining in these activities, and he usually accepts my stance. I'm not sure if it was out of pity for the silly girl searching for an imaginary friend or fear I may shout at him.

It's incredible how a dozen steps can feel like a mile. My chest pants and my mouth is dry. Why am I so nervous? Aithen's just a boy in class. Some of the goth guys I hang around with are a lot more menacing. I feel like such a wimp. *A sheep in wolf's clothing* my mother often describes me. Sheep? More like a lamb.

He looks up as I approach the desk, and I give a questioning gesture. *Please don't tell me to go away. Don't let this be a silly game to make me look like an ass.* I can't look him in the eye. He stands, pulling back the hood of his sweater, and says, "Yes, please do."

Oh, there they are good manners. Makes a change in this place; most boys here don't even bother to hold a door open for you or anything respectful. But Aithen does.

I sit beside Aithen and puff the bangs from my eyes.

Okay, what must we do? I skim through the worksheet and groan. *Describe three unique features of your lab partner.* Oh Hunneford, you're a pain. Are we seven or seventeen?

Aithen's hands catch my gaze. Long, slim fingers. He could be a guitar player or pianist, good at typing even. Tidy nails. I should say something to break the ice. I take a breath.

"Bit overdue but welcome to Hill Derry."

Really? That the best I can do?

"Thank you, Jayne."

He says my name with such warmth I falter.

The other pupils in the room are facing one another for the exercise, so I mimic this and turn to face Aithen. He's watching me intently.

My hand reflexively reaches to brush my bangs against the plate. It's hidden, but Aithen's so close, he may notice the scar. The ugly bump beneath my skin.

His eyes.

Violet. Like mine though Aithen's sparkle. Contacts? No, natural. You can always see the outline of lenses, and I really am looking. His dark eyebrows – crafted perfectly – contrast his fair hair. And his lips… I switch back to his eyes. I don't think I've seen this guy's face up close before now. Talk about hot. But something else, there's confidence in his expression.

Hunneford's right; who needs words when your eyes can tell you all they need to know? I can't stop my smile. His eyes shine, like a smile, and his pupils dilate. I could stay here in this moment for an eternity. Still, Hunneford gatecrashes the party as he perches on Aithen's desk.

"So, Jayne?"

"What, me, first?"

Hunneford smiles. "No, third actually."

I scan the group of quiet faces. I pace my response.

"Okay. Hard as Aithen is new and quite... reserved." It's weird to say his name out loud while he's sat next to me. I nibble on the inside of my cheek. "Erm, yeah... his name is unique, so I will say 'Name' as the first thing." I pass a fleeting glance at his lips, his mouth, so... "Soft."

The group laughs, and I cringe. I pretend it's deliberate, but I don't check to see how Aithen responds.

"Violet. His eyes, colour violet." I finish and lean back into my seat. "Sorry," I whisper to him.

"And you, Aithen; Aithen with a *'T'?*" Hunneford considers him and takes a few steps away. Hunneford is referring to the silent *h* in Aithen's name, hence no *th* sound.

I can see from the corner of my eye how Aithen looks at me then back to the group. His voice is calm and clear. "Okay, my three words for Jayne." My name never sounded so melodic.

"Beautiful."

The group gasps. My eyes flick wide, and my cheeks heat up. The piece of paper I'm holding is suddenly much more appealing.

"Violet, too."

Ever *heard* thirty eyes looking at you?

"Equilateral."

Silence. Then a few quizzical, "What?" from the group, but they immediately forget it and return to a hum of chat about his first word. There are whispers and sniggers from the group, and I'm sure I hear the word *crazy* or *nuts* in hushed, insulting tones. I dare not look up and catch anyone's gaze.

"Sorry back." He faces forwards, but did I catch a smirk then?

He called me beautiful; says nothing for a month and then? Is he toying with me? A silly stunt to make the weird girl go weak at the knees?

But equilateral? He noticed. I flick him a glance and stroke my cheek.

Even though I'm a black-haired girl with pale skin, I also have a sprinkling of freckles on my face. Three of which form the three points of an equilateral triangle. One above the centre of my brow line, and the other two perpendiculars below the outer corner of my eyes. These form my triangle points and appear no darker than my other freckles. Outside of school, I often enhance them with an eyebrow pencil. On a choice day, I will stick on small cubic zirconia to each point. The two things I like about my whole person: my eye colour and the triangle points.

I should have said kind words about him. I glance at him again, but my cheeks flush, and I avert my gaze.

Hunneford continues his presentation. I pay little attention to what he says. All I can sense is Aithen's presence so close. How did this ever happen? To go from ice cold to sweltering in one morning.

At least it's a welcome diversion from my other thoughts.

When the end-of-session bell finally sounds out, all I want to do is make an escape to allow myself time to calm down. I leave the room, and as I reach the door, I turn back to see Aithen. He's staring straight at me, so I smile.

Thankfully, he smiles back.

The sun in the courtyard chases away dark thoughts of missing people.

I can't wait for math class.

As I nibble on a sandwich, a tray of plastic cups spills over, and I jump at the sound. For a split second, I see the windscreen of the car buckling, from a year ago. I grasp the edges of the table and close my eyes to shield the memory of the accident. And all because of a silly crush.

Time is supposed to heal; people say as though it will fix your pain. It doesn't. What they should say is, we can't help you get over the sickening emptiness you feel right now. And we will not hug you for the next twelve months or wrap you up with comforting words to help you face waking in the morning and missing everything which reminds you of them.

Iain. He was the crush. A senior at seventeen and I, a junior at fifteen. A whirlwind romance of gothic bands, concerts, and pure bliss. But he also showed respect towards me and the boundaries of my youth. Yes, we kissed, but nothing more. He cared about me for me and not for *what he could get,* and for that, I loved him back like crazy. The next year brought college, and he left. His family moved away from Dereton shortly after. His graduate program in botany and plant diseases at Garland University is five hundred kilometres away. Not on the other side of the world, but it may as well be.

I lost it for a moment the day he left, and I stole Mom's car. I got it into my head to dash to the airport and, in a blaze of romantic glory, run into his arms and deliver a passionate farewell kiss. Instead, I steered the car into a lamppost a few blocks from home and awarded myself two weeks in the hospital. My badge is the small metal plate I now have in the front of my skull.

They did a decent job, and the scar isn't noticeable. But it feels like a mountain, and I cover it up with makeup and concealer. I wish I could hide the worried expression my mom gives me ever since. I let her, myself, all my family down that day.

But this was also the time Chloe became my soulmate. She was always there at the hospital, visiting me and often snook into the ward. The number of times security led her out – I'm surprised they didn't ban her from the premises. A smile escapes me. Chloe was so funny. She always had a quip for every occasion, often finishing people's sentences with an inappropriate ending. But her grey eyes would be deadpan and serious. The person she was mocking would be spluttering and recovering their position.

We had that thing where you could sit in each other's company without exchanging a word. Chloe shared my obsession with tattoos, but she was much more into body-piercings. She was very discrete about them and only wore studs in her earlobes when in school, but when you saw her away from the confines of rules and judging eyes… I miss her.

I flick away a tear as a funny day springs to mind. Chloe turned up to school wearing a cluster of rings in her ears, lips, nose, and studs in her eyebrows. Her eyes were like discs: she'd had a good night. I was ill that night, so I didn't go out for fun. Maybe I should have.

Chloe was ordered to the Principal's office, but when she returned, she was beaming. Our teacher asked to have a chat with the Principal.

"What happened?" I asked.

Chloe laughed and pretended to bang her head against the desk. Her black bobbed hair bouncing as she played.

"I think he's kinda sorry he started that." Her cheeks flushed.

I raised a fist to my mouth. "What? What did you do?"

"He tried the big I-am- Principal speech about rules and how we must conform." Chloe giggled, adding a deliberate pause as she threw back her head. "Then he *ordered* me to remove my piercings there, in front of him."

My mouth dropped open. "All of them?" I already guessed where she was going with this.

"Uh, huh. So, you know I can remove these things in a flash? I lost the face-hardware, but with just the final stud in my eyebrow, I asked him, 'All of them? Honestly?'"

The Principal's response had been a condescending, yes.

"So, I slipped off my top and bra." She laughed again. "And yeah, that kinda got him rushing to his feet to grab my top and cover me up. I'd already started to reach for my boob, and he said, '*Stop! Leave them!*'."

I laughed. "You're terrible. What did he do?"

"He looked like a tomato in a suit. '*Get dressed, Miss Bates!*'" She mimicked his voice and pulled this snobby, stretched expression, acting out how he must have appeared. "Then he made a sharp exit, asking me to return to lessons."

I'll give Chloe one thing, she may have rebelled that day, but she didn't push it. I think she was just high and wanted to play. She adopted a more covert stance after that episode. It had embarrassed her; it's not every day you flash the Principal. They could have expelled her, but it was daft.

I dab my eyes with a tissue and raise my gaze, smiling. The moment washes away, and my expression fails: three girls and a boy on a table opposite, watch me. Their cold stares ask silent questions I have no answers to.

———

A hand pats my backside when I pass through the classroom door, and I see Isla's sweet face. "You recovered from this morning?" She winks at me. "*Beautiful* girl."

I laugh away, my embarrassment. I don't want everybody talking about it, and I hope the word hasn't travelled quickly.

I take my usual seat, about three rows in front of Aithen when I realise I didn't smile or acknowledge him. He'll probably think I've snubbed him, playing it cool. Should I turn around and give him a wave?

Really?

No.

Okay, I can make an excuse to leave the room and then on the way back to my seat—

Durham interrupts my train of thought.

"Time for a quick-fire question session on calculus to get your brains warmed up. Then we'll carry out markups on the smart-screen." I like Durham. He's gentle, patient, and explains mathematical theorems as though reciting poetry. He always dresses elegantly for this school: three-piece suit, with a waistcoat. His only fashion faux pas is the ties he wears.

As is routine in his math class, I am the one to answer the quick-fire questions first. Either the other students cannot bother competing, or they hope I will finally get one wrong. Yes, I'm good at math, and today I'm on form, which is a bonus as I'm showing off in front of Aithen.

Durham asks, "Diff x to the power x?"

"X to the—" Aithen stops as our voices clash. I shoot him a glance, and he smiles. He opens a hand, gesturing for me to continue.

"X to the power x, multiplied by one plus log-e x." I consider Aithen again, and he mimics a little clapping action with his index fingers. *Oh, witty.* I respond with playful, squinting eyes.

Then comes the more exciting part of the routine, an activity I enjoy a lot. Durham produces a problem on a large smartboard, which a student must answer – solo. They can ask for help from the group but not from Durham. I'm poised for the first problem. *Demonstrate the Product Rule in calculus between two formulas.* Easy. But Isla is first to raise her hand and stand up. She clears her throat and looks towards the back of the room. At Aithen.

Is it me, or is she swaying from side to side as she writes? Her bright, giggly voice is like a young child telling a joke. Everybody likes Isla. Does Aithen like her? I rub the back of my neck while I watch Isla finish and return to her seat.

I'm already standing when Durham loads the next problem. Differential equation. Hmm, this could be an epic failure.

But I've committed to it.

I take the pen from Durham and review the equation. How do I appear from behind compared to Isla? Will Aithen still think I'm beautiful? I do a safety check on my top; don't want it riding up my back and having a wardrobe malfunction. I cringe as I realise I have rubbed my hips to check my clothes. No, don't be stupid, everyone smooths their clothes when they stand.

"Everything all right?" asks Durham.

"Oh, yeah. Deciding what to have for dinner." The group laughs, and the tension slips away. I scribble on the giant screen in front of me. Though it's tricky, I dispatch the problem within five minutes, and that puts a swagger in my step as I return to my desk.

Aithen is looking at me, and I don't want to let this moment pass. The motivation to leave my seat and answer the math problem resolved. Now I want to walk over to him. To feel wanting and passion again, like I had with Iain. I miss kissing and held in firm arms and having somebody to talk to about my mixed-up ideas. I want to be called beautiful again. Halting at my desk, I wonder what it would be like to kiss Aithen? I smile at him and sit down. He returns a broad smile back, and I don't care what the others think.

I look at Isla, and she beams at me from the side on.

Durham presents the next problem: one of his favourite examples designed to catch you out. It is a booby-trap question with no solution, and yet, Aithen raises his hand. I wish he didn't as these problems appear okay at first, but there is always an embedded red herring. I don't want Aithen to embarrass himself. This math problem has no solution; none of the professors at the university can even solve it.

I turn to Aithen, and our eyes meet. I offer a slight shake of the head when I really want to plead with him to sit back down. *You can't solve this!* I want to shout and save his embarrassment.

But then Durham catches Aithen's attention. "You sure?"

"Yes, I will give it a go." Aithen takes the pen. Durham stretches out in his seat and clasps his hands behind his head. Aithen writes in a clean and elegant script. Using various parts of the screen to hold aspects of the solution, he speaks. His voice is clear and confident. Not a hint of nervousness in front of the group.

I like having an excuse to watch him undetected. His body is tight and muscular but not like one that pumps iron in the gym. I can imagine him in a hundred-meter line-up in a track event. The back of his neck looks so kissable, and as he writes, I can see his triceps muscle pulsing. *He's* beautiful.

I've lost track of time. Aithen inhales and concludes, "… and hence as the first quadrant is tending to zero, the fourth is tending to the first. They evaluate to a regular null series. Quad two and lambda on three cancel out through equality. Thus, their division is equal to one. This is a singularity. Hence the answer is one. With lambda pursuing phase four: this is currently undefined, within the context of the original question."

Silence. I've missed most and understood less of what Aithen delivered. Durham sits bolt upright and ponders the screen.

"Has he solved it?" asks Jeff. "Is that, right?" someone else echoes.

Durham says nothing and leaves the room. What's that all about? The group erupts into conversation as Aithen takes his seat, his eyes downcast and his mouth crumpled.

When Durham returns to the room, he's accompanied by Mrs Forshaw, the head of the mathematics faculty. They ponder Aithen, then Mrs Forshaw presses a button next to the screen. A batch of A4 paper prints off before she clears the screen, and they both leave the room again. Okay, this is strange.

"What's up with that?" asks Steve.

"Aithen, was the answer, right?" Alan looks excited, but he overreacts to most things.

That sparks a reaction from Aithen. "Yes, sorry." He clears his throat. "But I guess I cheated a bit. I have seen the question before."

I'm not buying it.

He can't have seen this before. No-one can solve it. I think there's an award posted somewhere to solve the problem, in the math community. Aithen looks uncomfortable behind the facade. As usual, the psychology class reminds me: a person smiles with the eyes, not the mouth. Should I talk to him? I don't know. While the group discusses other things with one another, I approach his desk. He looks up and motions for me to join him.

"You okay?" I sit next to him.

He crosses his arms when Durham enters the room again, this time alone. I don't want to stare at Aithen, but while he rubs his forearm, I notice a glaze across his eyes. His lips quiver as he appears to mumble to himself.

Durham smiles, taking short, deliberate steps up and down across the front of the room. We await the verdict. Durham perches at a desk.

"Very good, Aithen. Yes, interesting use of who was it, *Zherkoslav*? I must admit those two theorems were, how can I put it? A revelation. If, of course, they were true." Durham searches the ground around him. "If only I had an Oscar for best actor."

The group exchanges questioning looks.

"But of course, your solution is a work of fiction, albeit an intelligent delivery. I'd say ten out of ten for the entertainment factor."

"Meaning?" Steve's always the first.

"Was it right?" More than one student asks this.

"Why did you print off the solution? Can we have a copy?" Well done, Alan.

Durham is tight-lipped, and Aithen says nothing, his eyes

averted and avoiding contact. Why did he get up and who is "Zh…" whatever? I can't remember the name.

Durham postures at the front of the class and smirks. "No, Alan. It's not the solution. Your classmate," his gaze settles on Aithen again, "simply delivered a cunning work of fiction."

Before I can speak to Aithen again, Durham issues a three-page assignment for us to be getting on with. We can work in groups or retire to the library if we wish to utilise reference materials. A few students exit the room to take up the library offer or, more likely, to leave early.

A small magazine plops on the desk in front of me, and Isla skims to the page she wants. "Those boots, this dress, what do you think?" She points to a page, then to the dress she wears.

As usual, it's a good match. "Isla, you could wear a plastic bin bag, and it would look good." I laugh.

We scan through the exclusive offers, and by the time I look up again, Aithen's gone.

I walk over and sit on the low ledge of the classroom window. The sun is shining out there. But my thoughts cloud any bright promises the light wishes to bring.

Today's been odd. One minute I'm beautiful to Aithen. The next he has solved an impossible math query or maybe has. For some reason, I believe him.

Maybe I should be chasing after him and not ghosts of imaginary friends.

CHAPTER FOUR

I used to dream about Iain and would wake up with a hollow longing, but now Aithen hijacks those fantasies. They are so vivid. He is lying there, smiling at me as I lower myself to kiss him. Reality is such a spoilsport and insists on snapping me awake just at the sweet moment before our lips touch.

Why is he in my dreams? A compliment and a smile, and I'm gushing over nothing. He could be playing a game for all I know. Messing around with the car-crash nut job. I scold myself at the thought. No, he was sincere that day.

If I'm truthful with myself, Iain left and took a lot of my confidence with him. He made me feel like I could rule the world. Nothing could touch or harm me, but then he left, and a lamppost jumped into my path and changed everything.

Kind words and actions tend to fall beside me, but harsh words always penetrate my shield, like they're amplified with molten steel. They sting and burn and deafen me to the kindness which often surrounds me.

My family, friends, even my doctor, are helping me to hear and feel good things around me. When Aithen called me beautiful, it was the loudest word I have heard in a long time.

But I have more important things to think about, and as I stand on the foot-walk, next to a detached house, I pretend to read a message on my mobile.

This house is where Laura lives.

I've battled a mental tug-of-war for the past week, but I must discover, once and for all.

The echoes of Laura's voice haunt me. She was so scared.

Why can't my delusions be unicorns and faeries?

As I trace the few steps up the path to the front door, nerves compel me to flee. I would feel less guilty if I were a burglar even though I've done nothing wrong. I search around me; I want nobody to witness the catastrophe I am about to unleash. I shiver away the uncomfortable memory of when I made a scene with Chloe's mom. The police arrived, and I was driven home in a squad car. Thankfully, no charges raised, but now I have a complaint in a file in police HQ. The car crash opened that file.

A dog barks in response to me pressing the doorbell. I can see a shadowy form break up the light inside, through the glass of the door. I draw in a deep breath. Be calm. You're not crazy. Just checking in with a *friend*.

The door squeaks open, and a small, white dog spins about, barking around my feet. Thank you, announce my arrival to the whole street, why don't you?

Laura's mom tilts her head. "Jayne? What brings you here?" She gently tussles the dog through the door and pulls it closed behind her.

At least she knows me, so I'm not nuts. "Sorry, Mrs Warden. I was looking for Laura?"

Her features become a strained mask, as though her mouth forgot how to smile.

"Laura?" She blinks several times.

The sting in my forehead compels me to move on.

"I'm sorry, Mrs Warden." I peer over her shoulder. The wind

catches the door, and the dog escapes to our feet again. She bends down to pick up the dog.

I know that house. The furniture. I can see the cabinet in the lounge, which houses figurines from movies. Mr Warden is a hard-core movie fan and collects many memorabilia. I've seen inside the cabinet when I came to one of Laura's birthday parties; many years ago, when we were friends.

"There is no Laura here, Jayne. Are you after Paul?" She places a hand on my shoulder, snapping me back to reality. Paul is, *was* Laura's brother.

"I'm an idiot," I excuse myself, waving my hands to dismiss my words. "I had a knock on my head a while back, and it still makes me mix up people and places."

She holds the dog close to her chest like a barrier; even the dog looks at me like I have two heads.

"I'm sorry. Ignore me." My laugh is not as convincing as I leave.

"Tell your mom I'll ring her later!" she calls after me.

Great. That's all I need.

I run my usual route through the forest; my pace falters when I notice two people jogging ahead of me. I recognise Aithen, but he's accompanied by another boy. Taller than Aithen – if that was possible – and white, cropped hair. Their pace is slower than mine, and they don't appear to hear my approach. I know that white hair.

Could I steer off course and bypass them? No, the trees are too dense here. A nervous buzz erupts in my stomach. Should I shout out to excuse my passing through? What if they accelerate and won't let me through? Do I try and push through anyway and risk a scene? Or hold back and allow them to dictate my pace? No, they can get out of my way.

I plod a little louder into the ground to announce my presence. This grabs Aithen's attention, and he raises an arm across his running partner's chest. They both stop.

Aithen watches me getting closer, though the other boy averts his gaze. It can't be him. But that distinctive white hair is a dead giveaway. Is he the boy with Laura?

Stupid human.

No, it can't be. It can't have happened. It's my head injury playing mental games.

My steps feel so slow and purposeful. Why do I feel like I've landed in one of those dreams where you're running through thick glue?

Should I say something to Aithen? Propose a smile?

I'm glad my face already flushes from the running. My pace increases as I pass them. If only I could be a menacing, athletic blur breezing past them.

I flash Aithen a quick glance, but a tree root distracts the smile from my lips.

Twenty more strides and the path behind me blends in the trees. My ears are sensitive to feet running behind me, but the only sound is my breathing and my own steps. I dare not take a break; I couldn't bear for them to catch up with me.

That white-haired boy. At least I haven't imagined him. But was it him who was with Laura? And why is Aithen with him?

I sit at the base of the hill. I'm not climbing that today, but I need to do something rash. The ache in my heart and the deluge of tears over the past month tell me Chloe was real. I can't accept my injury has created such detailed memories and thoughts. That's impossible. But it also feels like Chloe was too good to be true. Did I possibly invent her to plug the painful void left by Iain?

But why would I then create a friend, turned arch-nemesis in the shape and size of Laura?

My family, my doctor – I sigh thinking about Doctor Harris –

are trying to help me understand the head injury is creating thoughts, fantasies in my mind. But they're not listening.

I'm not seeing the odd image or having bad dreams. This is my waking reality.

And I honestly believe everyone is lying. I don't believe in conspiracy theories about government cover-ups, like Area 51 and aliens, or rubbish like that. But I am confident I'm being played the fool here.

Dereton is a small, naïve town, and I am sure I can slip into the school and access the admin office filing system. The school is always open in the morning on a Saturday. The library and sports hall used for assorted reasons. And the cleaning staff will have the offices unlocked.

There's nothing to prevent me from searching for Chloe and Laura in the school records.

The last time Mom gave me that look was when I woke up in the hospital last year.

Sitting on the opposite side of the desk in the school security office, grey walls press against my thoughts, and no windows offer distractions from the heaviness in the room. Talk about depressing and bleak.

The security officer is talking on the telephone to the Principal, his deliberate words and accusing glances, pushing me further into my seat.

Okay, so I got it wrong. I didn't know there had been a spate of petty thefts in this school recently, which resulted in heightened security and cameras in the office areas.

As the security officer flamboyantly places the telephone back into its cradle, he rests his hands on the table and clasps his fingers together.

What? I ask by tilting my head.

"Okay, Jayne. The Principal has decided, against my better – much, much better – judgement, not to call the police." He folds his arms and his chair groans as he settles back. "This time."

He watches me.

I mimic him and fold my arms, too. "What, you want me to applaud and thank you?"

"Jayne," hisses Mom. She pulls one of my hands towards her. "Just don't start."

I snatch my hand back. I don't mean to be so aggressive about it and could kick myself when I see the shock in my mom's eyes. I've noticed that telling look too often lately. The day I crashed her car is the day she lost her *little girl.*

Our family has always been so close and happy. We were bullet-proof, and nothing could interfere with the perfect balance. But then I changed all that. I flinch internally for a moment, as the wind-screen cracks in my mind.

The security officer arrests my thoughts. "Jayne. No charges are to be raised, but the Principal just wants a statement. Nothing more. Then you can go and do… whatever you do." His voice is lazy and condescending. "What were you doing in the school office?"

What do I say?

I'm an A-grade student, so can't pretend I would hack into the computer and raise my scores. I wonder what the Principal said on the other end of the call.

"Jayne?" presses the officer.

"Nothing," I respond weakly, but then clear my throat. "I was bored. It was a dare."

I don't look at Mom when she sighs loudly.

"A dare?" the security officer asks, dipping his chin. "So, you bypassed the security on a PC and prized open two file cabinets, causing criminal damage – I'll add – on a dare?"

I shrug. What else can I say?

"Jayne. The Principal can *suggest* no police action is taken, but it is in my right, my duty that I should report this." He pauses and tilts his chair back slightly, but then lets his weight fall forward with his hands slapping onto the tabletop. I jump at the sound.

"Give me one reason not to call them," he demands, his words quiet but commanding.

I look towards Mom, and I can see her stiffened posture is both defensive and agitated. She glares at me. "Just answer him, Jayne."

My hands are gripping the sides of the seat, and my heart is already thumping so loud, it wants to drown out my words. I can't have the police on my case again. It's becoming a habit now, and they will arrest me. Car theft and damage. The scene with Chloe's mom and me escorted home. And now this. What if I'm sent to court? What if the court asks my doctor for a medical statement? She'll say I'm crazy. Imaging people. Juvi-record and that's the end of my future if I'm not careful here.

"I was searching for my friends," I offer, weakly.

The officer retreats into his seat. "Your friends?"

"Jayne," Mom says under her breath, but it's loud enough to catch the officer's gaze.

"Where are your friends?" he asks. "Were they hiding in the office, too?"

"No," I respond. "They have gone missing from the school, from Dereton. And I hoped to find out something about them in the file systems."

There I've said it. Again. To another person.

His gaze widens for a moment. "Wait. You're not talking about this, who was it again? Chloe?"

My eyes snap to his when he says her name.

"You remember?" I plead.

"Yeah, I remember—"

"Then I'm not crazy," I declare and almost laugh. "Nobody

believes me when I say she's my best friend and that she's gone missing." I look towards Mom, but she's not smiling back.

Instead, she looks from me and back to the officer.

"No, Jayne. I remember taking you from your classroom, the other week when you had that... meltdown? About how everyone has been lying to you about your missing friend, Chloe?"

My heart plummets to my stomach.

"What? The... meltdown?" I can hear my shouts and screams from that day in class. The shocked faces.

"Oh..." I slump lower.

The security officer breaks the heavy silence. "Jayne. I realise something is going on here, about you, which I'm obviously not a party to." He sounds sympathetic for once. "But tell me then. Did you find any records on Chloe?"

I shake my head. "No, Chloe or Laura."

Mom squeezes my shoulder gently. "Let's leave it there," she says, gently.

I don't see the wordless exchange between Mom and the security officer. But in that silence, I am excused.

Mom asks me to wait outside for a moment, and I don't object.

I've said enough.

But in my head, I am screaming. For a split-second then, I thought someone had believed me. That I'm not going crazy and inventing people.

Just for that moment, I had Chloe back.

CHAPTER FIVE

Monday dawns with nervous anticipation. I half expect to see a police car parked in the reception lot, but there's nothing. I wasn't convinced the security officer won't call the police.

I hid away on Sunday out of doubt. Fear even. I took such a risk on Saturday.

Mom was careful and danced around the subject, but she didn't press. There have been one too many upsets over the past year and this weekend was not the time to stir matters further. Dad doesn't know.

I walk to the psychology class; butterflies stir in my stomach for two reasons. First, what if my weekend antics are public gossip? No, there must be rules about confidentiality and all that.

But second, despite the doubt and trauma of possible arrest, mischievous echoes from my dreams cause my cheeks to colour as I spot Aithen. He's deep in conversation with Hunneford outside the classroom. It's frustrating, I want Aithen to notice me.

I sit with Leslie and Tina as they skim through a college prospectus. It's still early days to plan for a degree, but no harm in seeing what's available.

Aithen walks past the three of us, and I gaze in his direction, but he doesn't even acknowledge me. He's dismissive of everyone. Alan gets in his path and Aithen stops, raising his hands like brakes.

"Oh." Leslie's exclamation voices my own inner irritation. I can't help but flush with disappointment as I take my seat, a few rows in front of his. This morning couldn't come soon enough. Two hours of deciding what to wear and finding everything not good enough and now, I feel cheap. Is this the start of being ignored? Forgotten?

Ever since that math class, Aithen has been wearing a troubled expression. The few times I've seen him on campus, he's always in a hurry. Like he bears the weight of the world on his shoulders.

Throughout the session, Hunneford eyes Aithen a little longer than usual. What's going on?

As I leave the building after class, I notice Aithen across the courtyard. He's talking to a boy I recognise. The boy turns to face me, and it's him, from the forest run. White hair, olive skin, and black eyes, cold and heartless. His stare passes through me, as though I'm invisible.

A shiver pulses through my body and goes with a mental slap, more like a punch.

Silly human.

A broken collage of memories, flashing through my head. I can see him and Laura phasing in and out of my mind, and it makes the plate in my head hurt. I rub the skin and let the thoughts fade away. Were they dating? Was it him I saw with Laura that night? No, it's not real. It didn't happen. I've seen her in a movie or whatever; before the accident. If only I could believe my own reasoning.

What are you looking at? I want to say it, but I hope he can read my expression.

I exchange glances with him; then I look at Aithen who seems to peer straight through me. He nudges the white-haired boy away, and I suck on my lower lip with anger. We can all play stupid games.

I'm dizzy as I leave school and head towards the doctor's surgery for my monthly check-up and chat. These memories make me nauseous, and I must talk about them.

———

Dr Harris types away at the screen, preparing my prescription. The plate in my head could be causing undesirable side-effects. It's a titanium composite, so she thinks a course of tablets will help matters. A doctor's surgery, an unknown entity until the accident, but over the weeks, the reception staff have come to know me. I find this place uncomfortable. The smells. The lights. Everything.

She hands me a slip of paper. "Take this to the pharmacy, and I've booked you in for a weekly check-up—" She raises a hand to my look of protest. "So, we can see how the prescription goes. You'll receive a text message to remind you."

She eyes me for a moment. "Anything else you want to discuss? You gave a hint at the start of the session?"

Do I want to answer this? I'm crazy, I know, and this will prove it.

"Okay. Now don't over-react but... Okay, I'm overdoing it." I laugh, trying to defuse what I am about to say. "I'm having more strange thoughts about people in school?"

"No, not those type of thoughts," I respond to her raised eyebrows expression.

Just spit it out. I'll explode if I don't say it.

"I remember someone else who doesn't appear to have gone to school? Laura Warden?"

Dr Harris appears to muddle the name over and then types at the laptop for a moment. She's giving nothing away, but I'm sure she thinks I'm nuts. She knows all about my Chloe meltdown in school, and the police summoned to her parent's house.

Harris smiles. "Unless she's seventy and a mature student in Hill Derry, then no, there's no Laura Warden you would know of."

This is not news; my own web searches found the elderly Laura. At least this confirmation is encouraging. Well actually, no it's not. It's like a conspiracy, and I'm the victim in the centre.

Harris' face droops as she considers me. "No, no other Warden here. Unless she didn't register? How long did Laura attend Hill Derry?"

Is this a test? Is Harris searching through my delusion for a weakness in my story?

"Could she have registered at another surgery?" I ask.

Harris motions towards the screen. "I'm accessing the district records here. Hospital and all surgeries, even the orthodontists, register on this shared system."

I bite my lip. Can we pretend I haven't mentioned Laura? "I think I have invented her, sorry."

Dr Harris clasps my hand with two cold hands. They're always cool to touch. "It's okay, Jayne. Just speak. I'm not here to judge you. The crash was a big ordeal for you." Thick glasses enlarge her sympathetic, pale-blue eyes.

"Head wounds cause all sort of issues, but so long as you can filter out reality, then you'll be fine. Don't worry, Jayne."

Why are memories of Laura and Chloe orbiting me? Mentally, I continue to be good at all my school subjects. Math and sciences are no issue. I recall the periodic table with ease, so the accident hasn't affected my memory in those areas. However, trivial things still escape my mind. I've forgotten nothing and yet, my mind created a brand new, detailed history of two people.

"So sorry. I feel like such an idiot." The chair squeaks as I stand.

"Don't worry, Jayne. I've heard worse. Just focus on the here and present. And if Chloe or Laura pops into your head, just

EARTH 101   41

remember they are the result of wires currently twisted in your head." Harris gives me a playful, gentle knock on my forehead.

"Before you leave." Dr Harris interrupts my departure. "Have you given any further thought on the group sessions I suggested?"

I haven't. Harris thinks meeting and talking with other people who have had a similar accident and experiences as me will help. More people to judge me? I don't think so.

"I need to think about it," I offer.

Saturday. We have a visit from my older sister Sarah, her husband Terry, and their two-year-old daughter, Louise. Lou's angelic little face and a chuckle provide a perfect antidote to my troubles. Her precious innocence envelopes everything when she's here. It fills the day with joy and sunshine.

Sarah first became pregnant at eighteen, while still at Hill Derry and living at home. She and Terry couldn't afford a place of their own. Thankfully, Mom and Dad were supportive. Sarah miscarried at three months. And then there came baby Matthew. I squeeze my eyes shut and shake my head to expel the approaching memory. I'm trying to invoke happiness, not more heartache.

Sarah and I have a close bond. Almost telepathic instinct. The loss made it even more devastating. The ache in my chest and over-whelming grief seemed to ebb from her and through me. I scold myself again. *Stop it! Happy thoughts.*

Visually, Sarah is the opposite of me. She has crazy, blonde hair often hurriedly stuffed into a bun with elastic bands and hairpins to tame it. Her green eyes are the same as our younger brother, David. He's fair-haired, too. Both Sarah and David look like my mom, with her noticeably pretty, rounded tones to their faces.

Then there is Emily, my younger sister, and me. Emily's eyes are ocean-blue and, honestly, she looks like a little doll. So cute, with black, pageboy hair. I inherited Dad's tallness, and while Emily has his olive skin tone, I'm anaemic. I guess somebody forgot to colour me in and instead, just splattered a few freckles onto my face. Probably didn't want to waste the paint.

Our family look like a patchwork of people placed under the same roof.

We get to spend the weekend with Dad. Then on Sunday, I go with Mom to drop Dad off at the train station. He's worked away during the week for as long as I can remember, so I cherish every minute we spend together. Despite the chaos I have caused lately, Dad always has my corner. Even when Mom raised the subject of my latest crime, Dad listened but carefully dismissed it.

I sometimes wonder what goes on in his head. Dad is so calm, and no matter what, he sees the bright side of me.

Watching Emily and David hug him goodbye, I wonder if they have the same worry I had when I was their age? A little girl's fear that one day, he might not come back.

The phone startles me out of my trance. It's Sarah.

"We didn't get the chance to talk much yesterday. How're things? Mum mentioned a new love interest in school?"

I forgot I told Mum about what Aithen had said in class. But when she caught me daydreaming and said, "I know that look," I was buzzing with excitement and couldn't contain myself.

But Sarah's question reopens the wounds I've spent the evening trying to close. Though already dry, I wipe my mouth and then my eyes.

"No," I say. "Nothing to report there. Just a misfire... I suppose." And then my face is streaming with tears. What is wrong with me? Am I coming down with a virus?

"You okay, Jayne?"

Breathe.

"Yeah, I'm fine. Busy week and no, nothing…" I trail off as my throat closes and I choke out a weak sob.

"It's nothing," I finally say. "My time of the month."

"No, it's not."

I exhale aloud. "I can't describe it but this stupid—" I don't mean that, "Aithen caught me off guard. He told the whole Psychology study group he thinks I'm beautiful. Childish, I know, and I don't know why he did it or why I'm so emotional about it all. I've known him for what, about ten seconds?" I wipe my nose with the back of my hand.

"Throttle back!" Sarah says. "Let it take its course. You've had a bit of an intense year, what with the accident and Iain. Yes, I am saying his name out loud, and I know you don't want to talk about him again." She pauses. "You're an emotional mess, but you're allowed to take compliments from another guy. Move on. Start having fun."

"I just don't get it." I sniff loudly. "Why would Aithen start something and drop it like a ton of bricks at the first sign of a math problem?"

This makes us laugh for a moment, as I give her a brief recap of what happened in the math class.

"Men say women are complicated. Trust me, Jayne the reverse is true. But you can't dive into a new relationship, expecting it to continue where you and Iain left off."

That stings. I am so over Iain now, but yes, I miss the attention. The looking forward to seeing him and just… being kissed. Loved.

"Yeah? But I want Aithen to talk to me. To look at me, once more." I dab my nose with a tissue. "I didn't feel like this when I first met Iain. There's something different about Aithen."

"He's got three legs?" quips Sarah. I know she's trying to diffuse my scattered thoughts.

"Oh, funny. No, I just feel like I've been waiting for him to enter my life." I sigh and run my fingers through the hair drooping over my face.

"You watch too many movies," Sarah responds, and she's probably right.

"I've even dreamt about him." Sarah doesn't interrupt. "I wish he'd pluck up the courage and continue where he began. Give it a chance to get to know me. To talk to me."

"To notice you, again?"

My silence alerts Sarah to back off, so we focus more on the doctor's visit instead. She also allows me to sound off about Laura and Chloe. I've already told her before about my phantom school mates and the details I remember about them. Still, she continues to have no recollection of them. There's no reason she would, as she knows hardly anyone at Hill Derry now.

My own voice sounds hollow as I recall arguments with Laura or the happy times with Chloe and the Goths. She scolds me when I recall my venture into crime and sneaking into the school office.

"Are you crazy or something?" she snaps. "You can kiss your future goodbye if you get a criminal record, Jayne."

"Well, obviously yes, I am," I retort.

I hear a deep breath on the other side of the call. "You've got to be careful, Jayne. You know I; we all support you in this. But not breaking the law. That's just stupid."

What am I supposed to say?

"I'll tell you what," begins Sarah. "You say these girls were in your class?"

I grunt in response, but then the tears flow as Chloe flows through my mind. I garble tearful words about how we used to people-watch in the mall, inventing stories about that couple over there, or that man talking in hushed tones to his friend, and so on.

All the while, the plate in my forehead stings, as though to give physicality to the painful memories.

"I can't cope with it," I drag a tissue across my cheeks and dab my eyes. "I don't mind the crazy, but I want Chloe back."

"I don't know what to suggest." Sarah's tone is quiet and comforting. "I wish I could wave a wand and bring Chloe into your life."

I press a palm to the stinging plate, moving my head left to right to ease the discomfort.

"I honestly believe that you remember Chloe. I'm not going to say she's imaginary or not important to you. It's like me, with Matthew." Sarah pauses. "I sometimes wake up and imagine hearing him crying, to be fed or whatever."

Sarah rarely says Matthew's name. This pulls me out of my reverie.

"But I know he's not there. Not here." Sarah pauses. I hear a sniff. Oh, no, Sarah. Don't go there.

"I'm sorry, Sarah."

"No, it's okay," she responds with a loud breath trailing. "The thing is. I never got to hear Matthew cry. Not once. But he's just as real, and his memory just… just as harsh to cope with." Her voice cracks momentarily. "So, I honestly believe that you believe in Chloe."

A moment passes, punctuated by our sniffs. I manage a short laugh to dismiss the silence. "Look at us two, getting ourselves in a mess."

Sarah echoes my sentiment.

"I need some sort of plan," I say.

"Then let's make a list of everyone you know in school, especially your class. You write it, and I'll do the same," Sarah suggests.

"And what will that do?" I ask.

"My list is independent of yours. If someone disappears – or appears – then we can cross-check our individual lists?" Sarah pauses for a moment. "It could give you peace of mind and if this is some sub-conscious thing—"

"I'm not making it up?" I blurt out.

"I didn't say you are," she says. "This can be our checklist."

I call out the names of all the boys and girls in my year, and we scribble down our lists. By the time we say goodbye, I am more in control.

I must stop worrying about everything.

Let whatever happens, happen, and stop all this nonsense about missing people.

At least that is the stance I offer to Sarah.

I will not give up.

I will discover what has happened to Chloe and Laura. That white-haired boy: I haven't invented him. And he was with Laura.

Sarah's words about remembering Matthew ring through my head. It's sort of not the same, but she recalls what it would be like to hear him cry. I remember a special friendship with Chloe and rivalry with Laura. And all because of head trauma?

I don't think so.

I know the world is full of so-called, crazy people. But are they all mad? Everyone is too quick to label and push aside those who make them uncomfortable.

I'm now one of those labelled individuals.

But I'm not mad.

Who else feels like this? I need to find another person, people even, who are going through what I am. And no, not Doctor Harris' group therapy session. I mentally roll my eyes.

Folding my laptop open, my fingers hover over the keyboard.

I need a search definition for this. For what though?

The web search engine offers various suggestions in response to my typing.

Missing people. Forgotten friends. Kidnapped students. Erased from existence.

Alien abduction?

CHAPTER SIX

A new school week and Hunneford paces with anticipation while we take our seats. What's he got planned now?

Hunneford stands at the front of the class with a big smile.

"Partner up as you were the last time."

The usual groans respond, and I freeze. I can't force this situation on Aithen again. I don't want to look at him, but I rotate in my seat anyway to look at Aithen—and he smiles. Not a full-on grin but an acknowledgement I'm here and exist. A start, I guess.

I lift myself slowly from my seat and give him a nod, and he reciprocates. Okay, let's see what Hunneford is up to.

As I sit beside Aithen, he rests his lower arms on the desk in front of us. He tilts his head slightly and flicks me a side-on glance. The fingertips of each hand tap together in a rhythm. Quiet but teasing. I don't know why.

Without realising it, I mimic his posture and rest my arms on the desk, leaning forward slightly.

We're so close. I can smell Aithen's scent. Clean. Warm. Seductive and my head is light, but in an enjoyable way. Not dizzy. No, quite the opposite, more alert. Hopeful.

"Take a good look at your partner," Hunneford claps his hands towards his knees, "as this is your new project partner for the end of year assignment."

He applauds himself and beams.

There are a lot of groans and words like, "Oh, I should have sat with…"

Aithen turns, and I'm glad he gives a short chuckle.

"I did not see that coming," he laughs, but his tone is mocking.

I want to shout out, *thank you Hunneford*, but instead, I return the laugh and say, "Don't get too excited. We don't know the project subjects yet."

We're not allowed to choose our own project but assigned randomly from a hat. Okay, not a hat but a sock, which I hope is clean. Aithen lets me pick from the garment, and I draw *Dinosaurs*?

"What am I supposed to do with that?" I ask Hunneford.

"Study. Research." Hunneford draws the words out deliberate and slowly, leaning forward to emphasise each one.

"And they have what to do with psychology?" I ask.

Hunneford beams. "It's not the subject matter, which is important, but communication. Working as a team. And presenting thoughts and arguments based on research."

I open my hands as a gesture of surrender.

"And about building relationships based on trust," Hunneford pauses and looks at Aithen then back at me. "You never know where it may take you." He smiles.

Great.

"We'll be fine," says Aithen. "This is something I know a bit about."

"Dinosaurs?" I lean back in my seat. "And you don't mind having me as your partner?"

"Not another person on this planet I would choose." He smiles.

I guess it'll be a distraction and a chance to get closer to Aithen. And in his head.

That friend of his knows something and Aithen will be my steppingstone to discover what it is. I've also got a handful of leads to follow-up from my web searches last night.

I'm not the only case of someone *mislaying* friends. Three people on a forum have described events like what I have been saying. There were all red-herring blogs and posts about missing people, but most were way too far-fetched.

People on this planet have this crazy fascination with aliens whisking them off to another world for probing and experimentation. Some were almost convincing, but I need reality here. Not some lonely dude in the middle of nowhere.

But there's this one person. They call themselves "*VioletlyAlone.*"

They do appear to be a girl and including the word *violet* in their name piqued my interest. Better still, they are a bus-ride, an hour away from where I am.

I don't know how to approach them with this.

They don't have a blog, but they do post a lot on the message board I found. It's filled with the usual conspiracy theories and other nonsense, but this *VioletlyAlone* appears to scratch for answers; raising questions about a close friend who has suddenly vanished.

But what grabbed me most from one post was where they wrote:

"... and one-minute Kelly was there and a flash of light later, she was gone.

Forgotten by everyone, but me..."

CHAPTER SEVEN

"You're going on a date?" Isla and Leslie practically ask in unison.

"No, it's research for our project," I respond into my mic. We have an online chat session, all three of us. "The movie has dinosaurs in it so—"

"Dinosaurs, my ass," laughs Leslie. "Tyrannosaurus Sex?"

Digital laughs all around.

"I'm so glad I can entertain you," I quip.

"Oh, come on, Jayne," butts in Isla, "One-minute Aithen's calling you beautiful in front of everyone and now…" she giggles, "he wants to *take you* in the cinema." She adds a sultry slant to the words.

More laughs applaud her.

"I don't think he sees me like that," I say, and that calms matters a little.

"Why not?" asks Leslie.

Because it's too good to be true, I think to myself. "I don't know. I think… I think Aithen's a bit out of my league…"

Squeaking voices chorus in response. All encouraging, saying how lucky he is and how so many boys like me and all that. But then Leslie steps in, with her pretend mature, calming voice.

"Take it easy and see where it goes. Don't let him pay for you at the cinema – be independent. Owe him nothing." She pauses. "Then suck his face off!"

Laughter.

"Get those puckers puckering!" chuckles Isla and exaggerates kissing sucking into the mic.

How helpful.

The cinema in Dereton is far from elaborate, having just three screens, and the foyer is a throw-back to nineteen-eighty, but the staff there are lovely.

I've kept my cool and dress more or less as I do for school: jeans, t-shirt, nothing fancy. It's a school trip – for two – and nothing more.

Mom and Dad may have to buy a new carpet, though, as I must have walked the distance of a marathon up and down the length of the lounge, waiting to leave the house. I'm ten minutes early, but I can't settle.

Marching along the high street, it's hard to focus on the simple task of walking. I accidentally bump into two people and almost a lamppost. *Get a grip, Jayne,* I remind myself. Be calm and no talking about Iain, missing girls and especially not Chloe, or anything else which may creep Aithen out. I grimace at my Chloe meltdown in class. What if he asks me about that? I chase away the thought and almost hit another lamppost.

This is a fresh slate for me, so time to forget the past for one evening and step forward to a happy future. But baby steps, no crashing through barriers.

I've also been debating how to break the ice with *VioletlyAlone*. My troubled mind shouts to dive in and explain what is happening. But I must tread carefully. Try and gain some common ground, trust. Then launch into the reason I'm contacting them. I can't just come out with it or else I will scare them away. Then again, if someone messaged me about this, I'd welcome the chance to compare notes. They may feel the same way.

So, I've registered on the forum page and kept it all legitimate and straightforward. I've *liked* a handful of posts, including those from *VioletlyAlone*. I've also posted funny pictures about current affairs and on-topic with what this mystery poster seems to enjoy. But not mentioning anything or responding to anything about missing people.

I need to break the ice first and speaking of which, I can't wait to see Aithen and there he is… with a girl?

Is this supposed to be a group thing? I'm sure it's not. They are standing close together, her back to me. She has auburn hair and is similar in height to Aithen—taller than me, and I'm 178 centimetres.

Halting, I watch her turn to face a boy our age, and I realise she is holding hands with him as they study what looks like a pamphlet. I'm such a fool.

The girl and boy exchange a few more words with Aithen and then walk away. I'm relieved to see Aithen's face light up when he sees me approaching.

"Friends of yours?" I ask. "I didn't recognise them?" Like I would know every single person in Dereton?

"No, just directions," he smiles. "Don't know why they asked me, I don't know anywhere around here."

Popcorn: the instrument of seduction. Fingers are reaching and accidentally finding each other in the darkness. I don't know if I'm hungry for Aithen's touch or the dry, sweetened bites.

His scent is clouding my defences again, gravitating me towards him. I wish I could rip the armrest between us away.

The whole audience jumps at the screech and the lurch of an agitated dinosaur.

The human prey is near.

Aithen reaches a hand to my forearm. To comfort me.

My body shivers and Aithen motions towards the armrest, and I raise it behind us, without thinking. What am I doing? Should I be encouraging closeness? Let's see where this goes. His warmth radiates close and greets a flurry of goosebumps in response. I close my eyes and thank the warmth which soothes the chill.

The big screen forces several more jumps, and Aithen grips me firmer. Is he scared? I chance a glance at his face, illuminated by the screen. His mouth is slack, and his eyes are searching the images in front of him. A soft gasp, as another scene shakes the audience. Even though I'd rather watch him than the movie, I become too lost in the film action and a hostage to Aithen's warmth.

As the end credits roll, I pretend to be interested in the closing credits and movie. I also suggest there may be a post-credit snippet of footage, foreshadowing a sequel. I want an excuse to linger with Aithen. It's hard to explain, but his presence is natural. I'm excited, but he brings a warm calm like I've known him for ages. It's strange.

The fresh evening air surrounds the click of our feet as we walk away from the hum and ding of voices outside the cinema.

"That was fun," I muse to break the silence.

Aithen laughs. "Yes, it was quite entertaining. Not sure if it'll help with our project, mind you."

"We could catch the train into the city, someday soon. Visit the museum for some inspiration?" It's been at least five years since I last went to the museum. History isn't high on my interest list. Still, I remember they had a half-decent collection of stuffed animals and plastic dinosaur fossils. If I'm honest with myself, I have a foot in the camp which says dinosaurs didn't exist. But still, that'll give me the chance to check Aithen out for the next few weeks.

We halt at a road junction. "I go left here," I say.

Aithen watches me. What's he thinking about?

"Yes, of course." His words are quiet. "Did you want to do anything else?"

I glance around the darkened windows of the street. I can't even force an excuse to have a coffee. Going to a bar and trying to talk over rowdy drunks isn't appealing. I'd like to be alone with him… to talk, hold hands, kiss maybe.

It feels like an eternity since I went on a date and felt special.

But this isn't a date, I remind myself.

"No, everything's closed now," I say.

He rubs his hands against his upper arms as though to warm himself. "Okay, I'd better go. Thank you for the cinema visit."

As he leaves, I say, "Yeah, you too. I'll catch you at school tomorrow."

And he walks away.

I watch him and can't stop myself willing him to turn back and give me a wave, at least. But he blends into the shadows and then, he's gone.

CHAPTER EIGHT

Midweek and we have a pass to excuse ourselves from classes to go on a field trip to the museum as it is course related.

"Have you never seen a train before?" I ask, watching Aithen inspecting the train we are waiting to board. I had to grab hold of him when he scrambled down from the platform to the rail line.

A disgruntled guard's whistle echoed my complaints. The guard pointed the finger at the pair of us but thankfully said no more.

"It's fascinating and yet so crude," says Aithen, crouched low as he scans the large steel wheels of the train. "They have rubber wheels in other countries and cities. It is a safer solution, as metal on metal breaking just doesn't bode well for safety." His expression drops like he's just remembered something sad.

"Maybe we should have done a project on trains?" I suggest.

Nudging him with my knee, I beckon to move on. "We can board, you know. Come on."

The journey is only an hour's duration and features a lot of turning and double takes from Aithen as varied landscapes breeze by. He genuinely is taken by the simplest of things, like a child travelling for the first time.

I had hoped this journey would have been a chance to chat,

about anything. Still, he's distracted by cows, chimney stacks, other trains passing in the opposite direction. But then he does the strangest thing.

"May I?" he asks, taking my right hand in both of his.

He holds my hand, palms up, and traces his index finger along my lifeline. Then across the base of all my fingers. He raises his gaze to mine while he describes a small circle in the centre of my palm.

"And you're a palm reader?" I quip, though my voice breaks as I speak. The sensation of his skin on mine is warm and relaxing.

"No, I wanted an excuse to touch your skin." With that, he smiles.

I look around the empty carriage, half expecting to be sitting in Hunneford's psychology class, and a group of curious faces watching, but it's just us.

"You're sweet," I respond, and can't stop my smile. "Can I ask you something?" I don't know where the courage is coming from to ask this.

He nods and holds my hand flat between his.

"Are you dating anyone?" There it is. I've asked *that*. I don't want to be wondering or chasing fantasies.

He releases my hand. "No, of course not. We're not allow— I'm not with anyone." His tone is defensive but calm, and his gaze avoids mine.

Resting his elbows on the table in front of us, he nestles his chin on clasped fingers. "I would never mess you around, Jayne." He rubs those soft lips against his knuckles then tilts a weak smile towards me.

We're not allowed? Is that what he was going to say? School peers do frown upon relationships, but there are no fixed rules about this. Maybe his last school was stricter. But who cares, he's single.

We head straight for the dinosaur department on the third floor. It's changed a lot since my last visit, but still surgically clean and echoey. If a mouse farted here, you'd hear it.

I shrink below the dark outline of a Tyrannosaurus. Its mouth could easily take me with a single gulp.

How scary would it be to see that for real?

"I've read they had feathers. You think they did?" I ask, looking at a small colourful, artists-impression model of a Tyrannosaurus housed in a glass box, next to the massive skeleton.

"No, that's a misconception due to fossil remains which look like feathers. They are a parasite which lives and feeds off the host. They're called Lyrenchallia and look like feathers or long hairs. A bit like a leech." Aithen stops at my crumpled brow.

"And you know this… how?"

His eyes dart about the room for a moment. "I read a lot, and that is a, a good theory. I don't believe in the whole feathers and birds thing." He laughs.

"Yeah, I've heard that part, about the birds at least. Something to do with the hip bones?" I suggest.

"No, that's also way off. It's purely a coincidence. Dinosaurs have no relation whatsoever to anything alive today."

Talk about pushy. Have I got a crush on a dino-train-spotting-nerd?

———

"So, Dereton. What brought you here?" We sit in the museum café area.

"I requested a semester transfer to expand on my learning experience." I blank out for a moment. A *semester*? Then he could be here for only another month? He notices my frown.

"Okay?" he asks.

"Yes, sorry. So how long do you think you will stay for?"

"I haven't given it much thought." Then a crooked smile appears, "but I think it could be a lot longer."

"How come?" I want it to be because of me; well, we all can dream. This guy is just so compelling.

He shrugs and appears to take an interest in the gift shop beside us. I always buy a souvenir anywhere I go, only to toss it into a box and forget about.

Don't shrug me, I want to say, but I curse myself. Get a grip, silly girl. Sarah always tells me to *throttle back*. I need that lever rammed into my chest.

"You haven't told me much about your old school?" A simple question but the wheels are turning. Is he nervous? Well, I am, so why shouldn't he be?

"Kay. I transferred from Kay."

"Wow! A bit of a step down for you then? No wonder you're so good at math and *everything*," I smile.

Kay is the best of the best schools. It's also about a thousand kilometres away.

"My favourite subject is history." He says sheepishly.

"History? Okay, that's unexpected. You seem to be good at everything?"

"No, only history, but I also like to understand the history of sciences, such as mathematics. Not so much the application of the mathematics, but its invention and the humans who discovered it across time."

Humans?

"So, you don't study zoology or other mammals then?"

He looks at me. He didn't catch my joke. Never mind, he may be quick but not altogether sharp. I change the subject. "So, when you're not a smart-ass in school, what do you like to do?"

"I love to travel."

"Really? Me, too, though I've only been to a few countries.

Where have you visited?" Anybody who can afford Kay will travel everywhere.

He nearly laughs, and it's lovely to see white teeth and lines on his face. "I don't like to boast, but I've visited a lot of places on this planet."

I laugh in response. "This planet? Why, which other planets do you visit?"

"This galaxy and a few others," he laughs. "It would be curious though, wouldn't it?"

"What? To travel to another planet?"

"Yeah." He watches me like he's about to say, *surprise! Here are two tickets to the Moon!*

Pondering the thought, I absorb the glow of his eager face. What does he want me to say here? "I'd be scared. Excited, yes. But petrified. Like... can I get back? I watch those space launches and all that energy, noise, fire and think... all that effort to leave Earth? We're not supposed to."

That calms his expression. "Why not?"

"I don't know. I love space; who doesn't? But I also think we should focus our efforts on our planet, instead of trying to discover or conquer others."

He gives a gentle puff of his cheeks. "Now that's deep."

I giggle. "That's the thing. The ocean is deep, and we know little about it, except it's wet."

"You're amazing, Jayne."

I'm taken aback slightly. What an odd thing to say, to which he follows with, "I'm glad I'm sharing this project with you."

It's Saturday, and I happened upon Aithen on the High street, sitting on a bench, and inspecting drawings.

"These are wow, Aithen," I gush as I scan through the pencil sketches of dinosaurs he has drawn. The shading is so distinct, and the images look more like black and white photographs.

"You sure you didn't bring a camera back to the Cretaceous period?" I chuckle as I browse through three pictures of a Tyrannosaurus, and then a Stegosaurus. They are stunning, and Aithen's theories on the animals, plants, and climate are unique. The stances and movement of the dinosaurs are not like I would usually imagine, slow and cumbersome, but quite the opposite. He sees them as swift, agile, and camouflaging beasts, ready to strike and defend in a second.

There are two close-up drawings of dinosaur eyes, but then I turn a page, and my breath catches. Aithen motions to snatch the piece of paper away, but I stop him.

"Don't," I say as I pore over an image of my face, in colour and hand drawn. The exact pencil strokes describe every millimetre of my skin, eyes, eyebrows, lips. Every freckle accounted for, and my expression is searching and a little haunting, if I'm honest. But it's me. He's barely looked at my face, and yet this detail is like he's known me for years. If it were only the back of my head – as in class – I'd understand. But this detail is unbelievable.

"Do you have a photograph of me from somewhere?" I ask.

Aithen fidgets, and his hand stays half-reaching. "I'm sorry, Jayne. Please don't think I'm strange or anything."

"Strange? This is amazing, Aithen. If it weren't my face, I'd say it's a beautiful picture. But you've caught me, like for real." I can't take my eyes away from the image.

"That's what I saw that day in psychology class, and I didn't want to forget the moment."

I quickly flick through the remaining pages, but they depict various plants. I return to my picture. The triangle-point freckles are ever so faintly highlighted, and I peer closer still. He's created a tiny star motif within each one. A tingle warms me and forces me to blink away building emotion, as the rush echoes of him saying I was beautiful. Maybe he did mean it.

"Can I keep it?" I ask but wish I didn't. I like to imagine him having it with him and looking at it all the time; missing me; hoping to see me soon.

His voice breaks, and before he can speak, I whip out my cell and take a snap of the picture. "Actually, you keep it. Thank you," I say, and our gaze locks. It's like we are back in Hunneford's class and we are inspecting each other's face, but now there is no one to interrupt the moment.

Clear, deep, violet eyes envelop me with sincere interest. Aithen has a way of looking at me as though recording the moment for eternity; like he doesn't want to skip a beat. My face heats up, and the flush forces a grin to appear on his lovely face.

I bite my lip and smile back. Dismissing the embracing silence, I say, "Thank you. The picture is brilliant."

"I'm glad you like it," he says, and for a moment, I think he'll reach for me, but then he stops himself. Should I continue the action? He could back away, and the moment lost. No, don't spoil it.

"What's your plan for today?" I ask, not wanting to suggest he spend it with me.

"A handful of chores and I need to catch up with friends."

Friends? I've only seen that white-haired boy. And I want to learn more about him. But discretion is critical here.

"From school?" I ask.

"No, from out of town," he responds casually.

Why am I so possessive with Aithen? I'm not clingy like this usually. When I was dating Iain, it didn't bother me when he hung with other people. I knew I could trust him, but Aithen and I are not dating. He's just some boy I'm doing a project with, and filling my head with his sparkling, violet eyes; both smart and gentle words; his tender mouth, everything.

He may be giving off signs of interest in me, what with the

excuse to touch my hand, and his focused, attentive nature, but I must be careful. It's all set within a controlled boundary. An invisible line which he doesn't want to cross.

Did he say something about this the other day, about not being allowed to get involved? Or something close to that. I should have leant in for the kiss before.

A stab of jealousy stiffens me, as I think of him wanting to be with other friends and not me, and I stand. "Right, I've got a hundred things to do, myself."

His expression is one of questioning wonder as he searches my face, gathering the drawings and standing in front of me. There's always a subtle pause between us. A void begging to be filled, but by what?

I wish he'd hug me or kiss me or do something. Anything. I'll do the rest from there, but I will not make myself look like a jerk should he back off.

Please don't pull away, the voice in my head pleads as I reach for Aithen's hand. "I love the pictures and especially the one of me."

He stuffs the rolled-up paper under his arm and takes my hand in both of his. "I love drawing you."

The sounds of traffic and people on the high street fade away as I watch him, drinking in his sincerity. I raise his hands towards my face and stroke my lips across his knuckles; then I kiss the back of his hand and smile at him again. "Thank you."

Allowing the moment to pass, I give him a gentle handshake, then our fingers part and the sounds of the town fill the void. As I walk away, I already want to run back to him, but I breathe in the strength to continue.

I must look back. Waiting until Monday to see him again is an eternity. When I turn around, he is watching me, still clutching the sketches. Smiling, I send him a wave, and he raises a hesitant hand, looking lost and longing towards me.

The rest of Saturday seems to course for a hundred hours, and sleep brings no relief. My repetitive dream of almost kissing Aithen is torturing me. Still, I'm also having dark night terrors of cold, wind-swept hills and a girl's voice, screaming for help. Laura's voice.

When I'm alone, both Chloe and Laura fill my heart with a smoky heaviness, which tightens my breathing. If I didn't know better, I'd say I have panic attacks. There's a tingling edge of adrenalin, which scratches at my heart and irritates the plate in my head.

They can't have been real. People don't just up and vanish into thin air. Well, not like this anyway. Their families would remember them. I've attempted a logical approach, considering what I am trying to substitute in my life, with the invention of these two girls.

What purpose do they bring to my life? People have imaginary friends, but I've invented two girls who are a close friend and a foe, and who have disappeared. Iain left, but I know where he is, and so does everyone else.

And there's little to no progress with *VioletlyAlone*. Whoever they are posting and respond to posts daily. Their words are often haunting and tinged with doubt. It could be me writing some responses. But whenever they write about friends, friendship, the same pattern of thoughts appears.

They are hurting deeply. You can't stifle the negativity which flows, and they're not trying to. Their words dance around the subject and offer discrete opinions. They also appear cautious and have a habit of saying things like, "*I dare not say too much, as anyone could be reading this, but…*" or "*Don't try to read between the lines here, but…*"

But I can read between their lines. I can insert the blanks, and everything they say could be written by me. This person is going through what I am. All the evidence tells me this.

But what are their theories? Do they have the answers?

I kick back the duvet as the pale, blue light of Sunday morning beckons me to run. My doctor reiterated there was no Chloe or Laura, and she will not lie about it. But what if she's wrong? There could be several reasons Laura and Chloe are not on her computer registry. I can't pluck any out of the air now, but there will be a logical explanation.

When I get back, I'm taking a chance and sending a message to *VioletlyAlone*. They'll either think I'm nuts or will reach out with both hands. I would.

I must discover the truth.

CHAPTER NINE

"Leslie, what's up?" I ask as we sit together on break.

Her eyes are bloodshot from no sleep, and her usually, healthy chocolate-brown skin looks pale and dull. She runs a tired tongue over dry, cracked lips, and her voice sounds raspy. "I don't know," she utters.

Leslie's not dating anyone, so it's not boy-trouble.

"Everything okay at home?" I suggest.

She nods slowly. "Yeah, all good there. I'm just goin' through somethin'—"

"Can I help?" I've never seen her this low. This is not the usual bubbly Leslie. She's been like this all week. For three days now, she slumps into her chair, having arrived late.

"Nah, Jayne. T'is something I've gotta figure out." She drags a worn tissue from the cuff of her sleeve and dabs at her nose. "I'll be fine."

I rest a hand on her stooping shoulder. "Something in school?" I almost whisper.

Her tired eyes consider me. "I know I can trust you. I know that for sure. But this is somethin' I 'ave to figure out for me-self."

"Well, if you need anything, anytime, just ask. Please?" I gently massage her shoulder, and her whole body appears to need comfort.

She nods and exhales loudly. "I'll tell you all abou' it once I get me-head around matters."

The sun dips behind clouds for a moment, and a slight chill surrounds her words.

"That day in class, when you were shoutin' about Chloe?"

I nod, eyes widening slightly.

"What came of that? Did you find her somewhere else?" Leslie asks.

She's not playing with me. Concern masks her expression.

I clasp my cheeks in both hands, and it's my turn to breathe out loudly. "No. I think I've had a nervous breakdown or something." I feign a laugh, but I don't even convince myself. But then it dawns on me. Is Leslie going through a missing friend thing, like me? How would I know if someone was missing from her world? Nobody remembers Chloe or Laura. What if I don't remember one of Leslie's friends?

"Don't take this the wrong way, Leslie. And no, I'm not playing some daft game." I must be sure I have her attention. "I realise my Chloe moment just added to me being the school weirdo. But are you missing anyone? Has somebody suddenly gone missing?" I cringe inside.

Her brown eyes consider me as she ponders my words. "No," she crumples her mouth, and her eyes glisten. "No, nothin' like that. I've just seen…"

She trails off and squints as the sun escapes its cover and shrouds us in warmth.

"Seen?" I ask. *Seen what?*

Leslie shrugs and waves a hand to dismiss her words. "It's nothin'."

She stands and stretches her back and forces a smile. "I'm just comin' down with somethin'. A bug or wha'ever. Makin' me feel delusional or wha'ever." Another fake smile. "Let's get to class."

Leslie is away for the rest of the week, but at least our teacher calls her name during roll call each morning. So, she hasn't vanished like Chloe and Laura. Leslie is always open about everything. This is not like her. I've sent her texts making sure she is okay, but her responses are short and of the sort, *"I'll get back to you when I feel better."*

Still no reply from *VioletlyAlone*. I've hinted in a handful of private messages, what is going on with me and my screwed-up world. I've done my best to not sound like a crazy girl but tried to supply potential scientific explanations to what is happening. I need her, or him, to contact me.

Together we may find a reasonable answer to this or uncover some government plot. Maybe I shouldn't be reading so many posts on that web site.

Then on Saturday, I am moping around the high street and almost slam into a red-faced Leslie, who's in a hurry.

"Oh, Jayne. Sorry. I was miles away there," she gasps.

I give her a quick hug. "Just glad to see you. You okay? Where you off to?"

Her face searches for an answer; she still looks worn out. "I've gotta meet someone." She stops as her gaze focuses behind me.

I turn, and it's the tall, white-haired boy. He's at the corner of the block, looking timid. But not close enough to shout to. Then again, what would I shout?

"Him?" I ask. "What does he want? Who is he?"

"That's Erek." Leslie looks anxious. "It's a long story and now's not the time, sorry." Her lips are trembling, and her gaze flitters between him and me.

"Are you okay, Leslie? I don't trust him. I need to tell you something about him." But Leslie interrupts me.

She places her hands on my shoulders. "Take my word for it, Jayne. You don't need to tell me anythin'. Keep away from him."

"What? What do you mean? Why? What's happening?" I can't bear the look of fear in her eyes.

She drops her hands and holds her palms out towards me. "Just don't worry. I've got this." She scans behind me impatiently. I follow her gaze, but the boy is not there.

"Leslie, don't. Take *my* word for it, he's not good. If Erek's bothering you, we can go to the police." So, now I know his name. It makes him even more real.

"Nah. That won't help." Her gaze plummets as she sighs loudly. "All the police on the planet couldn't help me." Leslie forces a smile. "I need to catch up with him. Honestly, I'll call you later," she says and departs at an abrupt pace.

"Call me when you get home," I say. "Or I'll call you later anyway."

Leslie turns the corner of the block and is gone.

I'm an idiot. I must go after her, but what if I'm wrong? She already is cautious and knows he's trouble. But what does she know?

Leslie is a lot more streetwise than Laura, so she'll be fine. And it's the middle of the day, so no nighttime shadows to worry about.

My thoughts snap away by an alert on my mobile. I've received a message from *VioletlyAlone* from that forum. I open the private message and rest against a wall.

Can't say much here.

Don't know who could be scanning messages.

I will send you an encrypted link to a private chat room, so we can speak more freely.

Say nothing to anyone about friends.

VA

My teeth chatter from the chill reverberating along my spine. I step out of the shadow and into the warm sunlight, welcoming its hopeful embrace.

Have I finally found someone like me?

CHAPTER TEN

I haven't spoken to Leslie, but she did send me a text message to say she had gotten home. It was a short message which didn't invite conversation.

What was she possibly doing with Erek?

It feels weird to know his name.

They can't be dating, but what do I know? I invent people out of thin air, so who says I know how Leslie ticks deep down?

No, I know Leslie, and I am sure Erek's dangerous. But why is he always with Aithen? I'm meeting Aithen for a coffee tomorrow – I look at my clock, 2 AM – today. And I'm not letting this pass.

My mind and feet have been pacing, waiting for *VioletlyAlone* to send that link, so we can chat. Where are they? Looking at their forum profile, they are close enough, so there are no odd time zones to contend with. Just an hour away.

My cell pings, and thankfully, it is the message. Considering I've been waiting for hours, I hesitate to press the link. What if this is a school prank? No, impossible. The forum was such a random find, and I contacted the person first.

I press the screen of my cell phone, and a web page opens after an impatient wait of ten seconds.

It's a featureless page with a banner, *Enc-Messenger*.

Never heard of it before.

The screen turns black and white text appears.

"Welcome to VioletlyAlone's Encrypted Chat."

The screen clears again, and the background is now dark violet.

"Hello?" I type, and my text is white, preceded by my user-name, *Elat180*. This refers to the angles in an equilateral triangle.

"Hi!" the response appears in yellow text, with the username *VA*.

Elat180: Are we introducing ourselves?

VA: No.

VA: We need to keep things short here.

Elat180: I think we're both going through a shared experience.

VA: Why?

Here goes nothing.

Elat180: Two of my school mates have disappeared.

I leave a pause if they want to jump in with a response.

Elat180: I saw your post about the flash of light? That happened to me, too.

The blood pulsing through vessels in my ears causes my head to throb, and the plate in my forehead stings. It feels like an eternity until the cursor flashes, showing the other user is typing.

VA: What happened after that?

Elat180: My friend, Laura, has vanished. I also—

VA: What have people said about her vanishing?

Elat180: Nothing. Nobody remembers her. Another close friend has also disappeared.

VA: Oh, my...

Elat180: Who have you lost?

Elat180: You still there?

It's a long minute before they reply.

VA: My friend for a few years now. The entire world has forgotten she existed.

I can't believe what I am reading, this can't be real. I massage my head.

VA: The memory is so painful for me.

Elat180: I'm sorry for you. It's so hard to face this reality. I thought I was going crazy, but no, there is you. There must be others?

VA: You're the first to reach out to me.

Elat180: What do we do now?

The cursor blinks then stops.

Blinks again and stops. This repeats for two minutes. I can't type while the other person is typing, so I wait, frustration building.

VA: Sorry. The pain is so harsh.

Elat180: Pain? Yeah, I know. It's so hard to come to terms with this.

VA: No, the physical pain. When I think of my friend, my head hurts so much.

I almost drop my cell, as I fumble to type a response.

Elat180: I have that, too. In the front of my head!!

VA: No way. Me, too!

Elat180: What is this?

VA: We need to meet...?

Elat180: Your profile says you are just an hour away from where I am?

VA: Is that your real location? You shouldn't do that!

Elat180: Only accepted connections can see my details. You're the only one.

VA: I still wouldn't risk it.

Elat180: So, how far away are you really from me?

VA: About three hours.

Still close enough.

Elat180: When shall we meet?

VA: As soon as possible.

Elat180: Okay, let's chat again tomorrow. I'm guessing you won't want to exchange cell numbers?

VA: No. Way too dangerous.

VA: You boy or girl?

Elat180: Girl.

VA: Me, too.

VA: I'll post a random historical date on the forum which will be the time I'll message you again. Okay?

Elat180: Yes. And thank you.

VA: Ditto!

The screen washes black and the message disconnects.

I hug myself against the shivers rippling through my body. I drag the duvet and wrap myself in its warmth.

Who is this *VioletlyAlone*? Assuming she is honest and is a girl, what's the connection with the pain we experience in our heads. Does she have a plate, too? I'll ask when I chat again.

This changes everything.

I'm not crazy.

Does *VioletlyAlone* know what has happened?

People can't vanish like this.

I need to understand her ideas on what is going on here.

But no comfort comes with the realization that Laura and Chloe are and always have been real.

CHAPTER ELEVEN

The gentle chill of the forest shrouds me, comforting the tears washing over my cheeks.

The fallen tree has been a seat for many hours of pondering and tears over the past couple of years. Leslie's sad eyes burn through my heart. Her fearful and broken voice shadowed her firm stance. But she's still here. I'm sure of that.

And *VioletlyAlone*. A random voice in the digital darkness. She's out there, alone like me in this thing; whatever it is. But we're not alone. We've found one another and could find others together. I'm more than willing to take my school crazy status and go public with this.

We can use social media to spread our word, and someone might see it. Other people experiencing missing mates will contact us.

Stupid human.

Erek.

VioletlyAlone must have an *Erek* in her life. Does she know or suspect someone of being involved with her missing friend?

Blowing my nose into a disgustingly wet tissue, I stand.

Get a grip, Jayne, the voice in my head commands. I'm meeting Aithen soon, so time to get my act together.

I run for home.

I'm in two minds about seeing Aithen again. He'll put my mind at rest, and his gaze will warm me and offer hope. But I worry how close he is to Erek. I mustn't make assumptions. Aithen makes me happy when we are together, so I am sure he'll have answers to calm me.

I love the aroma and sounds of the coffee store. The calm hum of voices, people enjoying their fix of caffeine and exchanging gossip with friends. And I love drinking in the hot guy sitting before me.

Aithen has that way of stealing the breath away from me and shackling negative thoughts in the bondage of kind words and a concerned expression.

"You don't seem yourself?" he asks, sipping on sparkling water with a slice of lime dancing on the surface.

I breathe in the steam from my cappuccino. "I've got to ask you something." I steady myself. Despite the urgency running through my thoughts, I don't want to break the surface of the calm waters around us. I don't want to spoil this moment of peace. Until Aithen appeared today, my mind pulled in a hundred directions. But I love focusing on him.

Leave it until after I've met up with *VioletlyAlone*? Get facts together before asking Aithen anything. If Erek is involved with the missing girls, or only Laura, can't it wait?

No. It can't.

"What's the story with Erek?" I ask and notice the discrete change in Aithen's expression. Not a look of shock, but his head ever so slightly back away, and his lips tighten.

I'm sure he's surprised I know Erek's name, so he must also know *I know something*.

"Erek," Aithen shrugs. "He's an ass." Aithen sniggers gently and that forces my smile, too. He looks to the side then back at me. "Why? What's he done?"

How I wish I could answer that truthfully. "He's giving me the creeps," I respond, reading Aithen's reactions carefully. "And I've seen you hanging with him? He's your friend?"

Aithen nods thoughtfully. "Quite the opposite. When we do these… student-exchange programs. We are assigned a guide. A *prefect* sort of individual."

"A prefect? Isn't that something from the past in some dusty, old school?" I laugh, but Aithen is serious.

"Okay, a chaperone of sorts," Aithen replies, but my frown deepens his already heavy brow.

"Erek is there to make sure we don't do anything stupid," says Aithen. His violet eyes search my face for a response.

"And if you do? Does he give you twenty lashes of the cane?" I chuckle, trying to lighten the mood. Aithen's reference to *prefect* is amusing, it's an old English school thing. "Or keep you away from unruly girls?"

"*Chaperone*?" I mock Aithen's continued defensive look.

"Okay. Think of Erek as a student counsellor," suggests Aithen.

"Counselor? Is that why I've seen him hanging with students from my school?" This changes the mood. Aithen stares at his glass, running his index finger along the length. What's he thinking?

"I can only imagine they have reached out to him, for personal reasons," Aithen says.

I bite the skin on the tip of my finger. Time to cause a ripple across the calm waters.

"Aithen. I saw Erek with Laura—No wait. I don't care what people say." I raise my hand as a brake to stop him interrupting. "Fine. I'm either crazy, or she is real. But the last time I saw her, she was with Erek."

Aithen rubs the back of his neck. "Jayne. I was there in the class that day. The day you accused everyone about Chloe?"

"That's because Chloe is real, too," I plead, but keeping my voice hushed in the buzzing coffee house. I grab the napkin stained from below my coffee cup and dab my eyes. I mustn't cry here.

Should I tell him about *VioletlyAlone*? No, I can't. I still don't know how close he is to Erek. But I must tell Leslie. I'll get the proof first, and then protect Leslie from Erek. She'll have to listen to *VioletlyAlone* and me.

Aithen considers me with those caring, non-judgmental eyes.

"Do you think I'm nuts?" I whisper.

"No," he replies, cupping my hands in his. "I'd say keep your mind open. I don't know what to say about your friends. I've got nothing. You're far from nuts, Jayne."

I'm listening, but the words dull from the warmth of his hands flowing into me and calming the waters again.

When we leave the coffee house, Aithen offers me a gentle hug, which I grasp for dear life. If I could stay in this moment for an eternity, I would. Why can't life be simple? Why can't I be normal?

We leave, and I scan my cell.

VioletlyAlone has posted her cryptic message.

Edgar Allan Poe – "Raven" 1st published

I search the web, and the year of publication referenced: 1845.

Five o'clock now. Less than two hours.

I can't wait.

CHAPTER TWELVE

The *Enc-Message* window presents itself again, and I type *Hi*.

VA: Cryptic question. How did you know to be here now?

Because you told me to, I think. But I get it. *VA* is careful and checking it's me.

Elat180: Mr Poe's bird suggested it. :)

VA: Okay, that's fair enough. I wondered how you may answer that.

Elat180: You okay?

VA: No. I'm scared. Paranoid. And honestly don't know who I can trust.

Elat180: Has something happened?

VA: No. What about you? Any developments.

Elat180: I don't want to say too much, but I suspect someone.

VA: ??!!??

Elat180: I can't be sure. But I am sure a particular person was there the night a school mate disappeared.

VA: You were there?

Elat180: Yes, and no. One minute I was there, but then I blacked out or something, and then they were gone.

VA: Did you see anything? Before blacking out?

Elat180: Yes. A flash of light.

No response. I wait a little longer before continuing.

Elat180: That's what drew me to your profile. It was that post about how one minute your friend was there, and a flash of light, they were gone.

The cursor blinks again. Like the last time, it's as though *VioletlyAlone* is typing a response, but then changes her mind. The cursor is stationary and then flashing again.

VA: Who do you suspect? Is it someone you know?

Elat180: No, I don't know him. He's new to the town I live in.

VA: Dereton?

Elat180: Yes. Does the name Erek mean anything to you?

The blank screen of silence is unnerving. I wish we could talk on a cell so I can receive feedback at once.

Elat180: Does it?

VA: No. No, I don't know that name. I don't want to say too much on here. I am happy to travel to you.

Elat180: When? I'm desperate to meet you!

VA: Same here.

Elat180: I'm also worried this Erek guy is hanging around with one of my mates. She looks a mess since hanging with him.

VA: Do you really think he's got something to do with your friend disappearing?

Elat180: I don't know, but he scares me. He has this creepy vibe going on.

VA: Stay away from him. I've got no idea what's going on here, but it's too much of a coincidence we have missing friends. I wish I could point my finger at someone, so hold onto that.

Elat180: I've tried to warn my friend about him, but I can't tell her everything. Everyone thinks I'm nuts as it is.

VA: You still in school? Or college?

Elat180: School. You?

VA: Finished high school but needed to get a job. Long story.

But I stack shelves, and nobody talks to me, so little chance of me slipping up about a missing mate.

Elat180: When can we meet? It's getting urgent as I need to get a plan together to help my mate who's hanging with Erek.

VA: What can we do?

Elat180: Two of us with the same story can back up the warning. I know she'll think we're both nuts, but I must try. I'm sure she could vanish at any time, and if this Erek has anything to do with it, then I need him to know. That we know.

VA: Be careful there. Don't do anything until we meet!!

Elat180: I won't.

VA: Okay. I'll get to Dereton for Saturday. I have the weekend off from work.

Elat180: Okay. Great. I can wait for two days. Do you know the area?

VA: No. But I did look at an online map and saw there's a harbour there? That'll be as good and safe a place as anywhere.

The harbour. I love it there, and the thought of meeting under a dark cloud unsettles me, but this is too important.

Elat180: Okay. Post a time like you did before?

VA: Will do. Now stay safe and don't speak to anybody!!

Elat180: Okay. Take care.

And she's gone.

Settling back into my chair, I play the conversation over in my head. Am I right to be accusing Erek here? This is serious, and I can't make such a huge mistake. My track record of late is not good, and to accuse a student counsellor from Kay may not be my best idea.

My cell sounds an alert. It's a text message from Leslie.

Help x

"Wow, Leslie. Are you stoned?" I ask when I hear Leslie speak. Her voice is thick and slurry.

She giggles. "Nah, I've 'ad a few drinks. I 'aven't touched the weed for abou' a year."

"On a school night? I take it you're off tomorrow then?" I ask.

"I can't be assed with school at the moment," she says. "Just too much rubbish goin' on aroun' me."

"Oh, Leslie. I'm sorry. Is there anything I can do? I hate seeing and hearing you like this."

I hear her swallow loudly from a glass or bottle.

"The last thing you need is to lose it to drink," I suggest.

She coughs out a laugh in response. "I don't know," she almost whispers.

"Is it Erek again? What's going on there?" I'm sick of thinking of Erek.

"Urgh, him. I jus' don' care anymore," Leslie slurs.

"Let me help you, Leslie. You're not alone in this." I keep my voice calm and words clear, to penetrate the alcohol haze.

"Oh, Jayne. There's nothin' you can do. Anyone can do on this planet." She exhales loudly with an added sigh. "I just wish I didn' see it."

See it?

"See what?" I ask. "Leslie, please. You can trust me."

"Oh, I don't know," she coughs and clears her throat.

"I'm not nuts Leslie. But if one of your friends have disappeared or something weird has happened, you can tell me. I'm not going to judge or anything." How can I break this wall of silence? I live with this doubt every day.

"You're not nuts, Jayne. No, we're all... what was it?" Leslie's words are vacant like she's talking to herself. "Stupid. That's it. We're all just *stupid humans*."

My blood runs to ice, and my heart pounds in my ears.

Stupid humans.

"W-what do you mean by that, Leslie?"

This can't be real. How can it be? People can't vanish into thin air and forgotten by everyone.

But for me.

"Oh, nothin', Jayne. Ignore me. It," she says. "I'm gonna hit the sack. I'm bushed."

Leslie ends the call before I can respond. I look at my cell and consider calling her back. She can't leave me dangling in the wind like that, but she's obviously not thinking straight.

I open the text messaging screen and tap in a string of messages.

Leslie. Hope you feel better when you read this. No big headache! LOL!

Stay away from Erek. Do that one thing for me!!!

I'm not nuts. I have found someone who can help – maybe. She'll be here on Saturday.

I met her on a forum, and she has a cool name: VioletlyAlone.

Hold in there. Two more days and we'll sort this out together.

Stay away from Erek!!!

CHAPTER THIRTEEN

Saturday morning and I can't shift Leslie and *VioletlyAlone* from my mind. The walls of my house press against me, trapping my doubts like a prisoner. I need to release my thoughts and escape. I'm not in the mood for a run, that's a first for me. But I have barely slept for the past few nights. I woke at 2AM this morning and have been awake since then. The coffee house will do.

I should have dropped a message to Aithen and ask him to meet me. His warm and assuring distraction would be good right now. But I won't be good company. I want to process everything I've learnt this week, but I also want to talk to someone about it all.

Leslie sent me an apologetic message the day after. I assured her there was nothing to be sorry for. What matters is her name called at roll call in school, despite her self-enforced absence. She'll be fine, I am sure of that.

What if *VioletlyAlone* is a weirdo? I'm not sure of my own thoughts and stability, but when Leslie said, "…stupid humans" the other night, it was too much.

Chloe was real.

Laura was real. And I'm convinced Erek was there when Laura vanished.

But just because he was with Laura that night, does that auto-matically mean he was there when she disappeared? I was there that night. I'm one of the last to see her alive. I did nothing, so who is to say Erek did?

I massage the stinging in my forehead.

The pain reflects my raw, grumbling stomach. I haven't eaten for two days.

VioletlyAlone's cryptic message posted to the forum page was, *Charles 5th crowned by the pope.*

A few confusing dates appeared, but the obvious one was 1530; hence she'll be here for half-past-three, this afternoon.

Butterflies scratch at my delicate stomach in anticipation of meeting her. Will she bring answers or confusion? I grimace when I sip my coffee. I should order something to eat.

I try to focus on the menu board through burning, tired eyes, but a commotion outside the coffee house grabs my attention. I *see them?* Erek and Leslie. Together. Arguing, by the looks of it.

Leslie is jerking her hands towards Erek, and her mouth exag-gerates whatever she is saying, but he appears distracted. Trying to ignore her. And now he watches a plane in the sky coming into land. I can't hear what Leslie is saying over the din of the coffee house.

She slaps him on the chest and then she holds up her cell to his face.

I taste blood from chewing the inside of my cheek. I gulp my coffee to rid myself of the taste and flinch at the sting of my chewed skin. What's going on here?

The table lurches when I stand abruptly, and my cardboard cup spins to empty the contents across the table. Cursing under my breath, I fetch a handful of napkins and mop up the liquid, my efforts quickly taken over by one of the shop staff, who ushers me away with thanks. I apologise for being so clumsy.

I make my way to the exit. This will not be an angry showdown, but something inside urges me to intervene here. I did nothing on the hill, *that* evening, but I'm doing something now.

As I pull the door behind me, I freeze in my tracks. An emptiness envelopes me, and everything is turning black. There's a silence so thick, it feels solid within my ears. I know I'm here, but I don't know where I am.

And then my eyes snap open again, and I'm helped up by the same girl, who just mopped my mess in the coffee house. *What's going on here?*

Leslie and Erek have gone. *I did see them, didn't I?*

My trembling fingers scratch at the plate in my forehead. I'm cracking up! I nod at the girl, *I'm okay* and stagger to a nearby bench. She hesitates, watching me, and I give a little wave to assure her she can go back inside.

What's with me? Is it a side-effect from the accident? Some post-traumatic thing? My heart is pounding in my chest, and I force a few slow, deep breaths in and out. I should have eaten. And slept.

My mouth is dry, and all I can taste is the metallic blood from earlier. I look up and thankfully, accept a paper cup of water from the girl in the coffee house.

The throbbing in my head accompanies the sting in the plate. Painkillers are doing nothing for me, and my face stares back at me in the bathroom mirror, like a sheet of white paper.

Dark rings around my eyes tell of haunted nights, and days. I've tried Leslie's cell number several times since I got home, but her voicemail is the only response. At least she's still there; hasn't vanished.

What was that outside the coffee house? A right and proper blackout. But the sight or dream about Erek and Leslie? No, it was real. I think it was. I could have dozed off.

I flop onto my bed, and my head spins. A vortex of thoughts swirl with Laura's lost voice and an empty school chair where Chloe sat, circling in and out of my consciousness.

Erek's dark eyes penetrate the fog, but I recollect a warm glow from Aithen's fingers caressing my skin to chase away the cold, dark thoughts. What is he doing right now?

I blink at my clock. It's still early enough for me to have a sleep before meeting *VioletlyAlone*. I set the alarm for two hours from now.

Alarm bells shriek within my failing thoughts. They warn me to check with Leslie, but I succumb to the spectre of sleep.

CHAPTER FOURTEEN

Where am I? What time is it?

Sunlight streams into my room, attempting to pull me awake. My clouded head can't focus my eyes on the digits. I grab for the clock but instead, knock it off the side table.

I curse myself as I snatch my cell from my jeans pocket.

"Oh, shit!"

It's four-twenty.

I pull focus and check for messages. None.

Kicking off the duvet, I scramble to the ensuite and splash my face with chilly water. I gargle with mouthwash and reach for my forehead as the plate burns with new urgency. Get dressed, I order myself.

Mom calls my name as I rumble down the stairs, but I can't pause. I must get to the harbour.

I'm so tired and gasping for breath as I run along the high street. Consider how much running I do; this should be easy.

I'm on my way, I chant in my mind, imagining *VioletlyAlone* waiting anxiously for me. She'll think I'm a lunatic who stood her up. Will she wait? I'm an hour late. It's not that far, and my breathing is already steady as I complete the run. I can see the boat masts, and I'm at the footpath entrance to the harbour.

I scan around me. Who am I even looking for?

There are at least fifty people here, but they are older, a lot older than I imagine she will appear. She could have lied about her age?

Take a chance. "V.A?" I shout towards the water but intending it for ears close by.

Heads turn, but there's no look of acknowledgement.

I shout again, this time giving a wave towards a collection of strangers over from me.

Nothing.

It's okay. Just the local crazy girl.

VioletlyAlone was scared. She said that. And me not showing must have been a nightmare for her.

I grab my cell and open the browser. I hope she will see this message if she is in town. She could be anywhere. I hope she's not travelling away. For all I know, she could be late, too. A three-hour journey could present many issues.

Logging into the forum, I bring up the private messaging screen.

When I type in *VioletlyAlone* as the receiver, a red cross appears with the text, *No such user.*

Urgh, I can't spell. I type her name again, more carefully, but the red-x message appears again.

"Oh, please," I gasp, dismissing the screen.

I enter the forum pages and search for posts from *VioletlyAlone.*
There are none.

I can't breathe as I open my profile page and the *likes* section. I've responded to a few dozen posts from other members, but not a single post from *VioletlyAlone.*

I crumple to a sitting position, on the ground.

Squeezing away the tears through tightly scrunched eyes, I already know she's gone.

They, it, whoever have gotten to her.

But what if she's just a phantom poster on the web? The whole thing was a hoax? A joke?

No. I can't believe that. What little we said, I believe in her.

And she's gone.

How am I going to tell...?

"Oh, please. No."

Leslie.

Do I dare look?

I can barely see the screen through the torrent of tears, trying to wash away memories, but they can't. Leslie's not there.

Nothing.

Not a single text or anything in the calling history.

I know she was real.

Am I simply crazy?

It dawns on me. The list? Sarah and I made that list. I must call her.

Sarah answers on the third ring.

"It's happened again," I say, my voice breaking and thick. "Another girl, Leslie, has gone."

I don't mention *VioletlyAlone.* Too complicated to explain.

"Woah a minute. Let me get my list," Sarah says, and I can hear her breathing as she climbs the stairs in her home.

Come on, I want to shout.

"Okay, go on. What name again?" she asks.

"Leslie. Leslie Wallace," I stutter.

"Have you got your list there, too?" asks Sarah.

"No, it's at home, but it's Leslie. I've been at school with her forever. You've met her loads of times." I clear my throat and plug the tears which want to erupt out of me.

Please, say her name is on your list.

"Jayne. It's not here." Sarah's voice is quiet. "When did I meet her?"

I smudge away a stream of tears. "But I read you the list the other night. She's been to our house dozens of times."

"Where are you now?" she asks.

"The harbour," I choke out.

"I'm going to go home. I'll see you there," I say to Sarah and hang up.

"I honestly don't remember her," Sarah says as she hands the two pieces of paper. Our written columns of names match, all except for Leslie: she's not on either list.

"I half remember all of those names you called out, but there was no Leslie Wallace," she continues.

I heave a loud sigh. "I'm cracking up." I blow my nose into another tissue and toss it into the bin next to me.

"There's always this boy with white hair. I saw him with Leslie and Laura."

"That's the other girl who disappeared?" Sarah looks sincere, but is she hiding what she thinks?

I nod. "Yes. I can't say if he was around with Chloe or not."

There's a slight drop, in Sarah's expression as I remind her of the third missing person. I dare not mention a fourth.

"And this boy, where is he now?" Sarah asks.

I shrug. "I don't know. Aithen knows him, so I can ask."

"Aithen? How does he know him?" Sarah stands.

"Student council, or whatever. For the exchange thing." I scan the lists again, willing Leslie's name to appear.

"Do we go to the police?" she asks.

"What am I going to say? Four girls are missing, and I have my suspicions on a suspect? Oh, and by the way, nobody else knows they ever existed." I massage my shoulders, but that irritates me. I slap my hands onto my thighs and stand.

"Four? What do you mean four?" Sarah asks.

"I'll tell you on the way. Shall we give it a go?" I ask her.

———

The last time I was at this police station was after my accident. A verbal caution but not recorded in writing.

Officer Johns looks like he is doodling rather than taking down notes. "And you say, Leslie was in your school, Hill Derry since you started there?"

I nod repeatedly. My head wants to jerk out of control. Sarah's hand squeezes mine. Why have I done this? I've recalled the story about Leslie, but Johns' poker-face is giving away nothing.

Does he believe me? Sarah and I agreed we won't mention *VioletlyAlone.*

"Dereton is not a diverse town, Jayne," he says, drawing out his words. "You say Leslie is your age and height, but with a dark-brown complexion?"

"Yes." It's true. Dereton is mostly a white community, with the weight of diversity from China and Japan. My dad's Japanese and Mom is the only Russian resident, and the black community is small.

Johns taps at his computer and sighs. "I know the Wallace family. Jacob works for the fire department. Unless there is another Wallace, but I don't presume there is." He trails off.

"Jacob and Martha have no children, Jayne," he adds, looking at me and then to Sarah.

My ears throb in time with my aching heartbeat.

"I must be imaging it." I resign the words to the void of the office. My throat tightens, and adrenalin urges me to run from this claustrophobic, judgmental prison.

Sarah squeezes my hand again while she exchanges a glance with Johns. They think I'm crazy. Maybe I am but tell my heart that.

Tell the memories screaming in my head; I haven't invented this. So many years of friendship evaporated into tears and doubt.

No-one remembers Leslie.

"Are you continuing to see the doctor, Jayne?" Johns asks.

I sigh and blink slowly.

"Can you not raise this with Mom and Dad, please?" asks Sarah. "I'm here as her guardian."

Johns considers me and then Sarah. "I'll have to notify the doctor about this. Just in case."

"Just in case?" I say, unable to control my tone. "What? Just in case I'm a crackpot or something?"

Johns raises his open hands. "I can only go on the facts, Jayne. You're telling me a girl is missing, from a family who doesn't have a daughter. You don't need to have a record for me to know who lives in this town. I know everyone, Jayne."

"Let's go," I say to Sarah. "I'm sorry for taking up your time," I direct towards Johns.

He stands and offers a hand. I shake it and say thank you again.

"Please pay your doctor a visit," he says as we leave the office.

How do I confront Erek? If I come straight out with it, then I'm sure he'll clam up, and I'll look the fool.

No. This will need tact, which I seem to lack lately.

But let's say for a second Erek is involved.

Does Aithen know anything?

CHAPTER FIFTEEN

Today must be the wettest day in Dereton. I've never seen it rain so heavy, as huge puddles pond together.

I love stormy weather, but even I didn't venture out for my run this morning. And it looks like many people have not bothered venturing out to school either. Roll call class is light in attendance.

My heart is already pounding, and my head won't let up in its complaining. Leslie is not here, and our teacher hasn't called her name or asked of her whereabouts.

"You dropped this," says Isla, offering my cell. "You okay?"

I glance at her and the mobile, but I don't want it. I can barely form the words to say thank you. Isla places the cell on my table and presses my shoulder gently, then returns to her seat.

The air is heavy between us and careful, discrete glances from Isla drive me further into the shadows of my mind. Where I want to hide. To protect myself.

I make my way to the girl's bathroom and splash water on my pale, tired face. Leslie has joined my personal missing person list. It's like a disease that eats away any happiness in my life. Any potential of comfort attacked and devoured and forgotten by everyone but me.

I've been in a daze since Saturday. I told Mom I have a stomach bug and I simply wasted away in my room, on my bed during the weekend.

"Jayne?" a voice asks me from behind. I turn, and Isla's eyes widen when she sees my tearful face.

Isla hugs me, and I can't stop the convulsions of tears.

"What's happened?" she asks. "Is it your family?"

I can't look her in the eye, but I step back a pace and watch my shoes. I swallow deeply. "Do you remember the online chat we had the other night? When you were all having a dig about Aithen and me going to the cinema?"

Isla doesn't speak, but I can sense her nod.

"Humour me," I croak. "Who was on the call?"

"Erm. You and me," Isla responds. "Jayne, is everything okay?"

"No. It's not." I say, quivering words passing through my trembling lips.

"Oh, come here." She hugs me again.

"I can't stay in school today," I say. "I'm heading up to the school office and then home."

"You sure? You shouldn't be alone?" she says, her voice slightly pleading.

"It's okay. Mom's at home."

Isla nuzzles the top of my head as she hugs me. Her grip tightens as my tears heave.

"It's okay. You'll be okay," she assures me gently.

But the sting in my head warns me to protect Isla. She can't be seen with me or else she could be next. I can't have another casualty of friendship.

I back away with a thank you and return to the sink. I look awful.

I try to smile. "Thanks, Isla. I'm such a mess."

"Do you want me to walk you home?" she offers.

I shake my head. "No. No, honestly. I just need to sleep. I was sick all weekend."

Her caring, teardrop-shaped eyes are too much for me. If I stay, I'll bawl even more.

Time to escape.

I hug her again. "Tell no one," I say.

"Of course not," she responds. "Call me any time. Okay?"

I nod and make my way to the school office. There's little sympathy offered there, despite my appearance. Well, I did break into their computer system and filing cabinets. But they hand me an excusal slip.

I head for home, but I can't face Mom and a hundred questions.

Instead, I send a text to Sarah, and she suggests I go there. It's only twenty minutes on the bus. And at this time of the day, the bus is pleasantly quiet.

We stop at a traffic light.

I raise my gaze and look out the window and into black, starring eyes.

It's him.

Erek.

And for the first time, he doesn't avert his gaze.

But he doesn't look menacing or disgusted as usual. His eyes widen, and his mouth drops open slightly. Do I look that shocking? Or is it because I see through his façade? Can he sense I imagined killing him the other day? I can't stop my grimace as I reach for the seat pole to pull myself up to stand, but the bus lurches forward throwing me back into my seat.

I struggle to look out the window again and watch Erek walking away and turning a corner.

It's pointless going after him.

I'm in no fit state to pick a fight with anyone.

But I will.

CHAPTER SIXTEEN

Tuesday brings sunshine, but my thoughts cloud by the anger brewing inside me. I should get an award for keeping my cool. I can't afford an outburst. Not here in school. I need answers.

I've lost the potential backup from *VioletlyAlone*. I wish I knew her real name.

The common denominator in this is me. These are my friends and maybe-friend. Why have they disappeared? If it has something to do with me, then am I at risk? I'm next?

I saw Leslie showing Erek her cell. Was she showing him the message I sent her? That would connect *VioletlyAlone* to me and all of this. But what did Leslie see? She said something about that twice.

I saw that flash of light when Laura disappeared. And so, did *VioletlyAlone*. But I also blacked-out. That light could have been a car passing or something. I also lost it when I saw Leslie with Erek. Is it possibly my head trauma?

What do I do about Erek? My mindset on Saturday mulled over ways to kill him. Maybe not the most natural and healthy thoughts, but I pushed myself into a tiny box of convincing myself, I had killed him. Hunneford has spoken about visualization, and I felt the anguish, the fear of killing someone and getting caught.

I convinced myself so well, I was vomiting into the toilet for an hour. That convinced Mom I was ill. If only she knew. So, I've imagined life in prison, until the day I die, and no, I don't fancy that option.

It all doesn't make sense. There's no reason for this. My family and friends can't help me. If they try, they will vanish, too. The police can do nothing.

I'm alone. And powerless against whatever. I don't even think it's Erek. What can some dumb-ass boy do to make people disappear? Cause amnesia in a whole town? Nothing.

VioletlyAlone didn't have Erek in her life...

But then she came to Dereton.

Is it the town?

How convenient that the police, school, doctors don't remember these girls?

And why only girls?

I shiver thinking about trafficking. No, surely not. Their parents wouldn't be a party to it too? And all the students? All part of it?

I close my eyes and shake my head at my own internal monologue. *Paranoia?*

A calm voice casts light into my wilderness," You okay?"

Today is designated *work on your end of term projects* day, so I'm sat in the school library with Aithen, on opposite sides of the table. Hand-written notes stack irregularly over the table, and I have tasked myself with typing. At the same time, Aithen highlights the notes: yellow is essential, and pink is a maybe, in the final draft.

I nod. "What is den-claric-uldine acid?" I ask Aithen, peering over the top of my laptop. I've done chemistry, and I've not heard of that one.

"It's part of the digestive juices of a dinosaur," replies Aithen. "According to some theories," he quickly adds.

The school bell announces lunch break.

"You lunching?" I ask him.

He stands. "No, I have to pop out. I'll see you shortly."

I'm not hungry anyway. But I'm empty. A shell of myself. And I wish Aithen was here. He says little, but he somehow grounds me.

I wander around the school grounds, but my mind has lost its way. I'm tired of the pain in my head; those stupid tablets aren't working.

Isla stops me on my way back to the library.

"You okay today? Didn't get much chance to speak this morning? And your cell was off last night," she says.

"Yeah, sorry. I needed to escape for a while. I stayed at Sarah's for most of the day and evening. Thanks." I hug her.

"What was it?" Isla asks, and I know she cares, but I don't want to lie to her.

"Oh, me being me. This plate's making me depressed lately." I point to my forehead.

She strokes the hair away from my face. "You can't see it, Jayne. Honestly," she comforts.

"I'm all over the place in my head at the moment." I smile.

"How are things with you and Aithen?" She looks at me sideways, flicking her eyebrows, mocking. "Saw you in the library with him, huddled close."

This stabs a little as I don't know where I am there "No idea. Stagnant?" I shrug.

"Hmm. We'll see. You had lunch?" She parts.

"No. Going back to the library."

I make my way to the library, and when I reach my table, my heart drops a little bit more. Aithen's laptop is gone, and he's scribbled a note on a post-it: *Could you finish with the notes? All looks okay and ready to go.*

I plop into the seat and resume typing.

Dinosaurs.

CHAPTER SEVENTEEN

Aithen doesn't show up in school for the rest of the week. I don't spot him around town either. Has he joined the numbers of my imaginary, missing friends?

When I think about Chloe, Leslie, Laura, and *VioletlyAlone*, my head stings, and my thoughts feel like physical throbs in my skull. Like someone is pressing their thumbs into the bone. But I'm not getting that with Aithen. I know he's still around; he's okay.

My visit with Doctor Harris was a nightmare. Officer Johns kept his word and said nothing directly to my parents, but he did contact Harris. Will she call Mom and Dad? I've pleaded with her not to. But there's some medical standard where the parents must be kept in the loop.

Harris hinted about some medical retreat I could attend, to help me *come to terms* with my life. I don't need to come to any terms. I simply want someone to believe me.

If Mom knows, then she's not letting on. And I'm not raising the subject with her.

Another Monday, dawns and my spirits are on the rise. Don't know where that is coming from, but I must see Aithen. I've got to talk to him. When I arrive at Hunneford's class, Aithen's not there. He must be running late. I know Aithen is on his way. Call it intuition, but he's about to—

There he is.

A quick nod at Hunneford and Aithen breezes by without a hint of a look in my direction.

Really?

Talk about blowing hot and cold.

"Projects due in next Monday," announces Hunneford. "But today, let's touch on forensic psychology…"

I listen for Aithen, but he's still. Silent. I desperately want to turn to see him, but I don't dare. What if I've done something wrong? I don't want to witness it in his eyes. Those beautiful, violet eyes which wash me away into dreams.

Speaking of which, my waking mornings continue to feature that ever so close kiss. I feel Aithen's warmth beneath me as we lay together, and I'm lost in his gaze. I'm not even sure if we are naked in that dream bed. But we're together and in love, and I lower myself towards his eager mouth—

"Jayne?" Hunneford's voice snaps me awake.

I'm startled as I look around me and the class is almost empty? "What?" My voice is weak.

"The bell went a few minutes ago." Hunneford smiles. "Every-thing… okay with you?"

"Yeah. Yes, sorry." I stand. "I'm sorry, Sir. It's been a tough weekend, and I was up late, very late working on the project."

Hunneford nods. "It's okay."

As I leave, he says to my back, "If you need to talk about anything, you know where I am?"

I turn and smile. "Thank you. Good lesson today."

Isla and few friends sit at a table outside, nibbling on crisps. I

EARTH 101   101

scan the area for Aithen, but he's nowhere.

There's math this afternoon, so I intend to say something to him. He's not playing this ignore-me game anymore.

Approaching Aithen's desk should be exciting for me, but the nerves are making my feet feel like I am wearing lead boots. He flicks me a glance when I rest my hands on either side of his desk.

"You going to ignore me forever?" I ask, keeping my voice barely audible as I know a lot of ears will be scanning for gossip.

"I'm not ignoring you," he mumbles back. "I promise."

I crouch so I can make eye contact, but he averts his gaze. "Erm, you are. You're fine one minute then off on one, the next."

His lips tremble, but he doesn't speak. Can't he even look at me?

"You're really childish over this," I say. "Can we at least have a conversation? What's going on?"

"Please, Jayne. I'm trying to work something out." He folds his arms tightly, continuing to look away.

That hurts, and my face flushes with a cocktail of frustration and embarrassment, wondering who witnessed this quiet stand-off. I return to my chair and give Isla's questioning look a shrug.

It's not fair. I've done nothing wrong.

And then to add insult to the burning mental pain, I spot Aithen with Erek when I leave the school grounds. Are you joking me?

They exchange words, and Erek departs. He casts an abrupt stare at me, his jaw clenched.

Next time, Erek, I tell myself.

Aithen catches my gaze, and I march towards him. He physically sighs. What is wrong with him?

"Jayne?" His lips tighten while he scans the area around us. I ignore that.

"I don't know why you're having a go at me, Aithen? I've done nothing wrong."

"I'm not saying you have—"

"But why all this blank-me crap? And why are you suddenly ashamed to be seen with me?"

"If you could—"

"Is this because of Erek? I've had to go to the police and make myself look like a complete idiot, because of—"

"The police? Are you mad?" Aithen asks, taking my shoulders in his hands.

"Well, everyone thinks so, yes," I say, shrugging off his grip.

"Jayne, you've got to stop this." The whites of his eyes add a plead to his quiet words.

"I can't. Four. Four of my friends are missing, Aithen." I stop myself crying.

Aithen raises his hands. "I'm trying to help. I told you we're not allowed to have relationships."

"Oh, come on, Aithen. Don't you like me?" I almost dread the response.

"I more than like you," he says with a combined frown and smile. "But you must stop these accusations. These thoughts."

I can't speak or else the torrent of tears will drown away my words. I watch him breathless.

"I'm on your side, Jayne. Take my word for it. You have to trust me. Please, give me a chance."

I stutter a nod and Aithen hesitantly, walks away.

I get it now. The rules about exchange-student dating. He's keeping it under wraps from Erek. It makes sense now.

But that's good.

For once, something is good.

I may be angry. Confused. Upset.

But.

He *more than* likes me.

CHAPTER EIGHTEEN

By Friday, I need retail therapy, so I head to Hill Derry mall with Isla and Sally, but a fire alarm scare interrupts our shopping fun. The centre evacuates and then given the all-clear forty minutes later. My friends exit for home, but I want some time alone.

The Mall eating area is quiet compared to normal. People come and go in waves.

I sit in the food court sipping on melon and kiwi flavoured water.

The review notes from today's cancelled physics class lay scattered across the table in front of me. Not because I'm digesting their contents but to make me appear busy.

Aithen.

I don't enjoy feeling weak about him. I've shed enough tears and lost nights of sleep over Iain. Why am I even torturing myself for Aithen? What makes him unique?

Everything.

He has a mature outlook on things, though there's his strange fascination with everyday objects, such as trains, or a paper stapler or hole punch.

He rarely laughs at jokes.

He's not chatty in class but what he says is so relevant. He's the smartest boy I have ever met. No small talk, only academia. An answer to any question asked of him.

But...

"Beautiful."

"I more than like you."

And that drawing of me.

I jump when a highchair knocks against a table. A young family settle themselves nearby. I smile and watch the young child – boy or girl – as it dives face-first into a pot of yoghurt. The parents are young, around Sarah's age.

Sarah mentioned Matthew the other day. It's almost four years since *that* day.

I cradle my forehead as I drift into the memory of that sad day. In my personal, private thoughts, I call it – the whole event – *the silence*.

After a troubled eight months and two weeks' pregnancy term – not forgetting two scares of no fetal heartbeat during ultrasound sessions – Sarah endured a fifteen-hour natural birth. I stayed with her throughout. A time of shouting, tears, laughter – yes, there was – and a whole mess of pushing and pulling.

You feel useless. You do nothing except pass the oxygen mask or offer water and a few words of encouragement at the right time. All special, though.

Matthew was born at 7:52 in the morning. He looked so small, covered in blood and other fluids. His little feet were bluish with white toes. I wanted to warm those tiny toes and could not wait to hold him and have him grab my finger. I've never seen a newborn baby up close like this before. I remember my tears welling up and how the excitement to be sharing Sarah and Terry's memorable moment engulfed me. Such a lovely feeling of warmth and happiness.

The midwife cleaned up his face, using a small suction device to clear out his nose and mouth. She used a towel to rub his back clean and seemed to give him a hard thump. I smiled at Sarah as she looked with excited anticipation at the medical staff.

Another slight thump and I waited for the first tiny wail to fill the room. The first call from your baby announcing their arrival for all to hear.

I waited.

Nothing can describe the hollow sound which filled the room.

The *silence* became deafening. My heart pounded; ears throbbed.

A minute seemed like an hour before the nurse hit the panic alarm. A medical team swamped the room and took Matthew away. Despite all their efforts, he did not breathe.

The silence.

I don't know which was worse, Matthew not waking or Sarah drifting away?

I press a palm against my mouth to stifle the groan.

Sarah deteriorated. Understandably.

But people weren't listening for her hidden screams.

I rest my elbows on the table and cup my face with my hands. I don't wish to share these tears. I don't care to see prying eyes watching me.

Sarah was still living at home then. Terry had found a job locally and worked all the hours he could claw together.

I came home from school to an empty house, but I could hear the shower upstairs. The sound encouraged me, as it meant Sarah was using it. I don't think she had washed her hair in two months; longer even.

But the shower didn't stop.

Even after I had called out a few times, there was no response.

A voice inside my head urged me to check on her.

I had finally heard her silent scream.

When I saw Sarah, the first thought burning through my head was, she's dead!

Blood oozed from the cut to her wrist, washing away down the drain from the water of the shower. The razor blade shone guiltily, discarded for taking a life.

"Sarah!"

I grabbed for her and brushed the hair away from her face with my fingers. She was sobbing, mascara-stained rivers down her face. I pressed against her wrist to stop the blood flow, and Sarah winced at the pain.

"I need to call an ambulance!" I shouted.

Through sobs, he gasped, "No, you don't. I can't even fuckin' do this right!"

She snapped her wrist from my clutches, and I could see the deep gash even more. The cut was away from her vital veins and along the side of her wrist. The blood flowed but wasn't pulsing the life from her.

I wrapped a towel around her wrist and held her tightly. Sitting together beneath the flow of the warm water of the shower, I rocked her trembling body and stroked her hair.

I sort of wish Mom hadn't come home and found us then, as everything went crazy… A voice nearby clamours for my attention.

"Chloe…"

"… Laura…"

"…deleted…"

The mists of the past crash into the present.

I snap my head up and sniff away the weakness, wiping my face with a grip of napkins.

What was that?

The hairs on the back of my neck stand to attention.

"… and Leslie."

I know that voice.

I stand, turning to where I imagine the voice came from.

Erek.

He sits bolt upright, opposite a heavy-set man, with his back to me. The man has thick, long hair, but he doesn't turn.

I see Erek's lips move as he mumbles something to the man.

He said *their* names.

"I heard you," I mouth the words to him.

Erek raises a hand towards the man and stands, too.

I grab a chair. It's heavier than I imagine, but I still throw it in their direction. It clatters and bangs against the man's seat.

Erek motions for the man to leave.

I immediately grab a glass from an empty table, and I don't care that I'm drenched by liquid. I aim at the man's head, but it bounces off his heavy coat and smashes to the floor. He exits from the area.

Voices shout, and someone calls for security.

But I don't care.

"I'm gonna kill you, you bastard!" I snarl. And I run for Erek. "I heard you!"

He takes a few tentative steps back and of all things, reaches for his wrist, but the coffee cup I have just tossed at him hits him across the cheek. The cup smashes, and he flinches from the blow and the splash of liquid from its contents.

I kick a table in front of me out of the way.

People shout further, and I am oblivious to the siren.

I don't care that it's only a rounded buttering knife, but I grab it anyway from an empty table.

I lunge for Erek, but vice-like hands grab my arms.

"No, you don't!" orders a deep voice.,

A thick arm wraps around my neck. I immediately elbow whoever is trying to stop me. I scream.

"Get off me!"

My other elbow delivers a grunt in response and heavy breathing. I kick out, but I catch the edge of the table. I shout with the pain.

I'm aware of two security guards as I catch sight of the light blue shirts and stainless-steel badges. "Get off!" I shout, but a third pair of hands wrestle me to the ground.

Thick saliva foams from my mouth and I don't care my nostrils flare and snot dangles in a disgusting string.

"You took them!" I shout at Erek. "You took everything!"

I struggle against the guards, but they won't release their grip.

"I want her back. You stole her!"

"Get off, me!" I shout at the guards, through tears and gritted teeth.

Erek stands wide-eyed, searching the scene unfolding in front of him.

"I want her back! You stole Chloe from my life! My life!" I plead.

A guard gasps, "We'll taser you if you don't stop!"

I hear that.

Like a flick-switch, I can suddenly see myself as though from the gathering crowd's viewpoint.

Oh, shit!

I relax slightly but not so much that the guards can subdue me.

I nod repeatedly.

"Okay! Okay," I surrender.

I watch Erek, as the guards wrestle me to my feet.

He looks to the guards then back at me. His face swells from the mug's blow, but the shock of my attack dismisses the pain.

"Sir? We need—"

Erek ignores the guard and exits.

My thoughts hit Earth with a huge thump.

I've fueled a whole new cycle of crazy-Jayne in school. Some people will lap this one up. A sharp echo stabs through my forehead as I recall Laura won't be one of them. She is usually the catalyst for most of the aggravation I have faced with her posse.

But I'd rather have that than her forgotten. She's still loved by her family and friends. Or was.

I hope no one here knows my family or me.

What an idiot.

But I heard Erek. He said *their* names.

And who was that man?

"Let's get her to the office," a guard says. I don't offer resistance. I'm led away.

When we reach the privacy of the office, one guard holds up the blunt knife. "You didn't have this, okay?"

"I wasn't going to…" my words trail away, and I bury my face in my hands, as the deluge envelopes me.

Two guards leave the room.

"Boy trouble?" the remaining guard asks.

I look up, and kind eyes regard me. He's a big guy, and I feel ashamed that I may have hit him with my elbow. His uniform is bright against his dark skin.

"I'm sorry," I offer through sniffs.

"Women are always the worse," he smiles. "Give me ten men any day."

That makes me laugh slightly. "I lost it." I frown. "The cops coming?"

He raises his eyebrows at me. "No. I think you've had a shitty enough day today?" He mimics, looking around. "And in this town, I'm sure the jury's already out, and your punishment will be the small-minded idiots."

He chuckles, and that makes me frown deeper, and I sigh, "That's true."

"So, who was the guy?" he asks.

"Trouble," I respond. "A whole world of trouble."

"Well, I'd say get Kung Fu lessons," he laughs "but I think you're already sorted!"

I laugh, too. "Sorry. I've never done anything like that. I'm really sorry."

"Nah, don't worry about it," he responds, warmly. "First bit of excitement we've had around here in a while."

My chest hurts as I breathe. Guilt? Probably.

"But for me, I'm sorry we had to get rough with you, Jayne."

"Oh, no. You know me?" I cringe.

He laughs. "Sorry, yes. But I know all you kids. That's my job." He waves a dismissive hand. "Now get your ass out of here. And behave yourself."

I offer my hand, and he shakes it flamboyantly.

I leave the office; the mall and it is like every pair of eyes watch me. Waiting for the crazy girl to blow up again.

When I arrive home, Mom does that thing with her mouth, where she appears to touch each of her bottom teeth with her tongue, one by one, as she considers what some gossiping friend has told her.

The disgraceful daughter.

"Don't!" she dismisses me before I can speak.

"I'm not hungry," I snap when she offers dinner will be ready in an hour.

I go upstairs to my room and cry.

I wake with a start. It's dark outside. The blue digits of my bedside clock say it's 2:55 am.

I lie there for a while, thinking about nothing at first. I watch the shadow of the leaves from the tree outside, dancing across my bedroom ceiling. Memories of the day course awareness through my sleepy head.

What came over me?

Obviously, what. Erek said their names. It's been building for days now. Despite pushing myself mentally into that visualization box, I still wanted to hurt him. Had I reached him; would I have tried to stick that knife into him? Doubt advises me it probably wouldn't have pierced the skin, but I had the intent.

There's no going back to sleep now, so I get up. I flinch as putting weight on my foot hurts. That's from where I kicked the table. I huff: the instep is swollen.

My body is stiff and sore. I open my pyjama top to inspect the damage in the mirror. I grimace at the ugly black and purple bruises across my shoulders, neck, and upper arms. They're tender to touch. I cover up again and make a mental note to keep back banana skins. I've read they help reduce bruising. Or at least speed up the healing process.

Was I that out of control? Three security guards and a heap of bruises say, yes.

I sneak downstairs and click on the kettle to prepare myself a cup of green and mint tea. I like the smell of the steam from the cup more than the drink itself.

I sit in the conservatory and gaze into the night sky through the glass roof.

The Moon is a sliver of itself. I love the Moon. All night sky. I can lie or sit for hours on a clear night and watch the stars. Now and then you catch the trace of a human-made satellite traversing across the heavens. It fascinates me. A better treat is seeing the space station pass over. It all looks so unreal, but when you witness it, albeit a small, shiny dot so high up, you feel a super sense of pride and wonder. What must it be like, to be there and looking down at our planet?

The sound of a key in the front door breaks my concentration. At this hour? Standing, I choke back a tear when I see it's Dad. He's home. I run to him, and he is holding me in his arms. Nothing can hurt me now. His arms shield me. Tears flow over my cheeks as he embraces me and strokes my hair. I already know he knows what happened, as he says nothing or asks anything. We sit down. He explains how Mom received a call from two people at the mall, but she left me to sleep: a smart idea. She called him, and he started for home straight away. It comforts me to know he made the journey for me; despite the shame, he must feel.

Mom and Dad have a curious relationship with me and my siblings. Emily and I are "Daddy's girls" whereas Sarah and David are so in Mom's camp. The way it's always been. But no matter what, we are one family.

Dad and I talk about what happened.

"Where were you when it happened? Mentally?" he asks, emphasising the last word. We've had similar chats before, though not on this scale of seriousness.

"I was thinking about Matthew and *that time* when Sarah…" My face melts into tears for a moment, but I gather myself together as Dad cradles my hands with his.

"It's tough, I know. But there's nothing you or anybody could have done to change things." His tired, sad face searches mine.

I'm annoyed by my actions. Dad doesn't need this in his life; I'm grown up now. Emily and David need the attention now, not me. But then he hugs me, and I'm reminded otherwise.

Placing his hands on my shoulders, "Why did you attack that boy, Jayne? Who is he? Has he hurt you?"

I suck in trembling lips and wipe my eyes. "No."

"I know I'm not always around, but I have noticed something is going on with you?" he asks.

I lean back in my chair, hands behind my head. "It's impossible to explain."

"Try me?" Dad asks. His eyes are red and droop tiredly at the sides.

I point to my head. "It's the accident. I imagine all kinds of crazy sh— stuff."

Dad raises a glance to my correction.

"I feel like I'm caught up in something…" I know I am, but he can't help. I must protect him from me. "But I'm trying to work it out… with the doctor." That's it. Add authority to my excuses. My lies. My deceit.

"Oh, Jayne," Dad hugs me. "Don't be alone in this. In anything." He releases me, and I stutter a nod, and he takes that as a hint to end the subject, for now.

We sit in silence, welcoming a broad, dark blue early morning light. "You should sleep," Dad says.

"You mean *you're* tired, lightweight?" I tease him.

He laughs. "Well, yes, but you can sit up for a few more hours and then sleep all morning and afternoon or?"

I nod in agreement. "Yes, I'll try and sleep, or else I'll pay for it on Monday morning."

"You are going to be okay?" he asks me.

I nod as my eyes well up.

He looks at me like I would Emily when she tripped and cut her knee. Then he hugs me once more.

Monday morning. School. Can I think about facing all those inquisitive looks?

CHAPTER NINETEEN

I'm expelled from school.

Conduct not becoming a blur, blur, blur…

Whatever.

Mom appears to have forgotten how to speak in English now. She has reverted to her mother tongue. This happens when she becomes angry and can't cope… with me.

Thankfully, I can roll my eyes in English or Russian.

But my tough stance and posture are a lie.

I hate myself.

Shame flows through me.

I've worked hard in school. My teachers are great, and I need a friend. Just one.

And she's there. Isla.

Only twenty text messages. A jumbled digital mess of things like:

"Some say ten guards tried to hold you down."

"You had a gun?"

"You threw a table twenty feet?"

I must call her and dismiss my superhero or villain status. No gun!

But Islas' sweet, childish voice grounds me. She reminds me I am me. And yes, I cry a lot, and so does she, but I feel saved. By her.

Shortly after lunch, Mom utters the words, "Teacher. For you."

Suddenly I am nine years old as I step into our lounge and Mister Hunneford is there.

Kids used to call him Hunny-Bun, as yes, he used to have a man-bun.

I still remember that day, when an ass-hole student tried to call him out, but Mister Hunneford said proudly, "Well, my husband likes it."

A strong statement in a small town. But thankfully, most pupils applauded him mentally.

"Sir?" I ask as I take a seat opposite him. It's strange having a teacher in my home. It's like someone has dropped a whale off. You see teachers in one place only, so they seem to become part of the school furniture.

He rests back into the chair my dad usually sits. "I just wanted to make sure you are okay?"

I shrug.

"Oh, school." He waves a hand dismissively. "Oh, to be young," he smiles. "Engines fired by passions beyond us elders."

"Is that a quote?" I ask. I'm still trying to work out why he's here.

"No. It's me saying, I don't care, Jayne. Something has awoken in you recently, and no, I don't think it is hormones." His gaze lingers on me. He dips his head and continues. "Keep on your path. Whatever it is you are fighting for, go for it."

How do I answer that?

He stands and straightens. "You are an A-plus, Jayne. I don't listen to gossiping fools."

I shake my head questionably, standing too. "So, you're not going to fail me?"

"Joking, aren't you? You're the best student I've had in years."
He leans in slightly. "The mall episode proved to me; you have
passion."

My jaw drops as he smiles.

"Now. Take time and relax. Heal. Whatever you need to do," he
says. And leaves.

I can't hug a teacher, but I'd love to.

"Thank you, Sir," I say as he departs.

Well, that was weird. But I still need to wipe away a stray
tear.

An A-plus? My project with Aithen obviously well received.

Oh, where is Aithen now? How will he react when he hears I
attacked Erek?

I hug myself from the shiver, pumping dread through my veins.
I lost it. Totally. But I heard Erek say the names. I didn't hear everything he said, but why would he say that? He also said something
about *deleted*? Is this why everyone else has forgotten Chloe and
the others? But I haven't.

And who was that man with the long hair?

I can't believe I threw a glass at him. A total stranger.

My heart pounds as the doorbell rings. What now?

I dare not look or answer the door, rocking myself as I listen for
voices.

I hear a man's voice, and it's sort of familiar. Another teacher?
Mom's face drains of colour when she opens the door to the lounge.
"Police. For you," she says. Her frown scolds me with no exchange
of words.

Officer Johns appears at the lounge door.

"I'll leave you to it," Mom says dismissively.

Johns shuffles into the room, looking towards my retreating
mom. He opens his mouth but then changes his mind and motions to
the seat opposite me.

I half stand but then settle back. Kicked out of school. Is he here to arrest me? I thought the guard said he won't be logging a complaint.

"Jayne," begins, Johns. "We're becoming familiar lately."

I fold my arms and nod. Say nothing. He's not here for my benefit. *You have the right to remain silent...*

I'm zipping it. You're getting nothing from me, Johns.

"Any idea why I'm here?" he searches.

I exaggerate a blink of the eyes and shake my head.

"Hmmm, okay," he says. "There has not been a formal complaint, but the episode in the mall—"

"Why are you here?" I ask. "There's no complaint, so why don't you go and do your stupid job elsewhere?" My tongue suddenly fills my mouth. I lower my chin so he can't see me swallowing nervously.

His voice dulls from the buzzing in my ears. The throbbing warns me to cool it. "No complaint does not mean; no action will be taken." He watches me. "Witnesses in the mall are distressed by your actions. I have no idea why the security team have not asked for charges to be raised."

My chest hurts from the subtle threat in his words.

"Witnesses say you were shouting a girl's name, Chloe?" he tilts his head in response to me tightening my arms further. "When you came to the station, you were talking about a girl named Leslie?"

I shrug. What can I possibly say? He doesn't believe me anyway.

Johns nods, thoughtfully. "Who's the boy with the white hair?"

I stare at the floor.

Johns sighs and blows air noisily from pursed lips. "I watched the security video, and I clearly see you aiming your *attack* at that particular boy."

This rips my gaze towards Johns. What does he know about Erek?

"Let me jump ahead one moment, Jayne. I'm not here to arrest you, okay? Something has happened with you lately, but your doctor is not willing to share personal details with me."

That's a surprise, but also comfort. I thought everyone is against me.

"But yes, I understand you are receiving treatment, so I won't push there. But you're high on police radar at the moment. See me as the bad guy if you wish, but I'm trying to prevent you from making a huge mistake in life."

"Bit late for that, isn't it?" I say, weakly.

"No, it's not. I just need you to help me, to help you," Johns offers.

I unfold my arms and bring my knees up to my chin, as I sit on the couch. I hug my lower legs. "I don't know what to say. I don't know what is real anymore."

"Jayne, neither I, any of my colleagues or the mall security team, know who the boy is from the footage. A total unknown and I'm not comfortable with that." Johns sits forward in the seat to press the words home.

"Now, you do know him. In whatever capacity. And I'm guessing from what has been said, and what I've now seen, this boy is connected to your lost friend or friends?"

I nod again. "But missing friends who nobody else knows existed."

"But I'll ask again," continues Johns. "Who's the boy. Give me a starting point, Jayne?"

"His name is Erek, and he's a student counsellor from Kay University. That's all I know." I must warn Aithen that I've spilt the beans on Erek. I don't care about Erek, but I don't want Aithen getting into trouble.

"Kay?" Johns' head jerks back in disbelief. "What's a Kay counsellor doing here in Dereton?"

"They have a student exchange program. Some students are here, and Erek's with them," I reply.

"News to me," muses Johns. "I'll need to check that and this Erek. You have a surname for him? Then again, I can ask the office at Hill Derry that." He stands, and I do the same.

"I don't know his full name. I'm not friends with him," I say.

"I can see that," smirks Johns. He halts at the doorway. "Please, try and stay out of trouble. If something is bothering you or you feel the need to attack someone, pick up the phone and call me." He reaches into a jacket pocket and hands me a card. "My details are on there, including my cell."

He rests a hand on the door handle. "Your doctor will want to discuss all of this a lot further. I think you need to open up more."

"I have been open with her," I say.

"More so then. It's time to nip this one in the bud, Jayne. Fix things and get yourself back in school." He leaves.

I flop back into the chair and bury my face in my hands, the tears sting with the fear and shame of what I've done. I don't want Mom to hear me cry, but suddenly her arms are around me, and I fall into her embrace.

"I'm sorry," I croak between sobs.

She strokes my hair. "The storm will pass. But I believe in you, Jayne."

"I'm crazy," I sniff. "Should be locked up."

"We're all crazy." I sense her smile. "You've hit a glitch. That's okay. You may feel like the world is against you today, but you'll be saving it tomorrow."

CHAPTER TWENTY

Tuesday and day two of my school suspension. Despite my crazy status, I've always had a perfect school record; academically that is. What a way to conclude my second to last year. How will this reflect on my high school graduation year, after the summer break?

Hunneford was supportive yesterday. Will the other teachers be so?

Mom suggested I go for a run, as I've grounded myself the last few days. No, the looks from the judgemental faces I'll encounter *out there*, have imprisoned me.

I miss Aithen. Something about him grounds me, calms the rage that burns fiercely lately.

Will he even speak to me when I see him?

Mom then reminds me I have an appointment with the doctor. Oh, dear. Time to pile on more doubt and guilt and convincing myself further, I probably need locking away.

"Are you sexually active?" Harris asks seriously.

I laugh. "Just come out with it, why don't you?"

Harris's face is unmoving.

"I'm only active when running, nothing else. No other activity going on," I say. Why would she even ask that?

She dips her chin and peers over the rim of her glasses. "But you have a new boyfriend. You've said his name, Aithen, at least a dozen times since you arrived."

Stammering, I say, "No, no, it's, he's just a friend from school." It dawns on me why she asked. I mentioned nausea and feeling faint, as a substitute for blacking out when people vanish from my life. "No, I'm not pregnant. You'd see from my blood test."

Harris smiles. "True. Let's hope it stays that way." She taps at her keyboard.

Harris plops her hands on her knees. "So, what's going on, Jayne? Friends. Boys. School. Police and now the unsettlement at the shopping centre. Your mental health is of concern to me."

I shrug and try to say something, but I'm running empty of excuses or reasons for anything.

"I still think you should consider controlled counselling," she suggests. "Part of a group or one-to-one with a specialist. Someone who has experience of the crisis you find yourself in."

"Crisis?" I quip. "I'm not in a crisis. I'm not a victim of whatever."

"Then what's happening? What's triggering you to break the law? Or search for missing people? The mall?" Harris's tone remains soothing, but the content scratches at my head.

"Is it still your missing friends?" she delves further.

"I don't want to talk about that," I reply.

"Just answer me this," Harris says. "Has anybody else disappeared?"

I dare not respond, but I see the knowing expression register in her eyes. She can read me like a book.

"Hmm. I see," she says. "How is your head now? Are the tablets helping with the pain?"

"No. Not really," I say.

Harris turns and types at the computer again. "Okay. Let's leave it there for the time being."

She turns again. "I'm sorry your school has responded as they did. But I am going to recommend they reinstate you as soon as possible. You need your friends around you and simmering in isolation is the last thing conducive to your wellbeing."

Yes, I do need my friends around me. But they've mostly gone. What did Erek say? *Deleted.* I don't raise this with her, but maybe Leslie, Chloe, and Laura are real, and everyone else is fake? *VioletlyAlone* was a virtual friend. How real was she?

I read somewhere we are all are a figment of one another's imagination. That in this whole world, *we* don't exist. Maybe that's true, and I've worked out a way to escape from mine?

Despite the overwhelming paranoia, I hold my head up high and walk towards the coffee house. A small dose of normality needed. Though that spoils by the sting of the last time I was here when I saw Leslie with Erek.

I remind myself I'm not the centre of the Universe. Life goes on. We're all a speck of dust and the outburst of some stupid girl already forgotten by time. For the small-minded, no, but who are they? Look in the mirror idiots.

The chatter of the coffee house helps me blend into life again. Peaceful. Fragrant. Calm.

"Jayne?"

His beautiful, violet eyes are sad. Concerned.

I stand. "Aithen. Oh, erm, hi."

"May I?" he asks, pointing to the chair opposite me.

"Yes, yes, please," I respond. "Y-you want a drink?"

"No. I'm fine," Aithen says, as he settles before me.

Oh, wow. I've missed him. But why is he here? Is this going to be a *"Don't ever talk to me again! You attacked my friend!"*

There's no anger or anything from him. We don't speak for what feels like an eternity, but I must.

"Aithen. I'm sorry. I'm sorry about Erek."

"No. Don't be," he says, shaking his head to dismiss my words.

"I just... I don't know what happened." I dip my chin. "I totally lost it."

"This is partly my fault," he says, like a confession.

"Your fault? What have you done?" I ask.

"Nothing. That's the problem," he replies. "I've allowed Erek to get to you—"

"Get to me?"

"It's tough to explain, without saying too much." He frowns and looks around us, then back. "You're going to have to trust me, Jayne. Have to trust that when I say nothing, I'm actually saying everything."

"Cryptic," I respond. What's that supposed to mean?

"Okay, here's the thing. I *could* tell you something, and it would answer all your questions. But then the first thing you'd say is, you shouldn't have told me that." Aithen says, using his hands to emphasise the words.

"Tell me what?" I ask.

He smiles. "It's a, how do you say it? A *catch-22* situation. I say I don't say. We end up in the same place."

"So, what can you tell me? Is it about Erek?" I need one answer at least.

"No. It's not about Erek. But he is trouble."

"Well, the police are looking for him now. I'm sorry, Aithen, but they came to my home. They saw the security footage from the Mall. So, he's on their hit list."

Aithen shifts in his chair. "They'll find nothing."

"Why? He's a student counsellor from Kay," I suggest.

"Oh, they'll find that's true. But they won't track Erek down," Aithen says.

"What is he a secret agent or something?" I laugh.

"Can you trust me, Jayne? Because I am going to trust you." How can I say, no to that expression? Those caring eyes?

"If I say yes, then what?" My question is innocent enough, but the wheels are turning in Aithen.

"For the time being, forget Erek."

"I can't—"

"You need to. I can't help if you are dragging innocent people into this mess." Aithen accentuates the words with open hands pointing towards me.

Help me? Innocent people? My friends?

"What is it you are trying to do, Aithen?"

"I need to protect you."

CHAPTER TWENTY-ONE

"Aithen. I need more than *I can't tell you or else I'll have to kill you* type of response here," I push.

He combs his fingers through his fair hair as he leans back in his seat, but then huddles towards me again. "Can we play a game? A bit like hide and seek?"

"What? Are we doing the hiding and Erek seeking?" I smile, but Aithen's expression confirms this is what the game is.

"Unfortunately, that is it. I need you to give me time to work this out. The more time you can give me, the more I can tell you," he says.

"But what's with all this cloak and dagger rubbish?" I ask, but Aithen's puzzled expression reflects he doesn't understand my question.

Is he trying to protect Erek or me? It's like every time I mention Erek, Aithen steers the subject away from him.

"Aithen, I've got to ask something."

"I'll try," he responds.

"Either I am well and truly crazy, or close friends of mine have vanished into thin air," I hang my head. How do I sound to him? He was there that day I had my Chloe meltdown in school. "I remember them and know them as clearly as I see you here."

Aithen places a hand on mine. The touch enchants warmth pulsing through my hand and calms my thoughts but races my heart.

"But I think Erek is involved. I don't know how or why. But I heard him say something about *deleted* in the mall?" I ask, keeping my voice low.

Aithen's thumb strokes the top of my hand. "I don't have an answer to that, I'm sorry, Jayne. And I'm not judging you either. I need you to trust me." He cups my hands in both of his to press home these words. "I want to be close to you. To help and protect you."

I run my tongue over my lips as I watch his mouth.

"But we have to be careful and not broadcast we are dating or anything," he says, but this springs my mental radar to red alert. In a good way.

Dating?

"What's funny?" he asks, and his smile mirrors mine.

"Dating?" I ask.

I giggle as his cheeks redden. His blush steals a beat from my heart, and my own face warms.

"Yeah, sorry," he falters. "You did ask me if I was seeing anyone? I think about you, all the time and I… I don't know. I can't stop myself liking you, a lot."

Where's this come from? The last thing I imagined today is *this*. He likes me a lot. My recurring dream pops into my head as I watch his lips.

"I like you, too." I manage. Our heads are so close, despite our eyes downcast. The sounds of the coffee house muted by my racing heart and thoughts. I want to make my dream real. Is it too soon to lean forward and steal a slice of that dream?

Aithen's eyes focus on mine. The violet spell envelopes me in sensual protection. Nothing can hurt me when Aithen is here. I believe he will prevent any possible harm towards me. I dare to edge closer, ever so carefully.

"You want me to clear them away?" a shrill voice asks.

The spell breaks.

We both turn to see the chirpy smile of the woman standing beside us, a trolley of cups and plates, teetering haphazardly in protest at the prospect of yet more dishes.

I nod, and she clears the table and gives it a quick wipe with a damp cloth, breathing heavily from the effort.

Just go, I shout in my head. Talk about spoiling the moment.

I thank her as she departs with a rattle and squeak of wheels. "Where were we?" I ask, but Aithen has sat back into his seat.

"Let's go for a walk," he suggests.

It's so lovely he always holds the door open for me to pass through.

"So, this hide and seek game," I begin. "Does it involve wearing dark sunglasses, wigs, fake moustaches?"

Aithen smiles at that. Wow, he does have a sense of humour.

"No, but we must be careful. A covert friendship," he says.

I halt and face Aithen. "Is this for my protection or Erek's?"

"Yours Jayne. I promise this is for you only."

"Then why do I feel like you're dangling a friendship… a liking me lots thing, when in fact you're just guarding Erek against whatever he has done?"

"You've got to forget Erek. I know that's hard, impossible even." Aithen rests his elbows against a railing and looks towards the harbour entrance. "But he can cause so much trouble. For you. For everyone."

I place a hand on his shoulder and turn Aithen towards me. He offers no resistance.

"Aithen, for some reason, I know something is going on. Everybody else in this town is oblivious. But before Leslie vanished, she told me more than once, she had seen *something*. And that *thing* was linked to Erek."

There's the slightest hint of a denial headshake from Aithen, accompanied by a sigh.

"My list of friends who have suddenly disappeared is growing. And I know I may sound crazy, but honestly, do you really think I am making this all up?"

He rubs his mouth, forcefully like he wants to rip away the words. "No, I don't. But I also can't encourage you to try and delve deeper. You've got to leave it alone, Jayne."

I nod for us to continue walking.

"Okay. You want to be friends, right? So, what does that look like? We're not exactly skulking in the shadows now, are we? Everything seems safe?" I ask, keeping my tone calm and playful, trying to defuse the tension which sizzles when Erek's name is mentioned.

"Oh, we're safe to walk along the high street. Go to school. Have a coffee, even. But an open display of affection, such as holding hands, hugging, kissing…"

The dream jumps into my head again.

"That would arouse concern and trouble," Aithen says.

I lean against a low wall of the harbourside. "And you've thought of those things about me?" I cough as my voice raises pitch.

Aithen's eyes searching around me makes me smile. He is shy. But then he looks at me, and wow, he looks at me as though he is speaking directly to my soul.

"Yes. All of the time," he says.

I stifle the gasp and swallow deeply, as I stand up straight. "Then let's give it a try. Being friends, that is," I quickly correct myself. I'm sure he's not planning to kiss me here and now.

"So, are we dating now?" I ask, trying to keep calm and not run around dancing for joy.

Aithen looks up as though thinking about something, then says, "Yeah."

I raise open arms towards him. "Can we sign it with a *friendly, schoolmate, no we're not really dating hug?*" I smile.

He actually laughs at that, and suddenly his arms are around me.

I squeeze him back and try to count the seconds. How long would I hug a friend for? Have we embraced too long now? But at that moment I know we will release, I plant a kiss on his neck, just below his ear.

Aithen's scent lingers as we pull away and intoxicates me.

"Woah," I laugh.

He raises his eyebrows and blows out air loudly. "And that was just a hug," he smiles. "But now you see what I mean? The difference between just friends and… that?"

I close my eyes and nod deliberately. "Yeah, I do."

Despite all the craziness going on in my life, how can I just forget it all in an instant?

We park ourselves on a bench.

"How does this work then?" I ask. "Our secret romance?"

"No more Erek, okay?"

I nod, reluctance visible from my response.

"For the next couple of weeks, and I know this is hard, try to stay below the radar of police and talk of missing people."

"But I can't just pretend they don't, didn't exist," I blurt out, but keeping my voice low.

"Yes, but you can't go running off to everyone and hope they are going to believe you. Nobody will. Ever," he says.

"I can't give up on my friends, Aithen. What if they're out there somewhere, and I'm the only one who can help them?"

"You're not," he replies. "I can help, too."

CHAPTER TWENTY-TWO

I'm not crazy.

And Aithen believes my story around my friends.

At least he says he does.

But it calms and reassures me they are real. Yes, they are still missing, but Aithen has given me hope. The fact one person believes me, and it's him, is like having an extra pair of hands to share the burden.

I recalled what happened with each, and he listened intently. It worries me he wasn't shocked by anything I said. Like he already knew the details. He can't, but he assures me we will solve this puzzle together.

The rules are as follows.

One: no more talk of or approaching Erek. He is strictly off-limits despite my continued protests. But it's that or Aithen won't help me. And what if Erek approaches me? I did attack him after all. Aithen advised me Erek won't. He has made sure of that, and I must trust him. It was all said nicely, but nothing is nice when it comes to Erek.

Two: I am to forget all talk about missing people. *What missing people? Oh, them. Sorry, just me hitting my head in the accident last year. Ignore me.* I hope I can convince my doctor, as I can't convince my reflection in the mirror.

Three: act normal. *Yeah, right.* I'm not at school, but that doesn't mean I can't call and meet up with friends. Let everyone see I am okay. Not behaving like the town weirdo anymore.

Four: we are *friends*. Dating, even. And that's nice. It's more than pleasant and an easy distraction for the play-acting of being a sane teenager.

Aithen is like a suit of armour to shield my mind and thoughts of dreadful things. I'm strong and positive around him.

But when I'm alone, and the shadows close in, I still hear screams in the night and the clawing of phantoms lurking and stalking my dreams, searching for me. Hunting me down.

And then the dawn breaks, and on cue, the kiss lingers in mid-air, waiting for contact.

I wake.

"Urgh!" I groan, kicking back the duvet.

Today's the day. Before I go to sleep, I am kissing Aithen. So hard, he'll pass out by the time I'm finished.

I relish a mischievous smile as I head for the shower.

The town bustles below us as we plant ourselves on top of Derr Hill. It is my safe place and always quiet, away from people, though the last time I was here, Laura vanished that night. A plane breaks the silence and chases away shadowed thoughts.

Aithen wants *normal* and for me to adopt a covert persona for a week or two? I'd love a bit of normality in my life, but how can I grasp that when I know Erek is involved in the cause of my missing friends? At least I think I do.

But Aithen hasn't said he thinks Erek is involved, only I should be careful there. Careful of what though? Aithen has asked for time, but what is he looking for? And how can he help me? Maybe Aithen hopes I will snap out of this delusional state. I don't know.

Aithen holds my hand, and my mind focuses on him. He's a welcome distraction, and it's nice to appreciate such a simple act.

I want Aithen to meet my family. Or is that too soon? If anything, I want to show them I can be normal, and not the girl getting into trouble with the police, security guards and school. Mom appeared happy that other day when I was talking about the boy in class who called me beautiful.

For once, it would be nice to see a look of approval from her, and Dad. I know they will like Aithen and will see I must be okay if I'm dating an amazing boy like him.

Maybe.

Aithen has become the reason I wake up and welcome the day. I thought Iain had taken my heart to college with him, but no, he took away the feelings of a younger me. My heart has matured and wants more. Aithen is inside my head, and he's welcome.

Ask him. He may say no, but then he could say yes. He's well-mannered and may want to meet my family. I'd love to meet his. What will they be like? He doesn't talk about them much. Then again, I don't give him the chance to speak. I need to shut up at times.

Aithen wants normal, then let's have a dose of that.

He's lying sideways watching the airport. Rolling him onto his back, I'm leaning on my elbow, above him. This is almost like the dream. I want to say so much to him and tell him how beautiful he is and how happy he makes me feel, but I'm lost in his violet eyes. He smiles, and I snap out of the spell again. I laugh as I'm already feeling clumsy without saying a word.

"You want food? With my sister and my… family? Sorry, scrap that." He continues to watch me, a half-smile waiting for me to proceed. "You fancy coming to my house and meeting my family?"

He smiles and raises his eyebrows.

"I'd love to meet your family. When?"

"Leave it to me."

I must plan with Mom and see when everybody is around, so it will be a weekend day. Still, right now, all I want to focus on is the low hum of traffic below us, screaming aeroplanes above, and the exquisite boy sitting next to me. His presence is electrifying. I place my hands on his hips as we kneel facing one another. I'm finally touching his body.

His face is so close; I want to grasp onto this moment. He's told me more than once he likes me a lot. Should I move towards him? Since *that* psychology class, those lips have tortured me for attention.

I fall into the depths of his violet eyes. Searching amidst my soul.

He said he's thought about kissing me. Does he dream about me, too? That first moment when our lips meet.

I need to kiss him. No more games and glances. My fingers want to touch his skin beneath his clothes. I realise his hands are mirroring mine and his fingers are rubbing my hips. Stroking upwards.

I run my hands up towards his shoulders, and he lets out a gentle breath. I hope he doesn't pull away as I move towards him; please. I must know of his intentions. Is he ready for this? We've only just begun as friends and dating. But his words and eyes are sending me signals.

He's so close. His nose strokes my ear lobe.

I edge my face towards his.

I'm just going to pull him closer and…

He kisses me!

Simmering desire pops. The first kiss is gentle. The next is more… passionate.

I don't mean to jump on top of him, but the tension built for a while. The memory of a hundred kisses explodes in my head. I've missed this, but it feels new, different, and yet, familiar. His warmth envelopes me as we kiss, and our hands dance across each other's body. I love the tightness of his arms when he pulls me towards him.

And as quick as it began, the wave passes, and we come up for air.

Regaining our composure, we can't help but laugh. It's been so long since I felt this flustered and happy.

When we finally arrive at the bottom of the hill, we steal one more kiss and stroll along the high street. Aithen brushes the back of my hand with his, and the touch is soft and warm. I want the world to see him with me. Of all people, why choose me? How long will he stay? Just a semester, he said. I chase away that nagging doubt. Enjoy this while I can.

I want him to like my family. I want them to meet him.

What am I going to wear?

———

Have I overdone it? Aithen's only seen me as *student* Jayne and not *me* Jayne. The goth girl who loves screaming bands of hot rock and vocals to melt your face. I'm not a hardcore punk goth with lots of black and white make-up, but this contrast to my daytime hours may be too much, too soon?

I have quite a few tattoos. It took some convincing, but Mom and Dad are quite liberal in many ways. So long as the tattoos are hidden and won't be frowned upon by the school, college, or a future employer, they have met me more than halfway with the decision.

Mom introduced me to a tattoo artist, Pauline, last year, and what started as a small mermaid, developed into an inked story and theme, defining my personal work of art. Mom's known Pauline for about seven years and boasts three small tats herself. Very discrete. Thankfully, Pauline is too and keeps confidence well.

So, I cover up at school and when running, but today, I'm wearing a skinny strap blue dress with small, darker blue spots on it; not a leopard-print but not far off. My right shoulder and upper arm are home to a colourful weave of butterflies, leaves, and stems. The colour scheme is blues, pinks, and greys, with a splash of pastel green.

I've also had colours dyed into the lower layers of my black hair today: blue, pink, and purple, but only the wind or chance can reveal their secret.

Pale – skin tone, not white – foundation. Black eyebrow mascara offers a gentle, fluffy touch to contrast my dark blue false eyelashes. The eyeliner is black with crafted tails at each corner, but the eyeshadow matches the dark spots on my dress. Plum lipstick. A light dusting of blusher.

Then I add three tiny zirconia with dark violet backings to high-light my triangle points. I stick them on with a skin glue I trust.

I spray the air with my favourite perfume and walk into its scent mist. The coolness absorbs into the skin of my exposed arms and shoulders. I eye the clock, still twenty minutes to go. Six o'clock seems so far away.

I need the loo; no, I don't. Nerves.

I could make an excuse and call off the whole thing? I peer out of my bedroom window, at the gathering outside in the rear garden.

My family.

No, this must happen. My family must meet Aithen. Selfishly, I want them to see him, to think I must be special and… yes, I want to show him off.

Everyone is here, including a few select mates. Isla, as always, looks stunning and adds the fizz and bubbles to any occasion. My Goth friends don't get her and why we are such good friends. It's good to have a few family neutral people here so Aithen won't feel too overwhelmed.

Isla passes me a glass, and I drink it down without looking.

"Woah there," she laughs. "You planning to propose this evening?"

I laugh as I cough on a shot of Jack Daniels – not my usual tipple, but it hit the spot. Am I so obvious? She knows I'm crazy about Aithen. He is all I talk about with her and I mean *all*. Down to the detail of how he drinks his water and runs and breathes, even.

He will be here at any moment, so I slip back into the house. My heart jumps when there is a knock on the door, despite me already expecting it.

Doors are amazing things. In stories, they open to whole worlds, the future, the past, the unknown. This door opens to the reason I breathe now. Why I woke up today and almost jumped four feet out of my bed with excitement. I'm the luckiest person on this planet at this exact moment; well, in my world anyway.

Aithen.

He is here, inside my house. This is where I get dressed for school. Eat breakfast, dinner. Hang out in my scruffy clothes with my family. My home and he is here.

"Jayne. You, you look amazing. So, beautiful."

He pulls me close and kisses me after I have closed the door. I'm oblivious to the embarrassing walls, lined with my family photographs, including me from nappies to last Christmas. I get this ridiculous idea to ask him upstairs to my room. Why? I don't know, but my thoughts are mischievous?

I kiss him again, and this time, I hope people notice us through a window or the open backdoors. I want them to see him with me. To see Aithen likes me and to know how much I want to be with him. I take hold of his hand and lead him to the tribe.

Straight away, Mom links arms with him and says, "Okay, handsome. You're with me. I trust you know how to prep salad?" And she takes him to the big, wooden table next to the cooking area.

My family do BBQ in a big way. I'm talking about freshly baked rolls in a clay oven, meat on an oversized home-made BBQ – built by Dad – and powered by gas and coal. It even boats a full rotary skewer for large chunks of meat.

They also like to introduce a touch of home or heritage. Mom always brews a pot of Borsch, which you can ladle into white bowls. She made the bowls herself and glazed them at a private kiln, or wherever you go to make bowls. She also includes a warm platter of Pelmeni and Blini, though she simply refers to these as pancakes. Hence, they are familiar to the locals. Her *pièce de résistance* is beef stroganoff. And the fact she stirs a piping steel pot of her speciality on a burner translates into this being a significant party. Mom communicates a lot via the medium of food: Aithen's important.

Then there's Dad. His contribution is kept to a minimum, as with all things, Dad. So, a tray of sushi is always first on a bed of ice. Then he'll slice beef to a millimetre thickness and invite guests to cook the incredibly tasty mouthfuls, one at a time. This simple dish is called shabu-shabu.

The women always gravitate towards Dad's food as it looks like you will lose weight by looking at it. Minimal, healthy servings.

I realise I don't know what Aithen likes to eat. How is that possible? He ate a bit of my blueberry muffin the other day and chewed on that okay, but I don't know what he may want. I'll let him find his way around the extensive menu offered by Mom and Dad.

Emily and David help Aithen. I'm surprised to see how patient he is with them as they *teach* him how to slice a tomato – the *right* way – and then cucumber. Fascinating to watch. He listens to them like he's learning how to do what they are showing him; it's funny.

Sarah sides next to me. "And you found him in which glossy

magazine? Why have you been hiding him?" She smiles at me with a raised eyebrow.

"It doesn't hurt, no matter how many times I pinch myself," I say, but then she does as such and yes, it hurts. We laugh.

"Honestly," she continues, "he must be a keeper?"

"I hope so," I say, and she hugs me. "Oh, Jayne. You look so happy. It looks good on you."

And so, the evening progresses, and Aithen is a hit. Without any forced effort, he blends in with the mood of the family. We laugh at what he finds *odd* about Dereton. The small-town aspect compared to the big city he comes from. He does so with such tenderness; no negativity for humour. He is an attentive listener, whether it be my dad or David.

I'm distracted from a conversation as I notice Aithen talking to Sarah and Dad. She is entirely dwarfed by the other two. Aithen is only just taller than Dad, who at 188 centimetres has a presence. He's not menacing, but the air around him clearly states, *don't mess with me*. But he's my warm and gentle teddy bear.

When there are moments of laughter in their conversation, it lifts my heart so much. It makes me feel excited, though I don't know what the subject may be.

Then the night creeps in, and I'm alone with him, sitting on the lawn and warmed by a small fire Aithen and Dad built together earlier. Boys will be boys.

Aithen holds me in his arms, and beneath a clear sky perforated by stars, I kiss him. Then I choke back a tear, but I smile. "Sorry. A great evening. I couldn't have wished for any better."

He smiles back, stroking my hair. "Your family are amazing, Jayne. I hope I didn't overdo it in any way?"

I'm glad he cares. "Of course not. It's been incredible."

"And you have quite the global family. Parents from across the planet?" He brushes a trailing strand of hair, which catches in my eyebrow.

"Yeah. Dad travelled a lot from his home in Tokyo."

"Yes, he said he used to sell bespoke parts for aerospace?"

"Yeah, he's sort of a mechanics scientist. He works independently now and in the project management side of things. But that's how he met Mom. During a stopover in St Petersburg. Chance encounter and boom, they fell in love."

We rock gently, with our arms around one another.

"And then they moved here? It must have been quite a cultural shock?" The shadows are hiding Aithen's beautiful face from me.

"Yeah. They wanted a safe and beautiful place to raise a family."

He kisses me. "It is beautiful."

"We are lucky to live here."

"Are you multilingual?" he asks.

"No, I wish. I can *get by* in Russian and Japanese, but I'm years away from fluent. They don't pressure us, though."

"That's good." Aithen rests his forehead against mine.

We giggle, keeping things hushed, as we sway to the music of the wind and our heartbeats.

Then I'm reminded I'm still living at home when my mom calls out, they will be off to bed soon.

We walk back to the house but rather than enter, I manoeuvre him via the side path. A lot more private and a place I can kiss him so he can't forget how my lips feel for a week.

As we come up for air, I realise he hasn't once touched me, seductively. He's always controlled, despite looking at me and my body appreciatively.

Does he think I'm hot? I dismiss the thought. He sends out the signs he does. Or am I too cold? He may assume I don't fancy him that way? No way. He must sense...?

I kiss him again, and this time, I massage his hair with searching fingers. Stroking his ears, I then run my fingers up and down his neck. Pressing my chest into his, this forces out a quiet gasp from him, and I kiss him harder. Control it. I want to send a hint, not be a tease!

But then he reciprocates by shrouding me with his arms and grinds me towards him. My breath falters. His body delivers a clear message on how he feels, having me this close to him. I want this, but not here, not now.

I take a pause and gaze at him. "Sorry," I smile. "You're special, Aithen." I want to say more, but I want to choose the moment wisely.

Our breathing is laboured as we kiss one more time. You're mine, Aithen, and I want to keep you here forever.

CHAPTER TWENTY-THREE

A week since the BBQ and I'm still away from school. Looks like they won't ask me to return until after the summer break. I can't complain.

There has been no sign of Erek, and an eerie balance has settled around me. My mind is in limbo regarding my missing friends. Aithen is padding the space that usually surges with cold, stinging doubt of Chloe, Leslie, Laura and *VioletlyAlone*. But they are still there, waiting for me to find them.

The weather warms and becomes more humid by the day. The charge in the air feels like the pressure building up between Aithen and me.

He continues to be careful and not take advantage. Having his hand in mine or running his fingertips over my bare shoulder makes me melt.

Even as I lie here now, looking down at him, having him on my bed is so compelling. I wish we were naked, but I also don't want to spoil things. It must be the right time and—

A rumble in the distance.

I kiss Aithen but stop when I hear the rumble again. The air blowing in through the open window is refreshing but dances with an earthy tinge. I know that sound.

"Get up!" I order excitedly. He looks at me puzzled.

"A storm. It's on its way!" I pull on my trainers.

I love stormy weather, and that's thunder I can hear. I run to the window, and there is a menacing canvas of grey-blue clouds. Hints of red pierce the sky as the sun dips below the horizon.

The conductor of the storm orchestra sends in the rain, and it's heavy. The sound is so loud when we step outside, and we have a moment of hesitation before we run towards our hill. I scream with laughter with the first flash of lightning surrounding us. The rage of thunder echoes in reply. We're saturated, climbing the slippery path up the hill. We reach the top, and the storm applauds us with more lightning, thunder, and more torrential rain. You cannot see the town below, but then the best thing happens.

An aeroplane joins in the chorus coming into land. I scream, and Aithen is laughing at us. Grabbing hold of him, I kiss him hard. I pull him close, grabbing his butt and he mimics me. I can feel his body so warm, firm and wet against mine, and I place his hands on my chest. He gasps between our kisses.

"Touch me!" I crave every inch of my skin to be touched by him. Every sense to be caressed. I want everything.

Aithen's scent wakes me. My bedroom is warm, and my mind races while I watch his sleeping face. I want to kiss him. Wake him up and shroud me with his passion again. But then a twinge in my lower stomach tells me I need to go to the toilet. His arms are not around me, so I stretch out and then feel a spasm of pain in my groin.

"Ow!" I whisper.

Our activities have made me tender. At the time, the feeling was soft and gentle, though matters progressed more physical. Amazing. Now I know what the fuss is all about? I get it, why people love. Why they exchange knowing, secretive glances at one another. I'm so happy this fantastic person wanted to share himself with me. To bring such pleasure to what felt like every inch of my skin.

His infatuation with my body heightened once I undressed – like he's never seen a topless girl in his life. Yes, okay, I have beautiful body art. A tattoo cradles the curve of my right breast. It follows the same theme from my shoulder: a thorny, twisted branch with small, red roses and a sprinkling of pastel butterflies. Heart-shaped leaves to continue the story of the art line.

He's not inexperienced. There was way too much knowledge of what he did. He could read my every breath or groan. Pure pleasure.

My body reminds me I must go to the loo. I stand in the darkness and mischievous goosebumps sweep across my naked body. Aithen's asleep, unaware of me. Tracing a finger across my tingling skin, this is new. A fresh wave of pleasure.

I step into the ensuite bathroom, without turning on the light. A moment later, I'm rinsing my hands and inspecting my darkened reflection in the mirror.

I don't know what I expect to see as everything is the same. No sudden glow on my skin or any noticeable change. Does this make me a woman, mature? The words seem strange but true. All those times wondering what will *it* be like and will I know *what to do?*

No, I didn't, but it all happened so naturally. That day Aithen called me beautiful, my perceptions changed. It was like he woke me up from a waking slumber. I was drowning in memories of Iain and my own self-pity. What else have I missed over the past year?

With Aithen, my senses are on a new level. More self-aware? I don't know. But I'm so focused on him and how I want him to make me feel.

Wanting him last night became a new sense to me, and nothing on this planet would stop me! A chuckle escapes me as I think to myself, I seduced him more than he did me. There was a kiss and…

I look once more at myself in the bathroom mirror. I thank myself I told him I love him. It came out as we kissed and again last night when we were in bed together.

This feeling of calmness is new to me, but then I shiver; it's cold in here.

I return to the room.

I slip back under the covers, and the welcoming warmth from Aithen's body meets mine. Aithen's arm slides across me. He's still fast asleep. I survey the muscle of his forearm as the dim glow of an external streetlamp lightens the room. I stroke his arm, and then there is a pale, blue flash.

What was that? Can't be my clock. My cell phone is in my jean pockets, hidden in the darkness of my room.

A second flash.

This illuminates the bedroom ceiling for a moment.

Again, but this time, the source catches my eye. It seems to come from Aithen's arm or wrist.

I examine closer. Is he wearing a watch? And this time I let out a muffled yelp, my hands smothering my mouth. Thankfully, I haven't woken Aithen.

About two inches above his forearm, a small screen projects from within his skin!

There is no sound.

I cannot make out the characters or any distinctive text on the mini projection. As soon as my consciousness realises, it is looking at something, the image vanishes.

"What the…?"

I rub the skin lightly where the image seemed to come from. Smooth. Warm. Soft. I pause as Aithen's breathing changes but then returns to a heavy rhythm as he drifts back to sleep.

I examine and massage the area with my fingertips, trying to feel anything odd.

Nothing.

Sitting up for a moment, I know I'm not dreaming. Aithen's arm falls away, and this makes him stir.

He wears no watch or jewellery.

I lie there.

Embedded technology? Not unheard of but not standard even in our so-called modern age. He could have a medical condition, and it's an embedded message if an emergency occurs. Like a diabetic or a person allergic to certain foods or drugs. This would alert a hospital before administering treatment.

But why would it pop up now? Is he okay? I could not read the screen.

The bedroom ceiling is turning a dark blue colour as the night is passing and day ascending...

Birds wake me with their song.

I don't remember falling back to sleep. I glance towards Aithen, and for a moment, a wave of panic grips me when I see the bed is empty. A sound from the ensuite tells me he is there, and I smile.

I gasp when he opens the door as he is still undressed. He smiles at my shocked expression and slides back into bed. This is lovely. I wriggle into his arms.

"Am I supposed to be *here*?" he asks, motioning his head out of the room.

I understand what he means. Would my parents mind?

I do a headcount of who is at home, right now. Everybody, most likely.

Still, I'm confident we won't have caught anyone's attention. We have a large house, and my room is furthest from the others. I can't stop the mischievous smile, which escapes.

"What?" he asks.

"Us." I hold his gaze and relish his eyes. Should I mention the screen? Do I spoil this moment? My fingers trail across the skin of his arm.

"You feel okay, Aithen? Need anything?"

He raises an eyebrow, pulls open the duvet, and checks himself out. Why am I blushing now? I slap the covers shut and laugh at him.

"No, I think I'll be okay." He smiles and motions towards the bedroom door again. "I could sneak out and make a run for it?"

"Oh, funny," I respond. "I had a weird dream about you last night..." I trail off, and he smiles questioningly.

"I'd swear I saw a screen pop up, from your arm?" I force a giggle and kiss his forearm. "Beam me up, Scotty?"

He smirks, but it's not entirely convincing. He prods at his arm, mockingly. "Yup, it's true. I'm really a cyborg. Sorry, I forgot to tell you."

I shove him. "Oh, smartass."

"You sure I'm okay to be here? Don't want to blow a fuse or spill any oil from my inner workings," he smiles. I love his smile.

"Don't worry; we'll be fine though let's not be too obvious, okay?"

He nods, and we snuggle up, chatting and giggling the morning away.

CHAPTER TWENTY-FOUR

Yet another school year is over. It came so fast. It's not fair I wasn't there to see the end of the semester. To not be part of the building excitement as the summer break approaches.

The two upper-school years always end two weeks before the general school term, which means I can enjoy this peace and quiet for a fortnight. At least I can share the excitement of my siblings. Emily and David are bouncing off the walls with school-break anticipation. Next year will be my final graduation year. I'm no longer the pre-senior, I'll be a senior. What a journey that has been.

Mom and Dad have also said I can investigate possible part-time work if I want to earn some extra cash. This is a possibility, thanks to my grade point average. I only need to complete subjects in the sciences, so I'll have spare time off and still graduate.

Where to look, though? I can't imagine I'll find anything in a hurry at the mall. But will people judge me on that day? I've kept my head low and become normal. No outbursts. Nothing. Model citizen. Yeah, right.

But now, I'm at home, with Mom. Dad is upstairs lying down, nursing a runny nose and streaming eyes.

My muscles are tired. In fact, I'm exhausted. I hope I'm not getting Dad's bug. But then I smile at the recollection of the other night. With Aithen.

But this morning, I'm once again Jayne the daughter, sister, and part of the humdrum of home family life. My mind is elsewhere, drifting in and out of Aithen's face; his voice; his touch.

Have you ever needed someone who just listens to you? No matter how scatter-brained your opinion, maybe?

That's Aithen.

He doesn't judge me or tries to out-guess what I'm about to say. But I wish he would trust my opinions and concerns about Erek. Everything is perfect if we can eliminate Erek from the equation.

At first, I thought Aithen was mocking me; feigning interest and understanding – Iain would often pretend – but no.

Not Aithen.

I can be speaking, and when I'm done, his expression is hanging on for the next word.

It's different.

Aithen watches and listens like a child with a teacher, telling tales of magic and unicorns and wizards and… Everything. I could be talking about buying socks, and he doesn't lose focus.

I often see myself as a leaf on a tree; one amongst so many in a vast forest. But Aithen only sees me. He's taken a snippet and placed it in a pot of good earth and seems to cherish *it*.

Me.

He's not overbearing, though. Quite the opposite.

I'd say the heavy comes from me. Aithen enjoys his own space and likewise gives me mine, but I grow anxious to see him. It would be comfortable to sit in a room and watch him, watching me.

Browsing web search results on my laptop for embedded tech-nology, I am recalling him stroking my skin, kissing me. Such a distraction.

There's nothing online which compares to what Aithen had in

his arm. Should I be worried? Maybe I did imagine it? If I can conjure up four people, then I can create a silly, little screen.

There's a knock at the front door, and Mom is there before I even have time to move. Her raised voice sounds excited, and there is lots of laughter and chat. Parcel delivery by the sounds of it. She approaches me and almost squeals when she hands me an elegant looking box with a transparent panel in it.

I sit up, and I peer inside the plastic window of the box. I gasp, and my heart races. Inside is a small, beautiful rose stem. A perfect, living replica of my chest tattoo. The number of butterflies is exact, not live ones but so realistic, all the same.

"There's a card," Mom squeaks.

I open it and recognise Aithen's handwriting.

I
Love
You
xx

He's finally said it.

Mom hugs me, and I enjoy her warmth. The absence of a response to me telling him that I love him rubbed against me recently. But that's just me bringing on the heavy again. He just needed some breathing space.

I send him a text message to say thank you for the beautiful gift and check he is free to meet me.

I task Mom with working out a way to water the rose stem. How did he find such a thing or a florist to make it? Mom doesn't realise the significance of this. Yes, she knows I have tats, but not all of the details. She trusts my choices and lost interest after my tenth visit to Pauline. I show her a lot of them, but a few are mine, my secret to keep. Aithen's fashioned rose is quite personal, a seductive gift. I love it so much.

But no response comes from Aithen. My emotions soared when I received his gift, but now, they are lying low with me in bed.

I repeatedly gaze at my cell screen, but there's nothing. I've raised the volume to max, so I don't miss the text alert tone. Every time it sounds, it's just a mate or worse: an advert. I don't want 40% off anything now, I want a call from Aithen. It's been four hours since I sent the text.

Where is he?

I type in another message and almost drop my cell when it rings.

"Is everything okay, Aithen?" I fear the answer, and though I can't see him, I can hear his breathing falter. I sense his caring expression flowing through my cell handset. It's like he is in the room with me, and a sad gaze is enveloping me from those tender, caring eyes.

His voice breaks as he speaks, but then he continues. "Jayne, there is no way for me to explain this and no matter what, I cannot begin to clarify what I'm about to say."

He's leaving, I know it.

"The timing is awful, I know but…"

He's speaking, but my ears have phased out his voice. My brain wants to protect my heart. He's about to tell me his plans have changed, and he'll be returning to Kay and … wait, what? My dad?

"What about my dad?"

He stops.

"Jayne, you have to listen, please. I know your dad is home this week and is due to travel back to the city tomorrow, Thursday."

I don't remember mentioning Dad taking time off to Aithen.

"And?"

"He must not travel." He says it quiet but firm.

"What?" I'm confused. "Not travel? Why?"

"You have to trust me, Jayne. If I tried to explain why you will get angry."

"Come on, Aithen. Is this some silly game? I mean it, not travel. Why? Because you say so?"

"Jayne. You can ignore me if you want, but you have to trust me on this."

"And you make this stupid revelation with a telephone call? If it is so important, then why not come to my house so we can talk about it?" I take a breath and a thoughtful pause. My heart is racing. Why is Athen trying to stir an argument? Is he forcing a breakup between us?

No, he can't be. The gift. The note.

But why drag my dad into this? Aithen knows how I am about my family, so if he is sincere, then what is going on?

"Are you splitting up with me, Aithen?"

I wish I could see his face right now. He groans. "No, Jayne. I love you, and I wish I could be there this moment but trust me, I cannot. I'm not in Dereton and before you ask... don't ask." His words trail off.

Okay, how irritating. Aithen loves me, but he is *somewhere* and cannot tell me where or why or whatever. Whatever game Aithen is playing, I'm not in the mood for it.

"Jayne, you've trusted me so far, and now I really need you to go beyond trusting me. I told you I need to protect you, remember?"

"Yes, but—"

"Well, this is me delivering on that promise. No matter how it sounds and how stupid it makes you look, you follow through on this. Everything depends on this now." He sounds desperate, nothing like usual.

"I don't know what to say," I choke back.

"You've wanted answers, Jayne. Your friends, everything?"

"My friends? What do you know?" I plead with a hoarse whisper.

"Everything," he replies.

Everything?

"Jayne, please give me this one day. Let me save you."

"But how does keeping my dad at home save me?" I demand.

"Trust me, Jayne." He almost whispers the words.

"Aithen. You need time to think and to sort your head out. I've got no idea what is going on or why you are so secretive and... I don't want to talk about this any further. If you're an ass, then fine."

I want to curse at him and tell him to go away, but instead, I say, "I'll call you soon."

I end the call and feel numb. No anger. No sadness. Raw. What have I done? I raise my mobile, finger hovering over the recall button, but I stop. Have we finished? What did I say? I was talking, but I wasn't listening. Why would he say such things about my dad and friends? I should have given him more of a chance to explain, but then, he didn't want to.

To protect me.

Where is he? Why all the secrecy? Well, I felt negative before – now hopeless. Should I pop down to see Dad? No, I'm too irritated. Frustrated.

I'll go for a run.

———

Early evening shadows and calm of the forest surround me. The silence is broken by my breathing and feet plodding into the soft floor of a natural pathway. The path is so familiar; I could run it blindfolded. I must clear my head. I always come here with my problems. The trees are good listeners though this may take several laps.

I'm angry, and I can't erase Aithen's words from my head.

What about my dad? Don't travel? And my friends? What's so special about tomorrow that Aithen can tell me everything?

Tell me what?

My feet falter, and I stop. I slam my hand against a tree branch. A stinging scratch erupts along my forearm. I kick the tree trunk with a snarl. *He must not travel?* What does that even mean? Forget it. I walk home with a slight limp.

I watch the water trickle through my fingers. The much-cooled water of the bathtub lost all the bubbles which foamed earlier. I lie there in a semi-state of wakefulness.

Whenever I feel down, Matthew creeps into my thoughts. After he was born asleep, I would not cry in front of Sarah or anybody, as it would be too selfish of me. I hid my own tears behind Sarah's hair as I held her and tried to hug away the pain of her loss. All too much. I had no right to mourn in public. Matthew was not my baby. But more painful are the memories of Sarah. Her before and after are distant. I wish I could rekindle that spark in her. Her new baby, Lou, has brought immense happiness to Sarah, but that other twinkle of light is missing.

The night after Matthew's burial, I sobbed in the bath and, of all things, the chilling water became a comfort. It was as though his cold, little body embraced me.

My white and wrinkled fingertips are as numb as my brain. I don't know how long I have soaked here, but every time I move my legs, a wave of chilly water flows around me. Time to leave my watery therapy and get on with matters.

After I dry, I dress in my bedtime clothes of loose tracksuit pants and a baggy top.

In the living room, Emily and David are head to head, competing in handheld games. Dad is in the study, on the telephone with work. So, I sit in silence, watching my younger siblings as they enjoy their usual match together.

It's peaceful, and I decide not to mention Aithen's call to anybody. When Mom brings in dinner, I take a bowl back upstairs with me. I chew on the broccoli; al dente how I like it. Should I call Aithen? I eye my cell and check for any messages. There are a couple but none from him. What did I say to him? How did I say it? I was so angry. No, I wasn't. I kept my cool. Am I over-thinking this?

No, I'm not. How am I supposed to react when he says that about my dad? What could Aithen know? Is he worried about the virus and whether my dad should travel? No, that can't be it.

I sleep for a while but then wake up, and my stomach is churning. Sitting bolt upright, I cough away the gag in my throat and my stomach cramps in response. I'm going to vomit. I toss away the duvet and slam my hands on the mattress as I retch again. Sweat beads across my forehead. Can I make it to the bathroom? Too late. I'm looking down at the mess on the quilt of my bed.

Urgh!

I act and grab the closest piece of clothing I have on the floor. I stuff it under the sheet cover to protect the mattress underneath, to stop the vomit seeping through too much. Disgusting.

I remove the sheet and clothing, carrying them downstairs to the utility room. Everyone is in bed. Not surprising at after one in the morning. Sixty-degree wash and time for a drink. I eye the alcohol cabinet for a moment, but no, not the answer. Green tea it is then.

I pour a glass of pineapple juice and gulp it down to get rid of the horrible taste in my mouth. Then I continue to make the hot drink.

"Make mine one sweetener, please?"

Dad. I smile and prepare him black tea.

"I felt sick."

"Or you were sick?" He nods towards the sound of the washing machine.

"Must be something I ate, or I'm catching your bug." I point at him, accusing.

We sip in silence. Now is as good a time as any to mention Aithen's warning. I've had time to reflect and soak and sleep and vomit, so it all seems trivial. Dad breaks my thought. "You and Aithen okay?"

"Yes, why?" I search his face. Surely, he didn't hear the conversation I had with Aithen?

"Oh, nothing. I noticed you were a little off today; earlier. You raced upstairs to have a call with him and when you came back down?"

"No, just this bug getting me down. I'm sure it will pass by tomorrow."

"Today, even," he says, "as it is Thursday now."

"And you have stupid work to go to." This is an opportunity to bring up the conversation.

"Well, yes, there is that, but there is also the fact I've decided to stay at home."

I almost laugh when he says this. "You? Throw a *sicky*? That's a first... like, ever?"

"True," he nods thoughtfully. "Don't think I've ever given myself the *day* off. Well, the doctor signed a sick note. So, hey, why not milk it a bit and have a lie-in when I'm feeling good again? Also, I'd like for us to go for coffee again? Been a long time and I have missed it, missed you a lot."

His baggy cheeks are sad and tired, so I hug him. I'm glad I needn't mention Aithen's dumb warning. He was wrong all along. Dad is off work, anyway, so won't be travelling. So whatever foolish game Aithen's playing can do one.

CHAPTER TWENTY-FIVE

The television is loud downstairs. Since when is the TV ever on in the morning and *at this time?* It's so early. Must be Emily or David watching kids' TV. I take my time brushing my teeth and getting myself into a tidy state.

I stand in front of the mirror. My vacant expression is tired and dark rings are chasing around my eyes. I look awful.

What's Aithen doing? Where is he and why isn't he with me?

There's something wrong, and I can't put my finger on it. It's like I'm walking solo across a desert, but I'm wearing a virtual game headset, and the real world is singing and dancing all around me. I can't see or hear it. But if I take off the blinkers, it'll be plain in front of me.

Dr Harris said something about a brain scan. I peer at the faint scar which zipped away the metal plate. Why is this stopping me from seeing the truth? From knowing fact from fantasy?

———

Mom and Dad are in the lounge, staring at the television.

Mom holds a moist-looking tissue in a tight grip. She's been crying. Dad is standing, hovering, unable to sit as he watches the news channel. Emily and David's voices shout from the garden as I scan the television screen text.

Trainwreck.

Eighty dead.

Head-on collision.

120 injured, some critical.

Life-changing injuries.

Mom blurts out, "All first-class destroyed. Not a sole survivor!"

Dad always travels in first class. The one luxury he allows himself when going by train. Mom guesses my next thought. "Yes, it would have been his train." She cries again, and Dad is holding her, his vacant, pale expression a mask of shock.

I grab hold of them both. I must feel their warmth in my arms. My mind is racing as Mom's body heaves with sobs and the screen flashes images of a long pile of steel and wheels. Carriages at the rear appear intact. But the collision point, with a lot of pictures blurred out, is a tangled pile of loss. A mess. A mound of destruction and death.

A passenger train hit a hundred-carriage coal transport train. This can't be real. How could it happen? My dad! I cry tired tears. I don't moan but can't stop the flow of water over my cheeks. My mind plays over the what-ifs of this tragedy. It's like the worst happened, but I already know it hasn't.

I raise my gaze towards the ceiling and think thank you. Dad did not travel. I'm glad I told him not to… No, I didn't. Dad decided he would take the day off. We even joked about it being the first time ever.

My tears stop and adrenalin races in to dry them up. Dad did not travel. He should not have gone. Aithen said so. He warned me. He warned me about what? How could he know?

For a split second – and I don't know where this thought comes from – has he had something to do with the crash? No! No, he hasn't. But why, how could he know about it or at least warn me about this?

I scan my mobile. There are no messages from him. Almost on cue, it rings. It's him.

I hug and kiss Mom and Dad then run upstairs to my bedroom.

"Aithen?"

"Jayne?" He sounds desperate. "Is everything okay? Your father?"

I interrupt him. "He's here. At home." I'm already fighting tears again. Aithen lets out a deep sigh.

"Thank you. I'm sorry for the strangeness, Jayne, but I had to warn you."

"This is all getting weird, Aithen. Did you know this would happen? If so, how? Why didn't you warn more people?"

Silence. Once again, I can imagine how he looks now; the wheels of thought ticking away.

"Who would listen?" He says it like a confession. It's true. I didn't listen, and I'm the one in love with him.

"I'm sorry for doubting you, but this is way off base in the reality department." I blow my nose into a tissue. "I didn't say anything to Dad."

"What? But how?"

"He took the day off by himself. I said nothing. I was upset yesterday, so I think he was worried about me."

Dad could be dead now, and it would be because I said nothing. The thought stings, but I need answers, proper ones.

"Aithen. Enough of the mystery. I must see you now and no excuses. Coffee house in half an hour. You promised me you'd tell me everything."

His sigh confirms this.

I end the call and take a deep breath. No more games. No more whatever is going on here.

I explain to Mom and Dad. I must see Aithen, and I will be

home early, but they tell me to take the day out. They must absorb the shock and want quiet time. I check on Emily and David. They know there's been a train crash but don't understand the significance of it all. I tell them to "play nice" as one of the other mothers will take them to school today soon. Yes, I know I could do it, but I have other matters to contend with.

It's time for answers.

———

The images from the television burn and twist in my head. Dad's decision avoided what could have been the worst day of my life.

But there's a pulse of anger coursing through my veins. Because of Aithen and what he didn't tell me. It's all too fantastic to be real. Either he's involved in this tragedy, or he boasts impressive abilities with a crystal ball. I'm rushing to him, but fear is accompanying the anger. How is Aithen involved here? The question echoes with every step.

Dereton is its usual busy self. Some people here won't have heard about the tragedy yet or won't be affected by it. I review the ongoing promise of a leisure centre as cranes and workers are busy constructing part of a roof. This work seems to have dragged forever, budgets coming and going. It will be good once completed.

I can already see Aithen outside the coffee house. Good. There's a collection of builders' trucks on this side of the road, blocking my way, so I cross the street and get away from the chaos of engines and big wheels.

When Aithen sees me, I wave and gesture *I'm crossing here*. He looks calm and happy; his smile evaporates the anger brewing inside me. He can't have done anything wrong. There's an explanation for all this.

Aithen's so gentle. And caring.

I'm about to cross the road when there is a splintering crash of metal. Sounds like a car crash, but I can't see where it is happening.

Oh, no. I'm nauseous.

No, I can't pass out here.

The threatening noise. Deafening.

My senses flash-aware for a second. I can see Aithen running towards me, but my vision blurs.

Why can't I move? I can hear nothing! I can't breathe!

Wait. I'm moving. Being carried? Floating. Or falling? Help me!

"You okay, Jayne?" Aithen's face is inches from mine.

Jerking awake, I gasp as I'm suddenly lying down on the ground. Scrambling to my feet, I push Aithen away from me.

I'm shaking, and I spin around. Where are we? No, I know where we are, on Cotton Street, but how did I get here. Why is everything so silent? So still? I touch my forehead. Am I losing it?

"What happened?" I welcome the sound of my voice, but it's so flat. Toneless. What's happening?

Aithen takes hold of my hands. "Okay, take a deep breath and close your eyes; trust me." I do as he says. What else can happen now?

This.

My eyes snap open as a warm breeze brushes my face. The air fills with the catastrophic explosion of metal hitting the ground. Where? Around the corner from here. Car horns complain, and people scream.

What, the…?

I rush to the high street and flinch at the scene. A crane spilt its cargo of steel pipes, which are littering the road. Aithen holds onto me, keeping me back from the carnage. Thankfully, it appears nobody's hurt, but there is plenty of damage to cars and shop fronts.

I raise a hand to my mouth. That's where I stood when the crashing sound started. I don't understand. How did I get away from the steel carnage? Sirens and lights hail emergency vehicles.

I pull back and stare at Aithen. He squints pity in his eyes, but also, he knows I want answers.

"Let's have that coffee to go," he says and takes my hand. I'm speechless and let him lead me. I can't catalogue this. The questions. Where do I even start?

I plant myself at the top of our hill. The high street is a buzz of emergency services and contractor vehicles. A carpet of red, blue, and amber flashes in the road below.

"Ever get the feeling fate is trying to tell you something?" I run my fingers through my hair.

Aithen holds me, but I must speak. I need answers to this and the entire day.

I stand and take a deep breath. "You've promised me answers, and I've been imploding for the past couple of weeks."

He's silent.

"I don't know what is going on, but it's all around you. My dad. My friends. Erek. This." I gesture towards the high street. "Then the other night—" I steady myself, that night was so precious, and now, it's becoming a negative memory. "I saw something in your arm. And I know we made a joke about it but—"

He stands, his brow creased.

"A screen popped up. And I know I was awake."

I brush his reaching hands away. "No. Don't try and avoid this. And please, don't do whatever you did down there." Did he stop time then? It felt the same as when I blacked-out, the time Laura and Leslie disappeared.

"I want to be honest with you, Jayne. In fact, I have intended to tell you everything the day I first met you."

He gives a sigh but then looks me straight in the eyes.

"I'm not from around here."

CHAPTER TWENTY-SIX

Apparently, *Koyorad*s have visited Earth for a long time. Their home planet, *Korudaz*, a massive world, similar in size to Neptune, is forever lightyears away.

It's the largest populated planet in the discovered universe. Aithen doesn't want to get into specifics about his world right now. I'm sure my expression is bordering on shock, wonder, and disbelief.

But most of all, *fear*.

I'm so scared, I can't decide if I should run down the hill to safety or beg him to spare me. But he's still, Aithen. He can't be an alien.

This is rubbish.

I've known him for weeks and weeks. He's a student. My boyfriend.

Now I know what Leslie meant when she said, *I've seen something*.

What did she see? What did Erek show her?

I've seen way too much today. Witnessed a news story train wreck which should have killed my dad. Steel pipes suspended in time.

This is… I can't cope.

I scan the ground around me. Except for some small dried-mud rocks, there are no weapons to utilise. No branches or anything.

If I try to run, Aithen can freeze things, like he did below. It was like drowning but with senses and emotions. How did he do that?

Aithen looks like *Aithen*.

But this is so off the scale.

I stand and raise my palms toward him.

"Jayne?"

"Aithen! Just stay away"! I manage as I take tentative steps along the path leading from the hill summit.

"Jayne, please!" he pleads.

My eyes bulge from their sockets. I have no weapons. I must scream and jump and grab someone's attention below.

Help me! I want to shout, but I know I won't be heard. If I charge down the hill and start screaming about aliens, who will listen? I can't run to the police. I'm the crazy girl from the mall. Doctor Harris' cold and caring eye stab my thoughts.

Someone must listen.

I must escape.

"Jayne!" Aithen shouts.

I spring forward, but already I feel my body enclosed like it's wrapped in a thick, claustrophobic glue, as time slows down… But I still hear my gasps for breath this time, not frozen like I was on the street below.

"Aithen! Release me…from this! Or I…I'll…F…kin kill you!" I demand through gritted teeth, but my limbs won't function.

I flop to the floor with my senses sharp.

Choking in a deep breath, I sit on the back of my feet. Spitting at the ground, I don't care how I look; still, I use a heel to wipe away the saliva.

"Jayne, I'm sorry, but you have to listen to me." Aithen lowers himself, so he is facing me, and he sits, too.

It's hard to explain, but he doesn't feel real anymore. I snatch a glance at him through my bangs. His worried expression searches for a response from me. But I sense a chilly aura, like the inkiness of space now courses through his veins.

"I can't help you if you're going to try and escape every few seconds," he says, his tone defusing my motivation to flee. "You want answers? I can give you that and a lot more."

This is the last way I thought I would respond to meeting an alien. I've read so much on space and the possibilities of how *we are not alone!* But this? Have I finally flipped, and my delusions have entirely absorbed all my common sense? How can I possibly be sitting here with an alien?

An alien?

"So, so you're from—"

"Korudaz," he says, keeping his tone clear and assuring. He said this before, but I need to hear the words again.

I reshuffle my position, so I am sat straight with my legs crossed.

"What did you do then?" I ask, motioning away from me.

"I froze time," he responds.

"Oh, of course, you did," I huff. "How do I even know that is an *alien* thing? You could just be some weirdo who has some drug or whatever to slow me down?"

I scan the street below and back to him again. "So, what exactly is it? How do you stop time?"

Aithen picks up a small stone and taps onto his wrist. I could be mistaken, but I'm sure something glows beneath his skin.

"Okay, take a deep breath. Keep your eyes open and watch." He tosses the stone into the air, and it's like we have dipped our head into the water. Everything halts in a split second. There's no sound. No breeze. But the rock suspends in the air. I can see it as clearly as my hand, which I can now raise towards the suspended object. I view the high street, and the flashing lights, blinking a moment ago, are either illuminated or off. Everything and everyone freezes, but I'm free to see and move.

He nods and the air returns, as do the sounds around us, like the unmute button is pressed. The rock hits the ground.

"What the...?" I pick up the rock and examine it. "I could see and move? Before, when I was down there, on the high street, everything froze." I search his wrist, pressing it with my fingertips. Nothing, only soft flesh.

"I can control a small perimeter and include you within. For everyone else, time stopped, but the people down there didn't notice a thing."

"So, will they feel sick, like I did?"

"No." He squints his eyes at me. "That appears to be peculiar to you only."

I roll my eyes at him. Lock me up now.

"This is not the first time I've experienced this, your time-stopping thing," I say, as my teeth chatter in response to the shiver running through me. "It happened the last time I saw Laura and Leslie."

No response from Aithen.

"That was Erek, wasn't it?" I ask, waiting for the usual understanding words which will offer comfort to help dismiss my screwed-up thoughts. To steer me away from Erek.

"Yes, it was," Aithen responds.

I snap my eyes to his. "That really happened?" I blink away tears.

"You're not crazy, Jayne. And neither are your friends and family. Or anyone," Aithen says. "Your friends are as real as you and me."

I cover my mouth and stand at the same time. There's no urgency to flee, despite my heart racing and chest panting. "What's happened to them?" I gasp. "Are they alive?"

"This is a hard one to explain. You'd best sit down for this," Aithen suggests, offering a hand to me.

I take it, and it's warm. Normal. Human and not alien.

"Why do only I remember them?" I ask.

"Now that, I don't have an answer to," he replies. "You should have no recollection of them at all."

"That's the thing, everyone else has forgotten them," I say. "Though there was someone else. A girl I met online."

Aithen considers me with genuine interest, I continue. "We were going to meet, but she also had a friend who suddenly vanished and *'with a flash of light'*, they were gone."

"Well that's news to me," he says. "Nothing to do with Erek."

Aithen's eyes squint in a fashion as though to try and remember something. "Where is she now? This girl you met online."

I sigh. "She vanished, too. We were supposed to meet here, in Dereton, but all her messages, the stuff on the forum, it all disappeared. I've heard nothing since."

The street continues to buzz below us. If only the people down there were witness to what I am learning.

"Where are they, Aithen? What has happened to my friends?"

"They've been *Deleted*," he says, almost spitting out the last word.

"Deleted? That's what Erek said in the mall?" I'm about to push myself to my feet but reconsider. I need to ground myself for this.

"This is going to sound as alien as anything ever could," begins Aithen. "But the number one objective to us visiting a planet is secrecy."

"Secrecy?" I respond, dipping my chin. "So, because you lot can't *keep a secret*, we pay the price?"

Aithen squirms, searching for a response. But I continue. "And this now means, you telling me this, I'm about to be Deleted? By you?"

His eyes widen. "No way. Not ever, Jayne. I'm honest with you as this is what I need to protect you from. I don't do the Deleting."

"Erek does?" I ask.

Aithen nods.

"And what makes him so special that he's allowed to do this? These are people, Aithen. Real people with lives. He can't just pull up in his... spaceship and start *Deleting* everyone." This is ridiculous.

Aithen places a hand to his chest and massages it as though easing a pain within. "When we visit planets, we are assigned, or rather, *they* are assigned to us. The visiting group."

"They...?"

"They are called Deleters. They observe us and make sure we don't do anything which will grab attention," Aithen says.

"Then why bother coming here if there is that risk?" I ask.

"Because we are fascinated with other worlds. Other civilizations," he says.

"It doesn't sound like it," I respond. "And you do all of this in a school, of all places?"

"No, not only schools. Mostly it's visiting various places and watching life," he says.

"But you are in my school?" I ask.

He nods.

"Why? Of all the places you could go on Earth, why here?" I ask.

"Truthfully, I was curious about the education system. Previous Koyorads—visitors have been to this country, so it was a recommendation. Nice scenery. Friendly humans—"

"I love your use of the word *humans*," I interrupt.

"Well, you are," he defends.

"And you're an alien," I remark with a raise of the eyebrows.

"And so are you," he retorts, mocking.

I never thought of it that way.

"Then why, Dereton? Smallest dot on the map," I say.

"Because of that word. Where I'm from, *deretone* means beauti-ful," he responds, and the memory of a sunny day and blushing cheeks pull at my heart.

I pant a louder breath. "Seems like a lifetime ago now. The day you called me that."

"But that's the thing," Aithen says. "I had to engage with you, and following the day you shouted out Chloe's name, to the class, I knew something was different with you. There's no way you should have remembered her. But once you did, I had to work out a way to protect you from Erek."

"And I remember Leslie and Laura, too. And whoever the online girl, *VioletlyAlone* is."

"I know," he says, nodding.

"Are they coming back? Can they be un-deleted?" I ask.

"Not normally, but *I* believe they can be," he offers, wiping away a stray tear from my cheek.

"And how do we do that?" I stand for a moment, and Aithen joins me, as a plane flies overhead, coming into land.

"This technology… I understand the concept. Firstly, only a Deleter can use the Deletion device. It's a hand-held unit, and it erases an individual from existence; as you now know." He pauses, waiting for my question, but I have nothing. "It was originally a medical-based technology, like Earth's cryo-freezing? Except this could take an individual and hold them in a genetic-digital suspen-sion. Imagine storing a person on a USB-stick?"

"That's impossible," I say.

"No, it's not," he responds. "This is not a data stick, it's a close analogy. But a side-effect was not only is an individual *stored*, their timeline across the years, from the point of existence, is stored with them, but erased from current awareness. They're forgotten."

"Then how would you know they are there, stored in the USB stick if they're forgotten?" I ask.

He smiles at that. "In a controlled environment, the medical or scientific team had one individual. They were all aware of the test subject. But when trialled with a patient, in a hospital, the scientific team became curious that relatives did not enquire about the patient. When they were called with an update, the relatives had forgotten them."

He opens his hands. "Hence, the Deletion device was created and quickly became a military project. With some applications in medicine."

"That's not normal," is all I have.

Aithen places his hands on my shoulders as he stands close, behind me. "It means they are somewhere, and not only in your head."

I turn to face him. A day ago, I would have given anything to be this close to him, but I can't help myself taking a step back. His hands flop to his sides.

"I am guessing from the mall, that Erek knows I remember my friends. And I'm certain he knows I blame him. So, why hasn't he done anything? I've gone to the police and told my friends, everyone about missing girls. But nothing from him?"

Aithen's posture appears to crumple slightly like a huge backpack just slipped over his shoulders.

"Because you're not a risk," Aithen's words barely register.

"But you said you need to protect me?" I ask, closing the space between us slightly.

His eyes well up, and he raises his gaze to the sky. "I do. I need to protect you from yourself."

I shake my head questioningly. "From myself? Why, what am I going to do?"

Aithen sniffs and sighs. "Commit suicide."

CHAPTER TWENTY-SEVEN

Aithen expands on the bombshell he landed on me. He appears sincere, but I'm numbed by confusion – I've never thought about taking my own life – and doubt. In a day, I've discovered alien life, and my constant mental battles with my missing friends could have a resolution.

It stabs my thoughts; I had forgotten about the train wreck. Aithen's warning about my dad. But I must hear what he has to say about me killing myself. He's wrong about that, so what else is he wrong about?

The journey from Korudaz to Earth takes about eighteen days. That's not because our planets are close, quite the opposite. The distance is measured in hundreds of light-years. I've read about this measurement in school, but a light-year distance is outside of my comprehension. But the Koyorad vehicles cover the distance at an incomprehensible speed.

"During the journey to Earth, I began reading through the assigned preparatory reading. We are placed in contained units which use various treatments to adapt our bodies to an alien planet's atmosphere. Hence, a lot of free time to study and prepare mentally," he explains, taking time to allow me to interrupt, but I only want to listen.

"It's easy for us to create records in any of your computer systems, so that was not important to me. But I wanted to know who I would be meeting when I turned up at your school." Aithen pauses, watching me. What's going on in his head? He's selecting his words carefully, like a doctor about to tell you, you have a month left to live.

"I read through the scripts and viewed pictures of the students in my target year and class... and there you were. Talk about smitten," he smiles, his eyes sparkling through tears. "I spent the next day's stalking you."

"Should I be creeped out by that?" I smile in return. We sit opposite one another again, and I stroke his knee as he speaks. The clouds have billowed above us, offering shelter from the sun, but these are clean and white, offering no threat of a storm.

"Maybe," he replies, "but I was caught under your spell. Your eyes; your smile. I read your blog posts, and that offer for a coffee seemed hard to pass up."

"Coffee?" I ask. Now, what's he on about?

"The subject of this particular blog was alien life, and do they exist?" Aithen raises his eyebrows. "You posted a short essay about how there must be aliens and if one should be reading this now, '... *then feel free to look me up and buy me a coffee. I dare you!'*"

My expression confirms this. "Oh, wow, I remember that."

"Yeah, so I did."

We sit in silence. A gentle breeze offers a cocktail of warm and cooling simultaneously, wafting a mild hint of grass and parched soil of the hill' surface, around us. The roar of another plane passing overhead grounds my thoughts again. The panic has passed, but I know there's more to come. *Commit suicide.*

"Go on," I request. Aithen's expression drops.

"I couldn't get enough, so I delved deeper. By the time we

entered your solar system, I knew everything about you. At least, everything you'd ever published publicly or was recorded otherwise on a computer."

"That must have been boring?" I muse. "But what about suicide? How did I do it?"

"With a razor blade. You cut your wrists—"

"No, Aithen, you've got it wrong. It wasn't me. That was my sister, Sarah." I stop for a moment, swallowing away the memory of the shower and hugging Sarah, watching the thin stream of blood dancing towards the plughole. "She tried, but only cut herself. Sarah didn't die." How could he know about that anyway? We told no-one. It's not recorded on any computer for Aithen to discover.

He looks away for a moment, the pain in his mind furrowing his brow. He faces me again. "It wasn't Sarah. It was you. Your father died, and you couldn't take it. You fell apart and in a matter of days, you... you killed yourself."

"My dad's fine. What are you saying? You've gotten me mixed up with someone else?" My voice breaks and I cough away rising tears.

Dad is okay.

He's safe at home. He didn't travel...

"Wait. Wait a minute." A ridiculous thought brews and fights for realization. But I push to dismiss it. The images on the television from this morning nag from the depths. "The train wreck. You told me to stop Dad?"

"Exactly," Aithen says, almost gasping. "Your dad would have died today. I had to stop it. To stop you."

My hands shoot to my mouth. I don't want to believe this. The other day, Aithen said something about how I would wish he didn't tell me the truth, had he told me. I wish I could un-hear this.

"This is impossible, Aithen. Okay, you can fly forever-lightyears across space, which I still haven't processed yet. But now," I raise a hand randomly, "you've saved my dad. And saved me? I don't get it?"

Aithen wipes the corners of his eyes and sniffs loudly. He stays silent.

"Okay, let's pretend for a moment this is all true. How could you know this? That train wreck happened today, and you knew about it. Now you're saying I'm going to kill myself in a few days?" And I thought I was the crazy one.

"Jayne, I'm really scraping the surface here, and while you seem to be holding onto your sanity now, I must be careful with how much I tell you."

Aithen waits for a nod to continue.

"What you refer to as lightspeed, we broke that hundreds of years ago. To us, lightspeed is like walking, but it was the stepping-stone to one of the big discoveries: time travel."

"You're joking?" I ask.

"No, but that's why I know so much," Aithen replies.

I heave from the tightening in my chest, pressing a hand against my sternum. Don't tell me I'm going to have a heart attack now. Slow breaths in, out. Aithen rubs my upper back. "Take it easy," he whispers. "This is way too much for anybody to comprehend."

The stabbing lifts and targets the plate in my head. I press a palm against it and massage my forehead with my palm, bending over where I sit.

Whenever the plate hurts, I must focus, imagining burning between the plate and bone of my skull. I visualise pouring cold water onto the flames and slowly, but surely, the pain sizzles away. This is taking longer than usual.

How could I have considered killing myself? Simple, the nightmare of my dad not coming home finally happened. All those years of childhood, dread suddenly realised. And in such a tragic way. But what about all those other lives lost? How many of their family won't be able to accept the news?

"Couldn't you have stopped the train crash?" I ask, through bleary eyes. "Save everyone else's dad, or whoever?"

"I couldn't," he replies, brushing my hair back with his fingers. "I realise this is too much hear, but I've had to be so careful."

"But so many lives?" I plead.

"I know it's tragic. A total waste," he says.

"You could have made the driver late? Stop it ever happen that way?" It seems so logical.

"I probably could, but we are not allowed to interfere. I have already taken matters too far as is. I'm trusting you with this, Jayne. But you can't say a word about it to anybody. Not to your family. No-one."

"But you said Erek ignored me because I'm a suicide? When he discovers I'm still alive and kicking, what will happen then? And why did he ignore me?" I ask.

"I convinced him you are an interesting subject for me to study. And you'll be dead soon enough, so why bother with you?" Aithen says, apologetically. "That is why I was so cold towards you when Erek was with me."

"A subject to study? Is that why you come here? To Earth?" The fear and doubt are brewing again. Adrenalin is rising and bubbling through my veins.

"Where I am from, we have a genuine interest in intelligent life. Even plant-based life. Some planets have nothing but bacteria. But when a world has *beings* which are like us, then that is fascinating," explains Aithen.

"And how many planets have human-like beings?" I ask.

He purses his lips but then relaxes his face. "About twenty so far discovered. But intelligent life? About a thousand."

"A thousand?"

"Yes, but you would probably call *them*, *alien-looking*," he smiles, at my wide-eyes expression.

I visualise images of bug-eyed Martians and all manner of alien concept images.

"One thing though," Aithen continues. "I've seen some of the artist-impressions of aliens created by humans, and there is not a single species of alien which has enormous eyes, or huge, round heads. I'm not sure where that idea has come from."

"So, what do they look like?" I ask.

"It varies. But for those who are not *humanoid*, they all reside close to one or more stars, just as Earth does its local star – the Sun – and hence there is no need to develop large eyes." He smiles wider at my reaction.

"How many are here, on Earth? Koyorads?" Asking this seems so weird.

"I don't know the exact figure, but I'm sure, across the planet, at least two hundred." He smiles at my slackening jaw.

"Two hundred? And all this is going on without anybody knowing?" I shake my head in disbelief. "So, 'Kay'. You studied there before coming here?"

His look is a mix between cringing and apologetic, "No, sorry. That was a white lie."

He coughs out a laugh. I'm glad he's finding this funny. This is ridiculous.

"And you have travelled to other planets?"

He nods.

"You look like us," I say as I grasp his hand and examine it: human, like mine. "What is a Koyorad? You're not a shape-shifter?"

That forces a smirk, "No, I'm a humanoid in most terms."

"Most?"

He rises and steps back. With straight arms, raises his hands level with his hips, as though to present himself to me. "Physically, I am human like you. Mentally not so, but I can still think as you do, but we are more intelligent by way of brain function."

My pulse races further. It's okay; I'm safe. He continues, "Genetically, we are about a ninety-eight per cent match."

I mull this over in my head for a moment. Everything around me is still the same. The hill, the grass, the chaos in the town below. The sounds. Everything is just as it always is—apart from Aithen telling me the impossible.

I spread my fingers and realise they are shaking, so I clench my fists and hug myself. Keep it together, the voice in my head comforts me. I close my eyes for a moment and open them in response to Aithen stroking my knee, once again sitting before me.

"How long have you been here? I mean you… as in yourself?" I don't like the thought of him not with me.

"About six months. We started in Iceland, then New Zealand. To climatize to the atmosphere."

I've always been curious about other lives in the Universe, reading various articles and books regarding UFO sightings, along with shaky video captures. But these Koyorads have been coming here for a long time, by the sounds of it. We are familiar to them, but for me, this is beyond a new revelation. This is the greatest news of our planet.

A hundred questions race through my mind, but I must process what Aithen told me. If I could run away and have the time to comprehend this, I may be able to reason it. A hint of fear ripples through me.

Shouldn't I be scared? I'm dating an alien. I've *slept* with an alien!

Conflicting thoughts clash in my head at the realisation of this. I've taken the contraceptive pill for a few years now, to curb irregular cycles and heave bleeding, so we didn't use any other protection? But what does this mean?

"Aithen. We slept together! Are you nuts? Do I need to get a check-up at the hospital?" For all I know I could be infected with some weird alien thing.

Aithen opens his hands towards mine. I grasp them with my own.

I'm holding an alien. But no, he's Aithen.

"No, we're fine," he replies. "We are both disease-free."

I pull a sour face. "Urgh! Don't say it like that. But how do you know that? I could have some *human* bug which you can catch and die from?"

He holds up his arm. "This told me." And the screen appears. It's not projected this time but illuminates under his skin.

My eyes widen. It's real. I'm not crazy. I think? I examine his wrist, but the screen just feels like skin, no resistance.

Aithen explains about the technology embedded in his arm. The devices are called *Meorlites*, and they are so microscopic, they would not register with any metal detector or similar device on Earth. They grant no superhuman powers, though stopping time is significant. Okay, so he can't pick up a bus or run at light speed, but yes, he can *actually* freeze time for a few minutes.

The Meorlite interacts visually, like with the screen I have seen in his arm, or – and this I have trouble grasping – from the mind. The device gives them information naturally. Like a thought. They can look at something and know if it is safe to eat or drink, or a contaminant can harm them. Call it fact-based intuition.

"This is ridiculous, Aithen. Considering what you know, knew. Why did you get involved?"

His serious expression returns. "Honestly, Jayne. I would never do anything to hurt you. I know it's safe. The thought of you giving up, someone so brilliant and beautiful as you. I had to do something. And the more I learnt about the real you, the more I have fallen in love. I had no intention of us sleeping together, but you over-whelmed me. When I'm with you, you make me forget who I am. Where I'm from."

I stroke his hair. Those same perfect violet eyes consider me desperately. How many people have fantasised an alien romance? Books are filled with them.

This is crazy. But Aithen's so warm and caring and here with me.

I believe him. And despite my fear and shock, I can't stop my heart aching for how much I love him.

Forget for an instant the fact he saved my dad and me, Aithen has trusted me. A pang of guilt reminds me I tried to run away in horror from him. Well, who wouldn't?

"You look exactly like us. Us *Earthlings*." I watch him.

"We are almost identical – but we have traits which define us quite exclusively," he says.

I tilt my head to the side. *Go on, tell me more.*

"Our average age span is three hundred years. Our eye colour distinguishes personality and skills from our world. A lot more than pigment." He cradles my face, so I am looking closely at him. "Think of it like a mood ring, which supposedly changes colour when you're angry or sad."

I used to have one when I was twelve. The ring's stone was always green or black. Yeah, black to match the mood I consistently carried around inside me.

"Well, a certain class of Koyorad will develop a particular eye colour, and this will dictate the life they lead; the work they will be good at."

"Class?" I ask. "What class are you with your violet eyes? What does this make you?"

"I'm a *Kurzite*."

I straighten, "A what?"

"A Kurzite. Call it a subclass if you want, but collectively, we are Koyorads. My skill is, amongst many things, academia and space travel." He clasps his fingers together.

"Space travel? Don't all Koyorads do that?"

"Actually no, not these long distances. It's a trait quite a few of our class, and I have."

Watching the high street again, little does anybody know what I know. It would be me, wouldn't it? How many billion people on Earth? And I'm the one dating an alien? Maybe there are others?

"How do I keep this a secret? I won't be able to stop myself from slipping up." I squeeze his hands.

"Jayne. I can't stress enough the importance of keeping this a secret."

I cast my gaze to the ground, combing fingers through my hair. "I know I'll slip up. This is big, Aithen. In fact, no, it's epic. We're not alone in the universe!" I open my arms as though preaching to a large crowd.

He sighs. "I understand, but you know the dangers now. Think of your friends. If you vanish, then there is no hope for them. For some reason, you can see past our technology, which is a good starting point. Together, I am sure we can solve this."

"What can I do? Some *stupid human*?" Erek's words sting my memories.

"You're far from it," replies Aithen. "It does make me consider. We're not supposed to get involved. It's drummed into us for weeks before we travel to Earth and during the flight here." He taps his head. "Don't get involved," he repeats. "The thing is the negative side of Korudaz are those who are extremely paranoid about other races. Fearful."

"Fearful? Of us?" I ponder.

"Yes, where I'm from, Koyorads are either overly interested in other worlds, which would make up a good sixty, maybe seventy per-cent of the population. But then, some condemn the whole space exploration program. The *nay-sayers*. They are the ones who would rather stay hidden or rid the universe of all intelligent life. Now they are the stupid ones."

"This is too much," I respond. Thoughts of a bright, warm world of Koyorads wanting to meet us excites me. But then I imagine a cold world where lurks black-eyed Deleters and angry faces, plotting to erase anyone, not like them. I'd never want to visit that planet.

"And it's not fair. Why can't we be allowed to know one another?" I search his worried face. "Okay, it's weird I'm from here, and you're from… Mars."

"Korudaz," he corrects, with a raise of the eyebrows.

"Wherever. You're a guy. I'm a girl. You know, it's all normal." Maybe a slight exaggeration, but I'm trying to reconcile this as I speak.

"But Jayne—"

"Yes, I know, Aithen. It's just not right. Not fair."

"I know. But now we need to plan for the next few days. We need to stay close together. Thankfully, you're not in school, so when I'm not with you, I intend to shadow Erek," Aithen says.

"When I attacked Erek, in the mall, he was with another older man?" I ask.

"Yeah, that's another bigger problem," Aithen says. "He oversees all activity on the planet. Call him the Deleter Manager, in simple terms."

"Does this get any worse?" I ask. "I threw a glass at him. I don't think it hurt him, though."

Something dawns on me. "Let's say we somehow bypass Erek and find a way to rescue my friends? What's to stop him jumping back in time, in your time machine, and doing it all again?"

Aithen nods, thoughtfully. "Good point, but despite how good we are at this, there are still strict rules. We're not allowed to visit a specific timeline twice."

"It doesn't sound like they, the Deleters follow the rules?" I say.

"Oh, even they do. As I said before, the planet is ruled by a larger population of sympathisers. The powers-that-be over-rule negative individuals. Personally, I am not sure the activities of the

Deleters is common knowledge of Korudaz. We have Kounsell organisations – factions if you want – who control the Koyorads. Most factions are good. It's a small number, especially those linked to the military, which upholds the bad aspects."

I sigh. "Why do I feel like I'm outnumbered badly? I want to run away and hide."

Aithen hugs me from behind and nuzzles my neck. I need the warmth more than the touch as these truths are ice cold to my core. I could stamp off in a fury, but where will that get me? Aithen said we can *sort this out*?

Can he fix what the Deleters have done? Can Leslie, Chloe, and Laura (and *VioletlyAlone*) be reinstated back to reality? What was it like for them? How did it feel? Being deleted?

I've seen Erek. He's nothing special. Just some lanky guy who…

"You two comfortable?"

Aithen's body stiffens.

I turn.

It's Erek.

CHAPTER TWENTY-EIGHT

There's a lot of posturing going on, but Aithen is the weaker there. I don't know what they're saying as the conversation moved away from earshot. I'm watching them both from the top of the hill.

I hear a few words, but not English. It sounds Swedish, Germanic but throaty simultaneously. They use weird hand gestures, one of which looks like a one-handed clap, using the fingers only.

I shiver against the cooling breeze and dark thoughts of what Aithen has told me. What can he possibly be saying to Erek, who is brandishing an angry purple bruise, on his left cheek? He barely acknowledged me and Aithen didn't give him a chance, marching Erek away from the scene.

How is all this possible? The Koyorads can stop time for a moment, but can they really erase a person from this world? It's impossible. But only I remember the girls. The deletion device can go back to the point a person's conceived and stop it. But why? Just to keep a secret?

I know so much; too much. Why has Aithen done this to me? Because he is sure he can help me, I assure the nagging voice in my head.

My cell rings. It's Mom, checking I'm all right. Erek is

watching me as I talk, so I profuse anguish with *whomever* I am talking to. Not that much acting is needed. Her voice croaks and every few words are punctuated with sniffs. I should head home and check in on her and Dad. Ending the call, I head towards Aithen and Erek.

"Right. I'm off. Mom needs me at home." I wipe my eyes.

Aithen's frowns. "Yes, you should. Tell your mom I said sorry for her loss."

Erek looks taught at Aithen. His chin juts out for an explanation. Is he sneering?

"Jayne's father. There was an accident today. A fatal accident." Aithen looks morose. Detached. He continues to eye the quieting high street.

"Right. See ya." I keep my face forward. I want to run and scream and hide. But I bounce along, testing my steps as I descend the hill. I slip around a corner and slam my back against the wall.

I gasp like I've been running. That was close. Was Erek convinced? I won't know until later. I can't call Aithen. He'll know when it's safe to contact me. Instead, I return home, paranoia following me like a shadow. I repeatedly peer behind me, sure I will spot Erek following, but the only shadows are those from the dipping sun.

I can't be alone, and this propels my steps faster and faster. I don't want to make a dash for it, but I want a door and walls between me and the outside world.

Erek could leave Aithen and come looking for me.

The ruse with Erek seems to have worked. For now. I've heard nothing from him.

Aithen is giving me space for a couple of days, to calm down. He'll be glued to Erek's every move.

I need the time to let the thoughts and revelations seep into my head. I'm scared to go outside alone. Even with Mom or a friend at my side, I am vulnerable. If Erek wanted to pounce, he can stop time and make me disappear; for good. But little comfort is offered at the thought I am safe until Sunday.

Erek expects me to fall apart and kill myself. I rub away the goosebumps on my arms.

Curiosity grows as the days pass.

Aithen calls and messages me every couple of hours. It helps that he is not the only visitor in Erek's party. There are three others. It baffles me that other aliens are within easy reach or reside in Dereton. I won't get the opportunity to meet them, which is probably just as well. Meeting two Koyorads is enough for me at the moment. What is curious is they don't meet up, to compare notes. What little Aithen has said suggests friendship and gossip between the visitors. Each has their own agenda and staying separate will prevent the potential for *mishaps*. I'm guessing "mishap" is code for Deletion.

"You said something about Erek tracking you all, the visiting party?" I ask him on my cellphone.

"Yes, it's the Meorlite technology again. I'm sure you've heard of nanotechnology? Well, this is more like yokto-technology. We're talking genome level. Erek can't read minds or anything like that, but his awareness of the team is like a seventh sense. He knows where we are and if we are in trouble," explains Aithen. "I suppose you'd call it a parental instinct."

"What if you're with me?" I ask. "Will he be able to register that?"

"He'll know where I am, GPS-wise. But no, he'll just sense I am safe. Calm. Happy. And not, thankfully, all those other thoughts and emotions I experience with you." I can sense Aithen's smile. Maybe I have a natural Meorlite instinct for him.

My thoughts darken again. My mood has been eclipsed many times today, Sunday.

"Aithen. What time is it supposed to happen? Me and… you know?"

"Can I tell you in half an hour?" he asks.

"Why half an hour?"

"I'll tell you personally," he responds. "Trust me, we can meet."

I'm not sure.

He's asking me to meet him at the Campus Green, an open field at the rear of the college grounds. Do we risk it?

My mind and body are starving for Aithen and more answers, but I must see him again. There was no hesitancy in his voice. It's worth the risk.

When I arrive, there are handfuls of students and families spaced out across the grassy area. Smoke wafts across the field, making my mouth water in response to the aroma of BBQed food. Hits the spot every time. The sun is low in the sky, and a calmness washes across the landscape. This is what summer evenings are all about, but I feel too exposed.

"Jayne!" Aithen beckons me over to him, and I break into a gentle trot.

I search my surroundings as I grab hold of him and plant a kiss firmly on his eager mouth. We have stayed apart for the last few days, and I'm hungrier for him than the food spitting for attention.

"We're fine, don't worry." He soothes my questioning gaze.

"Where's Erek?" I ask.

"He's with another member of our visiting party. So, we have a little breathing space." He straightens up, looking confident in himself, but this makes me laugh when he pretends to strut on the spot.

I place my hand on his firm, warm chest, and reach for the back of his neck with the other. "Come 'ere," I gasp, and I kiss him again. Alien or not, it's been too long. If I could empty this field right now, I would take Aithen where he stands.

He considers my face. "What are you giggling at?" he asks.

I open my mouth and run my tongue over my bottom teeth. "You," I say with a teasing, husky tone and give him a wink.

That triggers an unexpected but pleasant response: Aithen's eyes widen, jaw drops in wonder.

"What was that?" I ask. "I only winked at you?"

His eyes refocus on me, as though he was dazed for a moment. "I can't explain it. *We* don't do *winking*, ever. So seductive." He doesn't give me time to speak and smothers me with a long, slow kiss. His arms wrap around me and pull me against his body.

Somehow, we have forgotten we are in an open field behind a school and have an audience. It's so silent and still and… he's done it again!

I skim the scenery and realise nobody is moving.

Clouds of smoke hang motionless in the air. The licking flames of the fires are frozen, like a photograph. No sounds. No wind. Time is stopped. But not for Aithen and me. Thankfully, it's not accompanied by nausea this time. I must be accustomed to it.

He is wearing a mischievous grin. "This is why I asked you here." He touches his wrist and watches the empty space behind him.

Now what?

For a split second, I notice a faint haze behind Aithen. And then it's there. I gasp in disbelief. In fear.

Black. No windows. No flashing lights or sounds. It's not a saucer or cigar-shaped: more like a wedge with a rounded tip at the front, so you can tell which way it is facing. I would guess it's about thirty feet long and ten feet in height. It almost looks military.

Words can't escape my gaping mouth. Aithen guesses my thoughts as I reach out a hand. "Yes, it's safe to touch."

My fingertips stutter at the point of contact. The surface has a matte texture, but there is no friction at all when you run your fingers over it. It's smoother than silk and metallic cold.

"You park it here?" I ask.

He smiles. "No. I just summoned it from orbit."

"Huh?" is the best I can manage.

Suddenly, I remember where we are and snap my eyes to the still silent, frozen, unblinking faces around me. They can't see this. If they could, this would be a calamity on an epic scale.

"We should leave," Aithen suggests.

"Leave?" My breath is laboured. I squint my eyes and rub my forehead. My hand is wet, so I rub a sleeve across my face. "Leave where?"

He gestures his head upwards.

Up?

"I can't!" I don't mean to yell. "Sorry I can't do that. Can you even fly this thing?" I scan the exterior again. This is so alien. The blackness of the surface looks like it is sucking the light from the area.

"Yes, I've been flying these for years," he says.

"But what about Erek? The rest of your team? They'll know?" I can't comprehend this.

"I promise you; we all have one. This is mine while we're on this planet. My rental if you want."

The side of the craft cracks open. The entrance.

Aithen takes my hand. "Before I met you, you died today. I have changed history, and I want to replace that awful, negative moment in your time, with something special. This is the first step to your renewed life."

How am I supposed to respond to that?

…One giant step for Jayne.

Aithen holds my arm and leads me to the opening. Inside, it is quiet and dark, but once Aithen *starts* the craft, virtual screens and keypads appear.

"You can sit down." He gestures to a chair near him. I remind myself to breathe in and out. My head swims.

A deep hum followed by a small suction hiss draws my attention to the entrance area. The craft's door closes for take-off and the interior lighting changes from an orange tinge to blue. I give Aithen an inquisitive look.

"Cloaking applied. Lighting colour reminds us of this, so we know we're hidden from the humans or whatever may be watching."

His casual use of *humans* always fascinates me. He could be talking about potatoes or peas in the same way, though I don't feel like he's rejecting of us, more a matter of fact.

"Is everyone outside back to normal now?" I refer to those in the time freeze around us in the field.

"Yes, all back to normal. And we're hovering, cloaked about thirty feet above the ground."

Thirty feet? I'm not afraid of heights, but I didn't feel our rise. I can't imagine I am sat here, in the air and invisible. Really?

Aithen taps away at virtual screens. Pre-flight routine, I guess. He is using the Meorlite in his arm to communicate with the craft's computer terminal. Though he calls it the *kord*.

"So, can anybody fly this?" I continue to scan the enclosed space. I'm inside an actual alien spaceship. No odour. Sinister silence. Its featureless, matt surfaces offer no controls you can push, pull, or turn. When Aithen approaches an area, a collection of consoles and screens ripple into appearance. They disappear when his focus aims elsewhere.

"No, the Meorlite is essential," he responds. "There is the additional security step of bio-recognition." His voice is distracted as he watches the screens.

"Am I supposed to know what that means?" I ask, swallowing dryly.

"No. It means, only a Koyorad can fly this craft. If you stepped in here by yourself, none of the functionality would present itself. It would remain a non-working shell." He flicks away two screens, and they disappear.

The voice in my head laughs at me. This is unreal, but where are we going? Why have I willingly stepped into an alien spaceship? Nerves pull keenly at my senses.

I reach around my seat for the retention straps, but there aren't any. I don't want to interrupt Aithen. I'm sure he will offer to secure me once we are ready to start.

What will it be like? The launch. Will the engines fire up like a fighter jet and throw us back into our seats? The seats are padded, probably to absorb the pressure from the g-force which will result from a fast take-off. This is intense.

A tingling, nervous excitement brews increasingly in my stomach. The background hum of the craft lowers. The quiet before the storm? I clasp my hands together, trying to not appear scared. But I am. Using the back of my hand, I wipe away the sweat from my brow and upper lip. I can't control my shaking hands, and my knees bounce to the rhythm of nervous anticipation.

My head floats, and my mouth dry. Why am I so nervous? I have flown at least thirty times in my life, though not in an alien craft from hundreds of lightyears away.

Calm yourself.

"You okay?" Aithen is smiling at me.

"Yeah, sorry. Nervous."

"Well, this will be your first time in space."

"Space? I thought we would just… you know… fly about. Over town?"

His grin is saying otherwise.

Deep breath. I can do this? Astronauts train for years to do this, but I run every day. I should be fit enough?! My breathing is heavy. Loud. The blue darkness of the room is pressing on me.

"Can we open the windows, viewers, or whatever you have on this spaceship?"

Aithen taps into a console, and the *windows* become transparent. The glass changes from the opaque metallic appearance to pure, crystal clear.

My mouth drops open. My heart is racing. My brain screams, but it cannot create a clear thought. I stand.

The Earth.

I'm looking at my planet. My home. My world. Breath-taking.

I have never seen a blue so beautiful, so bright and then my eyes catch the brown and green colour of land, below partings in the clouds. Down there is my family. People everywhere are going about their days; evenings; night.

Aithen holds me in his arms, and I cry. Not sad tears, but in awe of my beautiful planet.

"I didn't feel a thing? How long was the take-off?" I ask as there was no hint we had moved.

"About four seconds—"

"Four seconds?" I sweep away the tears. "How is that possible?"

"We've done this for a long time." He's enjoying my shocked expression. "The drive dynamics – or engines, as you would say – have evolved for about a thousand years. We've got the science down to *an art*."

"What?" I respond to his smug grin.

"Human phrases are amazing. 'Science down to an art', the first time I have used that expression in a conversation. I like the relational development between the words *science* and *art*."

"Yes, us humans—" I over-stress the *humans,* "are good at such things. Turning a phrase from unrelated concepts. Oh, Aithen." I trail off as I consider the Earth again.

Despite my amazement at the view, panic flows through me. How do I get back? Can I go back? I understand the tremendous forces of gravity. Rockets develop so much energy to escape from the Earth's atmosphere. I won't be able to punch through the atmosphere, to return to my house. A hidden, tiny spec lost down there on the planet.

My head swims once more, and I sit. I can't tear my eyes away.

Aithen passes me a drink. "This will help," he assures me.

I swallow a sweet, pleasant-tasting liquid and stifle a burp.

"Sorry!" I laugh.

"It's normal, don't worry. An altitude rush, nothing more." He takes the glass out of my hand and kisses me. "Welcome to space."

My head clears again, and I approach the window for a closer look. I touch the pane, and I realise it is not glass, albeit transparent. It feels like a hardened gel, but the more you press against it, the more I sense a vibration against my fingertips.

Is it possible to tire of such a view? So, few have seen what I am seeing. Is it imaginable I'm here? I want my family to see this, too. For them to share this. I scan the entire world, and I wish every person could witness this. How would such an experience change the world? Would we still fight in our wars? Would we treat each other better?

Aithen beckons me over to a window on his side of the craft as he taps once more at a console.

I have seen it in so many news stories and pictures. A couple of hundred feet away from me is the international space station. I jump back away from the window, worried anybody on board will see me.

"They can't see us. The occupants don't know we are here."

With his words, I remember the interior blue light and I peer out of the window again.

The structure is a lot smaller than I had imagined. It's a mass of white blocks and tubes. So fragile, though the robust cables and bolt fastenings are strong in appearance. It's hard to believe there are people in there and they have no idea we are out here. The concept is almost dizzying. My people. My planet. Our achievements are incredible, and I'm looking at one of them right now.

My eyes widen with a surge of pride and bewilderment as I swear, I see a shadow or a blur pass by a window on the station.

The light is broken by a passing figure inside the lonely craft.

There are people there, right now on that space station. This is crazy.

"I thought it moved, orbited the Earth?" I ask. The station is motionless.

"Actually, we are travelling at over twenty-seven thousand kilometres per hour." Aithen lifts a hand towards another screen, which displays characters I cannot read. He taps in a command, then says, "Ask the computer to translate for you."

I shrug and respond, "Translate?"

The characters are readable and display our speed: 27,415.8912 KPH.

I laugh. "Scary." At this speed, what is keeping the space station together?

I'm standing firm as I watch outside. What about gravity? Why aren't we floating now? I have seen many TV segments featuring astronauts and pens and many objects floating around the cockpit once they leave the Earth's atmosphere?

"We're not floating?"

Aithen looks at me. "A long explanation but not one for now. We have also worked out how to create an isolated gravity field within our craft. Your scientists mimic gravity through centrifugal force. We do a similar thing but at a sub-atomic level. As with most things, time is the great dictator of all knowledge and learning."

He thinks for a moment.

"Think about how your computers have gotten smaller but more powerful. Well, we have done the same thing with our technologies. I'm sure you felt a little light-headed when we left the Earth's atmosphere?"

"I did, but I didn't know we had left the ground."

"And you felt light-headed when you stood up. I'm sorry, I forgot to plan for this. Space travel is routine for me and *alien* to you." He smiles at his use of the word. "Hence, why I gave you the drink. It stabilises blood within exterior zero gravity, along with cell oxygenation and other essential needs. Microbiology at its best," he smiles. "Also, no spinal elongation while in weightless space. Not a big issue for a short flight but over days or weeks, the spine can lengthen so we combat such effects, too."

My heart races at the mention of *days or weeks*. How do I get back? I can't exactly open the hatch and thumb a lift home. I stare anxiously at Aithen. "We're not leaving, are we? I can't go to Korudaz!"

He holds me and kisses my forehead, then lips. "No, no, don't worry. I'm sorry, Jayne. I forget how ridiculous this must be for you. This is just a quick sight-seeing tour. I should have thought this through more."

How to understand and accept any of this?

Aithen knows everything, and yet he's so young – and sharing this incredible experience, a fantastic secret, with me. I squeeze him tighter towards me. He gives no resistance as I plant a firm kiss on his mouth. Not so much a sensual kiss but more a way of saying thank you.

He holds my face in his soft, warm hands as he gazes into my eyes. It could be the craft's interior, but his eyes sparkle brighter, sharper than usual. Are there faint lines across the violet colouring? I try to focus on the grid; they are most likely a reflection from a console. His voice breaks my thoughts and inspection. "Are you ready to continue?"

"Continue? Where to?"

He points a finger outside. "The Moon. You've come this far, might as well visit your closest space relative."

So, this is what he meant about days or weeks. I can't be gone that long. My family, the police, will be searching for me. "I can't," I say, standing to look at Earth again. "I should return already. I can't just disappear for a week or so."

"A week?" Aithen asks. "We'll be there in less than a minute."

I sit for a moment. Aithen traces a hand on my back. His expression beckons for a response.

"Yeah, I'm fine," I whisper. "There's so much to take in."

I'm silent as I watch out of the other side of the craft. How do you describe the Earth? Words can't capture this vision. Beautiful and peaceful and blue.

"Let's do it," I say, and Aithen taps at various consoles.

I keep a careful eye on the space station. How fast do we move away? It's gone in a blink of the eye. I immediately snap back towards Earth, and it is drawing away from me, getting smaller.

My heart races. I am leaving. I can't return. I want my home, my family.

"Stop!" I shout and bury my head in my hands.

"Let's take this slowly," Aithen whispers, stopping the engine.

I continue to watch my home planet. A moment ago, it filled my vision.

Now, standing with my face close to the window, I see all the circumference of the planet.

"How far are we?" I ask.

"From Earth? A little over a hundred thousand kilometres."

"In what, ten seconds? This is mad."

"Ready for a countdown?" Aithen asks.

My blank expression asks, what?

"Estimated time of death was nine o'clock in the evening," he frowns.

"And I was alone, in the house?" I ask.

"I don't know the circumstances of why, but yes, you were." He holds me tightly in his arms, and we slip to the floor, continuing our embrace.

I can hear my heart beating in my ears, as Aithen kisses my head.

He doesn't need to say anything.

I feel it.

I know. I just died in that other reality. That other life.

But I'm here. Alive. And of all places, in space.

We sit together for about an hour, our craft hovering motionless within the emptiness of space. We discuss the day's events recalling the journey, the speed, and a lot of questions from me. I want to know so much, but I'm guarded with my questions as the more I learn, the more confusing it becomes. Aithen is so fluent in his technology like I would be if explaining what cell phones or microwave ovens are. He holds back on a lot of the detail, so as not to overwhelm me with too much smart science.

It's curious this tiny craft we sit in could make the journey from Korudaz to Earth, and back again. Yes, it would be a very lonely journey; I couldn't imagine doing it alone. You'd go crazy.

Aithen has the theory that I can remember the deleted girls because of the plate in my head. He flashes a pen-like object at my head and then inserts it into a machine for analysis.

He points at another display. "Without going too much into detail," he continues to read a load of images and scrambled text, "your accident and the plate appear to have switched on a strange side-effect."

"Go on. Give me the worse, Doctor Aithen." The garbled mess displayed on the screen means nothing to me.

"No, it's not bad. I can't perform a full diagnosis, but you can see past our technology.

"You remember deleted people. You saw my Meorlite. This is a first. It has to be something to do with the titanium."

I shrug. What can I say? It would be me, wouldn't it? I'm always weird.

Then we sit there in silence. Not awkward silence but more like wakeful sleep. Enjoying holding each other and allowing my brain to process the information. Outside of this craft is a vacuum of forever emptiness. It's like being dropped into a calm ocean, with no sight of land and no backup support whatsoever.

Space is so lonely. I could never be up here, on my own.

"So, you ready to make history?" Aithen smiles at me.

"History?"

"Yes. You will be the first human woman to go to the Moon." He mimics a fanfare and explosive celebrations with his hands.

First woman. How sad when you consider the history of space travel. "But nobody will know, and I can't tell anybody."

"Well, you could." He trails off.

I nudge him. "Yeah and the straight jacket would look lovely on me, I know." I wrap my arms around my body. "But yes, let's make history."

I have no time to reflect on the new journey when Aithen announces our Moon orbit. The speed is mind-blowing, and yet once again, I felt nothing. I'm sure every expert on Earth would explain how I should have disintegrated by now, but here I am.

I rise and view a bleak landscape. It's nothing like Earth. No blue. No clouds. Just lifeless, barren, grey land. The more I look, the more detail forms, along with areas of white and *blue* patches?

"There's no water on the Moon? I'm sure of that?" I ask.

"No, not a drop. You can see a land haze of sorts. The Moon has a weak atmosphere, and you see the internal reflection of the Sun's rays. You will often catch greens in the same way."

Well, I didn't expect any colours, so this is one for the books.

I'm not hit by the same sense of shock on being this close to our space neighbour. It's exciting seeing it up close. The familiar white glowing object from our night-time sky. But we are so far from Earth.

Aithen steers the craft towards the Moon's surface.

"We're not going to land, are we?" I hope not.

He laughs. "No, not today. That would send you over the edge. No, only a sight-seeing tour for today."

As we near the surface, Aithen arms the exterior lights. I watch out of the windows rather than using the monitors. See everything firsthand.

I gasp. Tears flow.

We're held stationary, about twenty feet above the Moon's surface. In the beam of light from the craft, I see it as clear as day – *Old Glory*. Planted into the Moon soil is a single slim, white stick. Attached to this is a flag of the USA.

All I can hear in my head are Neil Armstrong's words as he stepped onto the lunar surface so many years ago, and I am proud. Not for me but for him and all those people who had made the incredible journey to such a remote and distant place. I felt the anxiety of leaving Earth, what did they think? Hurtling across space. Did they wonder if it's a one-way journey?

A wave of bitterness sweeps across my memory. All those newspaper articles and documentaries, claiming the whole thing a hoax. How did these amazing, brave people put up with the insults? I gasp as the thought of our craft, so close to the surface, alarms me. "Be careful. Please don't disturb the footprints."

"Not possible, don't worry. No air or anything similar emits from the engines. We could be inches off the surface, and it wouldn't make a disturbance."

I settle and take in the new landscape. I move from window to window, looking at the Earth and then back to the Moon.

"So, what does this run on? Regular or unleaded?" I can't help but laugh.

The moment fades as I reconsider my beautiful home planet. That perfect blue globe houses a threat, waiting for me.

Will Erek already know I am still alive?

As of now, Aithen and I have broken the ultimate rule.

We have altered history.

CHAPTER TWENTY-NINE

It's already late in the evening, but I'm scared to leave the craft. I can't decide what is weirder, me sat in a cloaked alien spaceship, or having sent Mom a cell-message from a thousand feet, saying I'm with Aithen and will be home soon.

But this is becoming my new reality.

Dereton appears its usual self in the weakening light, as street-lamps spark to life and car head and taillights cruise the emptying streets. Just another summer evening with televisions tuned to today's unsettling events.

"Something's bothering me, Aithen." I flop into the seat next to his, but bend my knee and tuck it under myself, so I can face him.

"Just the one thing?" he smiles in response.

"It's the time travel thing. You've been able to see into my, our future here on Earth, so what else should I know?"

His mouth crumples in thought. "Well, as of now, you are alive and living a whole new life. Each second, hour, day is brand new in your timeline." His eyes don't meet mine.

He's hiding something.

"So, do you? Do you travel through time?" I ask, watching for minute flickers in his expression.

He nods slowly.

"And this craft, it can tell me about my future? Or you can?" I'm not even sure what it is I'm fishing for. Shouldn't I be thankful I'm alive? And even more so my dad is.

"I personally cannot just jump through time," Aithen says. "And neither can this ship, but… following a procedure – and quite a dangerous one at that – it can travel through time."

Procedure?

"I need to know, Aithen—"

"Know what?"

"The truth about me," I reply. "There's something else, and this craft can tell me. I don't know why I feel this, but I can somehow sense intelligence in here. Or am I just my usual crazy self?" I try to smile, but it's not convincing.

"I still can't figure out how you see through or detect our technology," he says, "but yes, this craft has an overly complex AI system. All our craft do."

"Artificial intelligence?" I confirm.

"Yes. But the computer here, I can speak to freely." He then issues a command in the Koyorad language, and a new panel appears at the front of the cockpit we sit in. It appears as an oval, virtual reality screen, with a pulsing, pale-blue neon border.

Aithen says something else but then looks towards me. "Okay, the computer will communicate in English now."

"Your language sounds almost painful to speak; quite throaty," I say. "It makes me want to clear my throat as I listen to it."

"That's your hearing. Koyorads hear tones on distinct levels to humans. What you hear as a rasping sound, is quite melodic to our ears. Call it a wavelength thing," Aithen explains.

"This craft is designated K5365, so that is how you address the computer," he says, and as though in response, the pale-blue border pulses to pale-green, and then back to blue. "Ask it something."

"What is the meaning of life?" I ask. There's no response from the computer.

"You need the K5365 first," suggests Aithen. "But ask it something you will know the answer to, as a test."

"Hmm…okay… K5365, when is it my birthday?" I jump as the computer emits a pulse, like a blink of a flash. "What was—"

"October fifteenth," comes the response from a deadpan, female voice. It sounds natural and not like a digital excuse for a voice, but it doesn't encourage conversation.

"Okay, how did it know that? And what was that flash?" I ask.

"You saw that?" Aithen wonders, his eyes pass over me like searching for an unknown truth. "This head injury of yours certainly is a curious thing. That flash should be outside of your visual scope, just like with the hearing differences. But to answer your questions, that was a scan of you, and the computer searched for the answer."

"And I have a record inside this craft's computer system?"

"Oh, no. There will be an index on the main vessel from when I looked at your social media on the way here," he gives me an apologetic smile, "but it would otherwise have connected to Earth's computer systems and found you."

"What, in like two seconds?" That's impossible.

"Yes. About that," he smiles at my gaping mouth. Still, it dismisses immediately when his focus turns to the Meorlite in his wrist. "It's Erek. Say nothing."

There's a brief exchange of words in his native language. I wonder what it is called? Aithen's expression is pained, and he holds my gaze as he talks towards his wrist. The *call* ends.

"This craft is the safest place for you on this planet. I need to meet Erek now and try to calm matters—"

"He knows I'm alive?" My heart already races.

"Yes, but let me fix this, Jayne. You stay in the craft, and it will be cloaked. Nobody in the whole universe can find you once a craft is cloaked, take my word for it," he assures, gesturing with his hands towards me.

"What can you say? He knows I know way too much," I gasp.

"Yes, but I am sure I can get through to him. Erek's not a complete Deleter robot. He may uphold and spout the rules, but he's weakened a few times of late."

"Weakened? Tell that to Chloe, or Leslie, or Laura and –"

"Yes, but he is not the final say in all matters Deletion," Aithen interrupts. "I think you met Erek's *boss* in the mall?"

"The man with the long hair? I only saw his back," I reply, the harshness of that moment stings my memory.

"That's Jerellone, and his role is to oversee all Deleters on Earth. Unless it's a life or death situation, he's the one who sanctions the Deletion."

I'm glad I threw that glass at him now.

Aithen continues. "Erek and I may not be friends, but he'll listen. I have to make him see sense."

I'm not convinced, but we immediately head to a remote, lakeside location outside of Dereton. Aithen issues a set of commands to the craft as we settle on the ground. It's so dark outside. No electric lights pollute the inky blackness.

"Will you be able to find your way?" I ask.

He nods. "The Meorlites in our eyes allow us to see without aid."

Of course, they do.

"So, stay here and don't panic. I've ordered the craft to remain enabled while I am gone, or else everything will shut down, with you not being a Koyorad. So, I have overridden that. I'll meet Erek a kilometre from here." Aithen searches the floor, as though he's trying to remember something.

I take his hands in my own. "Don't worry. Take a deep breath and let's fix this," I encourage. I'm sure he can feel my hands shaking.

He leans towards me and kisses me, then rests his forehead against mine. "You're safe," he whispers.

We exchange a brief hug. Aithen's scared and distracted.

He taps a panel by the exit point. The interior changes colour for a moment but then returns to cloaked-blue when the exit closes again. Deathly silence consumes the interior. I listen for the telltale sound of footprints, but there's nothing. An invisible craft is obviously soundproof, too.

The console screens and keypads glow invitingly around me; I can't decipher their contents. I don't belong here. Reaching for my cell phone, I consider taking a picture of the interior but think twice as the oval K5365 computer screen flickers momentarily.

I'll not get this chance again. What can the computer tell me?

"K5365. What will I be doing in five years from now?" Is that too vague a question?

"That is undefined." The cold, deadpan response arrives.

Let's figure this out. In five years from now, I should graduate college with my bachelors. I haven't decided which branch of science I want to study, so one way to discover.

"K5365. What subject will I graduate in for my bachelor's degree?" This is stupid. I'm talking to thin air.

"That is undefined," replies K5365.

Is anything defined?

"K5365. Do you know what a bachelor's degree is?"

"A bachelor's degree is an undergraduate academic degree awarded by colleges and universities upon completion of a course of study spanning three years or more," K5365 defines.

"K5365. Will I ever be awarded a bachelor's degree?" I ask. Maybe I'm doing this wrong. How could the computer know if I will complete a degree? It can't see into the future. Yes, these spaceships can time travel, but a computer is just a digital machine.

"No, you will not be awarded a bachelor's degree." The voice may be cold, but it's also authoritative.

"K5365. Do I have the potential to commence study for a bachelor's degree?"

"Yes, you do."

This is confusing, but then I peer out the panel, and while I see nothing, I imagine Aithen out there, talking to Erek.

"K5365. Am I going to be Deleted?"

"This has not been authorised." A glimmer of hope relaxes my heart slightly.

Not authorised.

Yet.

I run the fingers of both hands through my hair, combing it backwards. Let's be philosophical about this. Generalise then increment to increasing detail.

"Okay, K5365. Do you understand the future of humanity?"

"I do."

Not specific but I got an answer. I've often wondered about the future of human life. We seem to continually romanticise the demise of our species, with tales of Armageddon or zombie armies.

"K5365. When will Earth humans cease to exist?"

I roll my eyes mentally and await the undefined answer.

"Earth humans will cease to exist in two years, one month and three days."

My blood turns to ice, and I reflexively hug myself against the chilling threat from the answer. "How... how will that happen?"

No response.

"K5365. What will cause Earth humans to not exist?" I swallow forcefully against the adrenalin-fuelled gag.

"A Trenier, E1-90998712D, will impact Earth in two years..."

I grasp my mouth and stifle the cry, drowning out the response from the computer, as my stomach heaves. I can't be sick in here. Scanning around me, there's nothing to catch the vomit. I force deep breaths, in and out, coughing as the spasm in my stomach and chest heaves sickly.

"K5365. Is there drinking water available on this ship?" I croak through the gasps for air.

A glass beaker appears on one of the surfaces, and yes, it's filled with water. I gulp it down. "K5365. Can I have a refill of water, please?" The surface illuminates, so I place the glass back. It descends into the surface, and the reappears, filled again with chilled water.

I take a few sips and level-out my breathing.

"K5365. What is a Trenier?" I have an inkling what this is.

An image of a rock is presented in the void air between the computer screen in me. Lines map out a scale which seems impossible.

"A Trenier is a planetary debris object, measuring a minimum of two-hundred and fifty thousand kilometres."

How big was the one which *supposedly* wiped out or contributed to the dinosaur extinction? About fifty kilometres?

"K5365. How big was the Trenier which hit Earth?"

"E1-90998712D is eight-hundred and ninety-seven thousand, four hundred and twelve kilometres in length."

Is?

This computer appears to predict the future, but is this real? If it is, then Earth will be wiped out in July, two years from now. What am I supposed to do with this? Tell everyone?

"K5365. What is the current year?"

"R-2 and10-M-A, with respect to the current and actual time."

What's that supposed to mean?

"K5365. In quite simple terms, what are R-2 and 10-M-A?" I sigh.

"R-2 is the current year on Earth. 10-M-A is the current year on Korudaz."

Like that helps.

"K5365. What is the difference between R-2 and 10-M-A?" I believe this computer is broken.

"Ten-thousand years."

I stifle the groan. "K5365. Based on the current year on Earth, is Korudaz ten-thousand years in the future?" I rub my sternum, trying to ease the ache pounding in my chest.

"Yes."

I can't cope.

This is too much.

It means Aithen has travelled back in time. To me. But what's the real reason why?

Everyone on this planet died thousands of years ago, as for the Koyorads. Why bother coming all this way?

Not so long ago, Aithen would have woken on Korudaz. And I would be dust. A forgotten memory from a past and distant civilization.

I'm no more than a ghost.

A *stupid human*.

No wonder the Deleters don't care about us. We're already dead to them. We're nothing.

Why do the Koyorads come here?

They visit us like I did the dinosaur exhibit in the museum.

A curiosity?

I collapse to the floor and choke with the flow of tears.

Why, Aithen? Why have you gotten involved with me?

And why did you bother to save me, for the sake of two years?

How can you make me fall in love with you?

CHAPTER THIRTY

"Stay away from me, Aithen," I snap and brush away his hands.

"Jayne, what's happened?"

I consider him through a veil of tears. "I know everything, everything, Aithen." I motion a hand towards the computer.

He holds my shoulders. "What have you done?"

"I know about the future. Mine, the Earth's." I shrug his hands away.

Aithen exhales loudly. "I wasn't thinking. I'm sorry, Jayne. But I needed to see Erek urgently. I didn't imagine you'd do anything in here." He taps at a console, and the computer is dismissed.

"I just want to go home. I don't care about Erek or anything he plans to do…" I trail off.

Aithen lifts me into my seat, and the journey back to the college green takes seconds.

"I'll walk you home," he offers.

"No, no, don't. I need to be alone," I manage through my tears and sniffs.

"It's not safe for you to be alone," Aithen says.

I wipe my eyes and look up at him. "I'm already dead, Aithen.

You've been dating a ghost. I don't want to know why or…
anything. Leave me alone."

"But Jayne—"

"Just don't!" I raise my palms toward him. "I'm going home,
and I don't want to hear about Erek or anything."

I take a deep breath and walk away. My heart aches and wants
me to run back to Aithen, but we are broken. This is broken. The
entire world is broken, and I need to be alone.

The worst thing about death is you don't know it happened. You
imagine everything becomes hazy and then floating away into whatever. People write about *seeing the light* and a bright tunnel. It's all
part of life and is inevitable. We all die.

But not like this. Not everyone simultaneously.

My fingers tremble as I hold the empty cardboard cup. I drank
coffee over an hour ago, but I can't move. I don't want to. The last
time I visited the mall, chaos erupted. Compared to now, that was a
sweet and pleasant experience. Strangers and familiar faces give me
vacant or questioning looks. I don't care that my cheeks are lined
with tearful mascara.

It all doesn't matter.

I could get up out of my chair and throw it through the shop
window over there. Yes, security will appear, and the police will be
called.

But it's not important.

Nothing is. I'm not.

Everyone here is not.

We're all just a memory. We should be forgotten.

How can everything so right become so bad? Two days ago, I
ventured into space. But now I'm no more than a ghost haunting the
current reality of Earth. We're all phantoms in waiting. But we don't

realise our demise is racing towards us, hidden within the vast ink of space.

I welcome the warmth of the tears and dab my delicate nose with a wet clutch of napkins.

"You okay, dear?" A wrinkled, friendly face looks at the pile of discarded napkins on the table and floor. I'm not one for public exhibitions, but I'm numb. I stutter an, "Okay," at her and get to my feet.

Where can I go? Everywhere seems to have Aithen echoed from within. Home. The hill. The forest. The coffee houses. If I could peel off my skin, I would. I can feel his touch so vividly. I can see his face, hear his voice like he is here, now.

Even now, I can't accept the truth.

Forget all the aliens and spacecraft and Deleters. All insignificant compared to the truth. The ultimate reality, a nightmare I am living. I don't know if Leslie, Laura, or Chloe discovered this, but if they did, I'm sure they welcomed deletion from existence. I wish I dared to end it all now. I could find Erek, and I'm sure he'll accommodate me.

I leave the mall and lean against a railing in the harbour.

I watch a man wrapping up a sail on his boat. The harbour is quiet. The water splashes below me.

It's not fair.

As for the Koyorads, Earth was destroyed ten thousand years ago. A Trenier hit it, and all humanity wiped out. No, *everything* wiped out. This rock is on its way, right now. I could go to the police, press, NASA? Not a chance. I must wait. Like everyone else. I can prove none of this.

Well, I wanted to know about time travel, didn't I? I curse myself. Why couldn't I just be amazed?

It is clear why Deleters don't care. We don't exist to them. We are ghosts from another time. So, why bother? What if we discovered Koyorads? We're all gone soon anyway.

I hate Deleters. We're just a game to them.

Why did Aithen come to Earth? Why visit a relic from ancient history? And why date one? I cower to the ground. I am ashamed of my tears. Of myself.

How am I supposed to face another day? My family? I can't hide this.

I can't comprehend this.

I'm alive. I'm here on Earth, right now.

This is all real. But to the Koyorads, we are words on a page in an old history book. Just like a book, you ignore in school. I never found an interest in history. Well, maybe the Egyptians and Romans had a thing about them.

But if I imagine a person living in a house in 1465, I see a grey, bleary image of a life long ago. But in 1465, on any day, thousands of people lived their lives. Struggling. Working. Laughing. Loving.

If I jumped into a Koyorad spacecraft and travelled back to 1465, I'd see a living, breathing world.

What if I approached Erek? Does he have any compassion for us? He doesn't seem a warm person. His black stare rips through you.

What about the others in his group? There's no way for me to discover the other visitors. Could I force them to appear from the shadows? I have no proof and only my word: the word of a girl with a head injury, who is also treated by her doctor for delusions.

My family will believe me; I can start there. They've met Aithen, as has everyone in the school. But once I talk about aliens and how they've deleted Leslie, Laura and Chloe, my credibility will evaporate in an instant.

If only I took pictures of the craft or when in space. Then again, these could easily be doctored in our age of technology. I must give in to wait for a chance to prove something; anything.

I rub my head. The plate is itching me under the skin and making me nauseous again. I need help.

But who can I turn to?

This must be why Leslie and Laura were with Erek. Leslie said she'd seen *something* and whatever it was had scared her. They must have given up on life. Did they ask Erek to Delete them?

No, that can't be. I still remember the chilling echoes of Laura's voice, that night by the hill. Was she scared of Erek, or what she had discovered?

I can't continue hiding from the future. My fate.

I must find Erek.

CHAPTER THIRTY-ONE

A few minutes after Mom has left for the supermarket, the doorbell chimes. Do I even want to answer? It'll only be someone trying to sell me something. I descend the stairs lazily, hoping they'll have gone by the time I reach the door.

But no such luck. I open the door to a familiar sneer with dark, menacing eyes and white hair.

Erek.

At first, I want to hit him. Slam the door in his face. To run away from here. But I also want closure. I'm tired of hiding and fear. That doesn't subdue my heart, which feels like it is rattling in a cage.

What does Erek even see when he looks at me? A crumb of dirt? Speck of dust in his eye?

I open the door wider as a welcome to enter. If his intentions are Deletion, then let's get this over with.

I'm scared. Is this my last day alive? As Erek passes me, the scent is so familiar. Like Aithen's. Oh Aithen, what have I done? What am I doing?

"You want a drink?" My voice is shrill, lighter than usual. *Control yourself.*

"Water. Sparkling, please?" His face is blank like somebody forgot to draw the expression.

I bring a chilled bottle and two glass beakers to the table and sit down opposite him. I eye the glass bottle, filling the beakers. At least I have an immediate weapon if need calls. I grip my beaker firmly, to steady my trembling fingers as I sip in silence.

"How are you feeling today?" He tilts his head as though interested. The bruise on his cheek has faded, but it still lingers to remind me of that day in the mall.

I shrug. Why get into small talk? I consider the bottle again. If I throw it at him hard, it will break and distract him long enough for me to reach the door and run. But he can stop time.

He's here to Delete me, because of Aithen? Or what?

"Water, okay?" I ask. I must try and reach out to him.

He places his glass on the table, but then two taps on his wrist and…The room dims and dismisses the light streaming in from outside. Erek and I are separated by a translucent screen of charts, graphs, and data. I have seen the text before – in Aithen's spacecraft and on the Meorlite. I can't read the information, but I know a time-line when I see one.

Instinctively I say, "Translate?"

The screen turns to English, displaying a graphical trace of my family tree, along with numerous other data blocks. What is this?

Emerlie?

My great-great-grandmother's name on my father's side of the family.

Emily, my little sister.

Erek breaks the silence. "You've had a life-changing week or two?"

Loaded question?

Now I could have spent the next three days summarising the answer to his question, but instead, I respond, "Tell me about it."

There's no emotion from him. "I won't draw out the good and bad points of our planetary relationships—"

That's one way to put it.

"—but there are rules. And often those rules extend beyond what is acceptable to the continual scope of past and present reality-scapes."

"What does that even mean? Is reality-scapes a word?" I accidentally bite the inside of my cheek too hard.

"It is now," he responds.

I don't want to sit in silence and make it visible I'm inspecting the screen data. "So why are you showing me this? It's no big deal to trace a family tree. Is that the best you can do to try and intimidate me?"

He doesn't answer, so I continue. "Thank you for the information and light show, but why are you bothering to show me this?"

He hunches forward in his seat. "I'm here to correct the problem. A mistake."

"What? To Delete me?" Why did I say that? But this catches him off guard. His head jerks back, and his gaping mouth is wordless. Maybe he recalls the attack I launched on him at the mall?

If I disappear, I may as well say what I want. I'm revelling in the fact I've spoilt his surprise. Me. A simple human. Knows everything.

"Why have you let me survive all this time, Erek? I know about the suicide, but why should that stop you?"

Erek is taut for a moment and looks down to his right as though trying to recall a fact. He relaxes and leans forward. What's he thinking? Why the pause?

"Aithen convinced me to spare you," he mumbles the words.

"And you always listen to him?" I ask.

"No, I don't. This visit is the first time I met Aithen. But actually, it was the mall which changed my mind," Erek says.

The mall? "Why?"

Erek touches his cheek for a moment. "I guess you woke me a little. I've never experienced an individual responding to a loss as you did. You shouldn't even remember them."

"But I do," I add.

"It doesn't make sense. They have been erased from history," Erek says.

"But why have you targeted my friends? Why me?" I try to control the plead in my tone.

"I haven't. It's purely coincidental, nothing more."

"So, despite everything, you're still going to erase me?" I ask. "Erek, we're all dead in a couple of years anyway. Why bother?"

"You shouldn't know that—"

I interrupt. "Yeah, I know, I'm... what was it you said? A stupid human."

Erek's brow furrows. "I have no choice, Jayne. The order has been given." He stands and reaches into a pocket.

I eye the glass bottle again, but a shiny object in his hand distracts me.

Erek pauses, and he looks around the room. "Who else is here, in the house?"

I mimic his searching expression. "No-one. I'm alone."

Erek looks at his wrist, and I can clearly see the Deletion device he grasps. It appears as shiny obsidian, with the shape of a harmless, electric facial shaver. "Jayne, as a Deleter, I can sense the presence of a Koyorad, but I can't distinguish this individual. They are not from my visiting party."

"I'm alone," I respond. Aithen can't have snook into my house, Erek would recognise his signature from the Meorlite.

Erek looks at me, and his eyes scan the room and even look at the ceiling, then back to me. "This doesn't make sense," he says and raises a hand towards me.

"Erek, wait!" I shout, but his hand trembles.

"This is impossible," he says and plunges the Deleter device into a pocket. He rigorously taps on his wrist, repeatedly looking at me as he reads the details presented to him.

"This is… this can't be…" he mutters between the small screens which pop up and dismissed. He raises a projected screen towards me and shakes his head.

"What?" I ask. I place a hand on the table in front of me. The glass bottle is inches from my grasp.

"There's a Koyorad here. You're pregnant, Jayne," he says, and his hands flop to his sides.

Pregnant?

"That's not possible," I respond. "I take the oral contraceptive pill. I'm not pregnant. And I'm not a Koyorad."

"I know you're not, but how?" Erek is stunned.

"Obvious how," I remark.

"But Aithen can't get you pregnant. We take the equivalent contraceptive as a precaution," Erek says.

"Precaution? You telling me Koyorads have relationships with us stupid humans?"

"Yes, it's happened before."

"And they're always Deleted? For dating one of you?" I ask.

"No," he replies. "Only if our secret is revealed."

I roll my eyes at that. "Whatever. But I can't be pregnant."

"Pregnant?" A girl's voice fills the room.

Sarah stands in the doorway from the kitchen. She often enters the house through the backdoor.

"Oh, shit!" I exclaim. "What did you hear?"

"I just walked in and heard you say you're pregnant?" she jams fists into her hips.

"Hello," she greets Erek and then, "*We* need to talk," she demands.

She looks at Erek and me. "And I mean now. So, I don't care who you are," she raises her eyebrows at Erek.

Erek shifts nervously on the spot. This isn't going to plan.

I enjoy Sarah's candour, but I'm afraid – she could be Deleted, too! I must be careful here. This is my problem. I must distance myself from my family. It dawns on me my family have met Aithen. Erek's not planning to Delete them, too? No. If I go, it will be as if I never existed. But I must be careful.

"Okay, in the kitchen," I suggest to Sarah. "I need a quiet word here." I motion towards Erek.

Sarah sighs. "Okay, but now." She leaves the room and closes the kitchen door after her.

"Let me speak with her, okay? I'll say nothing. Then we can continue with whatever."

He lowers into a seat and responds with a slow blink. His face looks paler than usual. If it's a shock for him, he can't begin to imagine how this is for me.

Pregnant?

This must be a mistake, but if some high-tech alien from the future says your pregnant, they may just be right. Or is this a ploy? What if this is how Erek grabbed the confidence of Leslie and Laura. But did they have an intimate relationship with a Koyorad? I can't process this now; Sarah is waiting.

"You're pregnant?" Sarah states as soon as I enter the kitchen and sit opposite her, though her tone is angry. She shakes her head, disapprovingly.

"This is stupid, Jayne. Who's that out there? Is he the father?"

Erek, the father?

"Now, you're stupid. No, he's not." I can't think fast enough to form excuses or logic. A moment ago, I was about to be Deleted. Then suddenly I'm going to be a mom?

"Then why are you talking to him about being pregnant?" Sarah asks.

Good point.

I bury my face in my hands. There are no tears to brush away, but I wish I could wipe away this day. Is this how my friends felt before they were Deleted? Did life suddenly become too much to face?

No, I can't believe that. I didn't know *VioletlyAlone* personally, but I know how Chloe, Leslie and Laura were. Getting pregnant in high school brings a lot of negativity and shame from those around you, but would they still welcome having everything wiped out, erased? But they didn't necessarily face this same dilemma. Pregnant isn't the only thing to cause upset. Erek could have told them anything which was personal to them and their situation.

But I don't want a baby, so why would he invent that? The last thing I want is to risk what happened with Matthew and the emotional fallout with Sarah. And for crying out, I'm in high school! I have my own life to live without some baby messing it all up for me. And especially not an alien baby.

"You didn't hear the context of what we were talking about," I offer.

"Context? Well when I walked in, he said something about a *secret* and then you said *I can't be pregnant...* I'll ask again, who is he? And what's it to him about you being pregnant?" Sarah asks, the muscles in her jaw tensing.

I lean back in my chair. "He's no one, just a friend."

"I'm not buying it," Sarah retorts. "When I walked in, the pair of you looked like you'd seen a ghost. What's going on, Jayne?"

Oh, not much. Alien visitors. My boyfriend's home address is a few hundred lightyears away. I'm pregnant with said alien's baby. Usual stuff.

"Nothing's going on—"

"You're lying. I know you too well," Sarah interrupts. "What is it? Why can't you tell me?"

"I need you to trust me," I say. "Firstly, I'm not pregnant, and I'll take a test to prove that, okay? And secondly... well, there is no second. I'm okay."

No second?

No time more like it. Life on Earth is running out of time, and all I can do is rummage for excuses with my sister. Her forehead is creased with concern, and I rest my hands on hers.

I can't save her from the catastrophe hurtling towards us in space, but I can protect her from Erek and the Deleters. There's no time to consider my options or say goodbye. Erek's waiting for me.

Her saddened eyes watch me, and I fight back the tears which want to choke out the truth. But this truth will Delete her. In a moment from now, she won't remember me and may even wonder why she was sat here, alone in the kitchen when I'm gone.

Forgotten.

What brought her here today? I don't ask; I don't want to know.

It's time for me to face my fate.

"Let me get rid of him," I say, nodding towards the lounge.

I stand and hug Sarah, where she sits. If only I could smother her in hugs and kisses and gasp my final farewells. For all my family, too.

Where's Aithen? Why isn't he here to protect me from Erek? What if he has already been Deleted? Just because I remember Aithen doesn't mean anything. I remember Chloe and my friends, too.

When I walk back into the lounge, Erek stands. Sarah's right, he does look like a ghost has jumped out in front of him. But then a thought stabs my brain. I am a ghost, we all are. We died thousands of years ago.

He stutters the words, "Jayne, I'm sorry, but I... this... I need to..." His words trail off as he scans his wrist again and seems to search my face for an answer.

What's that supposed to mean? He's sorry? But there is a pain in his expression. Is he having second thoughts about this?

But I chill, as Erek raises a hand, and I spot the bright object he is holding.

"No, wait...!" I utter. Please, I need more time. Give me a chance to exist for a few minutes more...

I flinch when a blue pulse shrouds me for just a second. No sound. No wave of energy. What has he done? My breath pumps out in gasps. I'm choking. My mouth is sticky, and I wipe the saliva from my cheek. I curse at him and shout at him to leave. I watch Erek exit through the door as I kneel. My weakening arms try to hold me up off the ground.

I hear Sarah enter the room. This is too much.

"Jayne?" Her shout fills the room. My head.

What is going on? This is not fair. I'm not supposed to be living this life. A darkening wave of tiredness envelopes me. My limbs fail.

I don't want to sleep.

I don't want to leave.

Please. Remember me.

CHAPTER THIRTY-TWO

Darkness. I can hear a muffled sound, but I don't know what it is or where its source is. I'm thirsty, but I don't know how to call out for it. I can't move, or can I? If I can open my eyes, I can find my way... to where? To what? I don't know. I'm holding my breath, but the darkness is stopping me from breathing, pressing its confines against my face. Smothering me in blackness. *Open your eyes. Breathe.* I'm shouting the words, but no, I'm not. Wake up.

Aithen.

I snap my eyes open, and Sarah is still holding me, but now we are a heap on the floor.

"Aithen?" I gasp for air and say his name out loud. My head swims as Sarah's face fades the clears again.

She looks at me, both worried and puzzled. "What about him?"

"You know Aithen?" I ask and can't mask the desperation from my voice. "Me? You know me?"

"Erm, yeah! You okay, you lost it for a moment then?" Her face cracks a smile, but tearful desperation shrouds her eyes.

I'm here. I remember everything.

Sarah sees me.

I heave a loud sob, and Sarah holds me, rubbing my shoulder with a thumb.

I wipe my eyes as I look at Sarah.

"Erek. He was here then. Where did he go?" I ask, bringing my focus together.

"Oh, that guy. He left straight away. Talk about making a sharp exit as soon as things got a bit messy. Who exactly is he?"

"How long was I out for?" I'm not deliberately avoiding her question.

"Seconds. But you went so limp. I thought… I don't know what," she says, squeezing me. She stands and grabs a glass, fills it with water and passes it. I gulp it down.

I'm so thirsty. I can't think clearly. I gulp down another glass of water and immediately remember why Sarah is here.

"I'm not pregnant." I raise an eyebrow and almost feel light-headed again.

She manages to rise the corner of her mouth, but no smile is coming.

"What am I going to tell Mom and Dad?"

"You know I'll support you, but honestly, are you nuts? You've known Aithen for three seconds. I'm guessing it is his?"

"I can't be. I'll get to the store and pick up a test." I gasp, and she strokes my hair.

"You're still in school; you can't be a mom this early. Just… get that test, and I want to know straight away."

My head is spinning, pondering a schoolgirl-mom for a moment. Dropping out of school? Forget trying for a part-time job; I'll be busy cooking a baby in my tum and not graduating. What a mess.

How am I going to work this out?

What happened to Erek? I could see the physical turmoil in his face. Why should he grow a conscience now?

And what about the flash? It didn't Delete me.

So why did he leave and does he realise I won't be Deleted?

Could he have stopped the pregnancy? For a moment, I hope it's true, I'm off the hook. But then I recall how much hardship Sarah went through to be a mother, and I feel guilty.

But she wants it.

She always did. I don't need this. Not now. There's no point.

Why bother raising a child when we have only two years to live?

"If you are pregnant, then you need a plan, Jayne. This is not the end of the world. Yes, it's going to be tough, but you have to finish school." She looks around the ceiling as though searching for ideas. "And don't think college is off the menu. I'll babysit."

I cough up a laugh and swallow more water. "Babysit? College?" I cough once more as the revelations of Earth's end pass through my thoughts like a dark cloud, casting shadows on any plans Sarah and I are discussing. She'll be an aunt for a little over a year.

"What if I am and... I don't want a baby?" I ask and immediately wish I could claw back the words when Sarah's expression darkens. I already know she is reliving that day: *the silence*.

Sarah opens her mouth, but no words form. She dips her head, and I hold onto her.

"I'm sorry," I whisper. "I wasn't thinking then."

Sarah sits back and wipes her eyes. She coughs a single laugh. "No, you're right. That's my thing to be a mom. I was selfish then."

"No, you weren't. To be honest, if I am pregnant, then I would never do anything to harm my baby. I know I'm a cold, heartless ass at times, but I'll be an amazing, cold, heartless ass of a mom." I laugh, and it's nice to see Sarah's smile make an appearance again. "But yes, you'll be babysitting twenty-four-seven, while I'm out there partying with my posse."

"Deal," she replies. "But first things first, get that test. It's all theory between now and then."

Considering I felt like I was at death's door a moment ago, my head is clear, and I feel energetic, restless. But I must process this later.

"I will in a minute," I say. "By the way, no, Lou?"

Sarah casts a glance to the side, remembering why she is here. "She's at home with Terry. But yeah, I had a bit of good news. I've got a part-time job, and it comes with childcare as standard."

"Really? Where?" I ask. This is excellent news.

"Centre nursery as an assistant. They'll train me up and get me certified and all that. It's perfect," she says.

I hug her. "Oh, well done, you."

"Could be useful, too," she smirks. "I'll get a staff discount for potential spouse children."

"Oh, very funny," I pull a face at her and leave.

"And Jayne… you could never be cold or heartless."

I've bought a pregnancy kit. I'm glad you can scan these yourself at the checkout. No questioning looks to contend with. No gossip to reach the wrong ears. Mom is hoovering downstairs while I'm hiding in the bathroom.

It's surreal. The small window in the plastic tube displays one word: *Pregnant*. How is this happening? It's impossible. But Erek detected I am.

What will he do? I wasn't Deleted, but he must tell his boss, the long-haired man. Or will he? Is Erek going to risk himself for me? Is being pregnant more important than discovering the secret of the visiting Koyorads?

The darker truth tears at me: Aithen's the father. Forget the how – I'm pregnant to a Koyorad, an alien.

The plastic tube slips to the floor as I push my face into an already damp towel, muffling my scream. Why is this happening?

Aren't things bad enough? My cell pings and I snatch it up, drying my face.

It's Aithen. "You free?"

My cell rings when I answer *yes*.

"Jayne, you're safe? You're okay?" His voice is shaky

"Where are you?" I ask, walking back to my bedroom.

"In the craft. I came to get you today, but I saw Erek arrive at your home. I'm sorry, Jayne, but I really let you down. I didn't know what to do. If I tried to intervene, the Meorlite would have paralysed me," Aithen explains.

"Paralysed? How?"

"It's a defensive measure for the Deleters. They can't Delete another Koyorad, but their Meorlite automatically stuns one of us via our own, should we try to attack them. He would have sensed my arrival, anyway, had I gotten any closer. I told you previously? That seventh parental sense?"

"A bit *Big Brotherish*," I respond. "That's awful. But yes, I'm still here."

"Then what happened? I thought he had gone there to Delete you?" Aithen asks.

He doesn't know.

I eye the clock, just gone seven. Everything I do feels like suspicion hangs onto it, but that's my paranoia again. Mom will be fine if I say I'm meeting up with Aithen.

I haven't messaged Sarah yet, about the pregnancy test.

"I think we'd better meet, Aithen."

CHAPTER THIRTY-THREE

No-one could ever tire of seeing the beauty of the Earth. Aithen has activated a whole wall panel of the craft to transparent, offering a spectacular view of white, candy-floss clouds and deep, blue hues of the Pacific Ocean.

I've deliberately not broken my *news* to Aithen. Not yet. I need a few minutes before I hit him with that bombshell. And we need to re-bond from our argument.

"I'm sorry for my overreaction," I say.

"Overreaction? Don't be sorry, Jayne. The fact you're holding it together, after all, has happened to you lately is way beyond what anybody could manage." I've missed his words and support, so much.

"I still don't know how to process everything. I think my brain has shut down and I'm operating on auto-pilot at the moment," I offer a smile, which he reciprocates.

"Take it one day at a time," he comforts. "And if that is too much, then just an hour. You've so much inner strength and strong will. I'm starting to wonder if you're the human here."

"Oh, funny. All I seem to do is cry lately," I say.

"Better to let the emotions flow. It's when you bottle it all up, those complications emerge," Aithen says.

Sitting next to him on the metallic, dimpled floor of the craft, I stroke his open palm with my finger. I love to touch him. To watch him. He exchanges a warm smile with me, and I kiss his hand. He strokes my hair.

I move closer to him and brush my lips against his.

Looking into his violet eyes, I can't help but notice an odd grid-like matrix within them. I first saw it when he took me into Earth orbit, but I dismissed it.

"Aithen. Do you wear contact lenses?"

"No. I'm assuming you can see a net or web type of construct?"

I nod, looking at his eyes.

"Yes, they are… how do I say? Optical translators."

My questioning frown is enough to make him continue.

"No matter what I read here on Earth, any language, my brain understands it." He smiles at my open-mouthed reaction.

"So, you pick up any book, anywhere on this planet and can read it?"

That's a good trick.

"I should also add that we never forget what we have read once. The retinal Meorlite also stores the reading material in the brain's memory, like a computer."

"Okay, that is weird," I laugh and kiss him again.

"You said you had something to tell me?" Aithen asks as we settle back again.

"Hmm... yeah…" Time to spoil this mood. "I may outdo anything you have told me."

Aithen raises eyebrows to that.

I wish I could speak at lightspeed and fast forward this conversation, up to where we've gotten over the shock and can remain calm and loving, in this peaceful bubble, orbiting in space. Safe from everyone.

First, I give a brief recap of Erek's visit yesterday, until the point he detected a Koyorad, somewhere in the house.

"His Meorlite scanned me when he was about to Delete me, or something like that. But then he... discovered I'm... I'm sorry, Aithen... but I'm pregnant."

Silence. He stares at me with widened eyes.

"Please, say something?" I ask.

"Woah!" Aithen sighs and combs his fingers through his hair. "Oh, no, Jayne. I wish... I wish I could congratulate you, and me, but this is... oh woah..." He stands and offers a hand which I take.

We sit in the console chairs.

"Erek said it can't happen?" I ask.

"That's true. But how did he take it? Once he realised?" Aithen asks.

"I think he was more in shock then me," I reply. "He looked scared. But then he fired a beam at me."

Aithen's eyes squint as though unable to comprehend what I have said, but then they widen knowingly. "A beam. Did you see it? You seem to see everything else of our tech."

"Yes, it was a blue pulse of light. I thought he had Deleted me, as I went limp and fainted." I hate describing my constant weaknesses. Crying. Fainting.

"Oh, wow," Aithen says. "Well, this is a first and very Erek. He follows the rules to the book."

"Why? What's he done?" I ask, not sure if I want to hear the answer. "I'm still pregnant, as I took a test and it's still positive."

"That you are. No, he hasn't altered that. But he's followed protocol. That blue beam is a Tryborre—"

"A try-what?" More alien technology?

"A Tryborre. Erek has protected the baby. And you, of course. It's standard practice on Korudaz. It doesn't change anything in your physical makeup, but you've just become quite invincible."

"Invincible? Okay, so now I'm a superhero?" I'm sure this is not the case.

"Not quite. You're not bullet-proof or anything, but you can now slow time in the event of danger," Aithen says.

"What? I can stop time like you can?" I ask. It's scary, but surely this is good.

"Not quite. I can stop it on demand, you don't have control over it," he says.

"I don't get it?" I ask.

"If I held a gun towards you and pulled the trigger, time would slow down such that you'd be able to step out of the way of the bullet. Or say a car is going to run into you, then the same thing. But you still have to take action. Stay put, and the bullet or car will hit you."

"Cool," I smile.

"But don't let it go to your head. You can still be hurt by stubbing your toe or whatever, but not from a punch or kick, that will cause the time to slow down," he says. Still, he's fidgety, running a thumb over the fingertips of the other hand.

"And there's something else?" I ask. "There's always a negative."

He nods slowly. "A huge negative, Jayne."

I cross my arms and wait for this new terror. I'm not a Koyorad, so I expect the Tryborre will kill me or other.

"The Tryborre is safe for you, it's a gift in fact. But the pregnancy…"

"Don't give me deliberate pauses, Aithen. Spit it out."

"Unless we do something drastic, and the fact Erek has detected the baby as a Koyorad, then that comes with the side-effects of such a pregnancy," Aithen explains. "Cut a long story short, it could kill you if we don't act quickly."

I sigh. "Oh, what else is new? Do you ever get the feeling fate wants me dead?"

Aithen takes my hand and kisses the back. "It does look that way. But I intend to cheat death and save you."

"I want to believe you, but what is this new threat?" I ask.

"Two things. First is an enzyme which if not isolated at the right time, will cause irreversible paralysis and kill you once the baby is born—"

"Wait, if I'm paralysed, how can I give birth?"

"It's different for Koyorads. The mother does not push during labour, the birth canal and baby do this in isolation. It's an autonomic thing, and the entire process has been changed in our modern-day medicine practices." Aithen pauses, and I nod to continue.

"You need to be placed in stasis the moment the enzyme is about to react—"

"Isn't this a set date in time, like at twenty weeks or something?" Seems obvious but Koyorads appear to have a habit of missing simple details.

"No, if that was true then I'd know exactly how long we have," Aithen replies. "There is no set day in the cycle. It will occur after eight weeks, but it could be any second after that."

I'm trying to figure out how long it has been since Aithen and I slept together.

I can't.

"But how am I pregnant in the first place? I'm on the pill and Erek said you're, *on the pill*, too?" I ask.

Aithen frowns. "I don't know. Maybe it only protects pregnancy in a species. When it comes to you, everything Koyorad-related is deflected. It's just a random coincidence, but I have no way of finding out why here, on Earth."

He raises a sheepish gaze towards me. It's strange to hear him refer to us as different species, but I know there's no spite in his words.

"Why don't I want to know what is behind that look?" I ask.

"We don't really know how much time you have before the enzyme kicks in... and it takes eighteen days to get from here to Korudaz—"

"I'm not going anywhere!" I shout but immediately reel in my reaction. "I can't just up and leave Earth. There must be something the doctors here can do? We're not totally living in the dark ages, you know?"

"I'm afraid you are," Aithen responds but raises his hands to put the breaks on to my intended response. "I will never speak bad of humans, but honestly, you are at least a century away from the big breakthroughs in science and medicine."

"Then why can't you Koyorads help us? Instead of by standing our extinction, why don't you do something useful?" I rest my forehead in my hands. "Why can't you share your knowledge, if only a tiny bit?"

"It's not allowed. If we revealed ourselves to Earth, imagine the backlash?" he says.

"But humans are mostly peaceful..." I think of the wars, riots, the mess this planet gets itself into. How would we react to an alien race?

"We've tried it before," Aithen says. "Many decades ago. A planet with a population slightly more advanced than Earth was considered hopeful for some sort of alliance. They had nothing to offer us, but we opened up to them. It took exactly three weeks before they launched an aggressive, military attack against our visiting fleet."

"And what did you do? Blow them away?" I ask, imagining a powerful fleet of Koyorad ships blasting cities and lives apart.

"Nothing. Our ships were protected from their weapons. So, we cloaked and left them to their pending doom," Aithen explains. He rubs his mouth.

"What doom?" I ask.

"Coincidentally, like Earth's. There are many potential hazards out in space. Intelligent life is often wiped out before anybody can discover it. They either destroy themselves with nuclear war or rock the size of a country does the deed."

We sit in silence for a moment.

Do I have the luxury to relax, ever? Earth is dark from this position. I pay little attention to where, but it is nighttime over the land down there.

"Eighteen days, to get to Korudaz?" I begin. "I thought you are hundreds of lightyears away? Shouldn't that take like, forever?"

"Yes, but our vessels are rather advanced, and we employ methods which few have ever invented, let along considered possible," Aithen replies.

"So, we're talking lightspeed and all that?" I ask.

"That and a whole lot more," Aithen says, with a tight smile. "It's not important," he adds.

I stand and lean against the flat surface of the interior, watching out the transparent panel. "So, eighteen days there. Secure this enzyme-thing. Eighteen days to get back. Let's call it forty days? Can't you do your time travel stunt and get me back here the same day we leave?"

Aithen's humph is loud. "No, you're not getting this, Jayne…"

I turn to face him.

"Once the Koyorad Kounsell…" he spells the word to elaborate the difference between it and *council*, "are alerted to this, and I'm sure they now have, there's no telling what will happen. You can flip a coin."

"Why do I get the feeling I'll call heads to a coin with tails on both sides?" I retort.

"Thankfully, it's not quite that unbalanced. There are two Kounsell factions: one military, the bad, and one intellectual, the good. The good outnumber the bad by a good seven-to-one, but… the most influential, scare-mongers, work for the military." Aithen motions me to sit again.

"It's the good Kounsell who encourage intelligent life exploration and left alone, they would gladly help other intelligent life.

"But it's the Military Kounsell who uphold and set the laws and regulations. Koyorads are naturally paranoid, and the military propaganda machine paints other life as a huge threat. They are very convincing," Aithen explains.

This all sounds so dark and distant and not relevant. But I have a Koyorad baby, growing inside me, right now.

"Two things?" I ask. "You said earlier there are two things? The enzyme is one?"

"Yeah, that," Aithen answers. "Koyorad pregnancy term is twelve months, but when the baby is born, it won't be a baby as you're used to."

Do I even want to know this?

"It will emerge as a toddler, similar in size to a two-year-old human child."

"How can anyone survive that?" I ask.

"Until about a thousand years ago, they didn't. Having a child was a living sacrifice for the mother. A life for a life," Aithen says, and his expression reflects my own.

This is awful.

"That's so stupid," I say. "Why bother?"

"To preserve the species. Might sound daft, but Koyorads think differently about certain things. And because our life expectancy is long, then people consider children at quite an old age," he says.

"How long do you live for?"

"The average is three-hundred years. We age annually, just like you do, but once we hit fifty, then we stop growing older physically."

"So, how come you kick the bucket at three-hundred?"

"Our brain and the nervous system slowly but surely fails. Even our super-technology cannot prevent that," Aithen says.

I blink and shake away this distraction. "This pregnancy, how do you stop the mom from dying?"

"That's the process which resulted in the Deleter tool. A combination of stasis and time travel. The baby and embryonic sack are teleported out of the host parent and grown externally to the mother. The mother is frozen in time – Deleted – and the baby develops and is born on the respective date." Aithen pauses as I'm sure he can see my eyes have clouded over. I could already be frozen here. "Then the baby is brought back in time, the mother reinstated and there you go, instant baby delivery." He opens his hands.

"And am I supposed to understand any of that?" I ask dumbfounded.

"No. As far as you are concerned, once the enzyme moment approaches, you will go to sleep and as far as you are concerned, wake up an hour later and have a baby," Aithen smiles.

"And what about all that paralysis and pushing stuff?" I ask. I can't get my head around this.

"There isn't any. That's the point," replies Aithen. "We stop the enzyme action. That is the key to all of this. That is the killer. And no, we can't take you back in time to the minute before the enzyme kicked in."

"Why not?" I ask.

"It's not considered needed, and more irritatingly, it's not allowed," he says.

"Oh, don't tell me, the Military Kounsell?"

Aithen nods. "Who else? It's written into the law as a safeguard just in case something like *this* happens." And he gestures towards him and me.

"I've got to ask, Aithen. Why did you do it? Why sleep with me if there's a risk?"

"There isn't, though," he says. "Honestly, it's impossible for you and me to *make* a baby."

"But I have," I cut in.

Silence embraces us once more. I can't help but wonder what Aithen is thinking? I'm scared thinking about the never-ending list of dangers hunting me down. It's like I can't take a breath without some peril tracking me down.

I can't believe I'm even thinking this, but it looks like I have only one option. The last thing I ever imagined I'd say. "I don't know how Koyorads feel about this, but at the end of the day, I'm a human and I'm the one who's pregnant. It's my choice."

I take a breath, let the peril begin. "I'm aborting the pregnancy."

CHAPTER THIRTY-FOUR

Aithen is silent for a moment, letting my words sink in. At least, I think that is what he's doing.

"That's brave of you, Jayne and if I were in your shoes, that's exactly what I'd want, but—"

"There's no *but*, " I interrupt. "I'm not leaving Earth and hurtling through space to have a baby on a planet which, by the sounds of it, doesn't care much for anyone but themselves." I'm on the offensive, and I will not let Aithen try and talk me out of this.

This is not a knee-jerk decision. The last thing I want to do is face Sarah and tell her I'm getting rid of the baby. But I'll be honest with her, and if she doesn't believe me, then that is her problem. I'd rather stay here, and her hate me, than jump in some alien ship and vanish for however long.

"Oh, Jayne. You must listen to me," Aithen pleads. "It will kill you. The enzyme will trigger the moment you try to hurt the baby."

"But you said—"

"Yes, that's when the pregnancy has passed eight weeks, but any action to terminate erupts the enzyme automatically." His words are breathy, and I know he's not lying. This is not an excuse to trick me. Aithen's eyes don't lie; they are tearful and desperate.

My shoulders droop, and I dip my chin. "This is unfair. Of all things, why this?"

"I'm sorry, Jayne. We can't even test for the enzyme here on Earth, to see just how much of a Koyorad pregnancy is evident here. There's no reason to have to do so. This has not happened before."

"Erek hinted relationships have happened before?" I ask.

"I don't know. But I am certain no human has gotten pregnant with a Koyorad. That would not be kept undercover for long." Aithen places his hands on my shoulders and gently pushes me into the seat. I straighten and try to smile.

"How does this affect you?" I ask. "Will they come after you now?"

"Who knows? Erek hasn't tried to contact me, but I have been in cloaked mode all the time. I need to get you to Korudaz..." He raises a hand to stop my interruption. "It's not safe for you or me on Earth. At least if we can get there, then I can appeal to the good side of the Kounsell. I am confident they will listen."

"And if they don't?" I ask.

"Then we'll... I'll... I don't know. I'll take a medical team hostage... I honestly don't know. I just feel I can trust them to fix this," he tries.

"What if *you* Delete me? Store me away on that genetic-digital-thing? That way I'm forgotten to everyone? I'm assuming you'd remember me. Can't you then approach the Kounsell and see if they will accept this?" It sounds so stupid.

"Huh. It's actually a clever idea and would work. Still, I'm not a Deleter," Aithen says, his eyes searching the space around us as he processes my words. "I can't even use the device. Nobody has ever tried to hack one to enable them to use it, so I'm guessing it can't be done."

"What about Erek? He didn't Delete me but instead protected me. Is there the tiniest chance he might help?" Am I really thinking of trusting my existence on Erek? The same individual who has erased my friends?

"I don't know if I can trust him, and especially not Jerellone. They may detain me and decide to leave you here to die. The chance of a biopsy discovering the enzyme is near to impossible. Its chemical structure does not exist on Earth. So, it'll be death by complications of pregnancy."

I press my palm to my chest, as though that will stifle the pain. I breathe slowly.

"But I'm not giving up on you, on us. I love you too much, Jayne. I don't care that we are alien to one another. This may sound daft, but you pregnant proves we are the same. And it shows we love each other to share the most intimate moment." He holds me and kisses my forehead, my cheeks, then my mouth.

"I love you, Aithen. I'm sorry all of this has happened."

He brushes the stray hair away from my face with his fingers. His eyes glisten, and the caring warms me, settles the pain in my chest.

"What is it you humans say? *If it were easy, everyone would do it*?" he offers a tentative smile.

I try to laugh, but it's a weak attempt. "How do we engage with Erek?"

"I'll need to decloak and wait for the message. If he is looking for me, then I'll receive it immediately." Aithen's hand hovers over a console panel. "Do you want to stay, or should I drop you off at home? I don't know if I'm going to have to make a run for it."

"You're joking?" I respond.

He's not, and his hand remains poised to decloak.

It's late in the evening, and I'm sure Mom will be wondering where I am? Yes, she knows I'm with Aithen, but I can't stay out all night. Unless we have to high tail it across the galaxy. I dismiss that ridiculous thought.

"I'm staying with you. Hit it," I say.

The interior turns amber, and I already hear the blood pounding through my ears.

Aithen issues a command in his language, and I shiver when I hear Erek's voice, over the ship's speakers. I understand none of it, so I pay attention to Aithen.

His gaze flicks towards me and back to thin air, as he listens to the garbled message. Erek's tone is authoritative and commanding, but Aithen's composure is a mix of tension and disbelief, maybe? His eyes clear and widen as he listens, punctuating Erek's words with some of his own.

The call ends, and the interior returns to the safe blue of cloaking.

"And?" I ask.

"It's good. For once, I've got good news," he says. "The Koun-sell have sanctioned your safety."

"Which one? The good or the bad?"

"Both. That's the thing they couldn't let this pass. This is a first for Korudaz. Possibly a universal-first." A weight has lifted, and he straightens, arching his torso backwards. He gives a pleasurable groan.

"What happens next? Are they going to send a medical team here?" I ask.

But he shakes his head. "No, I'm sorry, that is not part of the deal. But we must take this. There's simply no other option."

"Can I come back, to Earth?" I ask.

"Would you really want to? You know what is going to happen here?" he asks.

"My family is here, Aithen. I can't leave them here to die alone."

"But why can't you survive? Do you honestly believe your family would want you to sacrifice you and your baby when you have a chance to live?"

I run my fingers across my brow. Can I really leave them to die?

In all reality, they already have died; we all have.

How can I and my baby, be the last remaining Earth humans?

Am I this selfish?

What if meeting me and my baby could alter the thinking of the Koyorads? I could change their minds, present a case to save humanity?

Jayne: the last hope for humanity?

"When do we have to leave?" I ask.

"Tomorrow."

CHAPTER THIRTY-FIVE

It's the middle of the night, and I wander around my family home like I've done so many times before. Mom says I would often wake up as a young child, and she would find me asleep on the downstairs couch or on the kitchen floor. No blankets. A silly, tiny girl curled up in a ball. The image makes me smile as I could soon have a whole life of discovery with my own child.

My own child.

Every movie I watch, the pregnant girl looks at herself side-on in a mirror. I'm doing the same, but so far, nothing. No bulge. I'm only a few weeks in, but should I be showing yet? Aithen said the growth will be exaggerated. Truthfully, I don't want to have a big stomach, but I at least want to see an indication – besides a pregnancy test – which tells me I'm pregnant. I'm sure my opinion will change once I see the bulge.

I'm so tired and should at least try to sleep.

I also need to visit Sarah in the morning.

How do I say goodbye, without uttering the words?

If I leave Earth and travel all the way to Korudaz, they're not going to let me go. Aithen hasn't said as much, but I'm not stupid. My baby will be a big deal to them. Or will it? What if they see this as a monster? A genetic mishap? I shiver, as the thought had not dawned on me.

Regardless of all this, I won't take this lying down. I must find a way to engage with the Kounsell. Is my baby the key to this?

I walk past the open door of Emily's bedroom. As usual, she's sprawled across her bed, quilt cover kicked aside, and her pyjama bottoms rolled up as she gets hot during the night.

I smile as I watch her exhausted looking face. Emily always looks like she has run a marathon when she sleeps as she is *out for the count*. Her fingers are twitching from a dream. She gives a deep breath then settles into quiet sleep again.

If I don't try, I won't see her grow up. It's bitter and sad. I wish I could explain to her why I'm about to disappear. I'm not doing this out of selfishness, but the goodbye will be too much for her. For everybody. If only I could explain, I'll be okay, and they should not worry about me.

But she'll be fine. I recall the advice she gave me when Iain and I split.

When you've been holding somebody's hand for a while, and they leave, then wash your hands carefully and think about washing away how their hand felt in yours. Then your hand will be clean, fresh, and ready for a new hand to hold onto.

She's smart and ahead of her years.

It's not fair.

But I can't accommodate my own pity or sadness; my head is occupied by so many thoughts of a journey to some distant nowhere. A planet filled with a race which isn't human. I'll be the alien. Is it possible there are others, other humans? Probably not.

To think going to the Moon was huge, but how terrifying is it to leave my own world behind as a distant memory? Everything here will be ancient history when I touch foot in Aithen's world.

Any person on this planet would want to experience this, but they wouldn't want to sacrifice their whole existence? The voice in my head argues: there's more than me to consider here. I have a baby waiting to be welcomed in my life, but it pains me to think my family here may never meet him or her.

This is a time for family, and the baby should be part of my wonderful family. I am not going to only lose a family, but they will lose a daughter; a sister; a *grand-something*.

David is a light sleeper, so I don't sit on his bed. Instead, I sit on the floor at his door and watch him sleeping. I want to scream out the truth. Wake them all up right now and tell them what is happening.

I flop onto my bed and welcome the cool pillows.

Forget the rules, I'm leaving a note behind. I can't just disappear and not tell my family; I won't put them through that.

Deep blue, early morning light seeps through the curtains in my bedroom. I place three pillows on top of one another as a comfortable rest. Reaching into a bedside cabinet drawer, I take out a notepad and pen. Settling back into the pillows, what do I write?

How do I say goodbye without mentioning aliens and the possibility my family won't ever see me again? The notepad rests on my stomach.

But I'll come back.

My eyes are so heavy.

Mom, Dad, Sarah, Emily, David. I'm safe. I'm coming back...

I must write...

I need you to know...

CHAPTER THIRTY-SIX

What did I do last night?

My head swims, and I could be hungover from a good night out with the gang. My room is dark, still in the middle of the night.

No, it was morning when I went to bed.

I bolt awake. Where am I?

Pressing a palm to my forehead, I scan the room around me. Featureless, grey walls enclose the silent, chilled room. What the…?

The bed under me is soft and rubbery but has no sheets or my lovely, comfy duvet. A thin, black sheet covers me. Surprisingly, it is warm to the touch.

I place my feet tentatively upon the smooth floor, as I breathe in an aroma of warm metal, like copper. It can't be…

They wouldn't…?

Approaching a large, square panel, the dim room lightens, and the panel splits and slides in opposite directions. I immediately flinch at the object hovering in front of me and cower further still as a huge siren bellows, like a deep, warped horn of a tractor-truck, sending my hands to my ears.

I squint at the grave, angry red object. A stretched pyramid, at least three metres in length and a metre wide at the base. The sharp endpoints menacingly at my face and I am suddenly immersed in a grid of red laser beams; up, down then left and right. A pulsing pitch accompanies the scanning.

The machine delivers the same aggressive, warped horn, and I don't know whether to run or scream or what?

A voice shouts a command at the object. Despite the fear clouding my senses, I know that voice, albeit not the words said.

It's Aithen.

"Raise your hands, like you would on Earth," he says, calmly to me.

I raise my shaking hands to level with my head, palms forward; Aithen does the same.

The red object scans me again and delivers a warped, pulsing tone that chills my core. Aithen slides in front of me, keeping the arms raised posture, and the machine scans him, too.

Another blast of the horn and the object pulses red laterally along its length, but then the red pulses wash to white then dismiss altogether.

I dare not move a muscle, as I follow Aithen's lead.

The corridor outside of the room is as bland as the room itself, except large pipes and cables run the length of the walls and ceiling. There are no other Koyorads around.

Aithen lowers his hands and turns towards me and motions me further into the room. The wall closes behind him.

I gasp as I drop my hands and collapse sitting onto the bed.

"What the… was that?" I choke on the words.

Aithen offers a small, glass bottle to me. "Drink this. It'll take away your sickness."

I snatch it lazily from his hand and swallow the acidy-tasting liquid. My stomach groans but the solution is fast working. My head already clears, and with it, the pain.

"That is a Deyloron. They are the Koyorad police," advises Aithen.

"So, we're under arrest?" I ask.

"No, it is here to guard you and monitor you. When a Koyorad is pregnant, they are assigned a Deyloron, which will monitor you for the enzyme point," Aithen explains.

I take a few more breaths. "Why am I here, Aithen? Why have I been taken before I could say goodbye?" I raise my hands when he reaches for me. "Don't."

"This is not my doing," he says. "No way would I want this. Honestly, Jayne, I intended to be with you and support you when leaving Earth."

"Then who has done this to me? This is abduction!" I shout. "I was coming to your stupid planet anyway. How can they do this to me?" My eyes sting with tired anger.

Aithen sighs and rests against a table. "The Military Kounsell have gotten involved. We're on a military vessel."

"Military? They couldn't send a medical ship, but can send this?" I ask.

"No, that's the thing. This was already here," Aithen replies. "But it begs why? There's no reason for the military to have any presence around Earth. From what I'm seeing, there appear to be four of these."

"So, it's a battleship or equivalent?" I ask.

"Yes, but more a small cruiser than a full-on destroyer. But it still shouldn't be here." Aithen's expression is worried and taut. He keeps clenching his fists, and his eyes are vacant, as he processes an inner monologue.

I can't decide if I'm more angry than sad. "How could they, Aithen? All I needed was one day: not even a full day. I wanted to see Sarah. But I also wanted to leave a note. Just something to stop them worrying about me."

"But that's the thing. The note could have caused more harm

than good—"

"So? They're all dead, aren't they?" I snap and force down a gag in my throat. "I wasn't going to mention this…" I swipe a hand around me. "I just wanted to let them know I'll be safe."

"I'm sorry, Jayne," he says, quietly.

I rest my elbows on my knees. "How come you had to raise your hands at that red drone thing?"

"The Deyloron? So, it could scan me and see I'm not a danger. If it thought I was, then it would paralyse me through my Meorlites."

"What is it with Koyorads and paralysis?" I ask.

"It's effective," he replies. "Thing is, a Deyloron is authorised for deadly force. It's not just an angry drone. It is judge, jury and executioner all in one box."

I rub my forearms. "That thing is so scary. And that noise it makes?"

"Yeah, you can't ignore it," Aithen says.

"And it's going to be babysitting me now?" I ask.

"Most of the time, yes. It doesn't need to be inside the same building as you but be assured, it will be close by. It's there for your safety," advises Aithen.

"Why do I feel like it's there to spy on and imprison me?" I reply.

"This is not how I saw any of this going," Aithen says.

"Are we in orbit? Can I at least take a last look at Earth?" I exhale loudly.

"I'm sorry, Jayne. You've been asleep for a few days." He closes his eyes and waits for my onslaught, but I can't fathom this out.

"Did Erek do this? Is he here?" I ask.

Aithen shakes his head. "He's still on Earth but will follow soon enough. This has been sanctioned by the Kounsell, this is their doing."

"They already hate me and have no consideration for how I feel or what I want," I say and punch the rubbery bed mattress. "How dare they touch me when I slept. And who do they think they are?"

Aithen sits beside me. "I'm probably the last person you want this close, but I still have to protect you. No matter how awkward the Military Kounsell make this, they aren't the majority."

"No, but they seem to be pulling all the strings. They've stolen me from my world. My family. My life." My tears warm chilled cheeks. "Three days, you say? How far are we from Earth?"

The change in Aithen's breathing indicates this is unwelcome news. "We left the Earth's solar system on the first day."

I scrunch my eyes at the thought, but further still, the painful idea my family will be distraught at my disappearance. What are they going through? How is Mom consoling Emily and David? They cried every day when I went away with the school for a week's field trip.

Picturing their sad little faces, I bawl into Aithen's shoulder. He wraps me in his warm arms and rocks me gently. I wish I could have seen Sarah. I've been her safety net and she mine, but she has Terry; he'll love and keep her safe.

I take the slightest comfort in knowing Dad is safe and I'm sure at home, but they've lost me forever, and I them.

There's not a chance I can return to Earth. Who was I kidding?

It takes a military vessel like the one I'm in to travel the vast eternity of space. Somehow, I'm not hijacking one of these, especially with those red drones, the Deyloron guarding me and everything.

I pull away gently from Aithen's embrace and offer a thankful smile.

Looking around the dull room, I ask, "This is my cell, then?"

"No, just a restroom. You'll be kept away from the crew—"

"What, in case I attack them?" I quip.

"Yes, exactly that," he responds.

I dip my chin. "I was joking."

"One thing you need to understand, Earth humans are considered a danger. A very violent race, as far as Koyorads are concerned," Aithen says.

"A danger? Then why visit Earth?" I ask.

"Why do people visit a wild pack of lions on a safari?" he says.

I manage to smirk at that. "Now we're lions?"

"To Koyorads, yes. The crew are nervous about your presence. Now I know humans are mostly safe, but the few spoil it for everyone else. I have been *instructed* to manage your medication and transition processes," he explains.

"Transition processes? Do I even want to know what that means?" I ask.

"Don't be alarmed, but you'll be sleeping a lot for this journey. Your body can't be exposed to the Korudaz atmosphere without enhancement. In the same way, any lifeform can't enter Earth's bacteria realm without some major genetic modifications. You need to be *altered* to be able to survive on the planet," Aithen explains.

The thought of sleeping is welcome. The less I experience this hell, the better.

"And you're allowed to do this alteration?" I ask.

"I'm not a medical person, but the process is done by machines. We use such things for most of our medical procedures. All I have to do is press a few buttons, and off you go."

"A minute ago, I was a lion, now I'm a TV-dinner in a microwave?" I quip.

I forgot what his smile looked like. "Funny. At least you packed your sense of humour."

"That's a thing, do I have anything from home with me? I didn't get the chance to pack anything," I ask.

"I'm sorry, but not much. They grabbed a few items of clothing and a washbag from the bathroom—"

"They packed my toothbrush?" I can't believe this.

Aithen hands me a small, waterproof bag. "I wasn't allowed to be there when you were… taken. They issued a squad to bring me in and… I can't apologise enough, Jayne."

My family will wonder why I've left most of my clothes. My bag has my wallet in it. My cell will be on the drawer next to my bed. I'll become a mystery and cold, authority in the shape of law enforcement will investigate my disappearance. They may even accuse my family of a cover-up.

I sigh, rummaging through the bag. Toothbrush and paste. A few hair ties. A small bottle of scent and a travel-size bottle of mouthwash. "It's not your fault."

"I'm afraid it is," Aithen says. "I should have left you alone. What if I did fall for you? We're told to stay away; don't get involved. But I did."

"It takes two, remember," I reply. "I could have ignored you, the same way I did with every other boy in school."

Do I regret Aithen? I don't know. Falling in love should not end your life and find yourself charging through space to another planet. It all seems ridiculous. I mustn't focus on this.

"You said a change of clothing? What?" I ask.

"Nothing flattering. Think of a one-piece, pilots jumpsuit? And cotton-like shorts for underwear. Koyorads don't wear briefs," Aithen says.

"Great. So where is this other room that I'll be sleeping and treated?"

"This vessel has eight decks, so we have one to ourselves. Mostly filled with storage compartments, but there is a viewing area, not that there's much to see out there." Aithen motions towards space.

"Lead on. I'm getting claustrophobic in here," I request.

Aithen stands. "Brace yourself, the Deyloron will be waiting for us outside."

CHAPTER THIRTY-SEVEN

I imagine stars and planets passing by like the buildings when I travelled by train. All I see is the blackness of space, a few stars in the distance. I recall reading you can't see stars when in space – not correct.

I love to travel, but this?

We're travelling at ninety-per-cent lightspeed, but there are no swirly cloud tunnels of light around us. No echoing engines to enhance the speed. Just the forever blackness of space.

I'm not in the mood to talk, but Aithen suggests I do some light preparatory study of Korudaz. Browsing through various projected screens, I discover Koyorads follow lifetime careers reflected by their eye colour. But there is a lot more to it all than a pigment colour. On Earth, we make a lot of reference to the eyes, becoming the doorways to the soul? Well, on Korudaz, they have found that, despite any effort to influence a Koyorad, their eye colour reflects their social standing, career suitability and personality.

Raising my gaze towards Aithen, I can categorise him as a *Kurzite,* due to his violet eyes. What colour eyes will my child have?

Food comes in the form of a smoothie for want of a better

description. It's cold and tasteless but apparently packs everything I could possibly need in the nutrition department. Desert is three tablets, which I will regularly take as part of my *transformation* process.

The primary aspect of this is the raised bed-station I now stand at. Brushed metal frame with a dark, spongy mattress. There are no visible controls.

"So, I lay down on this?" I ask and Aithen joins me. "I've only just woke up. I'll never sleep."

He runs a hand over a blank section of the frame, and an array of screens and panels appear, accompanied by a low-pitch hum.

"Yes. Lie down, and I'll commence the procedure," he requests. "It'll help you to sleep."

"Only you'll be in here in this room?" I ask.

"Yes, I can promise that," he says. "There's no lid or glass screens, so nothing to become unsettling. An invisible forcefield will surround you and contain the process."

"And I'll sleep?" I ask.

"Yes. You'll sleep deeply for the next week, but the system will feed and monitor you." He watches me. What is he thinking? How did we get here, all the way from a Monday morning psychology class?

"A week seems so long, but I need to be away from *this*." I look around us. "Just don't let them do anything more to me, please?"

"Honestly, I promise, Jayne. I've already let you down. Never again."

I watch Aithen as I lay there, feeling awkward, angry, and fidgety. I'll never sleep.

He taps away at thin air, warm air surrounds me, and the hum deepens pitch. The thumping in my chest calms like someone has turned the pressure off. Am I even breathing? A wave of calm ebbs through my muscles, and it's like the bubbling anger evaporates away.

So tired.

I manage to turn my gaze to Aithen and although I can't hear the words, I read his lips. Those beautiful, soft lips: *I love you…*

I wake with a start. Where am I? *What's this?* There are sucker-like pads on my forehead, back of hands, and shins.

How long have I been out? There are no clocks here.

I try to sit upright, but my head swims, and my head falls heavily onto the bed.

"Take it easy," says a calm voice, and Aithen presses a palm lightly to my forehead.

I can barely focus on him. I blink repeatedly, but my vision remains blurred. My throat is dry, and I try to croak out a word, but I can't. I point to my throat.

"It's okay. Lay back for a minute and let me take you fully out of stasis," he says.

The air around me begins to chill pleasantly, and I can hear my breathing. I clear my throat and cough. I blink continuously until I can make out precise details of Aithen's face. Gasping slightly, I need to sit up.

Aithen helps me rise and propped against his shoulder, he offers a glass of water. "Sip only. Don't gulp," he offers.

I try and cough against a salty-sweet tasting liquid. "Urgh. That's horrid," I remark.

"It'll help quench your thirst but also stop you taking liquids too quickly," he says.

I manage to drain the glass, and Aithen passes me a second. "This one is less harsh, and the third will be pleasant."

Coughing through my words, I say, "Thank you, doctor Aithen."

I peel off the pads and place them together on the bed.

"Welcome back. You've been out for quite a while," Aithen says with a smile.

"Really, how long?"

"Ten days."

"No way. I thought it was just a week?" Anxiety chases away the calm in my head and chest.

"It took longer than expected to make you Korudaz-ready," he says.

I frown. "I wish I could be excited about this, but I can't. I used to dream of this. Alien life. Otherworlds. But this is lightyears from my hopes."

"Reality tends to be the destroyer of dreams," Aithen reflects.

Turning towards him, "You getting philosophical on me?"

"No, just had a lot of time to think. It's strange how I spent the best part of my trip travelling to Earth researching you and thinking about you. Then the last ten days watching you."

"How has this compared with your dreams about me?" I ask.

"I wish... I wish I were human," he falters. "To have met you as an everyday person. And to love you without bringing fear or danger to you."

His eyes well-up and I wrap my arms around him.

"You're better than any dream I could have ever thought up," he continues. "I didn't exist until I met you, Jayne."

My smile greets the tears which hug the corners of my mouth. I kiss him. "Oh, I love you, too. I know I'm a mess and angry and everything. But you, I love you, no matter what. And I'm glad you're not a human. You're my Aithen."

"And I love you," he replies. "We're in this mess together. I know it seems impossible and scary. But we have each other. So, we'll take each hour together."

He reaches for the third glass and offers it to me. "Right let's get you up and ready. Not that there's much to do, but I have something new to show you."

I'm sat on the bed, towel-drying my hair. The shower system here is odd. You step in and step out and feel damp but clean. There's no water, just a mild humming sound with a scented fine mist, which lasts a minute and you're done. They also have dry shower systems, so these not only clean you but also the clothes you are wearing.

Opting for the dry shower, I don't want to wear one of the jump-suits yet and simply want to retain an ounce of my identity in the clothes I wear.

I miss the soothing sensation of warm water. On Earth, I could stand there in a shower for ages and simply wash away the day and bad thoughts. Sometimes I'd sing when the mood was right. But that's certainly not here.

"What are you watching?" I ask, noticing the screen Aithen sits at has a digital, swirling pattern with lots of symbols and lines pointing to various points within the rotating image.

"Best if you see it for real," he says.

The wall shimmers slightly and clears but remains a smoky, grey colour.

What am I even looking at?

Out there in the vastness of space is an incredibly bright circle of light. The inner edges appear to curve inwards, like the fingers of flames being sucked into a foreverness, but immediately disappear into a void of inky black.

On a planetary scale, I can't imagine how big the ring of light is. But compared to Earth and the Moon, they are a tiny speck of dust in comparison.

"Wh-what is that?" I stammer.

"A black hole."

"You're kidding me?" I ask, kneeling and run a finger over the transparent panel. The surface is vibrating strongly, I withdraw my hand.

"The panel is vibrating," I say, and it's now I feel a similar buzzing running through the floor below me. I press on the ground and raise a questioning raised eyebrow towards Aithen. Every few seconds, I feel a tingling pulse run through my lower stomach, like when you drive over a humpback bridge on the road. I retract my hand, pressing my abs to soothe the sensation.

"Yes, exactly. Not much travels through a void, but a black hole's signature certainly does. You're feeling micro-gravities on an exponential level," he explains. "A *black hole* is a light accelerator, which—to cut a long story short—translates to a time-travel engine."

So, this is how the Koyorads do it: travel through time.

"Wait a minute, are *your* black holes actually wormholes in space?"

"No," he replies. "Wormholes are the result of light speed displacement. In simple terms, they are the opposite of a black hole. A wormhole takes you back in time, black holes forward."

"Oh, I thought so." I smile. Of course, I don't know.

"So, a black hole. You're telling me this because we need to point the ship the other way?" I ask. Shouldn't we be shouting and panicking now?

"No," smiles Aithen. "We'll be passing *through* one."

CHAPTER THIRTY-EIGHT

What's it like to fly through a black hole? Loud. Terrifyingly loud. Like a million mirrors shattering all at once. With it came a stabbing sensation of tiny needles, coursing throughout my body.

I was drowned in darkness, blind to everything around me. Unable to see anything, I thought our time was up. Aithen had forgotten to warn me about it and once more, I'm waking up to see his worried face.

I'm so pathetic. All I seem to do is cry or faint or act as a weak person. Had you asked me to describe myself a few months ago, I would have defined myself as a strong woman who could be a warrior. Drop me in a desert, and I'd survive by feeding on lizards and digging up the roots of cacti. After recent events, I doubt I could survive a mile from the mall.

I rub my stomach. "Will the baby be okay after that?"

"Yes, don't worry. Scary as it is, the Deyloron continues to scan you and the baby. If there was a problem, we'd know immediately." Aithen helps me out of the straps from the chair I sit in. He has a nervous flicker in his eyes. *What's up?* I don't want to ask. I'm afraid to know the answer.

Aithen hands me a tissue as blood is running from my nose.

"I'm sorry again, Jayne. We need to be so careful. I forgot about the potential effects of the black hole on you."

I dab at my nose and flinch at the deep, red bloodstains on the tissue. "I'm falling apart," I say. "It's okay. I'll survive."

His frown meets my words as I scan around me. Is the room darker? All the monitors are off, and the lighting is more like a shimmering glow. It can't be actual light; it won't exist at light-speed; oh, my brain is warped.

My reflection catches in a mirrored panel, and wow, my eyes are angrily bloodshot. I really am a mess.

There's silence in the room and adrenalin flows through my veins. It's uncomfortable like a nervous itch in my blood. The buzz in the floor has gone, and this calm is unnatural.

"Jayne. You need to see this." Aithen holds his hand out, and I sit beside him. His look is telling, eyes cast down, then to me, then back to the blank console screen. I know the familiar look of unwelcome news.

Aithen enables the monitor. I'm dumbstruck, numb. I gasp and collapse further into the seat opposite to the monitor.

Time since leaving Earth orbit: 10,019 years.

I place my throbbing head in my hands.

There are no words for this.

I'm not angry. Not in shock. More, it's an emotional cocktail of mixed feelings. It's not like I didn't know about this. Earth was destroyed over ten-thousand years ago, in terms of Korudaz time zone. It all made little sense. The reality is so cold.

My family are long gone. Everyone on Earth wiped out. But what did I think would happen? That I could change anything?

For the first time, a seed of doubt sprouts to mock my hidden hopes. How do I expect to return to Earth? How can I be so stupid? I can't fly a ship like this through a black hole and navigate myself ten-thousand years to Earth. I'm so naïve. Pathetic and stupid.

It's odd, but I have barely shed a tear over the past couple of days. Maybe I've resigned myself to this existence, I don't know. It could be the transformation process I had also removed my sense of loss, sadness, caring? None of this makes sense.

It could be this cold, grey, featureless military vessel I am trapped inside of, draining away all potential empathy for anything.

Most of the time, we sit in silence. I'll stare vacantly through the transparent panel or browse screens describing Korudaz and its neighbouring moons and stars. Aithen busies himself with whatever he's looking at. He's still concerned about the Korudaz military in Earth's orbit. If he has any conspiracy theories, he's not sharing them.

Oddly, I am on this cruiser with twenty other Koyorads, but I've not seen the crew. One of the medical team did attend during my sleeping session, but I don't want to think about that.

How did they feel seeing an Earth alien asleep on their vessel? Is there any wonder or curiosity in us as a species? Aithen says there is enormous interest from the overruling Kounsell, but I'm not buying it. You don't allow a whole planet to be wiped out once you discover how it happened. One thing I am confident of, the Koyorads must have the technology to prevent such an apocalypse.

What if it did happen thousands of years ago? The fact the Koyorads continue to visit Earth must mean something. It all doesn't make sense.

But for me, personally, no matter how this is dressed up, I've been abducted; taken against my will.

I don't have a plan, but the sooner I arrive at Korudaz and assess any feasible options, I intend to pounce on them.

Aithen sits next to me on the floor. "How are you doing?"

I shrug. "Don't know. I'm numb."

"I don't know what the routine will be when we arrive at Korudaz, but I am confident we will be kept together," he says.

"How can you be sure? I'm not getting the feeling there will be a red-carpet welcome for me," I say.

"It will be a covert arrival," Aithen says. "I'm being kept in the dark about everything, too. This is a military crew, and they're not the most approachable. From what I've managed to glean from the few, they've been away from Korudaz for the best part of a year."

"A year? Orbiting Earth?" I ask.

"Apparently so," he replies. "And that is very odd. I feel a nervous tension from the crew. Not something I am familiar with."

"Could be space dementia or claustrophobic?" I offer. I remember something about this in a movie I watched.

"Could be," he says, his gaze peering into the darkness. "But it'll be nice for you to meet some nicer Koyorads."

I smile. "Aren't you the only one?"

"No, the majority are pleasant, and I think you need to see the other side of the Koyorads. Deleters aren't the best introduction to Koyorads," he returns my smile.

"I think those Deyloron are the scariest thing from your world," I say.

"Yes, they take some getting used to I'm sure. But there's one Koyorad I am looking forward to introducing you to," Aithen says, grinning.

"And that is?" I ask.

"My sister, Akeirlah."

CHAPTER THIRTY-NINE

"This is the first time you've mentioned a sister? Talk about keeping secrets. Any brothers or other family members I should know about? Pet dragon, maybe?" I ask, nudging him. It's nice to imagine a friendly face of a family member.

"No, just the one sibling," he says.

"Is she older or younger than you?" I ask.

"Older by four years, but she looks younger," he says. "I'm confident you'll find her a lot more pleasant Koyorad."

"Wow. This is nuts but good," I say. "How long do we have to go before arriving?"

"Any time now actually. We're going to come out of high-speed travel so the ship will go into secure lockdown." Aithen offers me a hand, and we return to our seats. The viewing panel solidifies again, and the interior becomes blue.

"Cloaking?" I ask.

"Safety measure," Aithen replies.

"From whom?" I ask. Aithen mentioned about other intelligent life on twenty or so planets? Do alien races rage war upon one another? "Is Korudaz at war with another planet?"

"No, but as I've said before, Koyorads are very paranoid," he remarks.

A buzzing sensation stirs in my stomach and travels up to my chest. My breath comes in pants, and I forcefully slow my breathing. Aithen places a hand on mine, which grasps the armrest of my seat.

"What should I expect when we arrive on the planet?" I ask.

"Secrecy. This is all going to be hushed—"

"No, I mean the planet and Koyorads. Is anything going to seem odd or very alien to me?" I interrupt. I've read a lot, but a lot of it has evaporated away from my thoughts.

"You won't see much, as we'll be landing in a nighttime zone. Just stay close to me and let's play this one out, step by careful step," he says.

"Will they place us in a prison cell or similar?" I ask.

"No. I realise things are isolated on this vessel, but don't let this bother you. You'll be okay," he comforts. "Right, prepare yourself."

The large panel clears.

My jaw drops.

I still remember seeing Earth for the first time and how beautiful and blue it was…

Korudaz!

It's right in front of our view and… it's enormous!

I see blue and purple; green and brown.

There are white clouds and landmass. Actual land on another planet. A world of Koyorads.

"Korudaz has a single ring?" I ask.

"Not quite. It was constructed by us; it is a collection of crafts which are linked together to form a protective, cloaking screen. We are invisible to anyone who may be looking."

Who could *be looking?* This paranoia must have a cause.

It is amazing. I can see the mining planetary moon of Neflorone and one of the stars – no idea which one – in the distance.

"And the water, is it blue or purple?" I suppose something should be weird about an alien planet.

"Blue only. The purple you can see is vegetation growth. Our predominant plant life has shades of green or purple on the land and green in the seas."

Interesting.

I'm buzzing, and I can't sit down. We are getting so close now, and I can see other craft out in space. A voice fills the room, though I still don't understand a word of it.

"What's your language called? Does it have a name?" I ask.

"What is the name of the language you speak here? Is there only one or more?"

"Khwutgh," Aithen says, tapping at a screen.

"Coat? Coat-the?" I ask, trying to copy what he said.

He spells it for me like that helps, but yes, it's called *Khwutgh*. "The leading sound is like the throaty sound, '*gh*' in lough. So, k-gh-oh-ten," Aithen explains. "Some say it like *coat-en*, depends on where you live on the planet."

"Coten will do for me," I say and make a mental note to self. "Is that your global language, or are there more?"

"Just the one language on Korudaz," he replies. "That's what makes Earth quite interesting; so many languages."

I'm transfixed by the number of vessels out there. There are hundreds of lights travelling at various speed.

"We need to buckle up as we are having an escort ship bring us in," Aithen says.

No sooner he says it, a large, grey, and menacing craft is on the right side of ours. There is no mistaking the purpose of that vessel; it's a military battleship from its appearance. I could swear I see large guns pointing at us.

"Hands up?" I ask.

"You're a human, and I'm sorry, but that translates to a dangerous entity as far as Koyorads are concerned," says Aithen.

"Yeah, you say that, but what am I going to do? Deliver a stern look?" I reply.

"Humans are one of the few alien races who would wage war on one another. They are considered by many as the most dangerous race of all time."

"Seems a bit unfair. We come in peace." I smile back at him. "What about the other intelligent life on other planets, are they all peaceful and loving?"

"Mostly yes," Aithen says. "Some have no interest whatsoever in space exploration, and yet they have the capability. Two have raged war on each other, but quickly realised they were at a stalemate."

This is fascinating. "And you've visited these planets?"

"Only two of them. The friendliest is also the most densely populated. It's a planet smaller than Earth but with double the population. The issues on that planet are resources," Aithen explains.

I can't imagine these other worlds, but I'm sure I'll learn more about them.

But now it's time for me to visit an alien planet.

Or if I turn this around in my head, time for an alien to visit Korudaz.

CHAPTER FORTY

I can't stop staring at the armed guard.

The gun he carries is enormous and it's pointed straight at Aithen and me. He is flanked on either side by a Deyloron. His body armour and overall height are menacing.

This is ridiculous.

Armed guards. Killer drones and a warship big enough to take on a country and wipe it out, all for one Earth human?

We're descending to the planet in a small vessel, similar in appearance to the one Aithen had on Earth, but this holds up to a dozen passengers. The pilot has not turned to regard us once, and the guard is the only other passenger besides us two.

I want to appear calm, but the hostile reception is chilling.

The guard considers me with brown, *Koryed* eyes, and they are bright. I try to smile, but he doesn't give me the impression he's open to niceties. I heave a sigh.

The interior washes orange and a hissing sounds accompany the opening of the craft's doors. The guard utters something to us, and Aithen stands. I attempt to do the same, but wow, my body could have a hundred weights tied to it.

Aithen links an arm through mine. "Different gravity remember," he says.

I did cover this in my *research*. The planet is pulling me down, and walking, standing even, is tiring. The gravity here is stronger than on Earth, but I didn't imagine this.

But I've set foot on another planet. It's exhausting, but I'm here, walking through featureless corridors on a distant world. The guard takes the lead, and the two, silent Deyloron follow, hovering aggressively behind us. I can't stop myself casting a cautious glance at them as we progress.

If only I could be outside. Grab some fresh air after days of confinement.

We enter a large hall which houses shelves of engine parts and all manner of boxes. The Coten language script hides the secret contents within. It reminds me of a mixture of Arabic and geometric shapes.

Our footsteps echo the open space, and we approach a table where two uniformed Koyorads sit. Both have the same brown, *Koryed* eyes as the guard. Brown eyes must establish a career path for the military. It's strange how this can define your future on this planet.

What is different is these two Koyorads have a gossamer shimmer to their skin. It doesn't glow, but it's like looking at someone through fuzzy glasses. A forcefield maybe? I'll ask Aithen when I get the chance.

There's a lot of Meorlite scanning and conversations around me, but I let the aliens get on with it. What else am I going to do? Complain and catch the next flight home, flicking my scarf over my shoulder as I go? No, maybe not – need to get a scarf first.

My washbag is placed in a clear box. They'll probably incinerate it as a potential source of germs. The innocent rabbit design on the side urges me to grab the bag and run. It's mine. My one of few items from home.

Each time a Koyorad looks in my direction, I can't help but cower. I'm exposed and alone on an alien world. On this world, Earth humans are either forgotten or feared.

I touch Aithen's arm for comfort and then…

That.

I feel it.

Again.

In my stomach but lower. Like a ripple of small bubbles popping in my stomach muscles. Then it stops, and Aithen looks at me. "You okay?"

"I felt it," I whisper and glance at my stomach, then him again.

His expression is blank; he doesn't understand what I'm talking about.

"I felt a kick!" I say, and his eyes widen. He squeezes my hand encouragingly. It's sweet, this is a private moment only we share, but it is spoilt by a dull beeping sound from one of the Deyloron. It's the one assigned to me. Monitoring my baby and me. Did it sense that unique sensation in my stomach?

I must go through a procedure to protect my eyes and skin. Having two solar suns, Korudaz is a bright planet, so I'll have to wear clear protective contact lenses.

Next, the sunscreen. Aithen will need similar treatment to restore his own protective barrier.

"Is that why I can see a hazy film around their skin?" I ask Aithen, keeping my voice as low as possible.

"Yes, we develop a natural sunblock," he replies. It's funny, but I forgot Aithen is one of *them*. But he's so different.

We enter separate rooms, and the first difficult step is parting with my Earth clothes. They want me to dress in the jumpsuit. I fold my clothes and step into a shower cubicle. There's the momentary quick spray of mist, smelling like eucalyptus. Warm air dries my body, and then a digital voice advises me to close my eyes and mouth and raise my arms slightly.

I jump slightly from a throbbing wave in the cubicle, which swirls up, down and around my body. Ten seconds later a single bleep announces the completion of the process.

All my skin has the same haze around it. I smell the skin on the back of my hand, but nothing.

Stepping into the slightly padded, snug uniform, the interior is pleasantly soft and cooling. These suits are not made for women, I curse as my chest is too constricted. I can't pull the zip closed. The suit fits fine otherwise but not the chest, so I tie the arms around my waist and slip into the bra and long-sleeved t-shirt I folded away. Guess I'll need these after all.

Sliding into flat-heeled ankle boots with anti-gravity pads to aid in my current feeling of heaviness, the result is excellent. They do the job correctly, and the sensation of being pulled towards the ground is relieved.

One quick inspection in a mirror and I'm both shocked by the gossamer sheen across my face and any exposed skin. Glowing with health? No, looking… alien.

I place the rest of my clothes into a provided bag and exit the room, finding Aithen waiting outside. He regards me and smiles.

"Yeah, now I look like E.T., too," I scoff.

"I forgot about the clothes," he says.

"Yeah, why so tight?" I ask. "I can't fit into it."

Aithen reaches in towards me and whispers, "Koyorad females don't have boobs. I thought you would have covered that in your reading here.'"

No, I didn't. "You're joking?"

Now it makes sense why he had the *apparent* infatuation with my chest. I just put it down to him being a typical boy, but no, he really hasn't seen boobs before.

I can't stop the laugh escaping me. "Why didn't you say? That's like, kinda big to leave out," I say. "Then again, you only told me about your sister a second ago."

"We'll talk more about it later," Aithen says, as a pair of guards and a Deyloron approach us. They look at the arms of the jumpsuit tied as a belt around my waist, and then I feel my cheeks redden as their gaze's rise look at the reason why.

"I'll need a larger size," I say, breaking the awkward silence.

Aithen says something to them in Coten, and I see acknowledgement in their faces and words.

We exit through a door into the bright daylight.

I'm on a distant planet, but it could easily be another country on Earth until you look up and around. Then the differences jump out at you.

I notice the lenses I'm wearing are shading my eyes slightly like those sunglasses which respond to bright sunlight. There is the equivalent of trees with smooth barks and straight, silver branches. The leaves are more like purple feathers. There's so much to take in.

Vehicles of varied sizes travel silently in single file across multiple highways in the sky, at least ten kilometres above us. Stranger still is a pale, grey section of the artificial ring, up high in the atmosphere. You can follow its length from horizon to horizon. To think that spans the planet is unbelievable.

A gentle breeze causes yellow, green, and white stringy plants to dance like they are in the water, their tendrils wafting about the air. And the roads, they are pure black but seasoned with sprinkles of silver glitter. I gape as a vehicle drives along, hovering above the ground.

"No wheels?" I ask, raising a hand towards the *car*.

"No, we use a magnetic composite in your ground road surfaces. The vehicle and road are equally charged positive magnetically; hence the surface repel, causing the hovering process," Aithen explains.

"Then how do they stop?" I ask.

"The vehicle converts it's positive polar charge to negative, thus drawing it's lower surface towards the road's, which delivers a braking effect. This is constantly happening to produce forward, backwards and sideways propulsion." He makes an action with his hands to mimic the concept.

"This is so strange," is the best I can offer.

And buildings – in the sky? Apparently, the material used in their construction has anti-gravitational effects, hence the structures float. Similar material is used in larger transport vessels and, like with the cloaking material, it all comes down to small electrical charges to control them.

Koyorads harness materials from the planet, but most mining occurs on the moon Neflorone. Other sources are Treniers, the giant rocks in space, and distant, remote moons. The wood-like material is synthesised and made as hard-wearing as required; they even make it smell and age like natural wood.

It's so quiet here, but in the background, there's a deep hum. A buzzing almost inaudible, but it's like a new sense.

"Is it just me, or can you hear a buzzing all around us?" I ask Aithen.

Aithen raises a finger towards the sky. "The ring. Most don't hear it, but you, being an *alien,* seem to have an odd perception of our technology." He smiles.

"Do you have, you know, shopping malls?" Well, I may need retail therapy at some point.

"Not here," responds Aithen. "If we need anything, it is delivered by *Terr.*"

"Terr?" I'm still recoiling from no mall.

"Terr delivers it to you. Pair of shoes or space transporter, a Terr is your friend." He laughs.

"And Koyorads make all these things in factories?" I ask.

"Most is done by machines. We have the equivalent of factories for the mass production of items, but few Koyorads need to work there. Those that do are usually involved in maintenance and administration," Aithen says.

One of the hovercars pulls up in front of us. Koyorads certainly don't go for detail with their designs. The vehicle is grey, silver and otherwise featureless.

"And where is this taking us?" I ask.

"Our accommodation," Aithen responds and smiles.

"With them two?" I ask, nodding towards the guards.

"No, just the one Deyloron," Aithen says. "But there will be guards assigned to the property—"

I cringe at that.

"No, but they'll stay outside our place," he continues.

Our place. I haven't given *us* a moment's thought all this time. I haven't given becoming a mom any thought even. How can I be so calm?

There's no driver of the vehicle which has been pre-programmed with the destination. Thankfully, the Deyloron escorts us from outside.

I watch the alien landscape pass by.

Buildings are single-story save for the odd additional floor now and then. Still, with a planet this size, space is not an issue, so inhabitants build outwards, rather than upwards.

"What's the plan?" I whisper to Aithen. There's no knowing who could be listening.

"First, I need to contact the Kounsell, the good Kounsell, and ensure they know *you* are here," he says, holding his tone, too.

"Why wouldn't they know?" I ask but can't stop my voice rising.

"I don't know," he says, running his hands through his hair. "It's all too hushed for my liking. I'm only glad they haven't insisted on separating us."

I don't know how I'd cope if that happened.

"I'll feel better once Akeirlah shows up," he continues. "That way we know they're not keeping everything under wraps."

"Have you contacted her?" I ask.

"Yes, as soon as we arrived, by Meorlite, but I've had no response yet. Thing is, *they* can easily intercept and block a transmission. So, my litmus test is her turning up," he says through gritted teeth. "Then, I can try and get a message to the good Kounsell."

"What's to stop you going to them personally?" I ask. "Can't you go to the building or wherever they are based?"

"I don't want to force a confrontation," Aithen says. "Everything is calm at the moment; despite the negative undercurrent I am feeling. I want to appear accepting of all this, that way there is less chance of a forceful lockdown."

"What, you mean like house arrest, or worse?"

"Exactly. I don't want to force the Military Kounsell to play their hand if they do have an ulterior motive. I say we look dumb and smile and be *so accepting and thankful* of everything," he says, ending with a mocking tone.

Shouldn't this be a moment of wonder and excitement? An alien is visiting a planet. An alien from a race which died out ten thousand years ago.

An alien with a half-Koyorad baby growing inside them.

CHAPTER FORTY-ONE

We are left alone for the evening, in a solitary but secure building. The perimeter delivers a forcefield which – like everything – grants access via the Meorlites. They control everything, like a planetary ID card. Two guards patrol the area, but they stay out of sight and won't bother us otherwise. The Deyloron hovers above the complex and delivers a loud blast of its distorted horn every now and then, as though to remind me, it is still there. Watching.

"Can that Deyloron harm me?" I ask Aithen. "I don't have Meorlites running through my body, so what could it do?"

"It can still stun you with a high-voltage pulse. It will already have scanned and detected your nervous system, so it will react accordingly," he says.

"I feel like a prisoner," I say, hugging myself and rocking gently.

"I do, too, but let's take this carefully. We tow the line and—"

I hold up a hand. "Is this place, bugged?" I whisper.

Aithen smiles and shakes his head. "No, that I can assure you. Koyorads are paranoid, but privacy is upheld with the utmost authority. Not even the Kounsell can override this policy. If such a device could be hidden here, the Deyloron would destroy it."

"What, even if the Military Kounsell did it?" I ask.

"Yes, exactly. The Deyloron have a set of prime directives, and those are upheld and controlled by an A.I. system. There's no interference by any Koyorad. The Deyloron can't be influenced by anyone. Yes, they can be requested to carry out a duty, but that is within the confines of directives," Aithen explains.

"Even the Kounsell are fully accountable and under control by the Deyloron," he continues.

"Surely there's an override?" I ask. "What's to stop the Deyloron taking over?"

"Truth be told, they already are in control. But so far, there hasn't been a single incident where the Deyloron were considered to have acted irresponsibly. It works for us," Aithen says.

"Scary," I say.

The interior of the building offers plain, white walls and exposed metal, tubular framework. There are four bedrooms, a kitchen – if you can call it that – and a large, open-plan lounge area.

"Don't take this the wrong way or anything," I begin, "but I'd prefer to sleep alone?" I cringe inside. I could be assuming here.

Aithen nods. "Don't worry, I understand. I think that's the last thing on our minds."

It's strange looking at this beautiful but hazy version of Aithen. His violet eyes are as perfect and sparkle with his smile. "Do I look weird to you?" I ask, casting a glance over my body.

"You look like a Koyorad, so that is a little odd," he says and leans in to kiss me. I accept, and it's lovely to feel his lips on mine and his arms around me.

We finally pull away breathless. "I might want to change my mind about those sleeping arrangements," I laugh.

I stand on the balcony outside of my sleeping quarters.

The dark trees around me radiate a silvery light. It's not the actual trees or branches that glow, but tiny insects living within or upon the leaves and branches. They are like small firefly beetles and during the day, they store the energy from the suns, like the solar lights you place in your garden. Then at night, they give off this mesmerising glow; it is magical.

Korudaz days and nights are not what I'm used to. Because of the two suns, Yettrelba and Quswania, the planet passes through two daylight phases. A standard day is forty hours here – equivalent to almost two Earth days. So, basically, Korudaz has two days and one night. How am I supposed to sleep here? It'll be like jetlag on steroids.

I view the night sky. The stars. It's so strange to not see the Plough in the night sky. I can't remember an evening of stargazing or waiting around for a bus, and not seeing the square with the tail trailing away. But in this night sky, there are different shapes.

For a moment, a thought passes me — like it does when you are away on vacation: what are *they* doing now...? My family.

But then the coldness of space reminds me they are not doing anything now. They have not done anything for a long time now. Not for years. Not for thousands of years. I survey the planet I'm stood upon. The lights of this civilisation are all around me.

It's so quiet here. No sounds of traffic, animals, or people. But there is the hum. An almost inaudible buzz in the far distance. It's a sound I've not heard before. More like a sound, I can feel. A pulsing wave. The ring up there in space.

I'm so alone. Reflexively my hand touches my stomach. Well, maybe not entirely alone. I recall the feeling earlier today when I felt the *kick*. It was like in a moment of emptiness, this little person wanted to remind me I have a new family to take care of me.

Aithen's warm hands rest on my shoulders, and he nuzzles the back of my neck. "How are you doing?"

"Erm, I think I made a wrong left turn on the high street." I laugh and turn to face him. "I'm scared, Aithen. I'm scared of this planet, the Kounsell, the everything."

On cue, the Deyloron above emits a chilling bellow.

Aithen holds me close. "I'm sorry. I wish I could replay this whole event and make it special."

I wipe my eyes. "What's going to happen? I'm assuming they will allow the baby to be born? But what then?"

"Well they've brought you here for a reason," he replies. "For all I, we know, it could be good. This must be a big deal to them, or else you wouldn't be here."

"But what's to stop them getting rid of me once the baby is born? If not before, when the teleportation-thing is carried out?" I ask.

"I'll stop them," Aithen says firmly. "Nothing will ever happen to you; I promise you that."

A shiver washes over me, and I indicate to go back indoors.

"You have to remember one thing; most Koyorads have little or no interest in Earth. They live here and have no care for what happens outside of the place they live. That could be their own street or town even. Most spend their whole, long lifetime not even leaving the city they were born in. So, they have no curiosity in other countries and no other planets. While we are what you would term an *advanced* race, we still have a simple lifestyle."

"But the good Kounsell, they are interested in other worlds and life?" I ask.

"Yes, and that's why we visit and learn about other races. It's just the Military Kounsell have an irrational bias towards Earth, in particular, "Aithen says. "I've said this before, but something doesn't weigh-up here. I need to investigate the military presence in Earth's orbit."

"And what can you do if you find out something?" I ask.

"A lot. Firstly, expose whatever it is. One thing you should be aware of, Koyorads listen to one another. Age is not a barrier to understanding and legitimacy here. I may be a younger member of society, but I have equal rights to any individual on this planet."

"And the military won't try to stop you?"

"Of course, they will," Aithen says. "But they can't prevent me getting an audience with the good Kounsell. Especially if they don't know what I'm up to." He gives a mischievous smile. "Discretion is key here."

"Well, I'm glad you feel confident. I feel lost," I respond. "I just hope I can go out of this building now and then."

"You can go out any time," he says.

"But I'm a human, not a Koyorad. Someone will notice?"

"We are out of the way here, and the *deliemous* helps your Koyorad camouflage."

"The del- what?"

He runs a finger along my glowing arm. "The deliemous. Sun protective layer."

It's true. My radiating skin and my naturally violet eye colour will help me blend in.

"It's weird. Anyone on Earth is curious about life on another planet. Even if that was bacteria," I say.

"Life on other planets is old news here. It's covered by the education system. Only a senior student with a particular interest will delve into life on other planets."

"What, like you?"

"Exactly. I have the same curiosities as you, and thankfully, I had the means to travel to Earth and meet you."

"Smooth talker," I giggle. "You're saying that to get me into bed."

"No, more like to *stay* in your bed," he laughs.

I kiss him and stroke his cheek. "So, when we meet other

Koyorads here, will they be able to understand me? What I'm saying?"

"No. Some will have their Meorlites programmed to translate what you say to them, such as the Kounsell and medical team. But sorry, best leave the talking to Akeirlah or me." I notice Aithen's expression drop for a moment. He's worried that Akeirlah hasn't been in contact yet.

"Still no word from her?" I ask.

He shakes his head slowly, and his mouth crumples. "No, and that worries me. But let's stay hopeful." He forces a smile. "She will get here. And when she does, we'll help you fit into this world."

"Scary," I remark.

"Smile and be pleasant. We will give you a few words to say, such as 'Kla' which is 'thank you' and 'Tugh' which is 'please.'"

This spurs me to attention. "Tugh? Sounds more like a belch."

He smiles in response. "You'll get the hang of it. We have various, interesting ways for you to learn this language or at least the basics of it as you can do so while sleeping. It is all non-invasive, but at least you will communicate a little after a few weeks."

More learning. Having to learn a whole new language and not speak English anymore, except with a handful of people? I could lose myself on this planet. It is all so large, and I'm so small.

CHAPTER FORTY-TWO

Considering a Korudaz day lasts forever, and the Koyorads live for such a long time, it's strange they do everything quick. Everything operates at the push of a button, whether it be the showers, food preparation or travel into space. All instantaneous.

Once more, I dress in bland, plain clothes, transforming myself into a soldier. I don't like it. This is a uniform, no doubts about it, and honestly, take away my head, and you could not tell if I was male or female. I like to dress like a girl, and I want my clothes to feel soft and giving.

I have an appointment with a medical person. Then the Kounsell.

"At least this one fits," I say, running my hands over my arms.

"Yes, we didn't talk about that," Aithen says.

"Yeah, the no boobs thing?" I ask.

"Exactly. Koyorad children, as I touched on, are born about the size of a two-year-old. They are not breast-fed. They eat a simple diet, which is like runny porridge, but this means women here have no need to develop in *that* area." He smiles.

"Do I look odd, weird to you?" I ask. "I must look abnormal in your eyes." I drop my gaze to my restricted chest. Even this looser suit is quite tight.

"You look beautiful and perfect and exactly like the girl, the human girl I am in love with," he says, and a hint of a tear tugs at his eyes.

I grab hold of him. "I love you, too. I'm sorry this is all so messed up, but we'll come through it."

He kisses my forehead then mouth. "We will."

Aithen slips a plastic card from a drawer and hands it to me. "Carry this as a temporary ID card. You don't need to show it or anything, but it has been coded with your access into the medical centre. A hovercar will take you to the medical centre," Aithen says, but I interrupt him.

"You can't leave me alone. Please, Aithen?"

He places his hands on my shoulders. "Don't worry. You'll be the safest person on this planet."

"How?"

"The Deyloron will escort you. You'll be fine," he says.

"But it's just a drone. It can't do anything against the military—"

"Oh, it can. One is assigned to you, but should anyone attack a Deyloron, there are several million more to turn up. And they also have their own large cruisers. I promise you; nobody attacks a Deyloron or the individual guarded."

Aithen searches my face, and I give him an assuring nod. "Okay, but you will be at the Kounsell meeting?"

"Yes, I'll take you there myself."

The hovercar takes a magnetised road through dense forest, filled with green, blue, and purple trees, all bearing the same feather-like leaves and shiny, black branches. I hear no sounds but for the hum of the car. I scan the branches for signs of life, but there's nothing. Not even birds. I enjoy the solitude and safety of the trees; it almost feels like home. But I know it's not.

I arrive at the medical centre. One thing Koyorads are lacking is any concept of aesthetically pleasing architecture. Set upon two floors, the building is little more than featureless, white concrete. I'm sure the material is something else, but it's bland.

The interior is more pleasing and features ground to ceiling glass walls and shiny, exposed metal. Treatment rooms have solid, white glass walls for privacy. What is welcoming is there is not *that* disinfectant hospital smell. No, this environment has a sweet odour, like fresh roses; it's pleasant.

A man and woman carry out a set of diagnostic scans. No needles, so that's nice. Everything is looking good, and they talk to me with eager eyes. Talk about two children in a toy store. What is odd is when they speak to me in English: their lips move, but the words are not synchronised with their mouth. It's like watching a foreign-language movie, and the dubbed voice doesn't match up. It's quite distracting.

They hand me a small vial of clear liquid with a golden lid.

"Take the dose before you sleep and please don't be offended, but humans can miscarry or—"

"Stillbirth?" I manage to force a smile.

They mirror sympathetic gazes. "This will prevent it."

I hold the simple bottle in my fingers. What would Sarah give to have had this?

The silence.

Matthew.

The bottle is no bigger than one of those tiny perfume samples you receive on a cardboard sleeve. A teaspoon of clear liquid which can save a life; alter a future. I dismiss a fantasy of me flying back to Earth before Matthew was born. Giving the bottle to Sarah and preventing what is to come.

The medics continue fussing around me and hovering screens. They bump into one another, as they reach for various liquids to administer to me or scan parts of my body with hand-held devices. It's nice to experience nice Koyorads, besides Aithen.

The medics have never experienced this *inter-galactic* pregnancy, and most likely won't ever again. And before I know it, I am asked if I want to see the baby, inside of me?

You don't need to ask me again.

I've seen these scans before with Sarah, but there's none of the gel on the stomach and a hand-held probe. The lady medic taps at a virtual console and a screen appear in front of my view. I see the clear outline of a tiny body, umbilical cord running from its stomach to me. And there, as clear as day, the small heart fluttering with life.

I sniff back loudly and gasp.

My baby.

"Do you want to know the gender?" the woman asks.

"You can tell already?"

"We could have told you a minute after conception." she smiles.

Do I want to know? Will it matter if I do or don't?

"Yes, go on then."

"It's a boy," they almost say together.

My throat tightens as my eyes glisten. A boy.

Sarah, it's a boy, I imagine saying to her and then I cry. But these are not the tears of loss or regret. Maybe some regret from the years I have been haunted by my little nephew. But Sarah has moved on. She's happy and I know why. Lou has filled the painful void and brought happiness to Sarah's life. Yes, Matthew will always be in her heart, but Sarah lives for her family, for life.

And I must do the same for my little boy. That little heart is beating for life, for me.

The medics raise their hands slightly in alarm. A crying alien is obviously new to them, especially when it's a dangerous Earth human.

I fall into Aithen's arms when he arrives.

"It's a boy, Aithen. We're going to have a little boy."

He squeezes me and kisses me, wiping away my tears with a thumb. "Great, Jayne. This is going to be amazing; I promise."

We hold each other and sway to an imaginary tune. I wish we could run away. I want my little boy to be safe. I know Aithen will keep us safe. I kiss him.

But next up is the *welcome* Kounsell visit, but I'm not looking forward to it. Too many rules and regulations. The Kounsell are those individuals who have insisted on this whole planetary visit, the abduction. They appear to be the holders of all cards.

When we arrive at a large, globe-shaped building – yes, we flew here – there is a large gathering at ground level.

It's hard to imagine such a gathering of Koyorads.

They push at one another, raising arms and placards in the air. There's an aggressive standoff towards a line of red Deyloron, which emit pulsing, white waves of light, acting as a cordon to the entrance to the building. I guess petitions and riots are going on here, just like on Earth.

Instead of landing the craft, Aithen cloaks.

"What's going on? Why have we cloaked?" I ask, searching his face and back to the crowd.

"They know you're here," he snaps, eyes wide and flitting between me and events outside.

"How do you know? Are they angry?" I see angry faces from my view within the craft.

"It's on the boards they hold. I realise you can't read it, but in short, they're asking why an Earth human is allowed here," Aithen says, steering the craft in a tight circle towards the roof of the building.

It is one of the only buildings which must be at least ten stories.

It's exterior adorned in a fashion of shiny, plate armour; huge spikes jut upwards towards the sky from the individual floor levels.

More like a fortress.

Even the windows have the appearance of solid steel.

"Will the Deyloron attack them?" I ask.

"They could, but it looks contained," Aithen says, as the craft lowers. "Oh, good," he adds as we hover high above the building.

"What?" I ask.

Aithen motions towards a large, triangular craft which appears at the upper part of the circle. "Good Kounsell has arrived."

"Is it really called that?" I ask.

I can see his features lighten for the first time. "For you, yes, but you can refer to them as the Gouhlde Kounsell; yes, a coincidence," he spells the difference for me and smiles, as is does sound like *good*.

"And you think they are here for me?" I ask.

"I hope so," he says, then dropping his gaze to the crowd. "How did *they* find out? It doesn't matter, at least you're not a secret." He presses my hand, and then we descend towards the white ship.

"We'll approach from the roof," he says.

I'm waiting with Aithen and Dzerklah, one of the assigned security guards. Security? Yes, I'm on protection detail. We're held in a plain room, and it is so weird to be ignored by so many aliens. They don't look at me or speak to me. Okay, they don't speak my language, but at least acknowledge I am here?

It's awkward speaking in earshot of the guard, as though my voice will be menacing and odd to him, but I'm curious.

"I have noticed that when a Koyorad talks to me, their mouth is out of timing with the words? What's going on there?" I ask Aithen in a hushed tone.

"They don't speak your language. Hence, those who may encounter you have had an amendment installed to their Meorlite. They speak our language, but their vocal cords emit English." He grins at my expression.

"Genius. Can't I have a language thing loaded so I can talk to you?"

He smiles. "Don't worry, you'll soon start to work on the language. I don't think you want a whole Meorlite installed in you."

The guard stands directed by a hidden prompt. Aithen told me a lot of Meorlite messages are sent covertly to individuals, so they arrive like a clear thought. Not so much mind-reading but mental communication. Koyorads are smart, it's a pity they are such asses with it.

I don't know why, but I imagined the meeting would be in a courtroom or similar ample space, but no, it's in a sparse office. Three Kounsell people sit opposite us – on the other side of a transparent screen. A protective screen? It all feels so unwelcoming. They are dressed in pale grey, flowing gowns, and it looks all out of date for such a modern, Meorlite-driven society.

If I had a place to go, I would get up and leave. The Kounsell bods are chatting amongst themselves and appear happy to ignore us. I give Aithen's hand a quick squeeze.

"It's normal, don't worry," he says with an assuring squeeze back.

Normal? So, these Kounsell people welcome aliens every day of the week? I know he's referring to their nature, but I feel more uneasy from mannerisms. I jump when a man speaks out – loud.

"Welcome, to Korudaz, Jayne."

The lips are off as standard. I must watch the eyes, not the mouth here.

"Bear with us as we await the arrival of Marrahmne Kounsell and a member from the Gouhlde Kounsell," he says, with a calm, deep voice. Pale grey eyes set in a tired, wrinkled face, consider me. He tilts his head slightly as though awaiting a response.

I have nothing to say but give a slight nod to acknowledge what he said. I turn to Aithen. "Who are we waiting on? Mar—"

"Marrahmne Kounsell. Just translate that to Madam Counsellor," he says.

I turn to see quizzical looks from the three men on the other side of the screen. Do they speak English? Maybe not.

Aithen nudges me as the door to the room opens, and we all stand. What is this school again?

An elderly woman and man enter. Both are dressed in the flowing garments, but hers are black and blue, whereas the man wears black and golden-yellow. His head is shaven smooth, and immediately he smiles at me.

That's nice. I return the gesture, "Hello." My voice sounds so small. We sit.

All eyes on the other side of the screen are grey, Korlevey-grey of a Kounsell birthright.

The woman watches me, and her chest rises as she takes in the sight of me. Is this going to be a staring contest?

The Gouhlde Kounsellor speaks, his words almost singing. "Welcome, Jayne. And what a marvellous sight you are. You appear so much like us."

"Thanks to our technology," blurts out the women.

"And congratulations on the most unexpected pregnancy of all time." His wide eyes inspect my stomach. He seems genuinely curious, but other eyes on that side of the table look at Aithen and me with bitter distaste.

The seat where the guard sits behind us squeaks as he shifts about; he must be as uncomfortable as us.

"I wish I shared your enthusiasm," says the woman. She squints at me through sour, greyish-blue eyes like she's chewing on a lemon. So, this is a *Korlevey:* they tend to uphold the office of power, such as local and central government. These grey-eyed individuals apparently live the longest, too.

Then the other man speaks. "And you have the appearance of a Kurzite, like Aithen. Quite a rare thing for a human," he says, referring to my violet eyes.

There's no feeling from them, and I want to stay silent, but manners are manners. "Thank you. Just a pity, the circumstances weren't different to experience a whole new world."

No flicker of a response.

"Circumstances?" she asks, daring to pout judgmentally at me.

"Yeah, circumstances. Like being abducted against my will—"

"Jayne," whispers Aithen, reaching for my arm.

The woman lifts her chin, but her words are halted when the door to the room opens again. What is it with this place?

Things become more uncomfortable. *Erek* and two other older men enter the room and sit nearby. These two men are unlike the others I have seen on the planet. Long hair and beards, but not a hair out of place, and dressed in smart suits. They wear silky, ruffled t-shirts under their fitted jackets.

I can't help but wonder about Erek. How did he get here so soon? He wasn't on the same ship as us. Then again, these aliens can travel distances and time forever quickly.

But it's odd. None of this would be happening had Erek Deleted me. He catches my gaze and immediately looks away. The bruise is a yellow shadow below his eye. His appearance has been altered to adopt the natural Koyorad sunscreen. It must be strange for him to see me here, on his planet, looking like one of them. One minute we're on Earth and now...

The conversation erupts. The Kounsell people bombard Erek and the other two men with questions. Every now and then, they call upon Aithen for an answer or input, but it is all a load of noise to me. They are not speaking English, which feels bad-mannered as I assume the debate has a lot to do with me, as shifting glances cast towards me and others in the room.

All this time, the Gouhlde Kounsellor remains calm, arms folded loosely as he observes the foray around him. He catches my gaze and furrows his brow. It's nice he notices I am here.

Maybe I'm invisible to the other Kounsell members? Or perhaps they are just rude. Ignorant. The voices are getting louder, and it seems like they are regurgitating the same phrases repeatedly. I know I'm the odd one out here, but please, "Can you shut the fuck up?"

Silence.

Right, yes, I spoke out loud. I don't curse often, and now may not be the time to start, but nervous eyes are on me. I didn't shout it, but you'd think I had from their expressions.

"Sorry about that, but shouldn't you include me in this debate?" I ask.

"Jayne."

"No, Aithen. Let me speak. I don't want to be here. After what technology I've seen on your ships and this planet, I'm quite sure I don't actually need to be here. But you lot insisted on ripping me away from my life, my home. If I'm not welcome, then send me back."

Erek is about to speak, but I flick him a stare which stops him. Yes, I know he spared me and has unwittingly protected me with a Tryborre, but... oh but what? There are no *buts*. I shouldn't be here.

"You finished?" taunts Marrahmne Kounsell. I notice she speaks English and none of the lip-synching.

"I have every right to be angry. *You*," I cast a hand around the room, "removed me from my world, and you are guilty of Deleting at least four girls I am aware of. What gives you that, right?"

Another outbreak of words clashes across the room, with most directed at Erek and one of the bearded men close to me. It dawns on me, he's the man who was with Erek in the Mall. Aithen said his name, but I can't remember it. But he's in charge of the Deleters when on Earth.

By the looks of things, the Kounsell are giving them a Coten roasting. The conversation stills, and the Gouhlde Kounsell man speaks; his voice immediately dismissing all voices.

"I didn't introduce myself properly. Please, call me, Myarve, Jayne. I fully appreciate your hostility towards this outrageous predicament, but we had to protect you and the unborn baby. Some decisions were made—" he looks towards the Military Kounsell members, "rather harshly and without clear planning. I will person-ally apologise for that and the shortcoming of those who have acted without any thought, whatsoever." He offers a smile, and I try to force one back in appreciation. Marrahmne Kounsell stiffens at his words.

"I understand you are aware of Earth's situation, albeit long past to us? Aithen has divulged an incredible truth to you, in your time, and that is the demise of Earth." His face creases with genuine concern and sadness. "We, the Gouhlde Kounsell, wanted to extend an offer of hope, a second chance for you to survive the inevitable."

"Couldn't you save Earth? Stop the Trenier?" I ask weakly.

He shakes his head, but before he can speak, Marrahmne Koun-sell interjects. "There are universal laws regarding interference with time-line events. The Trenier could not be stopped. If we were to do that, then why not prevent the extinction of dinosaurs on your planet? Humans would never have come to be. Which option should we choose?"

She is so cold. You can see the hatred in her eyes, burning with anger. Imagine if she was in complete control here?

"Why do you hate us so much?" I ask.

"We are wary of humans—"

Myarve clears his throat loudly, but Marrahmne Kounsell ignores him after a few seconds.

"You've seen the crowd outside. They are fearful of this decision and many who are aware, have been worried in the continued dabbling by the Gouhlde Kounsell to bring extinct civilisations to our current reality." She pauses for a moment, taking in the audience. "Over the years, the *modernisation* of your planet has turned it to ruin. Humans have become a clamouring nest of destruction. I know all about Earth in detail, and two things within their animal world defined humans for me. Those animals were ants and locusts."

I cross my arms. Here we go. Now *we* are ants. Locusts.

"Not spiders?" The first thing which came into my head.

"No, spiders are craft engineers and actually contribute to their natural world cycles. Whereas ants rage war. In fact, they are one of the few species in the universe that rage war on themselves. Like humans. Locusts. They use up all resources from where they set down. Once the swarm have depleted all useful resources, they move on and devastate a whole new area. Same as humans."

"It's so easy to point the finger." I return the stare of the woman. "Maybe you should train that judgement on yourselves. I can't remember the last time a human wiped out the existence of a Koyorad." I drag my gaze from her towards Erek and the two bearded men.

My words are arrested when she says something in *Coten* to the group. Aithen tenses and a sudden rush of raised voices cascade to and forth across the screen. What has she said? Her words only lasted about five seconds, but the response was immediate. I can't read what is happening here, as the expressions are looks of smugness, anger, and shock. Even the Gouhlde Kounsellor looks alarmed.

"What?" I reach for Aithen, but he, along with everyone else, return sitting.

"I'll tell you later," he says, wiping his mouth with distaste as he watches the woman.

Marrahmne Kounsell looks smugly around the room, waiting patiently for attention.

"I don't believe you have any bad motives or intentions. We are sure you have fallen in love with Aithen, and *that* love's reciprocated. I have no doubts at all. But you are a *human*."

I give a mild snort of a laugh and tilt my gaze away from her. I wait for the rest.

"Humans are like a virus. Take this girl, pregnant; another way the Earth Humans spread like a virus. She's here amongst us, she and her baby are here, and we cannot stop it. And all thanks to the Gouhlde Kounsell, Myarve." She dips her head towards Myarve. "It is fine for you to have overall control of the silly things, but I am in control of this planet's protection."

How dare she call us, me a virus! How dare they think so negatively about us. I could scream and shout and lash out, but I don't. I'm not willing to give her the ammunition she wants. I'm angry inside, but I feel so above her and her petty stupidity. My throat tightens, but I must be calm.

Gouhlde Kounsell stands. "I think that concludes this meeting," he says and taps on his wrist, which projects a Meorlite screen. "I'd like a quiet word with Kounsell, please."

I guess that's our cue to leave. I look to Aithen and his pained expression. "What did she say to you all?"

"I'll tell you in a moment," he whispers. "When we're away from here."

As we leave, Erek says something to Aithen, and I'm surprised to see Aithen places a hand on Erek's shoulder. I can't decide if that is encouraging or not. Deep down, I am more alone than ever. They are both Koyorads and I a human. The odd one out.

I half expect Aithen to suggest I travel back alone – maybe he wants to chat with Erek – but we return to the craft parked on the roof and a moment later arrive at the apartment. There's not even time to have a brief conversation.

I stand on the balcony, watching the twinkling trees around me and welcome the peace and quiet, and privacy from so many enquiring eyes.

"So, what happened?" I ask Aithen.

"Okay, this is hard. In fact, it's beyond unfair," he stalls.

"Just spit it out!"

"All travel to Earth is to end. That'll mean any Koyorads there will return immediately." He runs fingers through his hair. "And they are erasing the wormhole which allows travel back to Earth's past."

"Wormhole? I thought you called it a black hole?"

"They are two different things, remember? Wormhole takes you back in time, black hole forwards," he says, gesturing with his hands.

"Whatever. She said all that in a few seconds?" This can't happen. I must return to Earth.

"No, we communicate by speech and Meorlite, remember?" He points to his arm. "She had this planned. The message hit our minds as soon as she began speaking."

To think this message had been drafted and approved for consumption before I'd arrived at their offices. So sneaky and two-faced. She had no intention of offering me a welcome here. But if they are going to stop all means to return to Earth, what does that say about my future here? I'll be allowed to stay and somehow fit in with this human-hating society? Well, maybe not all are haters.

"How can they remove a wormhole? It's ridiculous."

He rubs his brow. "It's not. Wormholes, black holes, they are always moving. They are an object like any planet, star, debris. They follow simple rules, like any particle within a vast, open space."

"Just give it to me plain and simple. I don't want a science lecture." I shove him, so he knows I'm serious, but not forceful, so he knows I'm not angry at him.

"The condensed version? They'll push a black hole onto, or into the wormhole. The singularity… sorry, the whole thing will be a big bang, and they cancel each other out."

This is impossible. "They've done this before?"

"Yes. It was an accidental discovery, but aren't all the best inventions?"

"When you say a *big bang*? Is that in any way related to the whole universe creation thing? You know, start of everything from the big bang?" I mimic an explosion with my hands.

Aithen shakes his head. "No, sorry. That is purely a human creation concept. There was no big bang. More like a big push. But… it doesn't matter." He flops into a seat on the balcony.

I join him in the chair close by.

"When will this happen? This whole black hole, wormhole thing?" I ask.

"It won't be quick. This is a military operation, and while the Military Kounsell have a lot of leverage with decisions, they can only request the order. Our Gouhlde Kounsell and additional inputs from other sectors of security and social wellbeing will have to agree and action it."

"And will they? Won't they *welcome* the chance to stop the *threat* from us Earth humans?" *Last I looked the Koyorads were deleting us, not us attacking them.*

"I don't know why, but I have a feeling this will be passed. The Gouhlde Kounsellor didn't put up much of a display of authority at the meeting today. It is they who promote and support travel to other worlds and times, but something is off here. I couldn't help but notice he went quiet for a bit after Marrahmne Kounsell sent the initial Meorlite message to us all. I am sure she sent him and the rest of the attending Kounsell an additional message or messages."

"What happens next?"

"They'll have to agree with it. I'm quite confident the Kounsell will make a good argument about the threat of you being here. But there is a lot of red-tape and exploration work to ensure it is a viable solution."

"How am I threat? A solitary girl? Am I really that powerful?"

"It's not you in isolation. It's the fact you are even here. It's an impossibility that you are alive and on Korudaz. Koyorads will start to look at Earth humans again. The scaremongers will soon start to say words like invasion and war. Yes, there is a lot of fascination from some about distant worlds and their histories. Dinosaurs are a massive thing here. More so than humans, but what was considered safe in the past is now a reality."

"How do you feel about me, now that we're here?" I deliberately look around us.

Aithen reaches for my hand. "I love you, Jayne. That doesn't change. Korudaz, Earth, the Moon. I love you wherever we are in the universe."

I kiss the back of his hand and sigh. "I sometimes forget we are actually dating." I smile.

"I think we're beyond just dating," he says, and leans towards me, planting a kiss firmly on my lips.

I don't want to spoil this small moment of normality, but something is bugging me. "I saw Erek say something to you when we were leaving. Looked rather friendly?"

"Yes, it was a little unexpected," Aithen responds, his gaze vacant as his thoughts cast back. "He told me he's leaving the Deleter program."

"Can he do that?"

"Of course. Our eye colour defines us and career path, but we still have the right to choose."

I shiver as a chilly night on a dark hill travels my thoughts.

Stupid human.

"And you believe him?"

"I do. He said your recollection of everything, everyone has woken him from the Deleter curse." I can see Aithen notices I have chilled at the mention of Deleters. "I haven't lost hope at finding your friends, Jayne. It's ridiculous to imagine they could be restored, but so is an Earth human on this planet, right now. Erek may prove useful if he really is having second thoughts about matters."

"It all sounds too convenient to me," I say. "Why should he get away with Deleting my friends? He has a moment of regret and expects forgiveness all around?"

"There's so much more to it than that," Aithen replies. "Deleters are under stringent rules and orders. They enter a profession so demanding; they literally forget how to think for themselves." Aithen offers a weak smile. "Personally, I think the episode in the mall and you hurting Erek, may actually have woken him up. He was changed after that day. I'm not close to him as a friend, but I could see you had affected him."

I exhale loudly. "If it's so strict, how can he just change his mind?"

"Free choice, no matter what. It's usually a one out, one in routine, so someone has obviously volunteered for a Deleter role from another sector of Koyorad society—"

"What? A Koyorad without black eyes can become a Deleter?"

"It's rare, exceedingly rare, but it can happen. It all comes down to reprogramming of the Meorlite in that individual. Erek will always be considered a Deleter, but he will lose his rights to utilise the Deletion weapon and similar traits."

Who would want to become a Deleter? But I'm not forgiving Erek any time soon. If he appears with Leslie, Chloe, Laura, and the original version of VioletlyAlone, then I'll start to think about it.

"Something else," Aithen continues. "They, us, don't know about the Tryborre."

"What, the one Erek used on me?"

Aithen nods.

"But it would have appeared when I was scanned at the medical centre?"

"No, it wouldn't. They would not have been scanning for it; no reason to. You're a human remember. Why would you be host to a Tryborre?"

I shrug.

"When you told me that about Erek, I already had my doubts about what was going on with him. Yes, it is normal Koyorad procedure, but in no way human procedure; there isn't one," Aithen says.

"Wouldn't they read his thoughts or actions from the Meorlite?" I ask.

"No. Remember, it's not a mind-reading device but thought communication. It's down to the individual if they wish to send a *transmission*." Aithen touches his temple and motions his hand away.

"So complicated," I remark.

I swallow deeply. What if I can restore my friends? Can I begin to consider Erek an ally? But surely, we couldn't do this on Korudaz? Five humans on the planet would cause a war, considering how much these Koyorads overreact to everything.

If I could avoid the next question, I would and remain ignorant for a moment, but I need to know. "When do you think the whole black hole, wormhole thing will happen?" Please don't say it'll be tomorrow or a couple of days.

"A month tops. There will be resistance from the education sector. Still, the big problem now is a lot of Koyorads know you are here, thanks to that demonstration we saw and whoever tipped them off. It won't take long before most of the planet knows."

A month? Four weeks to learn the impossible and then form a plan from that. I need to figure out a way to return to Earth. Aithen said I can learn to fly, but can I fly all the way back to Earth? Through a wormhole, assuming I can ever find that again? But do I have to do this unaided? Aithen will help me, and now we might have the backup of Erek. No, I can't trust Erek.

I watch Aithen. Can I risk his life just because I want to go home? To return to a doomed planet. Let's say he did go with me, we'll both be dead in a couple of years from the Trenier impacting, and that's assuming the Koyorads decide to wash their hands of us. They may see it as an effortless way to tie-up loose ends.

But what about the baby?

A month from now, the baby won't be here. I can't leave while still pregnant with the threat of the enzyme reaction killing me. I hug myself, but then my arms are enveloped by Aithen's.

"Don't worry; we'll work it out." He lifts my hand and strokes my shimmering skin.

If he knew I was half-thinking about running away and leaving him, what would that look like?

If only his warmth could defrost the chill which flows through me. The clock is ticking, and I don't know where to begin.

CHAPTER FORTY-THREE

Dark deeds and negative thoughts of the Kounsell evaporate with the brightness of two suns. I have my *entry visa* into Korudaz, and I'm allowed a little freedom.

They have asked I remain within the area called Sicbyden, and it's obvious why they have chosen this area for me. It reminds me of home, and the forest near to the sea is a nice touch – even though this forest is different from those trees I first saw.

There are some patches of the sparkly, feather-leaved trees. Still, these more significant, darker green trees have huge, paddle-like leaves, leathery in texture. Running within the forest is like running with your head underwater. The air is so dense, and still, it oppresses all sounds and my ears pop, adding to the dullness around me.

The forest ground is quite smooth, like dark chalk and wisps of dust cloud our wake as we progress.

I haven't run for a while, so my breathing is more laboured than usual. Inhaling a bitter-sweet scent of aged, damp wood mixed in with a hint of something unsavoury, like a forgotten, humid, and moldy towel. It's not the most pleasant of smells.

Aithen is taking me on a tour of the area. I am relieved to exit the darkness of the forest as we jog along its edge. It's lovely to feel the fresh air and the wind on my face. Being cooped up in a spaceship and then a featureless apartment has been brain-numbing.

When we turn a corner, a gust of wind hits us, and the next thing I know is that I am cowering on the ground while a fierce growl, attacks my ears from all around. What is that?

My eyes dart all around us, looking for whatever animal that has come from, but Aithen is still standing.

Gingerly, I raise myself to my knees, but he continues to look calm. "What is that?" I gasp.

Aithen takes my hands and helps me up. "Don't worry, it's not an animal."

I search the trees, but that's all I see. There's nothing above us either.

Aithen leads me to a nearby tree with the large, dark green leaves that look like leather. They must be at least three metres in length.

Grabbing an end of the leaf, Aithen prizes it apart, and there is a distinctive tearing sound, like Velcro. "This is your monster," he says. "When the wind catches, then they—"

And there comes the huge bellowing roar again when another patch of the outlining forest is hit by a gust of wind. It makes me flinch, regardless.

"The leaves pull apart, and well, you heard it," he smiles.

"Wow! Scary," I manage to say. "I think I prefer the friendly, silver, glowing trees."

We continue our run.

I'm glad this area is secure from the mob. Only a dozen Koyorads know I am based in this location. Hence a breach will make it easy to isolate the culprit. But it doesn't lower my worries. The angry mob and the Kounsell. Not once did I imagine there would be such an aggressive response to my arrival. It doesn't make sense.

I investigate the sky and the airborne traffic streams and then at the massive, visible expanse of the ring, up there in space.

"Where's the Deyloron?" I ask. "I thought it had to follow and monitor me?"

"It's monitoring you via my Meorlite," Aithen says. "You are okay to request it to leave you alone, not follow you. But always carry this."

He hands me a slim, silver bracelet, which pulses green for a moment as I slip it on my wrist. "You get into trouble, tap this twice, and the Deyloron will appear immediately."

I'm tempted to try it out but decide against it. I want some privacy from Koyorads for a moment.

"So, where's your home?" I ask. "Where you lived before coming to Earth?"

"Not that far away. About eleven kilometres from here. But I've vacated that and what little I have will be delivered via Terr, when I request it."

In the distance, I can see snow-topped mountains, and they deliver a lovely, familiar sight. Also, there are two small unpopulated islands out in the sea. All covered with green trees, so again, a reminder of home and the view from the harbour.

I just wish I could do something normal like sit in a coffee house and relax. Browse around the mall, looking at clothes. I miss simple food. Everything here is soup, smoothies, miniature bowls of food consisting of weird-looking plants and a solid, soft substance like tofu. It doesn't even taste like chicken; I thought everything was supposed to taste like chicken?

The food is filling, but I can't imagine eating chocolate again. To indulge in anything. Koyorads are missing out on such simple pleasures. They eat to live and function; that's it.

I stand on the apartment's balcony area again, watching purple, green, and blue shades of foliage dancing with a light breeze. The warm air wafts a subtle, zesty tinge of fruit around me. Aithen passes me a glass of water.

"I've finally heard from Akeirlah," he says, and his face is glowing with excitement.

"Is she coming here?" It'll be odd to see his sister; something normal on this planet.

He nods. "She's on her way. Thankfully."

Okay, this is exciting. Meeting Aithen's big sister will be amazing. He's pacing the floor and smiling to himself. It's the first time I've seen him looking calm in days. What will she think of me? An Earth human dating her brother. Oh, no, a human pregnant with his baby. That'll make her the aunt.

Daunting.

No, this is great, and I need to meet another smiling face. It was nice when Myarve, the Gouhlde Kounsellor smiled at me, but this must be different. Akeirlah is Aithen's sister.

My heart flutters gently.

Calm yourself, my inner voice soothes.

I don't need to be told when she arrives, as the Deyloron emits a bellowing blast of horns and I hear the racing pulse of its scanning beams. I hear a young girl's voice shouting Coten at the drone, and it responds with several high-pitched bleeps, which echo around us.

It's unsettling, despite knowing it is supposed to be protecting, or monitoring me.

Aithen smiles. "Yes, that's her, telling off the Deyloron. Typical Akeirlah." He rushes to the main door to the apartment and opens it.

Aithen didn't lie, Akeirlah is young in appearance. She's more sixteen than what, twenty-three? She's tall, very slight of build, and beautiful, pale, gossamer skin of her hands and face. Even from here, I can see her bright, green *Koruzyte* eyes. Her shiny, black hair is cut short but is thick with hints of dark-red and green touches.

They both exchange a hand placed on the opposite shoulder; this must be how they shake hands here? Her eyes fall on me, and her beautiful smile is addictive, I can't help almost laughing. She's beautiful. I must look a mess to her.

"And this must be, Jayne," she almost sings the words, but there is still the slight out of synch movement of the lips. I need to get used to that. Akeirlah approaches me, and her eyes are level with mine. I sort of wish I were a little taller, but my thoughts are arrested by her hugging me.

I cough away a laugh and squeeze her back.

Akeirlah laughs, and it fills the room. "We don't do hugging here, On Korudaz, but you do."

She steps back and considers me further. "You look so like us, it's amazing. And way to go, Aithen. You picked such a beautiful Earth human."

That sort of stings, but I know she's not negative towards me. This must be crazy for her, but I'm lost in her positive, warm smile.

"Now, I'm sure Aithen is being boring and keeping to all the stupid rules, but that's why I'm here: to really show you around." She laughs at Aithen's expression. He looks dumbfounded.

"What's with the hand on the shoulder thing?" I ask.

"If—"

Akeirlah cuts off Aithen. "When it's family or a close partner, then you place your right, or left hand, on the opposite shoulder. If friends, colleagues, then as a mark of respect and friendship, then it's same-side hand and shoulder. Right to right."

It's funny as it's noticeable from her stance, presence, that Akeirlah is the older here, but she still looks younger than Aithen and I.

Akeirlah heads for the lounge and takes a seat. I enjoy her commanding style, as Aithen is quite timid around her. I guess he needs the support of his family at a time like this.

I quietly gasp away the thought of my own loneliness. I need my family too.

"Where've you been?" asks Aithen. "I messaged you when we arrived."

Akeirlah nods, cupping her hands together. "I've been held by the Deleters since you arrived."

"What?" snaps Aithen.

"They didn't harm me or anything, but they didn't want me near you or Jayne," Akeirlah says, and I hear a tremble of emotion on her voice. "It was awful. They locked me in a room. Just a bed and I've been going out of my mind, not knowing what was happening."

"It's the Kounsell," Aithen says. "They are not exactly happy to see *us*. Jayne's about as welcome as a Derglott—"

"A what?" I interrupt.

Aithen raises a hand slightly. "Sorry, they're another planetary race. Not necessarily hostile, but whenever they happen our way, their overall stupidity and clumsiness wreak havoc everywhere."

It's crazy to imagine Koyorads are familiar with so many other lifeforms. We certainly are not alone in the universe.

"Have you heard about the protests?" Aithen asks.

Akeirlah nods. "Yes, it's everywhere. Koyorads are already spreading the word of a human pandemic, an invasion, words like that."

"Pandemic?" I spit out. "That's not very nice, is it?"

Akeirlah smiles. "It's a typical reaction to the unknown. As if Koyorads need any excuse to be paranoid." Her eyes lighten towards Aithen.

He nods. "True. But I'd love to know who started it? Why?"

"Obvious," replies Akeirlah. "Has to be the Kounsell or, more like, the Deleters."

Aithen frowns. "The Deleter who was with me on Earth has resigned his post. Even he is starting to see through the rubbish spouted about humans."

"You mean, Erek?" Akeirlah's tone drops. "Oh, I heard about him when I was locked up. There was a lot of talk about his defection for some silly humans."

Ouch!

As if noticing my silent response, Akeirlah smiles at me. "Sorry, Jayne. That's all I've heard for the past days. Humans-this, humans-that. They're so obsessed with this. I know you're not silly."

Akeirlah sits beside me. "You're amazing and brave, Jayne. I could never do and sacrifice what you have. And that's why I'm here. I intend to prove to the Kounsell everything about you."

"How can you do that?" I ask.

"We all have a voice with the Kounsell," says Aithen, and Akeirlah nods in agreement.

"And you work with the Kounsell?" I ask Akeirlah.

She laughs. "Last time I looked, I'm a Koruzyte." Her voice has that same addictive chuckle and reminds me of Isla, my friend in school. My lovely friend, who is so distant and forgotten in this world.

"I work in development," Akeirlah continues. "I patch the software for those silly drones up there." She raises her eyes, and I realise she's referring to the Deyloron.

"You work with those things?" I ask. "I thought they are A.I?"

"They are, but they can still be improved. Their learning algorithms are quite perfect, thanks to amazing individuals, like me," she gives a fake, exaggerated smile. "But there's always something new to consider or cause potential confusion. Hence, that's where the development team come into play."

"Or damaged," adds Aithen. "If a drone is damaged, then a developer will diagnose recovery and so on."

"I thought they were all-powerful and can't be attacked?" I ask.

"Oh, they are quite so, but anything can be damaged in the end," he replies.

"Let's get out of here," suggests Akeirlah.

We stroll through an open park area, enclosed by a ring of the friendlier, sparkling trees. They appear dull now, but the light show will commence when the suns set.

I welcome, not seeing another individual in sight. There is no grass, but the ground is a patchwork of green, yellow, and silver-grey moss-like growth. This appears to be the Korudaz equivalent of grass as the compact plant appears everywhere. As we walk along, there is a hint of lime in the air. Our feet crunch on the springy surface.

"The more often you mix with the environment, the better," Aithen suggests.

It's nice not to be cooped up in the apartment. Yes, I want privacy, but I don't enjoy the sense of stir-crazy.

"How does it feel, Jayne, to be on another planet?" Akeirlah asks.

Good question.

"Alien," I laugh. "It should be exciting, but I feel so nervous like anything could jump out at me at any moment. Like those trees which roar."

"Triach," Aithen says to Akeirlah.

She smiles. "Oh, yes, I can imagine they would catch anybody out. I hate their odour."

"Yeah, it's horrible," I scrunch up my nose. "It reminded me of damp, black mold on Earth."

It's strange to consider Aithen and his sister. I'm strolling around a park with two aliens. Can life get any weirder?

"Do you get to see your two suns setting on the same horizon?" I ask.

"Not often, it is quite rare," Aithen says. "But it does happen twice a year, and it is a big deal."

"And one is due soon," says Akeirlah. "It is special."

"Don't worry, I'll make sure you don't miss that," Aithen says and brushes a finger over my hand.

It's nice to feel his touch. I also find it a little amusing that he tends not to hold hands. When we do, we tend to link our little fingers together, but he's entirely reserved around Akeirlah.

"How do I buy stuff here?" I ask. "On Earth, the best thing about travelling to another country is seeing the money. What does your currency look like?"

"There isn't any," Aithen replies.

"No money? Then how do you buy anything or earn a living?"

"It is given to us to suit our needs. There's no competitive market here and no stores as such that you are accustomed to."

"Why do Koyorads work if they don't earn a living from it? If they have no money, do they just take what they want? Like, steal it?"

"Koyorads are born with a potential purpose, defined by eye pigment?" I nod in response to Akeirlah's reaction. "So work, a career, is second-nature. We progress into roles and receive homes, transport, food, and clothing."

"No bills to pay," adds Aithen.

The concept is nice, but how odd? A world without money. No concept of millionaires or billionaires. No financial hierarchy.

"So, what about celebrities? Do you make movies, music here?" I ask.

"Celebrities, as you see them, no. They don't exist here; that would break the rules of elitism," Aithen says.

"Elitism? But isn't that what the Kounsell is all about? They control everything," I say.

"Hmm… that's control and management, not elitism. Here, on Korudaz, I have a voice. I can suggest and contribute to any discussion, even the implementation of new laws and regulations," he continues.

"But you don't have the final say? The overall voice?" I reply.

"That's why the Kounsell is there," interjects Akeirlah. "They gather and assess the details and decide or govern accordingly." She laughs, dismissing the severe tone of the conversation. "Let's liven up. No political talk; too grown-up and boring."

True. I don't want to think about the Kounsell. However, I would love to be alone for a day, so I can try and formulate a plan.

I know how the plan looks from thirty-thousand feet above: to get from A to B, where A is Korudaz and B is Earth. But there are ten-thousand years of time travel voyage in the space between the two points.

My inner voice is continually turning over all visual and audible inputs around me, trying to latch onto anything which could sow the seeds to a plan of action. But the void in my plan is as empty as space. How do I fill that vacuum?

"Aithen said we'll be flying together?" Akeirlah links an arm through mine. "Have you flown before?"

It's nice she likes to be close to me and not treat me like a threatening object. "Yes, but in a commercial, passenger aeroplane, not me flying it," I smile and gently squeeze her arm with mine.

"You'll be great," Akeirlah replies. "I bet you'll be solo in a couple of days."

"Me, solo? Erm, probably not," I laugh. "But I'll give it a go. Do you have simulators or whatever?"

"No. You'll pilot the standard K-100 class. Same as what we used on Earth," Aithen says.

"I can't fly that!" I respond, my heart is already palpitating. "I'm bound to hit the nearest tree."

"No chance of that. You'll be up there, outside orbit," Akeirlah says, pointing a finger upwards.

"In space? I'm not an astronaut." Fear and excitement begin to course through me.

"Me neither, but we fly from the age of ten. I'm sure you'll be an ace in no time," encourages Akeirlah. "And you'll have the best teacher ever. Me."

Funny how I didn't have any detail in my A-to-B plan a moment ago. Flying will fill in a lot of the blanks here.

But can I really do it?

———

Alone with Aithen again.

"I like Akeirlah," I say. "She's so positive, and so unlike most of the Koyorads I have met."

Aithen kisses me. "Yes, she has her moments. But I knew you'd get on."

"What about mom and dad?" I ask. "I know you said they are not necessarily like what I am used to, parent-wise, but will I meet them?"

"I hadn't even given it a thought," he says. "I can ask, though I've no idea how they'll respond." His eyes are downcast, head lowered as though in shame.

I lift his chin. "Hey, if they don't want to meet the scary human, that's okay," I smile. "I just thought they might want to meet the prospective mom of their grandson?" Still can't believe I am having a baby and it's a half-alien baby. I chase away the thoughts.

"I've nothing to gage this against. Not done this before," Aithen says. "They'll either care or not. I'll have to get in touch wherever they are."

"Off planet?" I ask casually.

"Most likely, but leave it with me," he says and repositions himself on the settee, so he is facing me more. "One thing. I want to strike while the iron is hot, with Erek—"

"But Akeirlah said to stay away from him; he can't be trusted," I say. "I don't trust him. I never will."

"I know, but there is no other way for me to discover much

about the Deletion process and certainly not the possibility of restoring people. I must give it a try."

"What happens if you dabble too deep and vanish? You're Deleted?" I control the plea in my tone.

"I can't be Deleted. Well, I can, but only the Kounsell could authorise the configuration of my Meorlite which prevents Deletion and the release of the few Deleter devices which can perform the task. It is not standard. I'll be quite safe and will be discrete." Aithen is calm, but his words carry so much threatening undercurrent.

Whenever I hear the word Kounsell, alarm bells scream in my head.

"I don't know if I want to risk you, Aithen. Yes, I want my friends back; they deserve that. But I can't lose you."

He holds me and kisses me. "I'm going nowhere. I'll tread very carefully with Erek and will assume he is still a Deleter unless he proves otherwise. And I'll feel assured knowing you are with Akeirlah. Your pilot training will be a perfect smokescreen for us."

"What from the Kounsell?"

"Exactly. Let them see us adjusting to life together on Korudaz. Flying is as normal as breathing here. You're being a normal, boring Koyorad. Not a scary, menacing human." He kisses me again.

"A scary... menacing... hot... beautiful... human," he repeats, punctuating the words with kisses, as we settle back into the settee.

CHAPTER FORTY-FOUR

Today, Akeirlah is taking me flying for the first time.

The Kounsell support this, as then I'm *out of the way* and can't be discovered or cause issues on the surface. This outcast status works for me. I intend to learn and build my plan, so let's get to it.

Once we sit in the craft, the interior turns blue. "Cloaking? Why?" I ask.

Akeirlah smiles. "I want privacy, and even *they* cannot get through the cloaking."

Ooh, naughty girl. I like this. I return the smile and wait for the take-off. Yes, I know I have done this before, but nobody could get used to it. One moment it's a sunshine day and the next, we are in darkness. In space. Nuts.

I stand and take in the planet. The ring is unbelievable, but then the dizzy spell arrives to arrest my thoughts. Humans aren't designed for space travel. Akeirlah apologetically hands me the usual shot of liquid, and I let out a gasp as I swallow.

"You'd think I'd remember by now to take the shot." I stare in amazement at the world. I have watched so many movies and looked at artist impressions of imaginary alien worlds. Now it is a vast, living planet right in front of me.

"When I saw Earth for the first time, it was breathtaking. But words cannot even describe this. Korudaz."

"Oh, thank you, Jayne." She hugs me. "I've never visited Earth. The chances are unlikely. I've watched many records and gone into virtual-reality experiences, though. It was amazing."

I laugh. "I'd love to try one of those." My head is still spinning from being in space.

"You should. You get the full effect: smell, sounds, wind, everything."

"So where have you gone, in the recordings?"

She ponders for a moment and then talks about New York, London, and Hawaii. Her voice appears to slur. Or is it me?

"Hawaii? How random?"

"It was amazing and so hot," she responds, and I can see from her eyes she recalls the memories.

"Well, I have never visited Hawaii but the other two, yes." I flick my head, trying to clear the grogginess. What's wrong with me?

Then she starts a drill on the craft we are in. This is an S-7598, bigger than the K-100 which Aithen flew on Earth. It is a four-person craft, but for now, two seats are stowed away. The controls are manual and vocal, with the Meorlites engaging in a lot of authentication requirements.

"So, I can speak my language to the craft?" I ask.

"Oh, yes. It could translate anything, but you need the authentication aspect to control things." Akeirlah holds out a hand. "And that is what I'll give you now. Hold out a finger."

I dip my chin. "A finger?"

"Yes, I'll inject a temporary Meorlite into you."

"No, you're not." I flinch away as she takes my hand.

She smiles. "It will hurt for about three seconds, and then we're good to go."

Hurt? Hurt how much? I can be such a baby. Just three seconds of pain then I pilot a spaceship – come on!

I hold out my left hand, and Akeirlah takes hold of my ring finger, pressing a pen-like object above the knuckle. There's a click, and she looks at me, questioning.

"I'm okay," I say. There was a little stabbing pain, but then again, I tend to have a high pain threshold. Or maybe it didn't work? At least my head clears a little. Maybe an adrenalin rush from the injection.

"Ask the ship to close all the windows."

"You sure it will it understand English?" I ask.

Akeirlah nods enthusiastically.

I tilt my head and say, "Close all windows." I'm sure it won't work, but a second later, we're enclosed in blue-blackness and Korudaz is out of sight.

Akeirlah laughs. "Back to the craft. It has a lot of useful features, some of which you will like."

We open the views again and cruise away from the planet, so we can't, or rather, *I* can't bump into anybody. The controls are simple to master. A pair of joysticks, though at first, it feels like that game of rubbing your stomach and patting your head, at the same time. Then, there is a point and click navigation.

You can click on a navigational map and a moment later – or two – you are there. Absolutely crazy. You can also ask the craft to take you to a location on the screen by reference or coordinates. If you have the necessary clearance, it will take you there.

Can it really be that easy? Can I enter Earth as a destination and the date?

I continue to listen, but my mind is drifting away. Returning to Earth will be simple. This ship can take me there. I remember when we travelled to the Moon, Aithen saying he could have made the journey without the mothership. I must learn. To focus.

But then my eyes blur. I squeeze them shut and blink, but my vision is spinning, like my head. My chest heaves as I begin to gasp for air. I can't form words but somehow gargle for help.

"Jayne? Are you okay?" Akeirlah's voice sounds thick and warped.

My vision fades in and out, and I sense a tremor running through me. I can't breathe!

Akeirlah grabs onto my wrists. "Try to calm down, Jayne. You're having a panic attack."

I try to cough, but no air is available to start the spasm. Akeirlah's voice is muffled. Why won't she let go of me? I raise a knee to try and push her away, but all I hit is air.

I'm growing weak. My lungs are burning, as is my throat, and my head sizzles with stabs of lightning. What's happening? The space liquid. It hasn't worked? I did take it, didn't I? Aithen gave me a spare vial to carry on me. It's in my breast pocket.

I want to ask Akeirlah to unzip the pocket and pass me the drops, but I can't speak. Through fuzzy ears, I can barely hear the rattle of my breathing.

The grip on my wrists is released when the cockpit is drenched in red, flashing slight and a digital voice speaks in *Coten*, then English: "Collision Alert!"

"Collision Alert!"

I sense Akeirlah jumping into the pilot seat, and there's a rattle of controls.

"Collision Alert!"

I don't remember opening the pocket and extracting the vial. Still, reflexively, I administer the drops and, with gasping breaths and clearing vision, I witness a series of amber flashes outside of the craft. There are no sounds.

Sweat is running down Akeirlah's brow as she stares out of the viewing panel, her hands gripping two joysticks, her knuckles white.

What just happened?

I try to stand, but fall back into my seat, but pull myself up again so I can share her view.

A hundred metres away is a motionless, silent cloud. In space?

"What's that?" I ask.

"It nearly killed us." She runs the back of her hand across her forehead.

"I'm sorry, Akeirlah. I went into a fit. I lost it there."

I rest a hand on her shoulder, and this snaps her back to attention. "What? No, that's okay, Jayne." Her eyes are distant, watching the cloud.

"Did the flashes come from the cloud?" I ask, motioning towards the grey mass.

She cracks a slim smile. "It was a ton of rock, to begin with. It would have destroyed us, so I blew it to pieces."

"This thing has guns?" I inspect the dark enclosure, clearing my throat as my senses sharpen again.

"This may be a *private* vessel, but all come with big guns. We can't open fire on another craft, but we can on those." She points at the dust cloud.

With a clear head and nervous excitement, I ask, "Can I have a go?"

She laughs at this. "Let's find you a rock. Won't be hard."

And it only takes a few minutes to find a stray target.

"Open aim," says Akeirlah. The craft's screen becomes an elaborate crosshairs targeting system. Lots of numbers and distractions to either side, but I focus on the crosshairs.

"Use the joystick controls." She beams.

I move the controls to get used to the movement and feel.

"And press to fire, when you're ready."

My fingertips stroke a trigger within the joystick, and as I line up onto the rock, I squeeze once.

There's no sound, but three orange flashes emit from outside of the craft. A quiet moment later, the rock I was aiming at is a cloud of dust, just like the one which almost killed us. It hangs there, neither moving nor growing. I sit back into the seat. I just turned about thirty tons of rock to powder. Could this be the answer to a question I had not even thought about? Could I change the course of history with this trigger?

This craft is so easy to fly, and if Aithen is right about the Tryborre, I can fly it alone. The ship will identify me as a Koyorad. The guns on this thing will destroy a Trenier, regardless of how big they are.

I could save Earth!

But the Kounsell clock is ticking. They plan to prevent all travel back to Earth.

Is it possible I could travel there, destroy the Trenier, then come back and save my baby? But what if the enzyme erupts during the journey to Earth? It would kill me, and I wouldn't save anyone.

No, it won't be that simple. The Koyorads can simply travel back in time and stop me.

The whole idea is foolish.

In fact, the concept of time travel is ridiculous.

If it were possible to prevent someone from going further past time, then that would be perfect.

"This is not real," is all I say as I target a smaller rock. I hit the trigger twice, transforming another rock to white powder.

"Why is this allowed?" I ask Akeirlah.

"We all have to protect the planet. We have a good meteor collision watch program, but often things can get close. So, they ask vessels to keep an eye out for fast-moving objects and well, blow them up!"

I laugh. Can I ever get used to this? "I take it the computer stops you from shooting at another vessel?"

"Yes, only the military can do that, but they rarely must as they can disable the craft remotely or give it a push. We can push things along with a pulse beam, but we cannot disable another craft."

Akeirlah asks me to buckle up. "Right, let me show you what this thing can do."

Buckle up? Hello, white-knuckle ride!

CHAPTER FORTY-FIVE

As I lay in bed with Aithen's arms around me, my mind wanders. I'm old. I'm not talking about the time travel thing. Based on such a calculation, I would now be in the thousands, age-wise, compared to Earth, but more like I'm aged beyond my years. What a strange expression. But I have learnt so much, and all I want is to feel like *me* again. To put on make-up, wear nice clothes, and to have a coffee. I miss coffee.

We shower dress, and I'm curious about the deliemous, the sunscreen. "Will taking the showers, or mist I should say, wash this away?" I run a finger along the back of my hand.

"No, you're safe there, don't worry. The *mist* will promote the deliemous and safeguard the protection," Aithen says.

Akeirlah is dropping off a learning-aid she was given when learning to fly. It is like any computer tablet I am familiar with and offers a series of lectures, in English for me, as refreshers. She's so thoughtful, and it's obvious she intends for me to fit in here.

How would she feel if she knew I was plotting to leave and steal a ship? I frown internally at myself, listening to her excited voice about early flying lessons when she was much younger.

"What are you two up to today? Something fun?" she asks.

Aithen and I exchange vacant glances.

"I'd like to do something fun," I say. "But let's keep it easy and uneventful?"

"Oh, Aithen. You're such a bore. Do something exciting with Jayne. I'm the super cool flight instructor, why not take her on a virtual journey somewhere?" Akeirlah bounces in her seat. She can be so cute and excitable.

Aithen sighs. "The virtual zones? I don't know. It's been ages since I went to one and they can be a bit unnerving."

"Okay, now I am curious," I remark.

"Take Jayne to another populated world?" suggests Akeirlah.

Yes, I exclaim in my head, and Aithen notices my eyes widen.

"No, I want to prepare more for that. And I don't think the Kounsell—"

"Oh, forget the Kounsell," interrupts Akeirlah, searching the ground around her, as though an idea will be written on the floor. She straightens, her smile beaming with a plan. "Take her to Earth…"

What?

"Take her to Earth's past?" she adds. "I'd force you to take me with you, but I have something to fix."

Aithen grins at Akeirlah's suggestion.

"What?" I ask them.

"Well, this may not be a walk in the park as far as the dangerous aspect goes. But as you know all about the time travel, do you want to see a dinosaur?"

My open-mouthed expression answers, but still, I gasp out, "No way. You're kidding? What dinosaur?"

He laughs. "Oh, you'll like this."

When you thought things could not get any crazier, think again. We are about to step into a world so distant and remote from all imagination. And yet we will be on Earth, but in no way will this be the planet I know. I am given another different liquid, so I won't fall into a major panic attack while we are there.

I want no repeat of that *moment* I had in space with Akeirlah. The fact I need to be artificially calmed is scary, but they are erring on the side of caution. And here is me thinking this will be a fun and relaxing thing to do; not when I'm involved. So much for my easy, non-eventful day.

We're dressed in pale-grey one-piece suits with incorporated boots and gloves. Our heads are sprayed with a fine mist which creates a transparent barrier around our heads. Like a spray-on helmet, but this allows us to breathe within the virtual environment.

"Remember, Jayne. This will be as real as though you are there." Aithen is fastening down straps across my back. "You will hear, smell, and sense everything. This is a lot more than virtual reality; this is a snapshot of actual reality from prehistoric times."

"Is this just pretend? Or are we actually travelling back in time, to be there?" Well, I may as well ask.

"Wow, no! Way too dangerous. To do so takes a large team and a lot of planning. Koyorads were killed carrying out recordings like this."

"But why?" I ask. "All I hear is how much Koyorads hate Earth—"

"No, not Earth," Aithen says. "It's the humans who they have issues with. Dinosaurs, on the other hand, are another story altogether."

"Maybe I should have dressed up as a Tyrannosaurus for the Kounsell meeting?" I quip.

The venue is a large circular building about two kilometres in diameter, and the actual virtual world measures about fifty kilometres across. I suppose this is a serious attempt to capture this virtual recording atmosphere on a large scale. We enter through a rather dull pair of sliding doors to a room with no light. I can't see my hand in front of my face.

Without warning, there is a bright flash, and an ear-piercing screech throws us both to the floor.

I'm not sure if I passed out momentarily, but I fumble in the darkness for Aithen, and his hands find mine.

"What was that?" I shudder, the chill slicing along my spine. My throat is parched.

"I don't know." Aithen's teeth chatter. "That was different." He swallows loudly, clearing his throat.

The blackness of the room becomes warm.

The confines of the room fade, and we are in a dark, dense forest, a jungle even. The air is so humid; it almost burns my throat and nostrils with a coarse smell of charcoal or damp wood. It is hard to explain; it is a smell I have never experienced before.

I gasp for air and Aithen passes me a tube with a spray nozzle on it. "Spray this on your face; it will help. You should already be protected, but I have to agree, it is hard to breathe in this landscape."

I do as he says, and the spray takes away a little of the heaviness of the air around me. This is so real, too real.

"You sure this is a recording?" I ask, rubbing together wet, gloved fingertips as I brush them against the leaf of an exotic plant. The air is like smoke in this place.

"This is not a rehearsed or pre-set recording. The animals and all life here will be as random as if we are there, so let's be careful." His eyes dart about the hostile vegetation.

I don't like the tone of urgency in his voice. "They can't kill us, can they? The dinosaurs?"

"No, but you could have a heart attack from shock. Take my word for it, respect this environment, it is dangerous. Your mind will believe it, the longer we stay here."

The ground is unstable and hard to walk on. If I had to run, I would not get far. The floor of the forest is springy but also snagged with roots and plants I have never seen before. They can only be prehistoric. We amble through the trees, and I'm almost holding my breath to be quiet.

There are so many strange sounds from invisible animals. Could be birds but then I remind myself they don't exist yet. Aithen stops and holds up a hand. My heart races. I check behind us, expecting to see the door we entered from, but all I see are trees, plants, and the dense, misty air. This is scary. I snap back to Aithen when there's a dull, deep vibration ahead of us.

I'm about to speak, but he motions his head. *Be silent.* He beckons my attention ahead. All I see are trees and darkness. There's the vibration again. It's not an animal moving; not the sound of feet but the sound of breathing. Deep, ancient lungs breathing. It is almost hypnotic in how the sound surrounds and penetrates my body. I mouth, *what is it?*

The first mouthed syllable in response is clear enough for me, and I duck down.

Tyrannosaurus.

It can't be?

I stay low and peer at Aithen. *Where?*

Get a grip. This is not real. But my heart is pounding. I'm nauseous from the dense air and the vibration of the breathing. *How close is it?*

Aithen gestures for us to move to the right but to keep low. We seem to struggle for what feels like an eternity before he speaks.

"Sorry, Jayne. That was too close." The whites of his eyes are more prominent. He's scared. "It is in hunting position, so I wanted to give us distance for a moment."

"Hunting position? Don't they run at thirty kilometres per hour to catch their prey?"

"They can, but it is rare. Those huge hind legs are for a different

purpose altogether. I'll show you, but let's get a little higher first."
He signals me to follow him, and we ascend a rather easy-to-climb
tree. It's enormous in width and looks to go upwards forever.

"Okay, down there. You need to let your eyes adjust, but there."
He points towards a large gathering of dense trees. I see nothing. A
scene of green and black and then…

What is that…? Oh no, an eye.

I trace along a bony brow, and I follow what looks like a snout.
It is huge! The head looks like the size of a small car, but I cannot
make out the shape.

"Can we get closer?" This is an ultimate first. To see a virtually
real, living, breathing Tyrannosaurus. I take two deep breaths,
knowing I won't be breathing much in a moment.

Quiet as possible, we gingerly circle the source of the deep
vibration. It is overwhelming. I utilise the spray twice to help me
on my way. Imagine living in this place for real. I know there
were no humans around then, but to be an animal of any description must have been so frightening. Aithen motions with his hands
for us to get lower as we approach a small opening within the
trees.

The light from the sun can barely penetrate this place. It may as
well be a cave with random, small holes in its roof. I jump and give
out a yelp as my hand is brushed. I look, but there is nothing. The
vibration halts and I hear a sound which turns my blood to ice. It's
not a growl or roar but a deep cough like the clashing of steel but so
heavy and distorted.

There's the slight movement of what at first appears to be a
snake. As I run my gaze along the length, I can see the snake
becoming broader and fuller; it's a tail. I trace along the animal's
back until I can see the head more. The Tyrannosaurus is dark
green, almost black in colour, and it looks like it's lying low on the
ground.

The dinosaur crouches low, and you can see the tenseness in the muscles of its legs. It's ready to pounce, to spring forward upon its prey. The small arms are hidden in the undergrowth.

I'm reassured slightly when the vibration of its lungs echo around us again; the colossal beast settles and doesn't consider investigating the sound I made. Is it sleeping? No. It's waiting. I want to run away, screaming, but the vibrating air freezes me. Aithen motions for us to move away again. My curiosity wants to stay; my survival instinct says to flee. This is not safe. How many Koyorads were killed when capturing this event? I can't bear to imagine.

But then a heavy, eerie silence blankets everything. The snap of a twig. A grunting sound, with the hint of a soft rattle. I can hear the throbbing in my ears. The colossal predator is deathly silent.

Something is coming.

Aithen squeezes my arm and touches an index finger to his lips. *Be silent!*

Another twig snaps. Grunting.

My heart pounds against my rib cage as I spot a big lizard. Maybe four feet tall and walking on four legs.

I don't see the predator lurch forward and spring death onto the victim. But the spray of blood, wood splinters, and leaves, which wash over Aithen and me, acknowledges its passing. My scream escapes and is answered by the deep, grinding cough of the tyrannosaurus.

We have our bodies and faces pressed into the ground. Can it see us? Smell us?

Ancient lungs vibrate below us as the animal tears and crunches on its prey. The speed and power of attack were sickening. I face Aithen for some assurance, but I see a mask of terror. He shakes his head and points with his chin to stay low.

My arms are bent below me, so with just my exposed hands, I lift them to ask, *what's going on?*

Another shake of the head, but then he indicates we should back away, on our stomachs, as slowly as possible. What can possibly happen? We're in a recording. I administer more of the spray, as the feeding becomes even more nauseous due to the odour from the dead animal. It may be a new kill, but the stench from its insides is repulsive.

I would say half an hour passes before Aithen speaks. Thankfully, the buzz of the jungle around us returns to regular volume. The predatory silence was unnerving.

Aithen wipes my face and passes me the cloth. He removes the blood and dirt from his own and his chest.

"How have I got blood on me? Shouldn't this spray-on helmet stop it?" I grimace at the cloth.

"There should be no blood. No nothing." He grits his teeth, searching around us. "We're really here, Jayne."

It takes a moment for the message to sink in, past the smoky environment, the burning tar odour, the stench of fear. *Really here*.

Then I freeze, and my lungs convulse. "Really here?"

"I don't know how, but yes. We are." He taps on his wrist, and I welcome the pop-up screen of the Meorlite. "I know it is safe to transport hardware across space and time, but never a living individual."

I examine my knuckle. I wonder if mine has a screen. Now's not the time. How do we get back? Can we? "Aithen. We have to get out of here. Can we get back?"

"I'm working on it." His fingers work furiously, sweat trickling down his face.

"How long?" I scold myself. *Leave him alone.*

He raises his chin, "Up!" he commands.

We climb. The ground is unstable and falls away at our feet, sliding down into the darkness. Alerting anything watching of our presence. But we march on. Aithen keeps monitoring the screen. I can only hope he is tracking potential threats, but I don't disturb him.

We must escape. How did we get here? I know I intended to return to Earth, but not sixty-five-million years in the past. My heart is like a golf ball rattling about a cage. A metallic taste flows about my mouth, forcing me to spit out. Thankfully, these spray-on masks are like a gas, so they permit substances to pass both ways. They were not meant for this environment.

We rest on a rocky ledge. The jungle still wraps around us, but for the first time, Aithen appears calm.

"Okay, I have a contingency plan." He continues as he taps on his wrist. "Please, don't be alarmed," he grabs hold of my hands, "but I have to leave you."

"What? No! You can't!" I keep my alarm quiet within the dangerous trees.

"Jayne. I can't travel with you. It's a teleportation module and must be piloted solo."

"Where are you going?"

"To get the craft, which brought us here." He rubs the back of his neck.

"What do you mean the craft which brought us here?" I ask. "We stepped into the virtual thing and... here we are."

"The fact you survived the journey is impossible," Aithen coughs as he speaks. "It should have killed you as you were not prepared. In fact, it could have killed me, too, and I think that was the intention."

"The Kounsell's done all this? To harm me?"

Aithen stares at me for a moment. "It's impossible to send an organic object, like us, to here. Yes, it was all a flash of light, but we have travelled here in a vehicle and then been teleported to our Earth location," he explains.

"But we entered a room, not a spaceship?" I gasp. This air is so thick.

"I'm sure we passed out immediately. What felt like a second was in fact almost a day. This has been a carefully planned attack—"

"Attack? For crying out loud, Aithen. What is it with the Kounsell?"

"That's assuming it was them. A lot of Koyorads know about you being there. Many potential enemies now," he says.

How can he be so calm? "You can't leave me, Aithen. I'll die here."

"No, you won't. I've scanned this area and anything for kilometres. You're safe, Jayne."

"And what if Mr T-Rex just happens by?" My teeth chatter, despite the humid air. I rub my arms as though chasing away the cold.

My feet are restless. I can't keep still.

"You have the Tryborre protection from Erek, remember?" His eyes are close and level with mine. "You won't give off any scent here and if by some chance something appeared, time will slow down. You can escape. But you won't need to. Trust me?"

"If I run away, how will you find me?"

"With this." His Meorlite.

"How long will you be gone?" I bite my trembling lower lip.

"No more than an hour."

I gasp. "An hour? Why so long?"

"The craft which brought us will be powered down and expected to burn up in the Earth's atmosphere. Even if it crashes to Earth intact, there are sixty-five million years to break it down and hide the evidence." Aithen exhales loudly.

The Meorlite on his wrist emits a ping and a blue dot pulses in the vacant air. "Okay, I've found the craft, so at least it is still above the atmosphere. I need to rush."

The firmness and warmth of his hug don't reach the chill of my core. I know I must let him go, but an hour? Here? It will be like a year.

I nod my head with a stutter. "Leave. Go. But please, hurry."

We kiss hastily, and as he grabs his wrist; he blinks out of existence. I scan the floor where he stood a moment ago, but he's gone. I fall to my knees and hug myself, rocking backwards and forwards and praying for him to return. Soon.

This jungle only appears to know one time of the day: nighttime. So many hoots, squeaks, pops, and snaps occupy the dense air around me. I jump at every crack of wood. Two of the calming spray pods have already been depleted. I have two more.

Every so often, a rancid puff of steam will wander my way, almost forcing me to retch. But I swallow away the fear. The terror. The bitter, dark isolation. What went wrong? It would take very advanced technology to send us all the way here. This must be the Military Kounsell's handy work.

But what an elaborate plan. Is this their way of saying I'm prehistoric, so get back to your own time? How horrible. Why have they bothered to bring me to Korudaz in the first place? It doesn't make sense. But I'm sure it is the Gouhlde Kounsell who wanted to preserve the life of the baby and hence me.

What about the angry crowd of protestors? Any of them could work at the virtual world installation. Have they targeted me? But why kill one of their own? Aithen.

I can't contain the yelp as a flash accompanies a sonic boom and warm air floods past me. But with the encouraging warmth of Aithen's arrival, comes the menacing, grinding cough of a skulking predator below.

This craft is different. Brushed silver and more rounded than the black wedge. It's bigger too, but I don't dare move. Another sickening cough below.

An entrance appears in the side of the vessel, and Aithen rushes towards me. "Get in!"

He barks a command at the craft as heavy footsteps charge at the soft earth, below us. It's making an attack. The ship emits a stabbing wave of strobes towards the monster, but this throws my coordination off balance.

Aithen's arms are around me, and he lifts me towards the opening of the vessel. Mild charges explode and pop under the vehicle and in a matter of seconds, we are twenty kilometres in space.

Somehow, I'm laughing and hiccupping with tears at the same time. I wipe my dirty face and saliva from my mouth. I can't cope.

Aithen sprays away the false helmet. He's dressed in the standard-issue Korudaz uniform, and there's one ready for me, folded on a chair. I dab my face with a warm cloth and then bury my tearful eyes into it. His arms are around me as I heave with the sobs.

"What the hell was that?" I manage through the slobber. I know I'll look a mess, but it was ridiculous.

We could have sat there for an hour, a day. Aithen's warmth seeps through me, clawing me back to reality. To safety.

When the little colour returns to my face, Aithen pitches in with, "So, you want to have fun with no drama attached?"

His false, crooked smile has me laughing. Then he does, too.

"It's not funny," I say, and we laugh louder. Hysteria, I guess.

We recover, and I explore this new craft. "This is different?"

"Not normally used for personnel travel," he explains. "This is different from the other in a lot of ways and will get us back to Korudaz, a lot quicker."

We're in Earth's orbit.

"Can we take a look?" I ask.

Aithen issues the command, and a large panel becomes transparent.

There it is. My planet – it looks different, but I can't put my finger on it. "It looks greener like there is more land?"

Aithen joins my view. "Yes. Sea levels are much lower, and there are no humans to level the forests."

I nudge him. "Yeah, but it's weird. That planet doesn't know what a human is and yet, one stood on it today."

"Yes, but you nearly didn't," he frowns. "I've had time to think, and it's now obvious, the Tryborre did its magic again and protected you and the baby for the journey. But that's encouraging, it means I can risk getting you back in one piece."

"I might be safer with the dinosaurs," I say. "We can start a whole new human race."

"Wouldn't that be a thing?" he smiles. "But we must return."

"What so that they can try and kill me again?"

"We have no choice. There are the pregnancy and the enzyme. I have to get you to a safe place, and I will report this to the Gouhlde Kounsell."

"They appear powerless to me," I say. "They're not the ones with the finger on the trigger."

"Maybe so, but the whole of the Military Kounsell can be replaced. The fact they have reacted to you like this can only mean the Gouhlde is making waves behind the scenes," Aithen says, a little hope lightening his voice.

"So, now we have to travel all that way back, over weeks and a black hole and…?" The thought of that journey so soon is not welcoming.

"Oh, no. We'll strap in, go to sleep and be back in Korudaz today." Something dulls Aithen's tone.

"Is there a risk? You said we're not supposed to travel in this craft?"

The colour from his face drains.

"We got here. The chance of doing so was one in a million. Same odds apply."

CHAPTER FORTY-SIX

My senses have been raw for the past few days. Ugly patches of bruising run across my body from the intense stress of the flight back.

Aithen and I were placed in medical stasis upon arrival at Korudaz. I was unaware of everything, but Aithen had set the craft to emit a distress beacon upon arrival in the planet's orbit. My appearance triggered the Deyloron assigned to me, and our ship was automatically protected by a swarm of these red drones.

The incident with the dinosaur has shattered my mind and concentration. I hear its breathing whenever there is silence, and the sickening attack on the prey accompanies night terrors when I sleep.

The stench of the jungle lingers in my nostrils, like a memory scratching for attention. I've been prescribed a safe remedy to help calm my nerves. Nothing which can harm the baby.

But my brain can't dismiss a hypothetical threat: what if when Aithen left to get his craft, something had happened to him? I would have been trapped in that place. Alone. Vulnerable.

Myarve, from the Gouhlde Kounsell, sits casually with Aithen and me. The medical gowns we wear are white and flowing, but I can't help feeling like I'm a child dressed in loose-fitting adult clothing. These gowns are over-the-top. I wrap it tightly around me.

The wrinkles on Myarve's forehead seem to burrow deeper as we speak. Caring, grey eyes watch us.

"This all appears an incredible overreaction from the Kounsell," he says. "I've heard their concerns regarding you, Jayne. But I don't believe they would go this far."

"Who else could it be?" I ask.

"Nobody has such resources," Aithen adds.

"There's a lot of noise out there, with the crowds, but you know what it's like," Myarve says, considering Aithen. "There are no complaints for a long time, and then a tiny thing triggers a landslide of opinions."

"How do we stop the threat? Another attempt to hurt Jayne?" Aithen asks.

"Or you?" I add, taking Aithen's hand in mine.

"I think it was an opportunist moment with the virtual zone," says Myarve. "Someone simply got lucky, in my opinion. By lucky, the pieces of a plan fell together, rather than were planned. I know this won't settle your mind, but it was a case of wrong time and place, or the opposite, depending on your viewpoint."

"Can you honestly say, the Kounsell are not involved in this?" I ask.

"No, I can't," replies Myarve. "But I also know they agreed to your transfer to Korudaz, to facilitate the safe delivery of the baby. If they wanted you to die, they would have kept you on Earth." His expression drops. "The enzyme would have killed you and had the baby somehow survived, then... its future was already doomed."

"Transfer?" I say, calmly. "You do know I was abducted? I didn't get the chance to say goodbye to anyone."

"And what would you have said to them? Your family, friends?" Myarve asks. "One option was to simply Delete you, which I am aware you are very familiar with."

I nod. "And then you could restore me here, on Korudaz."

Myarve nods slowly, watching me. "What if somehow, you could return to Earth? I don't know a scenario where that would happen, but would you want to return to a family who has forgotten who you are?"

Is he suggesting I have a chance to return to Earth? No, he can't be. Or have I been talking in my sleep, while in the medical centre? Have I spoken about my plan to steal a craft and leave?

"I'd suggest you keep things quiet about what has happened at the virtual zone," continues Myarve. "But keep aware of who is surprised to see you or acting nervous around you. Especially you, Aithen. You're familiar to more Koyorads, Jayne less so."

"What about the workers in the virtual zone?" Aithen asks.

"They've been questioned, and I understand they were genuinely distressed at what has happened," Myarve says.

"I'm not convinced," Aithen says.

"The thing is, the zones are not strictly monitored," Myarve says. "Individuals enter and can remain for hours, days. They've promised a full investigation, but what can I say?"

Sounds weak to me.

We are discharged a couple of hours later, and it's nice to wear the tight jumpsuit again after those gowns.

We return to the apartment, escorted by a Deyloron, and receive disturbing news: the plan to close the wormhole has been approved, despite resistance from the education sector. This is all I need. I am nowhere near prepared.

Akeirlah meets us with a hand on Aithen's shoulder and hugs for me. She even gives Aithen a hug, and it's funny, as he's quite taken by her gesture. Her teary-red eyes betray the worry she must have felt the past few days.

"They wouldn't let me visit you at the medical centre. What exactly happened?" she asks, stroking a few loose strands of hair from my face, and cupping my cheeks. "They said something about you leaving Korudaz?"

We sit in the lounge area.

"Where to begin," says Aithen, and then he briefly recaps the scary events. It's touching, watching Aithen looking at his big sister. Families are a strange thing and how they interact. It's the tiny gestures which only they share, like widening of eyes, or smiling at the wrong times. Laughing when something is deadly serious.

It's that trust. That special bond.

I miss my family so much. I want to tell them about a dinosaur, an alien world, and my baby.

"How did you know how to pilot a freight craft?" Akeirlah asks. "We don't learn that."

"Coincidence," Aithen says, widening his eyes. "I had a lot of time on my hands when travelling to Earth and stumbled across a manual and basic simulator. Probably the most important day I have ever spent."

Akeirlah agrees with our plan to keep things hushed. Let's smoke out the conspirators.

"I'm a nobody here, Jayne. But I'm from *here*. I'll mingle with the crowds. Especially those you said were demonstrating. More have popped up, but don't worry. None are near to you. You're secure here," Akeirlah says.

"Thank you, Akeirlah. I have Aithen and you, and no-one else."

CHAPTER FORTY-SEVEN

My stomach is swelling a little, and the thought is crazy. I still feel him kick randomly, but it is gentle, like butterflies in the stomach.

Compared with Earth pregnancy months, this is way too early, but the doctors assure me he is a lot more developed than I imagine. But best of all, the scans and tests have established I am having an earth-sized baby and will give birth to a small boy and not a toddler. Yes, I will have a little baby. Still, I must remember that his physiology is half Koyorad, and I will undergo the customary procedure for delivering the baby.

They are tight-lipped about this procedure, and I don't like it.

The threat with the enzyme point still applies, but they've assured me I am safe. The Deyloron is monitoring me carefully, so they encourage me to enjoy the experience.

Enjoy the experience?

What, when some crazed Kounsell and angry Koyorads are scheming to kill me?

"I need to understand the birthing routine," I say to Aithen. "Everyone here is avoiding the subject, and I have a right to know."

"I know, you're right, you do," he says. "The procedure has arisen due to the historical threat of pregnancy and labour. But you're not a Koyorad, so I think they are grasping for threads into the unknown at the moment."

"Why does that make me feel worried?" I remark. "I don't want some medics fumbling for ideas. Have they spoken to you directly about this? Behind my back?"

"No, of course not. It doesn't work that way here. The medical Koyorads only confide with other medics. All procedures are kept somewhat secret from the public, and if truth be told, we're not interested in such things. Leave it to the experts," Aithen explains.

"We're not like that," I say. "Us *humans* love medical stuff. We investigate the ins and outs of everything. I need to know what will happen to me, Aithen."

"Okay, I don't know the full detail applicable to you, but with a Koyorad, the sack which encloses the unborn baby is placed in stasis and teleported out of the host mother. This sack is then developed externally from her body."

"How does it survive without a blood source, feeding, oxygen?" I ask.

"All done artificially with the right technology. You must know us by now, a piece of machinery for just about anything," he says.

Aithen checks I don't have another question, so continues. "The mother is frozen in time, but the sack and unborn baby are sent forward in time—"

"Time travel again?"

"Yes. The baby is developed to the point of delivery and safety. It's brain functionality, and bodily functions are developed by many systems so that when it is born, it is mentally and physically strong and capable—"

"And is the size of a two-year-old," I add.

"The baby, still fully developed, is brought back in time and the mother woken," Aithen says.

"Wait, what?" I'm confused now. "So, the mother goes into the hospital. The fetus is teleported intact from her body. Because?"

"Its development size will kill her," replies Aithen.

"Yes, yes, I forgot that. She is frozen in time. The baby is fast-forwarded using time travel and is a toddler. This toddler is brought back to the day the mother entered the hospital, and both wake up together?"

"Yes, that sort of covers it," Aithen says.

"What happens to her after they have extracted the baby? That must leave behind some loose ends in her body?" I ask.

"Yes, the medical team will fix everything. She'll wake up fully recovered and feeling very unpregnant; no side effects or anything," he says.

I can't imagine that. Sarah could not walk properly for days after labour, and the stitches she had during post-labour were ghastly. I didn't need to see them, but I often heard her seething between gritted teeth when she even had a pee. I don't want that.

"But I'm having an Earth-sized baby. He will be tiny and soft and lovely," I say, my lips quivering.

Aithen hugs me. "Yes, and he'll be special."

"And ours," I sniff at the thought of a little person in my arms.

"This is one thing I'm not fearful of," Aithen says.

I kiss him. "So, I'll go to the hospital and see my baby on the same day?"

Aithen nods. "Yes. I know that will be weird, but yes."

It is weird. But what else do you expect on an alien planet?

"I don't feel like I've had time to prepare… mentally. I've been fighting for my survival lately, let alone thinking about being a mom."

"Yeah, it's been tough—" A bleep from Aithen's Meorlite stops him. He stares vacantly into the air, then to me.

"What was that?" I ask.

"I just received a message from Erek," he says, thoughtfully.

"*Him*? What does *he* want?" Why does this feel like unwelcome news?

"He wants or rather *needs* to meet with me?"

I shake my head. "Don't. This has to be a setup."

"No, I don't think so. Meorlite messages are not a straightforward text message. They can include emotional tone, and his tone is sincere, I promise you." Aithen stands and paces the floor a moment. "I can sense he's careful, too. The message has been sent covertly, so no ears or eyes, can intercept it."

"Which to me says the Kounsell is setting a trap," I stand, too. "You can't trust him. Akeirlah said so, and I'll always believe her before Erek."

Aithen frowns. "Yes, I know. But you don't just up and leave the Deleters like he has. And I don't believe for a moment it is because of your friends."

"He Deleted them, Aithen." I stand back from him. Surely, he can't be imagining a scenario where Erek is innocent here. "And don't tell me it is because it is something he was ordered to do. He is fully aware of his actions."

"Maybe so, but he still protected you," Aithen replies.

"Please, don't tell me you're taking his side now?" I swallow deeply. How can the warm, special moment we were sharing a minute ago be sabotaged by Erek and the stupid, scheming Kounsell?

"Sides? Jayne, I'm only on your side. But if Erek has information or some knowledge which affects you or me, then I need to hear about it. He knows where I stand, so I'd rather face whatever is out there than hide in ignorance."

"I don't like it, but okay, you go," I say. "But… if anything happens… I'll kill him."

———

I step out of the shower and enter the bedroom.

There's a small white bag on the bed, adorned in Koyorad symbols. I saw similar at the Kounsell building.

I open the bag and feel relieved.

Oh, Aithen.

My perfume. My favourite scent is here. I haven't seen this since I arrived on the planet. At least something cleared *Koyorad border control*. If there is such a thing.

I drop the towel – I don't need a towel as the shower dries you, but a habit is a habit – and allow myself a luxurious spraying of the fresh, sweet perfume. The mist across my skin is lovely and refreshing. I toss the usual jumpsuit back onto the bed and reach into a closet for something sweet and familiar to wear.

The jumpsuits come with several underlayers, some of which are like a black spandex material. Not much different from my usual running attire, but I need the legs shortened.

I grab a small laser cutter from the kitchen and make work of one of the thin under-suits. The cutter is like a metal knife with a pale-blue, laser inset into the blade edge.

There's never anybody around where I am living, so I decide to cut the leg and arm material, producing a one-piece short-sleeved, and legged uniform. Not perfect, but it'll do. The thin, tight material makes my tummy bulge look even more prominent.

How odd, but I don't care.

Today can be a bit of freedom-day. Get some sun on my skin and enjoy a gentle jog. I'll take a hover-car out and set it on auto-return. That way, I can run back. There are some quite deserted routes around here, so I'll just do five kilometres. I am pregnant, after all.

I pull on a jumpsuit as a precaution. If no-one is around, I can run back without this on.

Stepping outside the apartment, I scan the area for anyone, anything. A subtle wave of fear sweeps over me, but this is overcome by a small laugh breaking from me: I smell gorgeous. This is great. For the first time in so long, I feel human again.

My scent fills my nostrils and fires a hundred memories of home at once. It's quite intoxicating. But welcome and calming.

I hop into the hover-car and keep the roof closed over. The journey doesn't take long, and when I stop, I set the program to return the car back to the pre-set home location.

I step out of the jumpsuit and toss it back into the car. The background hum of the planetary ring, unfamiliar trees, and airborne highways stoke the paranoia, simmering beneath my personal high.

Be careful. You don't belong here.

"Bye car," I say and wave it away, as I park myself on a large rock.

Peace and quiet.

Distant vehicles progress across the bright sky, but I'm alone in this green and yellow wilderness. Just me, the Earth alien on a distant planet.

Alone.

Not safe. Danger.

It dawns on me how isolated I am. Where's the Deyloron? Isn't it supposed to follow me?

I stand and begin to jog.

I can't have been running for more than five minutes, but my breathing is coming in deep pants, and my skin is so hot. My feet stamp into the parched ground, and my vision won't stop blearing.

I stop and take deep breaths. The pregnancy must be sapping away my energy.

Let's go.

But within a couple of minutes, a nasty, musty smell is filling my nostrils, like singed hair. What is that? And then a sharp stab rips across my body.

"Ow!" I cry and stumble to the ground, shredding the skin on my knees. Blood wells to the surface and is met by a scalding burn.

I cry out again and grab my knees. My legs look red-raw and throb with agonising pain. There's smoke rising from my skin as the hairs and top layers of my skin dry and burn.

I'm on fire! I scream and scramble to my feet. How's this happening? I smack at my skin and try to run, but my energy is dwindling, and my vision is blinkered with tears.

My throat stings, and I wheeze through my faltering steps. How far do I have to go? Can I make it?

I fall to the ground again and scrape away the skin on my elbows and wrists.

I scream, but nobody will hear me.

The panic alarm. Did I bring it? My wrist is bare, no bracelet.

I search the slim pocket in the makeshift shorts with trembling fingers and find a small, metallic ring. It must be it. I must have packed it without thinking.

I scramble towards the shade of a solitary tree. Please, give me some protection.

Attempting to slip the bracelet over my wrist, it slips and rolls away.

I curse inside and reach for it, the searing heat from the suns tear a cry from my parched throat.

"Please!" I gasp and choke.

I grab the circle of metal and hold tightly.

Tapping the bracelet twice, I blackout.

CHAPTER FORTY-EIGHT

I jump awake in a bed.

I'm in a white-walled hospital room, and I'm wearing a white, plastic suit? I cough, and Aithen appears at the door. He hands me a glass of water and watches me drink.

My cracked lips hurt from the coldness of the water. My whole face feels tight and swollen.

"Thankfully, you had the alarm on you," he says, and I can see the worry shadowing his face.

Alarm? What's he on about? But then a waft of charred flesh reminds me of the heat and smoke of my skin.

"I'm sorry," I croak, "I don't know what happened." I take tiny sips and dab my lips with the cold, stinging water. I look at the suit covering my body; it even has incorporated gloves. "How bad is it?"

"You're fortunate, Jayne. What were you thinking?" he asks, his words trembling a little.

"I just went for a run. How bad is my skin, under this suit?" I'm going to be scarred for life.

"You could be dead," he sniffs out the words. "This suit will repair the damage."

"How long?" I ask through painful sips of the water.

"You'll be fine. This suit will regenerate your skin within a day; your face is already clear, though still puffy," he says, holding up a mirror for me to see.

I look like I've been in a boxing match. "I look awful," I respond, handing the mirror back to him.

"Jayne, they carried out an analysis and found traces of scent. I recognised your perfume from the material of your suit and the bedroom smelt of it. Where did the perfume come from?" Aithen's expression is pained. "It's not allowed and would remove the protective sunscreen you had applied."

"It was left in the bedroom," I croak. "I assumed you left it there as a surprise. The bag it was in had logos like what I had seen in the Kounsell building, so I assumed it had been cleared."

"There was no bag and no perfume," Aithen says.

I try to sit up, but my back stings and the skin pulls like it will split.

Aithen returns to sitting on the bed. "Don't try to move. You must lay still. I have a dose of medicine to give you, which will help you sleep for the rest of the day and night and will also stop you from moving around."

"Don't leave me alone?" I gasp.

"I won't," he says with a tender kiss on my head. "The bag and perfume are gone. Someone got the perfume in and out of there without the guard seeing."

"Who could do that?" I ask.

"Only you, me, and the security have an access key to the building. Nobody else—"

"So, it has to be the Kounsell or someone there? What about the Deleters? Could they gain access?" I interrupt.

"But why would they or the Kounsell?" he asks, standing and watching out of the window. "Despite their hostile reception, I know they wouldn't want to interfere with the baby."

"Then it's someone from that crowd of demonstrators? Akeirlah told me the protests are growing." I suggest. How horrible could they be? "Why do they hate humans so much?"

Aithen shrugs. "Scaremongers, who knows. But whoever it is; they know where you are staying, so we'll have to move you again."

I sigh at this.

Somebody seems bent on removing me. But in doing so, do they realise they would be killing an innocent Koyorad baby?

I'm so vulnerable. Open to attack.

Even having Aithen close does not seem to reach the depths of this feeling I have.

What have I done? Ran away from my life and lost everything on Earth. I should have fought much harder to stay. But had I stayed, I would have died along with everyone else, if not sooner from the pregnancy.

I need to escape from Korudaz before someone stops me.

Permanently.

"Aithen, how do I get away from here?" I whisper, as my throat can't handle the words.

He settles in close to me. "What from the hospital, or…?"

"From Korudaz. I want to go home, even if it is for a couple of years."

"But—"

"I'd rather die, surrounded by people who care and love me than spend another day here." I squeeze back the tears.

"You know that won't happen," he says, rubbing one of my gloved fingers. "Even if we could grab a ship, they'd stop us. But I'd stop us, too. I can't risk you and the baby."

"But I don't want to be here for weeks or months, waiting for the baby to arrive," I choke out the words.

"You won't be." Aithen sighs loudly. "The baby is coming today."

My heart jumps into my throat, and I feel nauseous from the rush of adrenalin, gripping my chest. All thoughts racing through my head urge me to flee, but my arms and legs are like a buzzing jelly.

"Today?" I gasp. "How? W-why? I'm not ready!"

I place an open, gloved palm on my forehead and search the room around me. "This can't happen today, Aithen. I can barely look after myself, let alone a baby. I can't—"

"It's okay," Aithen soothes. "Breathe. Calm down. Everything will be fine."

"But why today?" I ask.

"The episode with the... the fact you nearly died has triggered the enzyme point," Aithen says.

Oh, no.

I can't become a mom today.

"When's this happening?" I ask.

"You're stable from the sunburns, and the enzyme effects won't erupt for a few hours, but then you have to go into stasis," he locks eyes with mine. "I'll be here for you, Jayne. I promise. I've asked Akeirlah to come over after she finishes work, so you won't be alone."

"So, I'm going to go through that whole teleportation, time travel thing, today?" My brain is racing in a hundred directions. Every path leads to death or some complication. It's going to go wrong, I know it.

I sit up despite the pain and prepare to vomit. I wave Aithen away, but he places his hand on a shoulder and uses his other hand to brush away the hair falling across my face. I only cough, then wretch a couple of times, but I'm half thankful I'm not sick.

"I'm sorry," I struggle to say, settling back down.

"Don't be," he replies, holding a glass to my lips. "It's a huge shock. When they told me, I nearly passed out."

I laugh at that. "I keep forgetting how scary this must be for you, too."

"No, you're the one doing all the work," he says and offers a smaller vial of liquid.

"What's that?"

"It'll help you to relax. Consider it stage one of about a hundred stages. I'm allowed to give you this, the medics will do the rest," he smiles weakly.

I comply and swallow the sugary liquid. It reminds me of a thin syrup.

Within ten seconds, I feel a buzzing wave of calm, sweep over me. It's nice.

My vision is clear, and I take in Aithen's beautiful, violet eyes.

"Stay with me until I sleep?" I ask, noticing my words are slurring a little.

"I will," he says and kisses me. I hope my cracked lips don't feel horrible to him. "I'll never leave you. I love you."

I try to blink away the incoming tide of sleep, but the buzzing in my head is soothing.

The worried voice in my head calms.

He'll keep me safe.

Aithen, I…

CHAPTER FORTY-NINE

The beeping sound of a reversing lorry awakens me. Must be bin day and I've overslept. Glancing at my clock through bleary eyes, I see it's eight am. I can't work out if this is a school day or the week-end? I can hear Emily and David downstairs. Oh, get up, I tell myself.

Wait a minute…

My eyes snap open, and I sit upright in my bed. No, in the bed in the hospital.

I was dreaming. But I was there, and I could hear my family as clear as day.

I take in the alien room. Plain, white walls, dimmed lighting. Silent. How come I'm dressed in different clothes? I glance at my arms. No burns or signs of scarring. The sheen of the deliemous has returned. My legs are fully healed, too.

Where's my baby?

I stand and immediately Aithen is there in the doorway. "You okay?"

"Yes, Aithen. Where's the baby?"

"Don't worry; he is fine. They are making sure he is healthy and taking to feeding."

"Feeding? I thought I would breastfeed?"

Aithen settles on the bed. "Because of the medications you've had, they want to be sure there is no contamination which could affect the baby."

Apparently, they can synthesise my breast milk, and it will be one hundred per cent natural; well as natural as manufactured can be.

"Can I see him now?" I ask.

"Yes, he'll be here in a moment," Aithen replies, his gaze averted.

"What's—"

I interrupt myself catching my reflection in a full-length mirror. It's odd, but I look so healthy and my face? I look older. More twenty-two than seventeen. I raise the loose-fitting blouse of the hospital clothing. The suit reminds me a little of surgery scrubs.

All the sunburn bruising has gone. It is *me,* but my muscles are more toned, albeit not significant. My stomach is firm and flat. It is like an artist who took me and air-brushed all the imperfections away. I rub my fingers over the slight scar on my forehead, but it's no longer visible. I press, and there's the resistance from the plate, thank God. The plate may cling to bad memory, but it also protected me and helped me see through the Koyorad technology, so I want it to stay.

I turn to Aithen. "What have they done to me?"

He smiles. "Sorry, but it is a side-effect of the pregnancy. You have had a mostly human baby, but you have also had a Koyorad pregnancy and labour, so you've had the best of both worlds."

"Mostly? What does that mean?" I ask.

"He's more human than Koyorad. We don't know what effect the new genes will have on him, but only time will tell there," Aithen answers.

"But he's okay? Healthy?" I press.

"Yes, yes he's hundred-per-cent perfect," says Aithen.

I motion to my head. "They removed the scar?"

He takes my hand. "Yes. I hope you don't mind, but it seemed to bother you a lot? The plate is still there." He kisses my head and then my lips. "We need to talk." His tone drops, and I notice how tired the dark rings around his eyes make him look.

"Aithen? What's happened? Where is he? Is...? Is the baby okay?"

"Yes. But there was another attack. Against you."

I search the floor for an answer. "Now, what? What happened?"

"It's complicated, but the attempt failed."

I slump to the bed. I just wish they'd bring my baby here. Now.

"Okay, the medics changed things slightly, with the procedure. Instead of leaving you in stasis, frozen in time, they brought you forward with the baby, so that when it woke, you would be there. They weren't sure what to expect with such a small baby," explains Aithen. "Everything was fine. The baby calm. But during the process to bring you back, the building lost power."

I jerk upright. "Lost power?" I inspect my hands. "What does that mean? What could have happened? Aithen, please, tell me, is he okay?"

He rests against the edge of the bed. "He's fine, as are you... You would have been erased. Lost. The baby, too." His nostrils flare. "Thankfully, the birthing unit has an independent power supply. Seems obvious, but whoever it was almost got lucky. The backup supply is not meant to take such a power load, which is required for time travel procedures."

Tears wash against my neck as he sobs quietly. I cradle his face in my hands. "Aithen, please, what is it?" I plead with a whisper.

"Your life-support stopped," he chokes the words out. "Just for a moment, I thought I had lost you; you both." He hugs me tight, kissing the side of my head.

I squeeze him back. "I'm here. I'm okay."

"I'm so sorry, Jayne. This is why you can't feed him naturally. They had to administer drugs and processes to revive you." He sniffs loudly. "If it weren't for your Tryborre signature, you would have been lost to the time-tracking scanners." He kisses my head again.

We sit embraced in silence. I could have died. *They*, whoever they are, almost succeeded.

It's weird, but I don't feel fear about this. Nothing like the sensations I had earlier on when I realised I'm about to become a mom; today. Or travelling across space. Maybe I'm numb from everything.

I'm not going to let them ruin this day. They tried and failed. But they've robbed me of the chance to naturally bond with my baby through feeding. I curse the unknown entity in my head.

"Aithen. This has got to be the Kounsell? Who else would have access to the electrical grid on a whole building?"

"There's no such thing as a janitor or similar role. Such tasks are carried out by machines, drones." He stands and approaches the window, drying his face with a hand towel. "Things are becoming too dangerous, Jayne."

"But our baby, he's okay?" I wrap my arms around him, nestling my chin against his upper back. He reaches behind to hold me.

"He's fine." Aithen faces me. "I'd like to know his name?"

I nibble the inside of my cheek. "Only when he's here."

Aithen taps his wrist. "They will arrive in a moment now. You ready for this?"

How could you ever be ready for this? Time to clear my head. Cast away fear and doubt. This is our special moment, and I've come a long way to survive this.

I've been waiting for this, but now, everything seems to be happening way too fast. My baby boy is here and after formalities – there would be – we're finally alone with him.

I'm holding a baby.

My baby.

I gasp as my mind flashes to Matthew.

Cold. Blue. His toes.

Aithen's touch snaps me out of the shadows, and a little grunt brings my eyes to my baby's beautiful, little face. Aithen's hands are supporting mine.

"I'm okay," I respond to Aithen's worried look. "I wouldn't drop him."

My little boy is asleep and warm, and I can smell the softness and warmth of his skin. He bears a small soft spot, super delicate at the top of his head. He has light brown hair, and there are little white pores on his nose. His lips are bluish-red, but I know that's normal.

He makes small noises when he moves, and his mouth is so small and tiny. If you rub his arm or calf muscles, they feel like super-soft, smooth jelly. He is beautiful.

Aithen cradles us both. "Aithen, let me introduce Ethan to you." I allow my tears to flow freely. They're happy tears, and I'm not ashamed of them.

He smiles. "Ethan. A good name. On your planet, it means *strong or firm,* and interestingly, we have the word *etan*, which is close and means *to explore*. You and he are certainly explorers."

"It's my father's middle name, and it also reminds me a little of your name." I smile.

For a moment, Ethan's eyes open, and I notice they are silvery-white.

"Don't worry, it's normal," Aithen explains. "On Earth, your babies are usually born with blue eyes, but ours tend to be silver-coloured. His exact eye colour will appear within a few days."

I let out a sigh of relief. "I was worried he wouldn't be able to see."

"No, he's perfect. Like his mother." He kisses me, and for the first time since arriving here, the growing loneliness has faded a little, replaced by Aithen's warmth and Ethan's little face. This is one of the reasons I left Earth.

Setting aside the horrible attack, I wish my family could see this and be part of this fantastic day. I miss them so much, and yet, I'm happy.

Aithen passes me a small bottle of tablets. "These are for you, to help balance the changes you have gone through. You are human, after all, and your body could try to reject the changes."

I still feel uneasy about the whole body-makeover, and while it looks right, it doesn't feel natural. "So, I could what, revert back to myself or my stomach go into meltdown?"

"No, you will become fatigued and sick for several days and be susceptible to a virus. We don't have flu or colds here. Still, you would develop similar symptoms, but more exaggeratedly, as the effects are quite demanding on the body, human or otherwise. You have gone through the equivalent to twelve months of intense training in an hour. The body could go into shock."

I swallow my first pill with a glass of water.

"So, no colds or flu? What illnesses do you have here?"

"We don't." He shrugs his shoulders. "Our genetic makeup takes care of everything."

Ethan gives out a small groan and stretches out in my arms. He is wearing a white bodysuit and looks so tiny and peaceful. He makes all sort of strange faces, and I could sit and watch him for a lifetime. It's touching as theses bodysuits would have to be made specifically for my small baby.

"I'll want to give him a real bath. I know the showers here are quick, but I want to take care of him as a person, a human baby."

Aithen agrees. "Yes, I understand. You should also perform those massage techniques to encourage the skin-on-skin bond."

"So, you swallowed the parenting book, too?" I laugh at his eager voice and how Aithen's eyes are darting all over Ethan. It is incredible, though. A whole new person and *we* made him. I kiss Aithen, and then he reaches down to kiss Ethan.

"This is such a precious gift, Jayne. I love you and Ethan so much. Thank you."

I smile and trace my fingers over Aithen's eyebrows. "Thank you for putting up with me."

We lay Ethan down in a floating Moses basket that cannot topple over. He squirms and lets out a pretend cry. His eyes open and he seems to notice me, then Aithen. They close, and Ethan offers a cough and a shouting cry that demands attention.

"Maybe time to try feeding him?"

Aithen fetches a bottle that heats automatically at the prescribed temperature. He hands it over, and I tickle the soft teat against Ethan's cheek, and onto the corner of his mouth. I have watched Sarah do this so often, and he begins gulping away at the milk.

I let out a sigh and a chuckle. Ethan's eating. This is great. I'm doing it, me. I'm doing it, and he will be okay. I remind myself to gently rub and pat his back to bring up any air bubbles. After a few attempts, he gives off a small, gassy burp and my mind settles.

I'm sure the milk, bottle, and teat here on Korudaz will all be designed to not trap air or anything, but I want to do this the right way; the way I have learnt from my family. Aithen looks perplexed at my actions.

"I'm an aunt, remember, and older sister." I smile at him. "They obviously don't have everything in your books."

"You seem so calm and natural with him."

I laugh. "It does feel normal for some reason. Considering I'm a total idiot at times, this seems to fit okay."

"Yet again, you're amazing, Jayne."

"Okay, your turn." Aithen looks terrified when I lift Ethan towards him. "I have gone through labour, and you will be an active father, daddy-boy!" I laugh as Aithen gingerly cradles the tiny child and presents the bottle of milk to quite an eager little mouth.

If only I could take a photograph of the expression on Aithen's face as he watches his son feeding. His eyes are happy and tearful. His white smile beams and he's never looked more beautiful.

Our eyes meet. "Thank you, Jayne. Ethan is our miracle."

CHAPTER FIFTY

It is early in the day and not too bright with the two moons prominent in the early morning sky. It took me a while to realise it, but Korudaz is so quiet if you ignore the distant hum. I remember a similar level of quiet one evening when walking home from school. I could not explain why there was so little sound in the air.

Mom said it was due to bird migration for the time of the year, and their parting left behind a void of sound. Well, that is what this planet is like. No natural background sounds. No birds and the only thing which does fly is an insect which resembles a hummingbird crossed with a dragonfly.

We're housed securely in a private wing of the medical centre. Four security guards and two Deyloron protect the perimeter. Are they to keep me in or others out? I can't decide.

Watching Akeirlah holding Ethan is almost as comical and touching as it first was with Aithen. She looks like she is holding onto two dozen eggs, trying not to drop one. So funny.

I relieve her of the *aunty* duty and cherish the warmth of Ethan's little body snuggling into me. He sleeps a lot, but I know I should enjoy it while it lasts.

"Jayne. This really is amazing. Ethan is a universal baby, and what a bonus? Your gene was the dominant one here, with him."

"What do you mean?" I ask.

"We don't have small babies on this planet, so yours is somewhat unique. Different." She pulls a funny face at Ethan.

Maybe it is a deep curiosity, but Akeirlah always has that caring twinkle in her eyes when she watches me. I sense genuine concern from her.

"Akeirlah, I did ask Aithen, but what is the story on me and Ethan meeting your parents? Aren't they interested to see Ethan?"

She nods at me. "I get what you are asking. I know there is a term used on Earth where people say, 'It's not you, it's me?' It is us, honestly." She smiles as though reflecting on what she is about to say. "Koyorad relationships are not like what you had on Earth. Families don't live together once the children have reached our ages. We go to our schooling places, and the parents go to work; everyone gets on with their lives."

"So, you never meet up? Not even for birthdays?" I ask.

"No, nothing like that. It's not that we don't care, we just don't feel the need to," Akeirlah says.

"That's weird," I say. "I would have lived at home until I left college, if not longer. I love my family and... I really miss them..."

"Was it only because of the baby, you left Earth?" she asks.

I nod. "Yeah. I still can't see why a medical team couldn't have been sent. If they can send war..." I stop myself. Should I mention what I know about warships orbiting Earth? "If they can send students to Earth, you'd think a doctor could be included in the party."

Not the best catch on my part, but Akeirlah appears distracted by Ethan, and then Aithen enters the room.

Akeirlah strokes the baby's foot and then says, "Let me arrange a meet-up with the family. It is rather bad-mannered of them to not pay a visit at least."

"I did send a message, but no response," Aithen says.

I'm comforted Akeirlah wants to arrange things. Before I have time to think, I hear an older woman's voice on the Meorlite in Akeirlah wrist.

"I'll never get used to the technology," I say after them speaking in *Coten* and me not understanding a single word.

She smiles. "You will. And you're meeting them today. Dad will finish his shift soon. Mom finished her shift earlier today, so she is at home. They are about a thirty-minute flight away, so I'll come back here at six?" She raises her eyebrows at Aithen.

He repeatedly blinks for a moment. "No idea why she couldn't reply to me."

"Because I'm the oldest and they like me more," Akeirlah laughs. "And I'm not dating a human."

"Oh, very funny," he remarks.

Akeirlah leaves. It's nice that she referred to her parents as Mom and Dad, as such customs are not followed here. Neither is time measured in numbers.

Koyorads don't have clocks telling the time as we do on Earth, but they have created me a screen which shows the time as though in hours and minutes. It helps as their clock devices are all dots and dashes, like Morse code. I prefer numbers.

I welcome escaping the medical centre and travelling over and across a dense forest. The two Deyloron flank our sides. Large clearances of green ground open to interrupt the flow of the trees in places and unfamiliar animals are running about.

There are smatterings of buildings breaking up the landscape and small collections of houses. I can't help but wonder who is inside those buildings? What would they say or think if they knew I, a human, was flying over their homes? Are Koyorads discussing the visiting human in those buildings below?

What is the plan of the Kounsell? They can't keep me hidden away forever. The attack on the hospital demonstrates awareness of my baby. Now there are two humans on the planet.

It dawns on me. I haven't asked Aithen about his meeting with Erek. That day seems like forever ago now. I'll ask him later when we are alone.

We approach a white, isolated house with bronze glass windows, set within a large lawn of yellow and green growth which encircles the property. The nearest neighbour is the forest. Koyorads enjoy their privacy.

We touch down, and I breathe in a lovely scent as we exit the craft. I don't know what they are, but orange flowers decorate a small path, which leads to the front entrance of the house, and their aroma is terrific, like strawberries and a hint of pine. Summer and winter in one scent.

Akeirlah uses her Meorlite to open the main entrance and there they are to greet us. Aithen's parents. They look so *normal*. I don't know what I expected, but they both seem about fifty. They are staring at Ethan and me, and the glow of wonder is all over their faces. The dad has black hair, and the mom long, wavy, blonde hair; both have green eyes; same as Akeirlah.

"This is Jayne and Ethan," says Aithen and then repeats this in *Coten*. At least I recognise him speaking our names.

I feel myself ducking down slightly, and I don't know why, as I offer a handshake. The parents peruse my hand and me. Aithen speaks in *Coten*, and they immediately give a short laugh, then the dad takes my fingers and shakes my hand weakly. The mom quickly follows. They both say something, but all I hear is jumbled words. I must learn this language.

"Jayne. This is my father, Deqhlaw, and my mother, Serlariagh."

My cheeks flush as I say, "Tur-ket… ch… kur sikat." I'm trying to say *it is nice to meet you* in *Coten*, but I may have ordered a hotdog. At least they smile and respond in English, "Thank you."

The mom exchanges brief words with Akeirlah, who responds by linking my arm. "Let me give you a quick tour," she says.

I hesitate, not wanting to leave Ethan, but it'll be okay. Aithen will take care of him. Relax. Everything will be fine.

Most of the property is a single-story; only the sleeping area is on another floor. Then there is a basement, quite a flamboyant workspace.

"This is where my *father* works from home," announces Akeirlah. "Not that he is ever here. But it's his den."

"What's *father* in your language?" A simple question but Akeirlah's puzzled squinting eyes suggest there isn't one.

"We don't have such words. Not for mom, father, or dad. No sisters or brothers. No family, in fact." She shrugs her shoulders and raises her eyebrows. "I understand your use of Mom and Dad. And I realise Aithen calls me sister. That's quite sweet of him, but for your benefit."

Akeirlah sometimes delivers words with a snobby, judgemental tone. I realise she's not like that, but sometimes it can grate a little. I scold the negative voice in my head. Don't begin to find fault in your second only friend on this planet.

"So, if you're in one room and wanted to call out to your mother, what would you shout?" I ask.

"We don't," she says. "We talk to each other, face to face. Shouting to one another is considered disrespectful."

My gaze falls upon a pair of strange items. In a steel cabinet – it looks like a gun cabinet, with a clear front. There are two shiny, mirror-finished objects which look like large spark plugs, adorned with intricate pipes and wires.

"What are they?" I ask. "Look like some kind of high-tech guns."

"Oh, nothing. Something Dad will be working on."

We all sit at a table, and the conversation between the others is in *Coten*, which means I can't join in. I'm glad I have Ethan as a distraction, so I watch and cradle him while they continue talking about who-knows-what. My attention piques when I hear my name mentioned in the conversation, but they are not inviting me to speak.

I feel like the poor kid meeting the wealthy parents for the first time; like I'm from the *wrong side* of town. I'm trying not to be judgemental, but they are challenging work. They don't speak English and yes, I know I don't speak their language, but everything is just like at the Kounsell meeting. Cold. They do ask me about my family but avoid the bitter truth that Earth and everyone there is a distant memory. Surely, a planet this advanced should be more aware and empathic of other races?

They visit Earth. Directly or indirectly, they have met humans and no, we're not all dangerous. No more so than Koyorads.

But we are lightyears apart, even at this table.

They watch me as though on edge. I could be casually waving a loaded gun around from their appearance. No matter how I smile or the funny story I recall, setting the scene for friendly people, the audience before me is bewildered.

Aithen exudes warmth while translating my words to his parents, and Akeirlah has a relaxed posture, but the parents are taut.

Maybe I'm trying too hard.

As the table is cleared, Aithen pulls me aside. "Some good news. We don't need to return to the hospital. We have a new and secure place to stay."

"Oh, good," I say. "But how secure?"

"Not over the top. Two armed guards and a part-time Deyloron for the night watch."

"Not over the top?" I somehow manage to laugh as I bounce Ethan in my arms.

"We're taking no chances now," Aithen whispers. "And there's a lot we need to talk about."

"Such as?" I ask.

Aithen looks around us, then back to me. "Escaping Korudaz."

CHAPTER FIFTY-ONE

I stand at the bedroom doorway, watching Ethan's tiny body, as he sleeps in the cot. He's lying on his stomach, with his legs tucked under him and his bottom in the air. It's quite comical but cute.

How did Sarah cope after Matthew, especially when Lou was born? Did she notice those small things in Lou and wondered how Matthew would have compared? How scared was she when Lou was delivered? Did Sarah imagine Lou would have been born asleep, too?

I rarely spoke about Matthew. Maybe I should have asked Sarah more about how she felt. But I didn't. I couldn't bear the pain. Not only the hurt from his death but more so the vacant shell Sarah had become. That sudden moment when her eyes would glaze over, and her heart would falter, pumping cold emptiness through her veins and thoughts.

"You okay?" Aithen hugs me from behind, stroking his nose against my ear.

I turn and kiss him. "Yeah, just watching Ethan. Has the guard gone now?"

The security duo insisted on one of them checking inside the apartment initially.

"Yes. Took his time but he and the second security guard are watching the perimeter," Aithen says.

The calmness is lovely, but we have a lot to discuss, so we return to the lounge.

"So, then. Big revelation?" I ask. "Running away from Korudaz? How's that going to work?"

Aithen smiles and rubs his face. "I don't know, but we have to be ready for the opportunity."

"Has this got anything to do with your chat with Erek the other day? I didn't get to hear about that," I ask.

"Yes, albeit he is quite tight-lipped." Aithen pauses momentarily. Why do people do that? Okay, he's an alien, but get on with it. I nod for him to hurry along.

"He didn't tell me why he's left the Deleters, but he has information on your lab results when the medics took a blood test for analysis."

"What, they've confirmed I'm a female human?" I taunt but smile sarcastically.

"There's that, but we now know why you can see through our technology; why you remember the girls who have been Deleted," Aithen says. "It is the plate in your forehead and specifically so, the titanium."

"It's not just titanium though," I add.

"I know, but that doesn't matter. Titanium is safe in the human body, which is why it is used in so many medical procedures. Still, on a microscopic scale, your blood contains the metal. It is barely detectable, but it's enough to deliver the side effect you have witnessed with our tech." Aithen smiles for a moment. "You could say you have titanium blood poisoning, but because it is so inert, you'll never know about it."

"But that means anybody on Earth, who has a titanium implant of any type, would remember when a person is Deleted?" I ask.

"The girl I spoke to online, she called herself VioletlyAlone, she had a head injury, too. And she could remember."

"Not necessarily. The medics believe the location of the titanium source, relative to your brain, which has the *desired* effect... the higher concentration of titanium in that area is sufficient to stop the memory loss, in you. And I guess the other girl."

"And that's all Erek had to say?"

"He wants to meet us both tomorrow as he has something huge to tell us and it has everything to do with Earth."

"With Earth?" This sharpens my focus. "What did he say?"

"He didn't, which is irritating, but whatever it is, he's left the Deleters for, so I'd suggest preparing yourself for something bad." Aithen grabs my hand gently. "Don't worry, we can trust him. And we need to hear what he has to say."

"I'm not so sure." How am I ever supposed to trust Erek? Okay, he didn't Delete me but instead protected me with the Tryborre, and we're in his world now. "This all sounds too vague, and I don't know... where are we meeting him?"

"We'll pick him up in our ship and cloak. Go to orbit and hear what he has to say."

I mull this over. "What if it's all a trap? I don't feel safe, Aithen. Now that Ethan is born, what's to stop the Kounsell coming after me? I don't have the Deyloron monitoring or protecting me anymore."

"I hear you, loud and clear, and that's why I want to get away from here." Aithen stands and watches out the window. "When I saw my parents with you this evening, I've never felt so distant from this planet, this race of life.

"I realised even more how numb Koyorad society is. We don't have the family function. There's no such thing as closeness and caring. If I left this planet tomorrow and didn't return, nobody would miss me."

"Don't you have mates who you hang out with?" I ask. Come to think of it, I can't say Aithen has mentioned anyone he hangs with or hobbies.

Aithen faces me again. "I suppose you'd call them acquaintances, but no, not *mates* like you have. Even when studying, we do so in isolation. Korudaz is not a sociable planet," he laughs.

"It's like you all just live to work, and yet you have the opportunity to travel across the universe. You know, this should be the most amazing place to live. But it feels so empty. Devoid of all fun," I say.

"That's the thing," Aithen says. "The only time I've seen Koyorads come together and act like friends is when they're on Earth. When forced to socialize and act like humans, Koyorads become a nicer... *species*. We may be all advanced and what have you, but we may as well not exist. Earth is blessed, not knowing about us."

I stand and wrap my arms around him. "You're not like the others here. You care. You're warm, and I love you. I'm so glad you exist." I kiss him. "And Akeirlah, look at her. She's *normal,* and I'd have been lost if she weren't so accepting of me. Then there's Erek." A shiver passes through me, and I rub my arms. "Somehow, he could be changing. I'm not convinced, but if he could change, then... I don't know. Anything can happen."

I sit again. "And there's the Gouhlde Kounsell and your education people. They care, I think?"

"Not so much caring, but curious." Aithen joins me on the settee. "They are certainly not a danger to you or anybody, but I don't know how deeply allegiances go. The fact the Gouhlde Kounsell have agreed on the closure of the time-link with Earth is not a good thing."

"Could it be because they want to protect historic Earth?" I ask.

"More like preventing another *you* situation," Aithen remarks. "One half-alien baby is a curious thing, and an Earth human here is not dangerous, but you've seen the riots: the Military Kounsell. This planet is not open to the alien-immigration business."

"Take my word for it, I don't want to stay here, but I need to be sure, you are sure." Can I really take Aithen away from his planet? Aren't I doing to him what the Koyorads have done to me?

At least with Aithen, he wants to be with Ethan and me, and that is his motivation. Mine was potential death during pregnancy, and abduction settled the matter for me.

"I can't live on a planet where you and Ethan are under threat every day. Yes, it's easy to live in isolation; we would anyway, even if you were born here. But I don't want to be here. I want to be with you... on Earth."

"Going home will be amazing, but how will it work? Do we just jump back in time, to the moment we left Earth?" A thousand what-if questions race through my head, all of which I can't begin to process.

"We'll need a larger craft, and I'm not sure how easy I can get one of those. The small two-seater K-100 won't do, neither the four-person S-7598—"

"Why not? You said we could make the journey to Earth, albeit cramped, in the K-100?"

"Yes, but the smaller craft don't have the conversion units in them. The units which transform you genetically from one planetary atmosphere to another. You and I are safe for Korudaz and Earth, but Ethan is Korudaz born. He won't survive on Earth."

I hunch over, resting my elbows on my knees. "I hadn't thought of that. He would die, wouldn't he?"

Aithen rubs my back. "The air would be like poison to him, and your doctors won't be able to save him, even in an enclosed medical unit. He needs to be transformed first."

I kiss the back of Aithen's hand and flop back into the settee. "So, where do we get this other ship that has the unit installed?"

"I'm hoping we can get a portable unit, and that is where Erek will come in handy. He may not be a full-blown Deleter now, but he's still military," Aithen says. "This is half the reason I'm even considering giving him an audience. I'm not as gullible to him as you may think. He's useful, and if he has woken from Deleter-delusion, then I intend to capitalise on that."

"Can Akeirlah help us somewhere? She works in Deyloron technology, or whatever?" I suggest. "That must be useful somewhere?"

"I want to be careful here. I know she's not a threat and in fact, I think she'd come with us, but don't tell Akeirlah."

"Why? She can help us? I'd say the more, the better." If we are going to trust Erek, then we must have Akeirlah in on the plan. If anything, Aithen is planning to leave for good, he will regret not saying goodbye to her.

"No, it has to be you and me, only," Aithen says. "Akeirlah has been very gracious of you, and that makes me so happy. But she's still a Koyorad who has never left the planet. I must assume her alliance will remain here."

"We can trust a Deleter but not your sister?"

"No, I'm not saying that. If anything, I don't want to risk her. The fewer individuals involved, the better. Erek has already placed himself in the firing line by resigning that post—"

"Won't he be watched then?" I ask.

"Yes, I'm sure he will. But they'll still view him as a *company man*. He has carried out his duties to the letter," Aithen says, but this darkens my thoughts.

Carried out his duties.

That's why Chloe, Leslie, Laura and VioletlyAlone no longer exist in any timeline. Their memory is a shield for me. Protection from whatever smokescreen Erek and the Kounsell are conniving here.

Aithen is about to speak but then raises a hand as his Meorlite pings into action. He dismisses it a moment later.

"What was that?" I ask, watching Aithen's concerned eyes widen, and his nostrils flare slightly.

"I think it's safe to say we can trust Erek," Aithen replies. "The Deleters have been issued with a new weapon. This one can Delete *all* Koyorads. The Meorlites won't protect us, me anymore."

"So, this is a threat from the Kounsell?" I suggest.

Aithen nods. "Yes, it's too convenient; coincidental. Why issue such a weapon now? As a deterrent towards those thinking of siding with you?"

"But what do they know?" I ask. "I'm just the silly human playing mom and minding my own business."

"Yes, but they'll know you must be planning *something*. You've been attacked discretely a few times now and not complained—"

"I could go to the Kounsell and scream my head off at them?"

"But they know you won't, that's the thing," Aithen says. "They're quiet, remaining in the background here."

"They're scheming? How?" I ask.

"I have no idea." Aithen frowns and sighs. "They're playing it all too cool. But what are they up to?"

"I hate to say it, but it has to be Erek?"

Aithen sucks in his lips, mulling over my words. "I suppose he could be the voice of the Kounsell. *Tell Aithen we will Delete any Koyorad...* No, I don't buy that. Unless..."

"Unless what?"

"The two Kounsells would have to approve this weapon... but this means the Gouhlde Kounsell can be a target, too."

"No, I can't see that. This must be covert between the Military Kounsell and Deleters," Aithen says, pacing the floor.

"We could contact the Gouhlde Kounsellor we met at the meeting, Myarve. He seemed nice and actually smiled at me?" I suggest.

Aithen squints his eyes, a puzzled expression across his face.

"Sorry, who?"

CHAPTER FIFTY-TWO

A sleepless night.

Aithen has no idea who Myarve is. We've never met this man. I describe him in detail and the few things he said. Still, Aithen watches me with worried eyes, turning to fear with the realisation Myarve is Deleted.

We welcome Ethan waking for a feed and a cuddle to distract our thoughts. But peaceful sleep takes him to dreamland, while our waking nightmare scratches for attention.

"I guess I won't be running to scream at the Kounsell in a hurry," I say. "I'm sorry you don't remember. This is my reality."

"I have no recollection whatsoever," Aithen says. "I can't believe they've done it so soon."

"We don't know when though," I say. "It's only now I've mentioned his name. He's not forgotten to me, so it could have been any time after the Kounsell meeting."

Aithen runs his fingers through his hair. "True. Just because Erek has only just discovered it, doesn't mean his knowledge is real-time. I can't believe how dangerous this has become. But we must try and focus. And live through another day. We must try and sleep, too."

"You're joking? How can we sleep through this?"

"Oh, *we* have a tablet for everything—"

"I'm not sleeping and risking anybody taking Ethan?" I plead quietly.

"No, it's not like that. The pills put you to sleep, but you're aware. You'll sleep normally but just for a few hours." Aithen looks towards Ethan's room. "He can sleep with us."

"It's generally not considered safe to have a baby in the same bed as adults," I say. "Crushing, things like that."

"Okay. His cot floats, and we'll barricade the door to the room," Aithen suggests, but there's no smile to defuse the threat.

I stutter a nod. "Okay, yes. But then we meet Erek and find out everything. The last thing we need is to be half-asleep."

We push the bed up against the door, firstly wedging all manner of metallic objects in the small space below the door panel. If anybody is coming through there, we'll know about it. The windows are not glass, but a transparent forcefield, which Aithen assures me can't be broken from the outside. They can be deactivated individually from inside the room.

The small, white pill dissolves sourly on my tongue, and within minutes, I lose sight of the early morning, deepened blue light outside.

Satisfying grunts wake me. Aithen feeds Ethan, and my heart soothes at the tender sight.

"You're too organised," I croak. I hadn't thought to bring a bottle into the bedroom. "Thank you."

Aithen smiles. "You're welcome. I only woke myself a moment ago and thought it best to get this little guy fed and ready."

I stretch. If only we could have a quiet, lazy day at home. But of course, that's not happening today. It's odd, I don't know what today is? Koyorads don't name their days weekly, but instead refer to each day by a number; one being the first day of their dual-solar year.

"How many days are in a year here?" I ask. I've probably read this, but…

"Well, we have blue and red years, to correspond with our neighbouring stars. But we also have a generic year which is seven-hundred days," Aithen replies, as he dabs a tissue at Ethan's chin.

That's right, I remember that now. Korudaz circles the red star, Yettrelba, like Earth does the Sun. But Quswania, the blue and hotter star, traverses an oval path towards Korudaz and away again. The planet doesn't circle Quswania. At its closest point, the blue star doubles the temperature on the planet. That would be uncom-fortable.

"I take it you haven't heard anything else from Erek?" I sit up in bed, combing my fingers through my hair.

"No, nothing. But I'll assume he wants silence until we are meeting. No need to aggravate anything."

The bottle is almost empty. The synthesised milk has some interesting properties, one of which is the presence of tiny, digestible pods. These contain various vitamins, minerals, calcium and more interestingly, protein boosters. These small pods expand in the stomach and continue to feed like a time-release capsule. This means Ethan isn't hungry as often as would be the case with natural or powdered milk on Earth.

Maybe I should steal the formula and become a millionaire on Earth?

Maybe not.

We clear the barricade from the door and return the room to normal mode.

Aithen deposits Ethan on a soft, spongy mat on the lounge floor and I set up the weird toy Ethan loves to watch. It features variously sized and colour balls, which hover over his face and hands and deliver all manner of gentle noises and lights to lighten the wonder in his face.

He kicks his feet in the air, waving his hands aimlessly and coo's in excitement.

Wish someone gave me some sparkling lights to watch.

Passing Aithen a bottle of smoothie, I sip on my own. "I think we should leave straight away, but tell me something… what's your sister's name?"

Aithen is puzzled by this. "Akeirlah? Is this a test?"

I scrunch my mouth. "No, just checking."

Aithen nods. "I get it. If I remember her, then she's not Deleted."

"I'll ask you that every day, if not more often. Don't get annoyed by it," I say.

"No, I agree. It's a clever idea. I remember everyone else who has been in contact with you, I think," Aithen says. "But let's go with my family, who I do remember, and Erek. I also remember the others who came to Earth with me."

"Yes, but I don't know them, so we can't check that."

We quickly shower and dress, not that taking a shower here can be anything but quick. Ethan's ready and in his floating Moses basket, with the hovering balls and a few soft toys for distraction. And milk, of course with the travel bag. Children need so much stuff even if you're just going out for a short journey.

"Where's the K-100?" I ask as we step into the S-7598.

"Cloaked, just in case," Aithen replies. "You remember how to uncloak it?"

"Do I?"

"It's parked exactly where we usually keep it. Just wave your open hand towards the entrance. This is opposite to the bedroom window. I have programmed the K-100 to admit you and me only. If *anything* goes wrong, it is your safe place. Also, you won't need to issue commands by saying *K-100* repeatedly, at the start of each order."

"You could have told me this sooner," I gasp, controlling my voice aware that the two security guards are out of sight, but not necessarily out of earshot.

"You beat me to it," Aithen says, closing the door of the craft. "I was about to."

I nod my head, unconvincingly. "From now on, I want, I need a day's, a week's notice of anything you decide."

Aithen salutes me. "Sir, yes, sir."

I nudge him. "Oh, you're a smart ass."

Aithen sends a message to Erek and nods when he receives the response. "Okay, let's get this over with." The interior of the craft turns blue. "We can monitor the area before touching down."

We fly slowly, about fifty metres above the ground.

"Strap yourself in, just in case I need to carry out some odd manoeuvres."

My hands shake as I fidget with the straps and catches. Akeirlah helped me when we were in the K-100, but I wasn't paying attention. Not as tricky as I think: they are magnetic, and I was trying to attach the wrong parts together. I'm glad Aithen overlooks my fumbling.

"How far did you get with Akeirlah and the flying lessons?" Aithen asks.

"I found the controls quite easy. I've not flown a real helicopter or chopper, but the dual controls are the same, and I've played console games. The concept is quite similar. It's simply weird to do it all in real life. Oh, and with real guns," I say.

"You fired them?"

"Yes, we had an incident with a rock in space, but Akeirlah blew it up." I don't want to worry Aithen about my silly panic attack. The last thing he needs now is to think I may lose it in a crisis. I won't, the voice in my head assures.

"I got to blow up lots of rocks after that," I add.

"Good. We'll do a lot more of that today," Aithen says, looking concerned towards me. "I need to be sure you understand the navigation system. Again, it's not hard, and I'm sure you've already had a play with it?"

"Yes, the point-and-click screen? That's so scary. In fact, the whole idea of pointing to a place and setting a date? It just doesn't seem real," I say.

The craft slows further, and I make out the shape of a solitary figure on a hilltop, peeping out from the dense forest. His white hair contrasts against the matt-black jumpsuit he wears.

"Maybe we should try those guns out on him," I whisper. I know they won't fire at a Koyorad or craft, but I want to remind myself and Aithen of the imminent danger.

"The area is clear, or the vessels are also cloaked," Aithen says.

I peer through the windows around us. Why do I expect to see something when they are invisible? Maybe, just maybe my titanium contamination will see through the cloaking?

The craft settles, the interior flushes orange and my heart races.

We're exposed.

Vulnerable.

"Stay strapped in," Aithen warns. "Anything happens, and I am in space in a blink."

The side of the craft opens, and Erek immediately steps in and begins strapping himself into the seat behind me.

Blue interior and we are in orbit before his belts have clicked into place.

"Let's head towards Taiarlow," Erek suggests. "Will be a lot safer and quiet."

This is the second moon in the Korudaz solar system. It appears in view in a matter of seconds and is a ball of sparkling, pure white. I read about Taiarlow. It is a little bigger than Earth's moon and consists primarily of ice. It appears as smooth as a billiard ball, with incidental, silvery veins running haphazardly over its surface.

Aithen and I rotate our seats to face Erck.

"You two look awful," he says. It's only now I notice he says the words for real, none of the lip-synch thing. I wonder why he bothers to learn to speak an Earth language?

"It's been an eventful couple of days," remarks Aithen and he nudges me gently. "Ask about Kounsellor."

"Do you know what happened with Myarve?" My voice sounds hollow in my head, watching Erek up close.

Erek's gaze dances between us like he's not in on a secret joke. "And they are?"

"He was a member of the Gouhlde Kounsell," Aithen replies. "He's been Deleted. Only Jayne remembers him."

The realisation in Erek's eyes is apparent, as his jaw slackens. "Oh, my. So, they've already started."

"Started? Started what?" I ask.

"There's a lot of buzz around the Kounsell and Deleter seniors, aimed at the Gouhlde Kounsell," Erek says, his face grimacing slightly like he's tasted something terrible. "They are going off on numerous tangents over preservation of Koyorad culture and values—"

"Values?" Aithen cuts in. "The only value we have is hiding and being an ass with everyone outside this planet."

"I knew something was up, once I heard about the new Deleter device," Erek continues. "But in all honesty, what I have really discovered outweighs that, on a global scale." Erek regards me with renewed caution in his expression. It's the same stare he gave me in the Mall.

"You said… you said there's something about Earth?" My words stumble upon themselves.

Erek clasps his fingers together and rests his elbows on his knees. He hunches over as if to deliver a secret amongst conspirators. "Two things I need to share with you, and it's hard to know where to begin. I doubt you'll believe me, but here goes. Time for a history lesson…"

CHAPTER FIFTY-THREE

Earth. England. 1865.

The first Koyorad party to visit Earth chose a remote, country-side location, far from prying eyes in a city. The advantage of time travel afforded any choice of date. Still, this period felt safe to the Koyorads for the first encounter of humans.

The importance of this visit was deemed significant. Those chosen for the mission were picked from the highest ranks of the serving Military Kounsell. Not those holding an administration post, but the advanced war faction commanders.

This was not to be an invading party, but a secret, reconnaissance mission.

Initial reports from the team spoke of the ill-advances of the humans, appalling lousy health and the smells. Every report repeated the overwhelming odours encountered, whether from people, animals, buildings, or the environment in general.

Possibly not the best starting point for a visit to a populated planet.

The aim of phase one was a seven-day trial run, then return to the black hole. Perform the traverse through time, then implement phase two, returning a hundred years afterwards. And finally, phase three: a further hundred years on. All in a short space of time, of course.

The party was led by Gendeeryha Kaynballer.

He had successfully led the Korudaz army against three military campaigns, against other planets. Two were hostile attacks towards Korudaz, the third nipping a threat in the bud. That planet's ships didn't take off before ninety per cent of the Xellecorn population were wiped out. They didn't see the attack coming before it was too late. Had they realised, the incredibly advanced Xellecorn would have overcome the danger and saved themselves. The Koyorads would not have won that strike.

Gendeeryha became overly confident when on Earth during that first visit. Hour by hour, he considered humans with distaste, except for one.

He happened upon a young woman. In her twenties, lying on her stomach upon a blanket in tall, pale grass. Her auburn, wet hair glistened in the midday sun as she studied a textbook. Around her were placed various other books, some open and face down so she wouldn't lose her page.

"What are you reading?" Gendeeryha asked.

The girl ignored him, so he repeated the question.

She turned and squinted up at him, using one hand to shield her eyes. "And what it be you?"

Gendeeryha reached for a book, but she snapped it away before he could study it.

"Mine, I would thank you kindly, sir," she apologised, standing so he could see her clearly.

Gendeeryha was taken by her pale, blue eyes contrasting milky skin and deep, fiery-red hair.

"I… madam…" Gendeeryha faltered to offer a suitable come back.

The girl stooped to gather her books. Gendeeryha snatched one and offered it to her. He noticed it was a ragged looking book by Galileo Galilei; whoever that was.

"I will be thanking you as I bide my way, sir." The sweet girl offered a smile, turned, and walked away.

Gendeeryha raised a hesitant hand in farewell.

Who was she?

Little did he realise she was about to save his life.

Gendeeryha's presence in the spaced-out settlement had arisen fear and gossip. Who was this strange person, and why was he dressed differently from them? He must be from overseas, some said. He doesn't talk like us.

Others talked of seeing him with others dressed the same.

Was this a foreign invasion?

Why did they never visit the town hub?

Where did they go at night?

Some of the locals tried to follow the stranger but talk of magic suggested why they would lose the trail.

The stranger didn't go to church on Sunday.

They must be evil.

Unnatural.

A rider was sent to alert the authorities, and this individual happened upon a scouting, military exercise. Eight soldiers strong.

Gendeeryha was caught off guard. A victim of his own ignorance.

He was so busy trying to discretely track down the beautiful, red-haired girl, it blinkered him to the pending danger.

It was the seventh and final day of the mission.

Three of the soldiers trained their rifles towards him, but to the left, two young farmhands held trembling shotguns in his direction.

Gendeeryha could not run.

Should he reach for the Meorlite in his wrist, they would open fire.

He knew the craft, orbiting in space could save him in an instant, but how to raise the alarm?

"Stop!" a voice called.

A girl's voice.

It was her.

His gaze locked to her blue eyes as she ran towards him.

The soldiers searched the scene unfolding before them, tightening their grips further. The farmhand's barrels quivered more.

"Don't!" she called, her voice light and her breath coming in bursts.

The girl reached for Gendeeryha, knocking over an empty, rusting bucket and the shocking clang accompanied a gunshot.

CHAPTER FIFTY-FOUR

"Okay, that was random," I say, and Aithen reflects my puzzled look.

Erek glances between us. "The girl is Mary Wood... you know her better as Marrahmne Kounsell."

"No way!" I exclaim while Aithen delivers a simple, "What?"

"So, what happened to the general guy?" I ask. "He was shot and...?"

"Gendeeryha was not hit. Mary Wood took the bullet," Erek responds.

Aithen pushes back into his seat. "I'm the historian here. Why don't I know about this?"

"Top secret within the Deleters and Military Kounsell; upper levels," Erek responds. "I found out by chance because I was going to Earth. Only those who have had *business* with Earth and are deemed trustworthy may find out."

Aithen shakes his head in disbelief.

I wait for Erek to continue.

"Mary may have been a simple, country girl, but she was clever. Well-read. Way ahead of her time in nineteenth-century Earth—"

"Please don't tell me she's an alien, too?" I interrupt.

"Oh, no. She's human," replies Erek. "But she recognised an opportunity with Gendeeryha. Obviously, she had no idea who he was or where he was from. Just a good option happening by in a disparate town, in the middle of nowhere."

I settle back into my seat, clasping my fingers and resting my palms upon my head. "And how did Mary become head of an alien race, forever lightyears away from Earth, and in the distant future?"

"She saved Gendeeryha's life. He was smitten by her and quickly saved her back. A bullet wound is nothing for us to heal, despite how bad she was. In the end, she had been shot three times."

My hands flop to my lap.

"You call it the *Florence Nightingale effect*," Erek adds. "Gendeeryha nursed and cared for Mary. In her defence, I can't imagine how she coped with awakening on an alien spacecraft. In Earth's orbit at a time when homes didn't even have electricity, let alone a flying machine."

"I'd love to be a fly on *that* wall," I quip. This is more unreal than aliens and meeting a real, life Tyrannosaurus.

"But she did cope. Mary overcomes her fears and well… you know the rest," Erek says. "She had the backing of Gendeeryha and the serving Military Kounsell. We don't call it marriage here, but they become *bonded*. She was his apprentice, first officer and slowly, carefully, and surely, she rose through the ranks. She was adopted as a Koyorad, even having a full Meorlite threaded through her system."

"She must be so old?" I say.

"It's the technology," Aithen butts in. "It'll be slowing her ageing, but so will the planet's magnetic field."

"Magnetic field?" I ask. "What's that got to do with anything?"

"Aging is based solely on a planet's magnetic field, interacting with an individual's electromagnetic field. Every planet is different. Some are close, but Earth and Korudaz are different," Aithen says.

"Once *Mary* arrived in Korudaz, her ageing would slow down. Considerably."

"That certainly hasn't worked on me," I add. "I look older."

"You've had a baby," interrupts Erek. It sounds odd coming from him.

"Difference is, when I or any Koyorad is on Earth, our ageing accelerates and becomes the same as a human, and more. Our longer life expectancy shrinks considerably," Aithen says.

I can't let Aithen come to Earth and shorten his lifespan. That's too unfair. Too much of a sacrifice.

"If she's human, then why hate us so much?" I ask.

"She's a nineteenth-century woman, who lived at a time when society expected them to stay at the home, cook and make babies," Erek replies. "In those days, girls were not even encouraged to go to school. She had the self-awareness and respect to teach herself. But from what I've discovered, she has always stalked Earth. Its development over the years."

"So, she must be interested in it?" I ask.

"No, quite the opposite. I've read some of the journals she has written, criticising the evolution of humanity over the years. She sees humans as cancer, eating away at the planet. The wars. The political risings and global destruction of forests, icecaps. You'd think she would appraise the struggle for equality amongst women?" Erek raises an eyebrow. "She opposes that, too."

"But isn't that what she has done?" I ask. "She's escaped the shackles of a bigoted society—"

"Only to instil it on this planet's beliefs towards Earth and other planets," Aithen adds.

"Exactly," replies Erek. "The pairing of Gendeeryha and Mary was possibly the worse partnership in Universe history. He's a warmonger, and yet she views humans as the warmongers, but she sees them through distorted lenses."

"Wait a minute," says Aithen. "When did Mary come to Korudaz?"

"About four hundred years ago," Erek replies.

"Four hundred?" I ask. "So, she's what, about four-hundred and twenty years old?"

"About that, yes," Erek says. "In her position, it's safe to say she'll be around for a lot longer. I'm sure she's already had a transplant of vital organs, and her Meorlite will be of a higher level to maintain her longevity."

"I can't believe this," Aithen says. "It makes sense now."

"What does?" I ask.

"The time reset," Aithen replies, and I notice Erek stiffens to this.

"You think…?" Erek asks.

"Time reset? What are you on about?" I ask.

Erek opens a hand for Aithen to proceed. "Three-hundred and fifty years ago, the Korudaz solar system timeline was set to prevent backwards time travel beyond that point. In short, we cannot travel back into Korudaz history beyond three-hundred and fifty years."

"But you can travel back to Earth, ten-thousand years ago?" I ask.

"That's outside of the Korudaz system," Erek responds.

"So, she's done this to safeguard her position?" I can't believe her. How could such a toxic human gain so much power?

"Exactly," Aithen and Erek say.

"How can you do that? Set time like that?" I ask.

Aithen taps on his wrist and the Meorlite projects an image in the space between us. Weirdly, it's a familiar object, which looks like a giant, intricate sparkplug.

"I've seen that before," I say.

"Where?" Aithen laughs but then realises I am serious.

"In your father's workshop. There were two there. What is it?" I ask.

"It's called a Timepost. Think of it as a bookmark. You launch a Timepost at a point in time and once set, nobody can travel beyond that. Yes, you can travel up to the time, but no further into the past," Aithen says.

"Well, isn't that breaking the time rules?" I ask.

"No, it's not. It's preserving time. Timeposts are not a Koyorad invention but are a requirement of all races able to utilise time travel. That's how we ensure saving Earth can't be undone. I should add, the Timepost only affects the immediate planets around a central star, in your case, the Sun. So, it is localized."

"Can't they simply destroy the Timepost? Blow it out of space and then travel back to wherever?" I ask. "What's to stop them parking on the border where the Timepost is effective, and sending a homing missile?"

"No, once set, it cloaks. You'd have to know the exact thousandth of a second it was set and location of course. It can't be detected either once cloaked, naturally. It may be small technology, but it is powerful. It even has a protective forcefield, so is quite indestructible. Oh, and it is password-protected when you set it."

"Password protected?" I laugh. "What, *password123*?"

"How about *family?*" Aithen smiles. "But that may be useful, knowing we can grab hold of one, or two if needed." I catch a discrete glance between Aithen and Erek.

What was that?

I don't like the thought of secrets between the two.

"Putting aside for a moment, the fact Mary Wood is Marrahmne Kounsell…" Aithen looks around, still trying to process that revelation, "you said there were two things. What's the other?"

Erek's turn to settle back into his seat. He searches the area for something.

"What are you looking for?" I ask.

"Just making sure there's nothing obvious you can throw at me," he responds with a faint smile. The bruise has faded completely.

I give a breathy, "Huh," bracing myself.

"This is where the bad part comes," Erek begins. "I'll cut to the chase, as I don't want to dance around this—"

"Get on with it," Aithen and I say in unison.

Erek takes a deep breath, his grave expression considering the audience.

"Earth was deliberately wiped out by the Military Kounsell."

CHAPTER FIFTY-FIVE

Aithen and I remain silent.

Erek's opening words have rammed my heart in my throat. I can't breathe, let alone speak.

"The Koyorad scientists always seek new wormholes and black holes. There's a huge team solely dedicated to this branch of exploration. When they discovered the wormhole, KT-5192, they hadn't realised the significance of that timeline which brought them to Earth."

Erek stands and rests his forearms on the back of the chair, continuing to face us.

"It was during a routine visit, purely educational-based, that the travelling party stumbled upon a piece of space junk. Anything not purely mineral-based will always raise an alert on the scanners—"

"What was it?" I interrupt.

"A relic but it was a machine launched many years ago. What brought alarm to the visiting team, or rather the Deleter members, was a modern and advanced tag, which accompanied the object," Erek says. "The tag was an advanced piece of technology created by the Xellecorn."

"Wait... aren't they the ones who were wiped out by Gendeeryha? Well, mostly?" I ask.

Erek nods, slowly, emphasising the fact. "After the war with the Xellecorn, they fled their planet. It was destroyed and uninhabitable, but nobody knew where they went. There were rumours across the various planets, but the Xellecorn went undercover."

"Why would they tag a piece of space junk?" Aithen asks. "That was giving away their potential location. Or at least a lead to their existence."

"What was this tagged thing?" I ask.

Erek taps his Meorlite rigorously, running through a series of authentication screens. I guess this as he grits his teeth, "Too many passwords."

A virtual image appears in the space between us, and I remember this from a science class in school. A dish with a box attached and a long arm, jutting outwards and away from the object.

An Earth object.

To confirm my thoughts, a human voice fills the craft. A child's voice.

Hello from the children of planet Earth.

Bonjour tous le Monde.

Hartelijke groeten aan iedereen.

Herzliche Grüße an alle.

Erek taps again and the same – a familiar – message repeats:

Hello from the children of planet Earth.

"Voyager," I confirm.

I've heard these recordings before, in science class and when watching numerous programs about space. Voyager was a small craft sent to explore our solar system and now deep space. In lower school, my class performed a presentation based on the voice recordings. I had to speak the Russian and Japanese segments.

"It took a while, but the Military Kounsell intelligence team were able to crack the Xellecorn encrypted message and disarm its self-destruct, of course," Erek says.

"I have a feeling I know what you're going to say." Aithen rubs his mouth.

Erek nods again. "It was a calling card to other Xellecorn advising them there were at least ten-thousand hidden on Earth."

"They look like us then?" I can't imagine even more aliens on Earth. They really have been *among us.*

"This explains a lot," Aithen says. "The military presence we saw when leaving and more so, why the continued visits to Earth. All under the disguise of Koyorad students wanting to experience other worlds and life."

"Oh, the students are real, as were you." Erek blinks deliberately at Aithen. "But yes, that was used as a cover for the real covert operation: track down any Xellecorn."

"And if found?" I ask.

"Delete them, or anybody found to know about their existence," Erek replies.

"But I thought… aren't the Deleters supposed to be preserving the secrecy of Koyorads?" I ask.

"There is that," Erek says, "but that was rarely the case on Earth."

This can't be right. Can't be true.

"I'm sorry… I'm so sorry, Jayne. But your friends were Deleted because of their friendship with a Xellecorn. One of them was one." Erek's nostrils flare, and he swallows deeply.

What?

"What do you mean? How is that even possible? Billions of people on a planet and I happen to know three who knew a Xellecorn? One was one?" I plead.

"In most cases, the human… the person does not know. Once we realised how close the relationship was, then action was taken," Erek says, hanging his head. "The thing is, it's not a coincidence at all. The Kounsell managed the chosen locations, based on intelligence of potential alien activity."

"Who was the Xellecorn?" I ask.

"Fiona. That was her Earth-name. You knew her as *Violetly-Alone*," Erek confesses.

Fiona.

Now, I know her name. And she was an exiled alien.

What happened with Chloe, Leslie, and Laura? How did they discover the truth of an alien species?

Erek continues. "She used the platform on the web to find anyone who might know the location of another Xellecorn. The narrative based on missing people, albeit for a single individual, was code for them to find one another."

"But she gave me the impression I was the first to contact her?" I suggest.

"You probably were. The Xellecorn were scattered and living in fearful isolation, under the radar, but they intended to trigger a global reveal. Their technology was cloaked and hidden all over the planet, neighbouring solar system of moons and planets. Whoever was in charge intended to reveal their presence to all those on Earth," Erek explains.

"Would that have been a friendly or aggressive reveal?" I ask.

"Friendly." Erek raises his eyebrows. "They would have brought an end to Earth's suffering. We're talking incredible advances in medicine, technology, you name it. Humanity would have been sprung forward millennia."

"And the Kounsell did not want that," Aithen says. "This is ridiculous."

"But Earth is forever away from Korudaz. Where's the danger?" I ask.

"Nip the Xellecorn in the bud. Once they made their presence known, the Xellecorn would be visible to everyone on Earth. That's the beginning of dangerous army and add to that, the military capability of Earth, which will have access to weapons beyond compare, you can imagine what is going through the minds of the Military Kounsell."

"But all of the Xellecorn can't be military?" I ask.

"True. Of the ten per cent who survived, I'm sure the military numbers were small. But any force, which could potentially take retribution against the Koyorads was considered too much." Erek must feel less cautionary, as he retakes his seat.

"I'm going to guess the end here," Aithen says. "The Trenier which hit Earth…?"

"The Military Kounsell propelled it to Earth," Erek replies.

"The, what…?" I gasp. "No, they can't have. Where are these Treniers? In the asteroid belt?"

"No. They're in orbit around Jupiter," Aithen says. "But that's the thing. Think how big that planet is and yet, it's gravitational pull has no effect on the Treniers."

"One of their properties is an anti-gravitational effect. They are quite common around gas giant planets," Erek adds.

"And you say the Kounsell ordered for the Trenier to be given a shove towards Earth?" I can't believe this.

"But why did the Xellecorn let it hit Earth?" Aithen stands now, resting his hands on a console desk. "They had more than the required capability to destroy a Trenier. The craft we sit in can destroy one; even a K-100."

"Because the Military Kounsell followed the same protocol used by Gendeeryha when he attacked the Xellecorn planet," Erek replies. "It was cloaked."

I choke and force down a gag in my throat.

Cloaked?

Aithen flops back into his seat and reaches for my hand. "That's a lot of effort to cloak a rock that big. It must have taken them weeks."

"They didn't see it coming?" I whisper coughing.

"On Earth, they did see it, but it was minutes away from the impact." Erek's words almost washed away by the blood pumping through my ears.

My head spins.

Thoughts of a shadow eclipsing life on Earth.

We didn't stand a chance.

Nobody did.

Hello from the children of planet Earth.

Voyager's messages of hope became a war cry to the Koyorad Military Kounsell.

How do I cope with this?

I have no home, no family. How horrible was their death?

I don't want this! One truth too many. Too many realities.

Hello from the children of planet Earth.

My family. I miss my family. I miss my world.

Hello from the children of planet Earth.

I'm so alone.

I want them to meet Ethan.

I must save them. They should have lived.

Hello from the children of planet Earth.

I'm so angry.

"I could kill her!" I growl, visualising the soulless, grey eyes of Marrahmne Kounsell, Mary Wood.

It's not enough to drown out the billions of screams from that day.

"We can't just let her get away with this?" I say, remembering Ethan is asleep, controlling my voice.

"Exactly," says Aithen.

Both Erek and I look towards him.

"I'm not going back to Earth for a sight-seeing tour." Aithen folds his arms with a smug smile.

"We're undoing this."

CHAPTER FIFTY-SIX

I understand now why Erek left the Deleters. Discovering this attack was the final straw. He'd already been weakening by the realisation of my relationship with Aithen and the fact I could remember my Deleted friends.

Aithen feeds Ethan, and I grab a moment alone with Erek. Certainly, didn't imagine this day... ever.

"Just because I'm no longer associated with the Deleters doesn't mean I can't get them back," Erek says. "Your friends still exist in a sense."

We're parked in a small clearing within a dense forest back on Korudaz.

"Why did you do it?" I ask. "You must have had doubts?"

His eyes shift towards and away from me, shame cast across his face. "I was an emotionless robot. We're raised with such single-mindedness. I loathed all life away from this planet. Visiting Earth was the last thing I ever wanted to do. Turns out it cured me."

"I'm sorry—"

"Don't," he interrupts me. "If you're about to apologise for the cup..." He strokes his cheek. "I needed it."

I laugh. "Actually, I was going to say I'm sorry you were born a Kordet. You seem to have too much heart to be a Deleter."

He cracks a smile – that's a first – showing appreciation that I know who he is and not just the label, *Deleter*.

"I realise you don't have families here, but either way, you have parents," I say. "How do they feel about you being a Deleter? Are they Deleters, too?"

"No, we don't follow the family-thing here on Korudaz. When a child is born a Kordet, they are immediately taken away and raised with a surrogate family. Again, not a mother and father scenario, but more like a boarding school with a small number of children attending," Erek explains. "Female Koyorads don't have children often, so non Kordet children may be placed in the school—"

"And they become Deleters? Wouldn't their eye-colour conflict against that decision?" I ask.

"Normally, yes. But then their Meorlite will be altered. This amendment with the brain-washing training produced a Deleter." Erek shakes his head in disgust. "The crazy thing is when a mature Koyorad elects to join the Deleters. Now that is the odd thing."

"Aithen said someone has taken your role as a Deleter, so that made it easier for you to leave?"

Erek nods thoughtfully. "Yes, that was the strangest timing. But it has facilitated my leaving." His gaze is downcast. There's something he's not telling me.

"What else?" I press. "I can see you're holding something back?"

"I've told you and Aithen all of this as I won't remember much in a few days. Part of leaving the Deleters requires a security mind-wipe."

"What?" I gasp.

"It's for mine and the *Deleter's* protection. I know way too much, so it's the rules."

"That's awful. And this is happening when?"

"They haven't given me an exact day, but it will be soon," Erek says. His expression softens. "Just so you know, each of your friends showed amazing discretion and bravery. Despite meeting a Xellecorn, they didn't betray the confidence."

A tear escapes my eyes, and I smile. "Thank you."

"I do mean it," he continues. "I had already begun to doubt my actions after Chloe. Humans are different."

"Stupid?" I taunt with a smile. It hurts to hear Chloe's name.

"Yeah… sorry again," Erek frowns. "Stupid Koyorads more like it."

Aithen joins us, and we sit on the fresh, soft, purple ground. It reminds me of heather, but the scent of the forest reminds me of grapes of all things. Or maybe melon.

"I guess you have a plan?" Erek asks.

"I'm making this up as I go along," Aithen shrugs. "But I'm a quick thinker. The fact the Kounsell are closing the wormhole works for us. That stops that traffic and threat. We can travel back to Earth to a date before the Trenier hits. Destroy it and all Treniers near to Jupiter. Set the Timepost so it can't be undone."

"But what if we show up and there's a Koyorad army sitting there?" I ask.

"We'll choose a date that's safe," Aithen says. "I'm sure you can find that?" Aithen looks to Erek.

"Yes, that won't be hard to do," Erek taps at his Meorlite. "Koyorad visits tend to follow simple logic. Earth-wise, they always visit in a year divisible by five, such as nineteen-seventy, twenty-fifteen, whatever. So, we can pick a date outside of that."

"What's the significance of that?" I ask.

"Easier time-line calculation across the wormhole and black hole," Erek explains.

I mimic slapping my palm against my forehead. "Whatever. Then what?" I ask. "We save the day and…?"

"We wait for the Xellecorn to reveal themselves," Aithen says.

"They were going to do so. When they do, I'll let them know I'm there."

"They may be hostile towards a Koyorad," Erek states.

"True. I'll just have to be careful. But I'm hoping I'll have another Koyorad with me?" Aithen dips his chin, watching Erek.

"What? Me go back to Earth? I appreciate the sentiment, but no, I'll be more useful here," Erek says.

"How?" I ask him.

"I can't find your friends if I'm on Earth. Their existence is on Korudaz. I've got a promising idea where, but it's how to extract and restore an individual. That's the trick, and I have no idea how to do that."

"Thanks to Jayne, we know where Timeposts are and easily accessible," Aithen adds. "My *parents* are off-planet, so no challenge there."

"And you know how to engage a Timepost?" asks Erek.

"Yeah, stick it in a dump-chute and eject into space. It sends a message to the ships' console, and you arm it with a password."

I'm lost in this conversation. Let them get on with it. I'm glad it won't be me ejecting Timeposts into space and whatever.

"I need to find a portable conversion unit for Ethan. Make him Earth-ready?" asks Aithen.

"That's military," Erek says, concerned. "Even I can't get you that."

"I've got to try, or else we can't land on Earth," Aithen says. "If there are Timeposts so freely around, I have to find a conversion unit."

"And you're sure the ones in your *father's* place work?" Erek asks.

That puts a dampener on things.

"He's an engineer, that's his job. Fix stuff. We have to assume they work," Aithen says.

The voice in my head is nagging me. Saving everyone is one

thing, but I can't let Aithen stay on Earth. But I need him. We need eachother. Is there another planet which has life-like humans? Koyorads and Xellecorn are like us. How many more worlds have human-like populations?

But I want to see my family again.

Oh, shut up! I quieten the voice in my head.

I need to focus on the here – a distant alien planet – and the now – ten-thousand years in Earth's future.

"Silly question, but what's your sister's name, Aithen?" I ask.

Erek's gaze bounces between us.

"Akeirlah," Aithen says. "Jayne is checking she hasn't been Deleted."

"Hmm." Erek nods. "That's original."

It's strange seeing Erek in this new light. This reborn individual.

The aggressive, coldness has warmed, despite the ink-black eyes. But now his white hair and pale, gaunt expression no longer threaten. Truthfully, he reminds me of a punk rocker more than an alien hitman.

"Do you think she'd come with us?" I ask. I'd love Akeirlah to see Earth in real life.

"Probably," Aithen says. "But as I said before, I can't risk her, too. This has now hit serious to the billionth level. She's smart, but she's also a bit scatter-brained."

"No, she's not," I laugh.

"Honestly, she jumps without looking," Aithen smiles. "Many think she's brave, but no, she's fool-hardy. She'll take a chance and ask questions later. We don't need that on this mission."

"On this mission!" I mock, widening my eyes.

"But I'll feel better knowing she is safe here," Aithen says.

He and Erek tap away at their Meorlites, searching for a potential conversion unit.

"I don't want to be the silly human here, but I assume you have considered the medical unit and maybe the birthing facility?" I ask, cringing inside at my silly suggestion.

Erek's fingers freeze, and he watches Aithen, who looks to the side.

"Never thought of that," muses Erek. "The birthing unit?"

"Me neither. Genius, Jayne," Aithen says.

Screens float and disappear as they fidget through options.

"Less to little security," Aithen says. "I can invent any number of scenarios for why I am there should I be caught... I'm worried... first baby... first half-alien baby... what do I do?" He smiles. "I think it'll work."

On cue, they both stop tapping.

"Okay, we have a plan," Erek says. "Aithen, you *try* and get that conversion unit. Jayne, pop to the *parent's* house and grab those Timeposts. But be careful."

"They won't be there, but there are Koyorads and Deyloron around, so play it cool," Aithen says. "Don't use the K-100 or cloaking. Use the hovercar. You're paying a visit to the family home."

"And if I am caught?" I ask.

"You're just a nosey human," Aithen replies.

"And if I'm caught with the Timeposts?" I add.

"Don't be caught with them," Erek interrupts. "Otherwise that will be game over."

"And what about you?" I ask Erek.

"I don't know. I guess I'll just sit here looking pretty," he says flatly, but that forces me to laugh.

"Now, you have a sense of humour?" I ask and Aithen joins the laughter.

"No, I'll monitor the communication lines. If yours or Aithen's name is mentioned anywhere, I'll warn him," Erek says. "For the next couple of days, I still have low-level access to the Deleter network, but that'll be sufficient for any alerts."

"Okay, first thing first," Aithen says. "We need to have a serious crash-course in space. Get you up to speed."

"I'm sure I can fly. I'd rather get on with things." I don't like the idea of us losing focus on the plan. "You can fly blindfolded. We'll be wasting time."

"You're the backup plan, Jayne. I need to know you can escape this place," Aithen says. "Just show me what you can do, and we'll have a play with the navigation system."

He's right, of course.

I just hope there isn't some crazy scenario where I'm the one piloting our escape.

CHAPTER FIFTY-SEVEN

The nicest thing about space is the quiet. The distant hum I always hear on the planet surface is driving me nuts, so this peace provides much-needed relief.

Aithen and I have spent five hours solid running over the piloting and navigation.

Nothing significant but things like how to target an object while flying at speed, countermeasures built into the craft, and a little more on cloaking. The guns can't be used when cloaked, and Aithen repeats this. Is that a lesson or a warning? I can't tell.

I impress myself when I navigate through a scale-four meteor field. Level four means the rocks are about ten kilometres apart, and the scales go to two hundred, which means I'm still a little bit way off expert here. Again, I take every achievement as it comes. Aithen is at scale eighty; he can navigate a path through fast-moving rocks that are a kilometre apart. It all comes down to speed and density of the rocks in the collection.

We're parked in space, and Korudaz emanates in glory as a backdrop to our conversation.

"I'm impressed," Aithen says. "If you were to take an official test, I believe you would pass."

I smile. "Okay, here's a thing. We get to Earth, blow up the Treniers, set the Timepost and… live happily ever after, waiting for a Koyorad military invasion?" It sounds so stupid to me. "I'm no expert, but I'm sure that horrible woman from the Military Kounsell won't let this go."

"The thing is, we're going to cause a ripple, no, more like a tidal wave by carrying out this plan. And yes, we may save the Earth from the Trenier but what's to say some other global catastrophe doesn't occur? If we get away with this, we won't be able to play games with the technology."

"But isn't it good to do something useful with it?" I say.

"Maybe so, but we have to be careful. What scares me is the current state of Korudaz will be thousands of years in the future, when we arrive at Earth. Just because the wormhole and black hole are destroyed, does not mean the Koyorads can't navigate a course to Earth," Aithen explains. "Yes, they would need an exceptionally good reason, as even with the advanced technology, it would take them at least ten years to reach Earth. You and I would never know about it; we'd be long gone."

… long gone.

"That's morbid," I say.

"But true. Even if we both live to be a hundred, it's a blink of the eye on the cosmic scale."

"Okay, let's change the subject," I remember as a child when I realised how finite life is. The thought of no longer existing; not being alive. The world going on and on, until I'm not even a memory. I hate the idea of death.

More so, the idea of a life not given a chance to spark to awaken. Matthew born asleep was the potential for happiness and love stolen away. The silence of that day fills my dreams often, even now. Cradling his tiny, light, cold body.

"Jayne?" Aithen soothes me back to reality.

"Oh... sorry," I smile, wiping away the tears on my cheeks. "Just a flash-back moment."

"Where were you then?" he asks.

"Whenever I think about death and... you know. I think of the day my sister's baby was born... dead."

"Matthew," Aithen responds and holds me for a moment. Then he kisses me. "I forgot about that. It must have been so tragic to experience that."

I nod. "It was. I'm haunted by it. Sometimes, selfishly, I wish *I* could have a security mind wipe like Erek."

"Oh, he told you about that?" Aithen asks.

"Yeah, we had a bit of a heart-to-heart chat about things. It was actually quite good."

"Erek has changed so much. You saw him on Earth... he was a total ass, but then I see *today* and... who would have known."

I watch the planet, and despite the negative which resides down there, below the clouds, it fills me with wonder. If only I could stay here and enjoy a happy life with Ethan and Aithen. If only Earth was safe for my family and friends, and me dating an alien was a regular thing.

Imagine a parallel universe where I can pop back to Earth and catch up with everyone, then return to Korudaz. All normal. Nothing weird.

"Obvious question, but when are we leaving? For Earth?" I ask.

"I'd say, tomorrow." Aithen frowns. This must be impossible for him. "If we wait too long then there's more chance the Kounsell may prevent us from leaving. I'm sure the only reason they are ignoring us now is because of the plans to destroy the wormhole. That's a huge operation."

"I still find it hard to believe they can actually do that." I'd love to see the reactions to Earth scientists when you explain a black hole and wormhole can be destroyed. "But, Aithen. I'm worried about you going to Earth and cutting your life short."

"What, would you rather I lived two hundred years of misery on Korudaz?"

"No, but… you know. It seems unfair to sacrifice your years." I dip my head.

Aithen lifts my chin. "I'd rather spend one year with you than a lifetime without. Zero sacrifices."

We kiss but the moment's peace is interrupted by Aithen's Meorlite.

"What is it?" I ask as Aithen's eyes widen, and his jaw drops.

"It's Akeirlah. The Deleters have her."

"Where? Can we save her?"

"They are based on an island, and it's guarded, and no, we can't try a rescue attempt." Aithen begins tapping at virtual consoles. "We have to kick off our plans now. I'll drop you off at our home, and you grab the hovercar." He sends a message on his Meorlite. "I've asked Erek to go with you to grab the Timeposts, so I can't risk you."

"And where are you going? You're not going to Deleter-central, are you?"

"No, there's nothing I can do about that…" he closes his eyes and shakes his head. "This is ridiculous."

"I know. Akeirlah's harmless, but she did become my friend," I say.

"No, it can't just be that. It's the Kounsell going off on a tangent." Aithen uncloaks the craft and steers towards the planet. "We leave today with whatever we have."

We land next to our building. Despite the panic, it is touching that Aithen referred to this place as *our home*. But it's not. It's temporary. Very temporary.

And we're leaving today.

"What about the two security guards? They might stop us?" I peer around us but can't see them.

"Just act casual," Aithen warns. "I thought of them and have asked Erek to... there he is."

Erek's hovercar parks beside the one assigned to us.

"Where are you going?" I ask Aithen.

"To the medical centre and see if there is a conversion unit there."

"Is it safe? They could come after you now that they have Akeirlah?" I ask, looking towards Erek at the same time for possible advice.

"You're not mentioned on any watch-lists but then again, neither was Akeirlah," Erek says.

"Okay, you two, the Timeposts. And yes, grab them both." Aithen climbs into the car. "I'll see you back here."

"How long will you be?" I ask.

"Not long. If I don't find it straight away, then we'll just have to leave without it and sort something out later," Aithen says.

That plan sounds as hollow as his voice. But he'll find it.

I know he will.

CHAPTER FIFTY-EIGHT

Erek drives, and I sit in the back with Ethan in his basket.

I don't think anything will surprise me again.

Me on an alien planet, with my half-alien baby and chauffeured by a Deleter.

"Everyone flies here, why did we decide to take the hovercar?" I ask.

"Less conspicuous. Yes, everyone flies, but air traffic is closely monitored. We'll be quite ignored in this car," Erek says.

We park the car behind a clump of bushy trees.

"Now, remember. You're just visiting the parents with the baby. Nothing weird to see here." Erek looks around us. "I'll stay out of sight until you need me, okay?"

I nod and begin walking, casually towards the house, my heart thunders in my chest. Ethan's basket hovers next to me at my side.

Watching the house in front of me, I expect the front door to open and quizzical looks from Aithen's parents. There's no way to see through the bronze glass, but I know it's deserted. They are both working, up in orbit, and it is so tantalising to be this close.

Will my appearance here be recorded? Are the homes alarmed? Doors are not locked here. The Meorlites grant entry to everything a

Koyorad should have access to, such as their homes and vehicles. I've visited before as a guest, so will I be allowed in automatically?

Only one way to find out.

I approach the front entrance. I'll say I was passing and—

The door opens with a gentle push.

No alarms!

I close the door behind me, and the dark reception area is unwelcoming. I shouldn't be here. Is the property tracking me? Are the Deyloron on their way? I head towards the basement area. I can't stop myself holding my breath. Even my thoughts seem too loud for comfort.

I'll think of an excuse if caught. I'm just visiting.

The door to the lab.

The interior is visible through a clear panel. Then I notice it. I'd missed it previously, but there, a keypad next to the door. It houses symbols instead of numbers. Oh no. How do I get in? Everything is so pristine and blank. No hints what the code could be. Will Erek know?

I reach for the pad. May as well press a couple of keys, and... to my shock, the door opens. I touched nothing; I shout in my head. As I step into the room, I realise the pad had nothing to do with the door. I laugh at myself, nervously. This is too much.

Settling Ethan's basket upon a table, I take a breath.

The cabinet with the Timeposts is at the back of the room. Maybe it will open automatically, too? I rush to the cabinet and reach for one of the large devices, but my fingers hit a cold forcefield. It hurts.

My fingers trace around the edge of the cabinet, searching for a switch, but there's nothing, just smooth metal. No wires or pipes leading from the box. I try lifting it. Solid. That's not going anywhere.

The room is busy with lots of machines and parts for whatever, but there's nothing to hint it's a means to open the doors on this thing. It looks like a medicine cabinet with transparent doors, but how do I unlock it or disable the clear force field?

Simplify. The Koyorads may have loads of technology, but everything is simple. Straightforward. I'm over-thinking this. I stand in front of the cabinet. What can I see? My reflection. I curse my flippant thought. It's a metal-framed box. Two doors. A clear force field. No wires.

I throw back my head and laugh. My reflection?

It's glass. It hurt my fingers because the force field is glass.

I tap a knuckle on the transparent door, and yes, it's glass. Or at least the equivalent. I hope it's not bullet-proofed or similar.

Time for breaking and entry. I am taking the law into my hands. Please, don't let there be an alarm now.

I gather soft padding and lay some on the floor and then place more against a glass panel. Here goes nothing.

I strike the door with a massive tool, but it bounces off the material. Oh, come on.

The Timeposts are inches from my grasp.

It's time to take a risk. There's no time to be gentle about this. Aiming for the base of the glass, I drop the padding and swing hard at the door. Nothing again, but I flinch at the sound of a bleep.

Turning around, I scan the room for any clue. What made the sound? Another bleep. There's a screen over there. I approach it, and two icons are flashing. I can't read the Koyorad script but can one of these open the cabinet? Is it a panic switch? Taking a deep breath, I say, "Translate?"

Nothing.

I could bring the craft here and blow the doors apart. This is irritating now. I jab my finger at the icon on the left.

The screen dismisses, and now what? Everything looks the same. I'm sure I've just engaged an alert to the armies of Korudaz, but hey, why not? I fling the tool in my hand at the cabinet, and it bounces off and falls to the floor. I sit next to it, on the floor.

I hate this.

I don't want to ask Erek for help as him entering the building could set off an alarm. I've been here before, and I'm sure he hasn't. But I must open the cabinet. We have to risk it.

The building is probably surrounded by the Deyloron and army and the Kounsell. They're all waiting for me to walk outside and the judgement, the shame is waiting there, too.

I'm an idiot! I press my hands against my forehead. Simple, remember.

I stand and glimpse my reflection in the glass of the cabinet. Why am I so stupid?

"Kghurt!" You must create the sound of clearing your throat, with a slight cough while saying the letter *K*. So, it's *K-ert.*

The cabinet doors *open.*

All I had to do was say, "Open" but in *Coten*. Always simple. Duh.

For once, something is simple, but that thought is arrested by the booming horns outside the building. The Deyloron are here; at least two of them.

I close the cabinet door and take Ethan and myself upstairs to the sleeping wing of the building. I hear a voice but can't understand the words.

Looking through the one-way glass, I see Erek, hands raised, barking Coten at two Deyloron, which hover and scan him with their red, lasers. His body illuminates with the grid pattern of the laser light.

I have no idea what he says, but he's putting up a good front. Is he scared? Surely, they won't stun him?

Their distorted blasts fill the air further. I may not speak Coten or Deyloron, but they're going to attack!

I snatch Ethan from the basket and run for the stairs and out of the door, clutching him in my arms.

"Stop!" I shout, as the pitch of the Deyloron rises. "Stop!"

I stand between Erek and the aggressive torment of the red drones, their angry blasts deafening. I duck and shield Ethan away from the Deyloron and gasp. I see Erek is already cowering beneath the angry horns of the drones.

There are four high pitches, and the red lasers turn to blue, then green.

My body shakes all over as I face the blinding lights of the Deyloron.

"I'm a human. Earth human," I shout. "I'm authorised to visit here." I know I'm not, but I must try. The house would have scanned me. I'm an alien with the only half-alien baby on this rock. These killer-drones must know I exist.

The laser grids envelop me, then Ethan alone.

"Leave her and the baby alone!" Erek orders the Deyloron, and he stands between me and the rage of the lasers. His arms raised, and he blankets Ethan and me with his shadow.

"Erek, don't!" I cry.

He dares to toss a rock at the Deyloron closest to him. "Attack me! They are innocent! Stun me!" He spits as he shouts at the cold, unhearing machines.

A second is like a minute as the horns blare and lights flash. A racing sound emits, like unimaginable weapons charging to fire.

Then a deathly silence.

My ears ring.

I dare to peer over my shoulder, shielding Ethan. Blue lights pulse the length of the Deyloron laterally.

With a *whoof*, they depart.

I turn to a shaken, wide-eyed Erek. "You okay?" I ask.

He stutters a nod. "Yes… yes… thank you. That, that was a… they don't normally show up unexpectedly like that. Two at once and *ready to go*."

"I think I may have triggered an alarm when forcing open the cabinet," I offer.

"Yes, that could do it." He brushes his knees off from the dusty ground. "How did you know that would work? That they would stop?"

"I didn't." I raise my eyebrows and scrunch the side of my mouth in a dumb fashion. "You didn't need to stand in the way like that. You saved me once; it was my turn to save you."

"Save you? How?"

"The Tryborre. You could have Deleted me but instead, grew a pair and protected me." I smile at his puzzled expression.

"Not sure I know what *grew a pair* means, but I just followed procedure," Erek says, but he has *that* look. I don't know how, but I know when he is lying.

"Yeah, keep telling yourself that. I know you meant to protect me, and I won't ask why—"

"Because of your friends. Chloe. Laura. Leslie, and Fiona." His face is stone cold. I almost wish he could have a tear in his eye as he says it. "I'd made enough mistakes towards you. Turned your world upside down. The least I could do was protect you and your baby."

I clench the inside of my bottom lip with my teeth and try to stop the tears. But my mental dam is made of tissue. I sniff and wipe away the tears.

I do that stupid snort thing when you try to hold in a good solitary sob.

"Who would have thought I'd save a Deleter one day?" I laugh through my tears.

Erek smiles and woah, his eyes actually glisten.

"Right. Shall we grab these *easy to get with no complications, Timeposts?*" he laughs.

"You bring the hovercar outside, and I'll get them," I say. "I left Ethan's basket in there, too."

"Oh, and just so you know, the cabinet can only be opened with a Coten word… Kghurt," he calls after me.

I'm glad he doesn't see me roll my eyes.

"Thanks!" I call back.

Placing Ethan back into the Moses basket, I rush to the lab and grab hold of a Timepost. It is light in weight. So, I grab them both and push the cabinet doors closed with my shoulder.

I'm out of here.

The basket follows me automatically. When we get back to Earth, I might *invent* these and sell them.

"Okay, ready?" I ask Erek.

He turns towards me, and his face is paler than usual if that were possible. His lips move, but no words sound.

"What is it?" I gasp.

"The Kounsell have ordered the fleet to close the wormhole tomorrow. They are readying as we speak…"

"No! They can't!" I gasp. "We have no time."

"That's not all." Erek squeezes his eyes shut, and his brow furrows.

His grave look prepares me for the bad news.

"The Kounsell have arrested Aithen."

CHAPTER FIFTY-NINE

Erek shakes my shoulders gently, snapping me back to consciousness.

"You have to focus, Jayne. You're now the plan. You must leave today now. Use the K-100. It's easier to manoeuvre."

"What? I can't leave without Aithen. I can barely fly the ship. No way I'll make it to Earth from here." I press a palm to my forehead. "And what about the conversion unit? Ethan can't go to Earth without it?"

"You will, you can make the journey," Erek assures, his tone firm and commanding. "You set the date and location. The craft's computer will do the rest. Always stay cloaked."

My hand flops to my side. "And the unit?"

"Aithen will bring it. You can send and receive communications while cloaked, and they are scrambled."

"Who am I going to message?" I ask.

We load the Timeposts into the hovercar. I place Ethan in the back, too.

"Aithen will be able to send a message to you once he is in range. Failing that, it will be when you're both in Earth's orbit."

"But how do you know you can free him?" I ask.

"I don't, but I need to get to Kounsell HQ and find out what is going on. It may be just a misunderstanding, and he can leave straight away."

I can't leave Aithen locked away in some cell or wherever. But if I stay, I'm going to be arrested, too and any plans to escape Korudaz and save Earth end as of tomorrow. Can I be this selfish and leave him?

But if I stay, can my conscience survive, allowing billions of lives to be wiped out?

If I leave, I save Earth. But how can I live without Aithen?

"Jayne, we can't wait around." Erek's voice snaps me back to harsh reality. "I'll help him. Somehow he'll be free—"

"But the wormhole is gone after tomorrow. What if you can't?" I ask.

Erek shakes his head. "I have no answers here. I don't believe the Military Kounsell can achieve this in a day; take my word for it. We've got more time, but you need to leave urgently, and I need to tell you about the Timepost."

"How do I set the Timepost?" I ask.

Erek points to two buttons on the metallic object. "Red button turns it on. Blue button arms it to be ready. You then ask the ship's computer to open the dump-chute, and you place it in there. Then you ask the ship to eject the Timepost. It will transmit a message to the ships' console—"

"And I set the password," I remember this from when he and Aithen were talking about our plan.

"Yes. Simple as that and you'll prevent time travel backwards from that moment. Just make sure you're in Earth's orbit, just to be double-certain," Erek advises.

How am I supposed to do this? My thoughts are like a house of cards, and the bottom card has just been swiped away. I'm trusting Erek to free Aithen and then for Aithen to grab the conversion unit for Ethan.

I just want to scream, but what use is that? I'll still be trapped in this situation and not making progress.

"Please, Erek. Try and get him away today?" I plead.

"You take the hovercar," Erek says. "I need to get to the Military Kounsell and fathom out what they are doing. I *will* get Aithen out, and he can follow after you."

"If I take the car, how will you get to the Kounsell building?" I ask.

"The Terr will send me a vehicle," he replies, his eyes scanning around to match the thoughts running through his head. "The ship will have all you need onboard. Remember to take the space-drops, and then you will both need a shot for travel to and after the worm-hole. The ship's computer will guide you here. Ask it anything."

"Do I have clearance to pilot the ship alone?" I ask.

"Yes, Aithen set it all up for you, just in case," Erek replies grimly.

...just in case.

"How about family?" Aithen had suggested for the password.

I power up the hovercar. "I'll need to grab Ethan's stuff but otherwise... how do I know you can get Aithen?"

"I don't know for sure, but he, we haven't done anything wrong. They don't know what we've been planning—"

"Maybe they've guessed?" I interrupt.

"I think if you don't leave now, right now, the window is lost," Erek says, calmly.

"And they're closing off the wormhole. What if Aithen can't escape in time?"

Erek shrugs. "I can't guarantee anything, Jayne. But you must save yourself. Save Earth."

I consider the Timeposts and Ethan. Erek's right, but it feels so selfish leaving Aithen behind. And I'm risking Ethan's life. No conversion unit means he can't go to Earth. I can't leave him on Korudaz.

But this is my only chance to save Earth and put things right there.

"Please get him," I beg Erek. "I'll be setting the computer's date to two years before impact. On the day we left Earth."

"Make sure you set the date for the day after you left Earth and certainly not any time before," warns Erek. "We don't need two Jayne's in the Universe."

"Didn't think of that," I shrug.

"That will allow for travel time from exiting the wormhole and reaching Earth. You alone complete the cycle." Erek takes my hand and shakes it gently. "It's been an honour, Jayne. It's a pity we didn't meet under less hostile circumstances."

"Thank you, Erek. Please, stay safe."

I engage the hovercar to return home. I don't turn to watch Erek disappear from view.

CHAPTER SIXTY

Paranoia greets me as I approach the building.

There are no Deyloron or similar *welcoming* party. Still, my footsteps echo and join the thumping heartbeat in my ears. Barely able to swallow as panic dries my mouth, I carry Ethan in his basket.

Shall I move the Timeposts now, put them in the K-100? No, I'll only be a minute.

Entering the apartment, I am both shocked and overjoyed. "Akeirlah? They let you go?" I gasp.

Lowering the basket to hover at hip height, I offer to hug her, but she backs away?

Her padded jumpsuit is black and her eyes, they look darker green than her usual bright, sparkling, welcoming gaze.

"Is everything okay?" I ask. "I heard the Deleters arrested you? And now they have Aithen. The Kounsell have arrested him. What's going on? Have you heard anything?"

"I don't know, Jayne. What is going on?" She folds and unfolds her arms. Her feet are restless.

Taking a seat, I feign calmness. Akeirlah is safe, but I can't mention I'm about to leave Korudaz. I can't risk her being taken by the Kounsell. Oh, no... the Timeposts are on show in the hovercar.

"I don't know what is going on. I heard about you and now this with Aithen. It's the Military Kounsell. They've got it in for us." I watch Ethan as his feet kick against my open palms. Can Akeirlah hear my heart jumping with adrenalin? I must show composure.

"Firstly, I wasn't arrested by the Deleters, so I don't know where that has come from," Akeirlah says, slightly pursing her lips.

Is she angry?

Then again, I don't blame her. I know there's no family thing here with Koyorads, but she's sure to be angry with the Kounsell over Aithen.

She spins on a heel and casually approaches the open doorway to the hover-car. Please, don't go near, my mind pleads.

She freezes.

Oh, no. She's seen them? The Timeposts.

"I know what you're planning, Jayne." The calm in her voice is menacing, as she speaks with her back towards me. "And I can't allow this."

"Akeirlah. You know why I must do this." I approach her and pull on her elbow, so she can face me. But she snaps her arm away with an angry grimace.

Her face is featureless and cold, like a statue. Her menacing eyes are almost like... Erek's.

"Akeirlah? You know about my family and me. Earth. What's wrong?" I plead. Why should she turn on me now? Someone's got to her?

"You're too dangerous. You and *that* baby!" Sourness rips through her words. "What did you expect? We'd welcome you with open arms?" Her eyes burn through me. The anger. Torment. Fear?

My head quivers as I try to form a sentence. What? Where's this all coming from? "Who's got to you, Akeirlah? This is not *you* speaking."

"Who has got to *me*? You! You, Jayne. When I first heard about this, I honestly believed it was a hoax. A joke. That's why *I volunteered* to join the Deleters when the fool, Erek, gave up his post. He's such a conflicting, weak idiot. Like so many of the insects on this planet." She's pacing now.

"You... you joined the Deleters?" My words trail off. None of this makes sense.

I scan the apartment. No weapons I can use, and if I make a run for it or try to rush her, I don't know if she'll hit a panic button to summon the Deyloron or... she could have a Deletion device? Ethan is too close by, so I remain standing in front of his basket.

"Akeirlah, I can see you're agitated, but can we talk about this? Calmly?"

"I am calm, Jayne. Now I am calm because I can fix what I have been trying to correct since you got here." Her eyes widen to my gaping expression.

"It was you?" My broken whisper produces slow nods from Akeirlah.

"With the approval and full support of Marrahmne Kounsell." Her sarcastic tone is light and annoying.

"You do know she's a human, don't you?" I suggest, looking for a weakness in her mental armour.

But she tilts her head sideways. "And I'm a Tyrannosaurus."

The words are as bitter and dark as the stench of that ancient jungle.

It's pointless reasoning the human point with Akeirlah. "All those elaborate plans, just to get rid of me? You failed each time. You're pathetic, Akeirlah."

"But I'm not a poisonous virus, like your human scum." She spits at the floor. "If I did nothing, *he* would breed." She points at Ethan while she wipes away the saliva with the toe of her boot. "This planet will be full of humans in my lifetime. We'll have wars and destruction within a couple of generations. You think I'm going to sit around and watch? Let it all unfold as you grow like a tumour on my planet?"

"Then let me leave," I plead. "We'll be gone for good. The wormhole and any means of travel to and from Earth end tomorrow—"

"And we want all loose ends *Deleted*," Akeirlah snaps. "Yes, we were very elaborate, to disguise the plan to remove you and *that* baby. I played my role well, don't you think? For some reason, Marrahmne Kounsell wanted to keep us all as one and appease the Gouhlde Kounsell, but then we've decided otherwise."

"All this for one, no, two humans? We're really that dangerous?"

She nods.

"Out of curiosity, why did you inject the temporary Meorlite into me?" I ask.

"So that we could isolate you in the Virtual zone. Tracking Aithen's was standard, but a silly human, like you, doesn't have anything to lock on to. But then we did and sent you, and stupid Aithen, off on your dinosaur safari." She slips a hand into a pocket and produces a chrome device. It looks like a small hair clipper, minus the cutting end.

She raises it towards me. "The space-drops: a failure and a stupid rock was your timely saviour. But I'm very patient."

It makes sense now. She tried to suffocate me, or whatever, during our first flying lesson.

She paces left and right, keeping the device pointing at me. "I send you and that lump, Aithen, back in time, and of course, you bounce right back here." She rolls her eyes.

"I can't take credit for the power outage, which was a member of the Kounsell who bumbled that one up." She looks past me and towards Ethan. I back up, to mask him from her evil stare. "But I did break the secrecy about your arrival, under the instructions of Marrahmne Kounsell."

"Listen to you. You're so proud of yourself, aren't you?" I scoff at her aggressive stance. I'm not going to appear weak. I don't have a plan, but I must buy me time. This is a standoff I can't hope to win. She may as well have a loaded gun pointing at me. Though a gun would not remove all memory of me from consciousness and existence.

She'll get away with this.

She is poised with confidence. This is a win-win for her. But why now? Why does fate love to throw a spanner in the works?

"I'm immensely proud. You are so gullible, Jayne. You let me in, but then I made the mistake of losing focus on you while I underwent the Meorlite conversion. It appears I was off target too long. And Marrahmne Kounsell wanted me to complete the task. Complete my initiation as a Deleter."

"Akeirlah, I never wanted to come here, to Korudaz. I was abducted and taken against my will. You're blaming me for some-thing the Kounsell ordered. I'm not supposed to even be here."

She sighs, tapping her foot. "But here you are. And that!" She may as well have spat again, as she looks towards the basket behind me.

"I don't believe this is you, Akeirlah. You're warm and caring. I trusted you."

She rolls her eyes. A dull click and the end of the device glows. "I'm deleting you and your disgusting baby."

Could I throw the table at her? I'll be too slow.

"You can't!" I shout as I begin to move towards her. If the device is going to kill me, time should start to slow down if I'm in extreme danger, because of the Tryborre. It would typically be removed after the pregnancy, but the attack at the birthing unit meant I was isolated and normal procedures not completed.

I reach for her wrist, and my fingers scrape against the device. But she moves so fast, sweeping my forward leg with a sharp kick, and pushes me to the floor, smacking my head against the low table.

"Bye, Jayne," she taunts. Her words are unravelling through my spinning head. There's a bright flash, and the soundwave of her words trails into a distorted slur like someone just hit the off switch on a vinyl record player.

With this comes the silence, as time immediately puts the brakes on. Grinding slower, the beam from the device breaks into streams of white shards, like glass spears. The pulse stops inches from my face, and despite this pending horror, I can clearly see Akeirlah.

Her mouth is open in a silent scream. The beam is coiling back, as though it hits an invisible rubber force, and rebounding towards her. This doesn't make sense. There's no air or sound, but through my cloud of terror, I am aware.

The pulse begins to envelop Akeirlah. I don't know why, but I try to reach out to her. My mind is operating at half speed and my limbs a fraction of this. I was able to dodge a bus, but this is different.

Like a click of the fingers, I am stood there panting in real-time, sweat running down my brow.

Akeirlah and the device have vanished.

Deleted.

I inhale loudly. No! What? Why? "Akeirlah?" I shout, startling Ethan. He begins to cry. I cradle him in my arms and can't contain the stream over my cheeks. No. It can't be. She didn't know about the Tryborre. I bury my face in the blanket, covering Ethan's little body. I don't want to upset him further with my own tears.

The Tryborre protected Ethan and me.

The energy force rebounded and hit her. I can't believe it. I calm Ethan with gentle kisses and stroke his soft head, rocking him gently.

I must flee. Escape. The echoes of fear and the unwelcome sniff of tears accompany my auto-pilot mode.

Can I do this? I may get ten feet before the military stops the craft or blows me to pieces. Should I risk Ethan's life for this? His eyes flicker to sleep. Innocent.

I must.

I quickly pack supplies for him. The milk can be created within the craft from small pods, so no bulk there. You load a pod into the processing machine, and it's as simple as that. Nappies come packaged in tiny pouches and roll out to full size as required. We need enough for several months, as I don't have a plan when I get to Earth and have completed my immediate tasks.

My mind is surprisingly calm, considering I was almost Deleted a few minutes ago, but my heart and breathing are racing. Have I thought of everything? I know *where* I want to go and *when*. I must do it.

And now for the worse part.

What if the craft doesn't recognise me? This is my first time alone.

Yes, the Tryborre protected me, but does it really present me as a Koyorad to the K-100?

The dark wedge of the craft decloaks as I approach. It stands ominous and silent in the evening light.

Will it work? I walk purposely towards the sealed entrance and expect to hit metal, but there's a hum, and the doorway opens. But will it engage? Will the lights come on?

I step inside and gasp; the room is lit, and several devices click to life. I cover my mouth to smother my laugh.

Okay. Step one: check.

I strap Ethan into his basket and onto a seat of the craft, then the essential supplies. Essential less one conversion unit. Please, Aithen...

I rush to the hovercar and grab the two Timeposts. My pace quickens from imaginary blasts from the Deyloron.

I place the two objects inside the craft and hold my breath for a moment, listening to the pulse in my ears. I breathe out slowly.

"Close entrance." I close my eyes but open them when I hear the hiss and a clunk.

Step two: check.

I have about thirty more steps to consider, but this final one is the most important. "Engage cloaking."

I almost scream when the interior encloses in blue light.

Step three: CHECK!

If I can cloak, then they can't stop me. I can leave right now, and there's nothing they can do. But can I fly?

I take a sip of the liquid, which allows for us to be in space, and use a dropper to give Ethan his dose. K-100's computer will set a reminder to warn when we should take another amount.

I hope he stays asleep, for now. I will have too much to take care of while I prepare for the long flight. Hope so, anyway.

I sit inside the craft and engage the take-off procedure.

This is it.

I have the forward panel clear, so I can see the apartment.

What am I doing?

Oh, Aithen. I love you. Honestly, you make me feel so alive and happy, but my heart also has a hole in it the size of a planet. May sound philosophical, but it is true. The fate of an entire world is in my hands, and what am I? An insignificant speck of dust in the Universe.

Please, Erek. Save Aithen.

For all I know, Aithen could already have left. But he would message me?

I engage the orbit mode, and daylight turns to the darkness of space. Can you ever get used to it? I set the craft to face away from the planet. I don't want to watch it grow smaller. I'm leaving behind Aithen, and it is hurting. All the space-drops in the universe can't control the heavy feeling, but I cannot hang around. I have a tiny window of opportunity here. Can I outrun everybody in this craft?

I ask the navigation computer to confirm an estimated time

when it would be on the far side of Jupiter and invisible to Earth, two years before Trenier impact.

This takes longer than I anticipate as the computer finds it hard to understand the parameters I'm requesting. I need to factor in the time it takes to get from Jupiter to Earth so that I arrive at Earth at the time we jumped into the black hole.

Aithen has programmed the computer to speak with a female voice. It is a sweet, calm voice but too relaxed when trying to negotiate what is such a complicated set of instructions for me. But we finally get there and yes, it sounds right.

I laugh as the navigation device advises we should travel through a wormhole, as this allows for negative time travel. It reminds me of car navigation saying do you want to include a toll road?

Issue command flashes on a screen in front of me.

I raise my left hand and point at the screen. "Go!"

I sit poised in silence, waiting for an alarm to sound or for the craft to come to a sudden halt, but there is nothing. All I can hear is the throbbing in my head. I draw in a deep breath. I must calm down. Should I risk going to sleep?

Duration of the journey is eighteen days. Maybe I should have learnt how to pilot one of those freight vehicles which can make the journey in a day. Maybe not.

I have the craft locked down. Having a window panel open makes me feel too nervous. Yes, we are cloaked, but I want to see nothing. To hear nothing except for the natural sounds of the vehicle and Ethan. My body is cloaked in fear to match the blue of the craft. Can I trust the computer to guide us safely? There are so many things we could hit. Destroy the ship and us in it.

I mourn the nice Akeirlah, not the evil one which schemed to kill me. I can't reconcile any of it now. She was so manipulative. Convincing.

I try to distract my mind from other thoughts, anything. Aithen.

Home. My family. Korudaz. Matthew. Death. Emptiness. I'm so lonely. We're going to die. We'll hit a comet, and the craft will tear apart. How long will it take to die in space? When the vacuum sucks the life out of us?

"Oh, shut up, Jayne!" I shout at myself and punch my thigh. It brings tears to my eyes, and as I cradle my head, dragging my hair back, I laugh.

Yes, I'm cracking up.

My leaving and theft of a craft will give ammunition to the Kounsell's distaste for humans and me. As if they needed any more motivation. But no-one will know Akeirlah is gone. Deleted. The device vanished with her.

The computer warns us when we approach the jump through time and the wormhole. No way do I want those sounds again. After taking the pre-jump medicine for Ethan and myself, I place earplugs in both our ears and brace for the acceleration.

It feels like a nervous butterfly buzz in the stomach, and the crashing sound is still there but muffled. It sounds more like nails scratching on a board in school. Talk about harsh. I place my palms over Ethan's ears to add more protection from the noise. He is smiling at me and kicking his legs.

And then we are in silence again, and with bleary eyes, I read the date display on a screen. Sixty-four years from Earth orbit and the figure is decreasing rapidly. There are no tears now. This is the final leg. If I can control my trembling hands from fatigue and fear, I'll be happier. I haven't slept. Okay, maybe dozed a little, but I would bolt awake as the crashing sound of metal would be just a dream. A dread. Night terrors ripping us apart.

"Are there any other vessels near to this one?" I ask the computer.

We are alone.

Could it be so easy? Surely the Koyorads would have contacted a crew based on Earth by now? They wouldn't be able to see me anyway, but then, maybe they are also cloaked, and I can't see them. I know I can't fire the guns when cloaked. That will be my most vulnerable point.

But there can't be any craft. They will have returned to Korudaz. The wormhole will be shut by now; assuming they went ahead with that operation.

I open the front-viewing panels as I'm minutes away from my rendezvous. Jupiter is menacing in the distance, with its complicated multitude of rippling storms running laterally across its surface. I can't see the trademark circular storm present in so many images, so it's on the other side now. I'm not here for the view though; I'm here for the collection of rocks before me. The Treniers.

They are so huge.

I disengage the auto-pilot controls as I want to do this myself. Fear may course through my veins, but I'm confident I can control a hovering ship, moving barely at pulse speed.

Time to face the cause of destruction to my home. The clock is ticking, and for all I know, the Koyorads could arrive at any moment and spoil everything, but I need this moment, now.

The computer identifies the first target Trenier. I steer towards E1-90998712D.

Earth did not stand a chance against *that*. My craft is like a tiny dot against a rock the size of a US state. It's terrifyingly huge. I engage the reverse thrusters and allow a long distance from the menacing, shiny black Trenier, which reflects incidental portlights from the craft, like deep, dark obsidian. The reflections remind me we're not cloaked.

What was it like, the last day on Earth? To be looking up and seeing it approach at such high speed, too?

I jump when an alarm sounds out, and multiple screens display *Collision alert!*

What?

The Koyorads are here?

"Collision alert!" says the computer in her calm voice.

"Where? What?" I shout, opening all viewing panels and looking around anxiously.

"Collison alert! Impact in seven, six..."

"Help me!" I shout. "Evasive manoeuvres!"

I see three orange blasts emit from the craft and then the screens clear.

I gasp. "Are we safe?"

"Object destroyed. Alert cancelled."

"Why couldn't you do so in the first place?" I urge the computer. "Engage scanning for other dangerous objects?"

"Scanning already enabled."

"Engage automatic evasive manoeuvres?"

"Enabled," the computer replies.

Cradling my chin in my hands, I stand and look out of a rear panel. A small cloud of dust hangs in space behind us. It doesn't move; it floats there as a reminder of death.

Space is a dangerous place to be, and Jupiter's gravity will attract all kinds of random rocks. That was a close shot. To make it all this way and to accomplish nothing. Just imagine.

I turn and eye the mass of the great rock. I've already taken too long. I disengage the cloaking, and my fingers are already twitching from nerves in the amber-lit interior. I'm a sitting duck now.

"Okay, engage weapons and target on E1-90998712D."

"Clearance, please?"

You're joking?

Password?

I stare at the console and controls in front of me. I take hold of the joysticks, but there are no triggers to fire. What?

"What do you mean by clearance?" I ask the computer.

"A clearance code is required to engage with a significant time-line object." If I get past this, I intend to have emotion built into her voice. It is too calm for this situation, and it is making me angry.

"Please, I have come this far. I must save Earth." Why am I bothering to plead with a program?

"Clearance, please?"

So, this is the final defence. To stop me or anybody from changing things. It is so unfair. I'm here, and I'm such a fool. They let me escape because they already knew I'm powerless. How would I know what word or expression is the key here? And it will be in *Coten*. I have learnt a lot of the language but nowhere enough to communicate confidently with a lifeless computer getting on my nerves.

"Clearance, please?"

Surely Aithen would have thought of this? But then, he intended to come with me. I'm not supposed to be doing this alone.

"Clearance, please?"

"Oh, shut up!" Disabling the voice control, I glimpse the display panel with the same message on it in blue text. I'm not giving up.

Looking at the interior of the craft, is there an override switch? Not likely, but this thing must be a nuclear weapon and more. I gaze through tears at Ethan as he will become an innocent victim of my plan. I can run this craft into the Trenier; but will I destroy it?

I would save billions of lives. I'm scared for Ethan and me as I know my thoughts are not rational. Am I brave? Can I really do this? Now?

I enable the voice control again.

"If I crash the K-100 into E1-90998712D, will it be destroyed by the explosion?" My voice falters as my mouth is dry and tastes horrible. I haven't eaten for so long.

"Clearance, please?" is the calm response.

"Will E1-90998712D be destroyed if I crash this ship into it?"

My chest heaves. My heart is racing. A sick, nervous buzz runs through my stomach.

"Clearance, please?"

"What is the product of the integers two and four?" I must see if the computer is stuck in a loop.

"Eight."

Okay, so it's not. Is there a way to explain what I want to do without clarifying I want to destroy the Trenier? I can't end Ethan and my life on a gamble. I must know I can save Earth.

"Please, help me. I must destroy E1-90998712D!"

"Clearance, please?"

"Bitch! I must help everyone—"

"Clearance, please?"

"… on Earth."

"Clearance, please?"

"Why can't you understand? I must save Earth. I must save my—"

"Clearance, please?" the voice interrupts, but I continue my sentence, regardless.

"… family!"

I gasp as the triggers press against my fingertips. One of the many words from Earth with no corresponding translation in *Coten*.

Family.

"How about family?" Aithen asked me the other day when I suggested a silly password.

What else would it be for Aithen to have configured the craft for me? He probably had this moment planned, and when the ship asked for the password, it would have been a happy and simple one, just for me.

Oh, Aithen. I wish you *were* with me now.

"Weapons armed."

"Is the craft a safe distance from E1-90998712D's blast wave?" I ask. Better be safe now.

"Confirmed."

I press and hold in the triggers in both controllers, and a stream of orange blasts travel towards and hit E1-90998712D. I gasp for breath and almost scream for joy when it rips to pieces and creates a plume of black, grey, and white dust. I target the other Treniers and watch them become only a cloud between Jupiter and me and all beyond.

Ethan is crying as I rock him after startling him awake.

"Shhh… sorry, Ethan… I'm sorry."

I laugh through my tears. Ethan looks at me with wide, blue eyes and pursed lips. He is bouncing as my body heaves with my joyous sobs. I can visualise Earth so far away and the people all there unaware of what is happening here, now.

People will be relaxing, working, or commuting.

Children will play and laugh.

There will still be sadness and grief and anger. But there will be life and existence. There will be families and friends all enjoying each other, and there will be Mom, Dad, Emily, David, Sarah, Terry, and Lou.

I wish I could bring back Laura, Chloe, Leslie, and even the Xellecorn, Fiona but they've been Deleted. That's a problem for me to solve, another day. But for now, the rest of my friends will go to college and enjoy music.

The world will go on.

CHAPTER SIXTY-ONE

Ethan sleeps soundly having just been fed.

Peace emanates throughout the blue interior of the craft and Earth fills my tearful view.

What do I do now?

There's no sign of Aithen. I dare not transmit a message for evil Kounsell ears could be listening.

But what about the Xellecorn? They're down there, somewhere.

What would the computer do, should I initialise a message to any neighbouring Xellecorn? Surely there will be strict protocols against that?

But I'm exhausted, both physically and mostly mentally. I need to sleep for a bit, but first, I must ensure my handy work can't be undone.

And I'm making sure it is the case. This must work.

I place a Timepost in the dump-chute after requesting this be opened by the computer. The red button, then blue button.

I return to my seat. "Eject Timepost."

"Set Clearance, please?"

I laugh with relief. No drama, for once.

Now it's my chance to set a password. I won't use the same

word *family*, but I have a password nobody could ever guess. I type the characters into the console and enter the requested details.

This can't be reversed. I watch as the Timepost floats away from the craft, and with a small flash, it disappears. So simple. And disturbing. I have amended the time fabric of the local cosmos here. I wonder, what if there is another disaster waiting to happen? How will this affect the future? I have read and heard so often in fiction that time should not be altered; butterfly effect and all? Well, this is space, and this is a vacuum, so no butterfly wings to cause havoc here.

I smile and cradle Ethan, kissing his warm head.

On a day like today, it's hard to imagine Earth will be saved…

By me.

Jayne.

"Okay, little man," I soothe, placing Ethan in his basket and enabling the hovering, glowing orbs he likes to watch. "Time for us to go for a ride."

I turn the K-100 away from Earth. It's strange as while I can't see or hear the planet, I sense it like it is a chorus behind me.

Erek said the Kounsell won't be able to close the black hole in a day.

I hope he's right.

Punching in the coordinates and date of arrival, I take a deep breath.

Saving Earth alone, is not enough. I want my friends back and more still, I need Aithen.

I'm coming for you, Aithen. If I can save a planet… I can do anything.

"Go!" I order the K-100.

AFTERWORD

Upon publishing this story on 20th July 2021, to mark the 50th anniversary of NASA's Apollo 11 mission, the storyline of Jayne being the first female human to visit the Moon will soon be achieved by a woman in real life. There is much excitement with the space program, and humans are on their way to the Moon again.

There is mention this could be as soon as 2024.

I look forward with excited anticipation to hearing the words of the first female human to set foot on the surface of the Moon.

ACKNOWLEDGMENTS

Even an author working in isolation will generate an editorial team around them. My ongoing team has undoubtedly helped me deliver this story.

Special thanks go to my friend Julia Sincock, who proofread this story's early drafts and to Eve Terry, who inspired me to complete this story; I hope you are well and happy.

Andrei Bat has produced such incredible artwork for the book cover and patiently transformed my jumbled thoughts into a beautiful work.

The audiobook has been dramatised by the wonderful Jessica Duncan, and she adds a whole new aspect to the story telling.

My first editor LJ Lawless took my painfully bad first draft and was genuinely kind and supportive with her feedback. Next, I worked with the amazing Julia A. Weber. Her input transformed this book in so many ways; I certainly learnt lifelong writing lessons from her.

Finally, to Sara Starbuck. Where would I be without you? Your honesty and out of the box thinking helped me transform the book's final draft, which I am confident tells Jayne's story in its best form possible.

ABOUT THE AUTHOR

Emae Church is an emerging author of young adult Sci-Fi, and lives in England, UK.

This is Emae's debut book which begins a new universe of story telling.

 facebook.com/emae.church
twitter.com/emaechurch

Lightning Source UK Ltd.
Milton Keynes UK
UKHW011842090621
385229UK00001B/75